PAPA BEAR

Shift Work 1

Alex Silver

CONTENTS

COPYRIGHT

SYNOPSIS

Raising a kid on my own wasn't the plan. Then again, neither was falling for the first shifter I allowed to get close to me after my ex left me with a newborn.

I've always been a solitary bear, and that suits me fine. Until a remodel at the zoo where I work showing off my shifted form to an admiring crowd turns everything upside down. Bramble moves into my habitat and after a rocky start, he worms his way into my heart.

My daughter, Myra, is my entire world. Being her dad doesn't leave much room for romance, but Bram is one persistent bird when something shiny catches his eye, and somehow—impossibly—to him, I sparkle.

Papa Bear is an M/X omegaverse mpreg romance with a grumpy genderqueer single parent bear shifter and a sunshiny raven shifter who wants to fix everyone's problems for them. CW for infertility in a side character and parental abandonment from Ty's ex, bullying of Ty's child over having a single parent.

CHAPTER 1

Ty

The line for my morning coffee is standing still. All thanks to the person in front of me who can't make up their mind. My inner bear wants to growl at the delay as they chatter on to the patient barista at the register.

"Hm, in that case, I'm not sure what to get. Do you recommend the Polar Bear Plunge? It's peppermint mocha, right? And Santa's Reindeer is caramel apple flavored? Are you certain you're out of the pecan caramel crunch?" the annoying obstacle to my morning brew asks, gesturing at the menu board.

I glance between the indecisive shifter and the pastry case full of baked goods, all too aware that I'm running out of time before my work shift. The person ahead of me is still taking their sweet time ordering. I am not amused.

It's not that I'm late. Not really. I mean, if I was in my bear form, I'd be hibernating instead of slogging through the morning commute. As it stands, I should make it in on time. I'm just desperate for the hit of caffeine that the customer in front of me is keeping me from getting.

My therapist—back when I had time for one—suggested deep breathing when I get stressed out at this time of year. One heavy inhale just fills my nostrils with the enticing coffee aroma that makes me want my morning brew even more.

There are subtler undertones too. Avian, canid, and maybe a feline shifter? They're hard to parse in my human form and with the overpowering aroma of coffee filling the air. I can pick out notes of sweet honey, pastry, something tangy with warm vanilla, and the mix of human smells and irritating artificial fragrances. I usually stop at a cafe inside the zoo, where I work, but they are remodeling several buildings during the winter slow season. So my usual fix is closed and the other option is clear across the other side of the arctic loop.

I prefer to avoid passing the polar bear exhibit. I've got something of an unspoken agreement with the alpha who works there to stick to our own turf. Another alpha bear's pheromones are irritating, to say the least. So here I am, at Wild Bean, the coffee shop outside the zoo gates. Where they don't enforce a shifter-friendly fragrance-free policy.

The confusing jumble of scents irritates my bear. I can feel him just under the surface, growling to come out and deal with the problem. He'd probably scare the wishy-washy obstacle to my morning coffee fix right out of the cafe. Unfortunately, he might also scare away the staff who can get my coffee for me.

Besides, shifting in public like that isn't socially acceptable. The act of shifting is generally something private, not to mention questionably legal in a place that sells food. So I resist the impulse. I doubt anyone here would appreciate real bear fur in their bear claws.

A donut actually sounds delicious to my hungry inner bear. I deserve a pastry for keeping those instincts in check. The gooey honey crullers I spy in the display case will do nicely. I was planning to skip the donut this morning, but, well, sometimes the best way to handle life's minor frustrations is to treat yourself. Bears need their honey.

"It's for Bram." The person in front of me must have finally decided. They give their name to the barista with a flirty lilt to their voice. As if it's a shared intimacy and not standard procedure. Whatever.

I harrumph, eager for them to get on with it already as I wait for them to pay. They take an extra moment to dig out cash for a tip even though they paid by card. I don't want to warm up to them, but that little gesture must mean they aren't all bad. And there is a certain grace to their movements that I envy. Bram—if that's even their real name—pivots and moves aside so I can order.

Bram does a double take when they see me, eyes traveling up my body like they are memorizing my bulky build. The indecisive shifter gawks at me, and I take in the mismatched array of costume jewelry that puts my eight-year-old's collection to shame. Their aesthetic reminds me of a pair of glam jeans from the 90s.

I bet this Bram could pull off having an ass covered in rhinestones. With their lanky build and strutting poise as they walk gracefully to the pickup end of the counter, I can easily picture it. I stare after them for a moment too long before stumbling up to the counter to order.

My preoccupation with ogling Bram's assets leaves me feeling wrong-footed. It's not as though anyone expects a bear to be anything other than lumbering, but sometimes I think it might be nice to be less noticeable. Not so broad and imposing in stature, like I'm towering above the crowd, a beacon that draws unwanted eyes. In either of my forms.

I place my order, pay, and move aside. Except, just as I'm going to stand in the waiting area, Bram gets their drink and whirls toward the little counter next to me. I should have expected it. That's where they stock creamers, sugar, and various coffee fixings. Bram isn't paying attention though, so they slam into my chest. I let out a surprised 'oomph' at the impact and reach for their shoulders to steady them.

Bram squawks, like a startled bird, as their hot sugary brew sloshes out onto their hands. I get a whiff of dusty feathers, citrus, and vanilla, then time seems to slow as their drink tips toward me. Before I can react, the burning sensation of most of their beverage splashing me in the chest hits. I brace myself as the wave of coffee, sugar, and peppermint has my bear coming to the surface, ready to react to a threat.

I hold back, barely. The strong mint scent soaking into my shirt as Bram clucks apologies obliterates my sense of smell.

"My poor ruined coffee!" Bram flaps their hands. Definitely an avian, as though their scent left any doubt. "And your poor ruined shirt!" They grab a stack of napkins and pat ineffectually at my chest. "I am *so* sorry."

"It's fine," I grumble as I push their hands away from my person. I don't need some stranger feeling me up before I've had my coffee. It's really not fine, but I only have to wear the sopping wet shirt until I get to the black bear enclosure at the zoo to start my work shift.

"Well, if you're sure, I need to go get back in line. This is going to make me late for work." Bram sighs, then goes to rejoin the line. That leaves me dripping in a puddle of sugary sludge as the barista calls my name for my latte and donut. I take my order with an apology for the mess on the floor and leave an extra tip for their trouble, even though it is completely Bram's fault.

Birdbrain. Avians have never been my favorite. They stick to their flocks for one. Bears are more solitary. We just don't have the same values. I sip my heavenly brew. It's not as strong as my usual order from the zoo cafe, but it will do.

I devour my cruller on the short drive between the cafe and the zoo's employee parking area on the other side of the street. As I enter the back area of the zoo to make my way to the bear exhibit, I chug what's left of my latte. My usual keeper for the American woodland loop greets me as I rinse my empty travel mug at a water fountain outside the enclosure.

"Morning, Bob." I tip my head toward him.

"You're running late again, Ty. That time of year?" Bob teases.

"You know it." My bear doesn't actually hibernate, but I tend to be hungry all the time and tire more easily in the fall, going into the cooler months. Once winter sets in, it doesn't affect me much in my human form, but for now, I'm seriously dragging. Hormones are no joke.

"Well, the gates are about to open and our keeper talk is in half an hour, so get a move on."

"Ugh." I groan. Keeper talks mean crowds

coming to gawk. I mean, that's what I signed on for when I took this job, but I prefer when the crowds are more sparse. Winter is the best season for being a zoo exhibit. Ever since shifters came out to the world at large, most zoos have contracted with local shifter populations to keep their exhibits staffed.

It means steady income for shifters, keeps static wildlife from being exploited or mistreated, and lets the general population learn about nature and conservation. A win all around in my book. Not all of us agree, but that's the beauty of the system; we don't have to. Shifters who don't want to be in a zoo can take on different jobs.

As to how they pay us a wage to sit around and look pretty, well, for one, we don't have the same round-the-clock care requirements as our static counterparts. For another, visitors will pay more for the sort of displays shifted animals will put on for them. I've been a bear for the Willowdale Zoo for the better part of a decade now, and I've got no complaints. Or at least, no more than anyone has about their job.

"On the bright side, we've got in some lovely herring for your morning snack. If you give them a good show, I bet we can spring for more of those blackberries you like." Bob grins at me.

"And smoked salmon?" I wheedle, licking my lips at the thought of one of my favorites.

"Sure, that too. It's your hungry season. We'll

keep you well fed."

"Wouldn't want my bear to get any ideas about snacking on the visitors." I wink at him. It's a joke. I wouldn't actually harm anyone, but some guests get weird about being around my bear form. That's another reason I like my job. Being a zoo exhibit lets people get used to me instead of fearing my furry self. Every bit helps with staving off restrictive dangerous shifter regulations.

Bob laughs at my joke and I duck into the employee only area to stash my travel mug in my locker along with my clothing. I leave the door propped open and hang my wet shirt up on the corner so it doesn't soak my other clothing. The mint is less irritating now that it's had some time to dry and dissipate.

Once I've stashed my things in my locker, I let my bear take over. The shift is quick, a brilliant flash of intense pain as I reshape my entire being into my second form. Muscles burn as they take on new shapes, bones aching as they crack and reform. My head throbs as it expands. I drop to all fours and shake out my coat to ease the prickle of thousands of bristles of fur sprouting to fill in my warm winter pelt. One more big shuddering shake to relax into my second skin, and I'm good to go.

Bob comes in to open the door to the enclosure and I lumber out into my area. It's a nice replica of the sort of territory my bear would prefer in the wild. I got a hand in helping to design some of the enrichment areas when I first took the job. There are trees to climb and mark and a cozy den for me to retreat to when I've had enough of the visitors. I even have a nice artificial river area that they sometimes stock with actual fish for my supper. The river flows throughout the woodland loop and I can smell the other shifters close by.

I also catch whiffs of the visitors, though the thick glass between me and them helps cut down on the human scents, making them more bearable.

Bob follows me into the exhibit to get everything ready for our keeper talk. I can't respond to him in this form, but he shares all the juicy work gossip, anyway. We've worked together long enough that he knows I still understand him in this form.

"Oh, I almost forgot. You're getting a new enclosure mate this week."

I growl plaintively at that. I dislike sharing. Bears are territorial at the best of times, and more so when we're preparing for hibernation.

Bob scrubs his fingers into my thick fur consolingly. It took him a long time to be comfortable touching me in my animal form, but we're friends now and I know he means it as a comfort. He's alright, for a static. "It's only until they finish the remodel on the forest pavilion. A couple months, tops."

Oh no. The forest pavilion is an interactive exhibit, one where the animals can move freely among the human visitors. Meaning that most of them are small, friendly, and prone to communal living. Birds or rodents. Maybe it's a raccoon? Those aren't so bad. Might steal my fish. I go to get a drink from the river, as if I can stake my claim on it that way.

"Don't sulk. They're just moving a few of the raven shifters in here. They need a good place to perch. Freya, the alpha, said she likes the look of your trees." Bob gestures toward my favorite back-scratching tree. The trunk has *just* the right curve to fit my back, and the bark is the perfect texture. It's mine. I should scent mark it again.

"You should barely notice them," Bob says.

I'm not a fan, but Bob is right that if I *have* to deal with an interloper, at least the ravens will probably stay out of my way. Mostly. I huff and snuffle at the concrete rocks next to the river, looking for any snacks that might have hidden in the crevices here. My breakfast donut won't hold me over for long.

Bob chuckles. "I do not envy you that appetite. Here."

He tosses me a few of the glistening silver fish, and I gobble my treat. Tearing into the snack distracts me from the irritation of having to share my workspace with a stranger until it's time to show off for the sparse early morning crowd gathered for our daily keeper talk.

CHAPTER 2

Bram

My day is not off to a great start. First, the coffee place was out of my favorite latte flavor. And it all went downhill from there. I'm very late by the time I wait in a morning rush line twice for my coffee. It was necessary, after a big brute of a bear slammed into me and spilled my first cup. Sure, I could have paid better attention to where I was going, but he wasn't there when I went up to the counter to get my drink, and then bam! I turned around and walked right into this hunky—no hulking—wall of muscle.

I end up having to park in the furthest reaches of the visitor lot since the employee lot is full by the time I arrive. The zoo frowns on taking visitor spots, hence having us park as far away as possible while remaining on the zoo grounds if the limited employee spots are full. And then, when I finally make it to the forest pavilion to start my day, there is a big yellow closure notice on the employee entrance. I try the door anyway, but of course it's locked.

I spend several frustrating minutes trying to track down one of the pavilion keepers to figure out what is going on, but none of the ones I know are here. In the end, I have to text one of my fellow corvid shifters from the exhibit to get an answer.

Bram: Hey, where is everyone?

Freya: Didn't Jolene tell you we have today off?

Jolene is one of the pavilion keepers who works with us.

Bram: No. Why?

Theron: Oh, my bad. I think she asked me to pass along the message on Thursday, but I totally spaced. Sorry, B.

I don't know the other two raven shifters who work with me all that well. They're from a different rave. Okay, so I might be the only one in my flock to call it a rave, but I like that one. Way better than the other things statics call us. There's nothing unkind about me, thank you very much.

Anyway, we do most of our socializing in bird form. I'm pretty sure the names that Freya and Theron use at work aren't their real ones. Since we belong to different flocks outside the zoo, they haven't shared that information with me. My flock doesn't really approve of my career choices. They would rather shifters had never come out of hiding. But I enjoy getting to put on a show and having my raven form admired by a crowd of adoring onlookers.

Freya: They are getting things set up to transfer most of us to different exhibits while they do the remodel. I guess there was a scheduling conflict with maintenance and they weren't ready to confirm our temporary spot yet. So we took PTO for the week while they set up for us.

Bram: Great. Well, I'm here. Now what am I supposed to do?

Theron: We can shoot you Jolene's cell number so she can find a place for you for today if you're already there.

Bram: Sure, thanks.

I take the number and give Jolene, the head keeper for the pavilion, a call. She answers on something like the tenth ring. I wince. She must be busy with the remodel and she probably won't appreciate me bothering her.

"Hello?" Jolene answers in a clipped tone, but that's her usual businesslike demeanor. She probably isn't mad at me for calling. I still duck my head and try to make myself smaller as I huddle near the employee entrance to the pavilion to talk.

"Hi. It's Bram."

"How can I help you, Bram?" Jolene's tone

warms slightly.

"I'm just here, and I guess our exhibit is closed? No one told me."

Jolene huffs. "Okay, that's not a problem. You can head home or we can find a place to stick you for the day. Which would you prefer?"

I already made the hour commute, and I need every penny I can get to help Winny. My sister's medical bills aren't getting any smaller. Flock helps each other, but I'm one of the few working in the human world and making a good human wage. It's not even a question. "I need the hours."

"Right, your sister. How is she?" Jolene's voice softens and I'm pretty sure she really is sympathetic to my family situation.

"Fine." I rub my temples. Nothing about it is fine. Winny is miserable, so I revise my answer to be more accurate. "Hoping we can raise enough money for her surgery by the time they give us a date so she can actually get it."

"Is that looking like it will happen?"

I shrug one shoulder, even though she can't see me. "Your guess is as good as mine. I set up an online funding thing."

"Text me the link and we can share it around the break room. We take care of our own here," Jolene says.

I suppress a snort of disbelief. Sure. They take care of their own, but they couldn't even bother to tell me directly that I'm not wanted today.

"Thanks, I'll do that." I roll my shoulders, the

motion an echo of twitching my wings to resettle my feathers in my other form. I'm not being fair, Theron was supposed to tell me. And I do recall a notice of the remodel starting soon, just not that the switchover was today.

"Well, since you're here, come meet me near the black bear enclosure. We are planning to add some extra perches and shades to the public area and locker space to the back room for you three. We just wanted to give Ty some time to adjust to the idea of sharing his exhibit space with other shifters."

"Okay, sorry for the trouble," I say.

"It's fine; I'll meet you by Ty's habitat in five. Sound good?"

"Yeah, thanks, Jolene."

I hang up and make my way along the paths toward the black bear enclosure. I rarely have reason to enter this part of the loop. Bear musk smells, plus Ty, the alpha black bear who works the weekday shifts, has a reputation among the smaller animals of the pavilion as a territorial grouch.

I've never so much as had a conversation with the other shifter. Mostly, I keep to my kind. Birds of a feather and all that. But I need all the hours I can get to keep up with the hospital's payment plan.

Not to mention putting aside a little extra for the surgery fund. So I'll just have to make the best of an unpleasant situation.

CHAPTER 3

Ty

Bob told me I'd be getting enclosure mates this week. He didn't mention the changes started today. And of course the feathery pest chooses my perfect back-scratching tree to perch on. Makes a beeline right to the topmost branch as soon as Jolene, one of the pavilion keepers I don't normally have much to do with, lets the feathered fiend inside.

It's galling. I pace under the tree, rearing up to rub against the trunk every so often, hoping the featherbrain will choose somewhere else to roost. They caw at me instead of relocating, wings flapping to maintain their spot when the tree sways under my weight. Apparently, subtlety is lost on them.

Bob tries to distract me from my irritation with the new arrangement by bringing in a forage toy. He tosses them into the artificial stream near the front of the enclosure. The splash tears my attention away from the raven shifter's irritating presence. Since my efforts at dissuading the bird from using my favorite tree have failed, I go to investigate the object bobbing in the water.

It's a frozen pumpkin. And if experience with these matters is any guide, the gourd will be stuffed full of other yummy snacks too. All I have to do is fish it out of the water and gorge myself on yummy deliciousness. Bob certainly knows my weaknesses.

I bat a massive paw at my prize. It dunks down into the water, floating away from me in a drunken wobble. Another swipe pushes it out of reach from the shore. There's a log sticking into the stream, so I make my way toward the food, trying to snap it up with my jaws this time. The stem breaks off in my mouth. I spit it out with an annoyed roar.

My efforts are attracting a crowd along the glass walls of the enclosure. Although, to be fair, my irritable pacing all afternoon already had more people lingering near my exhibit than usual for this time of year. I'm normally fairly sluggish and content to lounge in the straw of my artificial den once the weather turns cold, still visible to the zoo's guests, but boring.

Well, I'm not boring today. Today I'm perched precariously at the end of a spar of wood, dangerously close to overbalancing into the cold water to get a treat. I overextend on my next swipe, distracted by the crowd and the loud croaking caw of my new enclosure mate.

At the last moment, I twist and find myself balancing on a boulder midstream, all four paws nearly touching since it's not a very wide rock. This is pointless. Once I have my balance, I rear up and roar my frustration at the treacherous pumpkin. And Bob for making a fool of me.

The raven finally swoops down out of my tree and glides in to land on a branch protruding from my log. They then hop delicately onto the floating pumpkin and cock their head to regard me. I want to growl at their insolence. As I watch in annoyance, they set sharp talons into the pumpkin and dig their beak into my snack, gouging open a hole to the tasty flesh.

I lower back down to all fours and search for a way to get closer without plunging into the shallow water. It's cold. The raven eats several more mouthfuls of my food, then takes off with a nut salvaged from inside the pumpkin in their beak. The pumpkin bobs toward me, bumping against my rock. It's easy to swat it into my mouth and grab hold of the indents the raven's beak made. I carry my prize ashore and tear into it to get the choicest bits of filling. Bob and the other keepers always supply snacks. I hurry to claim them before my rival can return to try taking more of what is mine.

While I eat, the steady staccato thump of my enclosure mate slamming their stolen nut into the rock formation above my den echoes around me. I growl a warning at the irritating featherbrain, but that doesn't stop the noise. Not even cracking open their treat does that. Quite the contrary, they squawk and croak and generally make a nuisance of themself. The raven goes back to the pumpkin scraps I left eviscerated on the shore of the stream once I'm a safe distance away. I watch them flapping around the habitat to hide some for later.

That might make for a small silver lining to my day. In that misery loves company, and retrieving the hidden food before it spoils will give Bob a taste of my irritation at this new arrangement. It better be as temporary as he led me to believe. Sharing my territory is unbearable.

When the loudspeakers along all the walking paths chime their warnings that the zoo is closing, I can't get out of my fur fast enough. As soon as I'm through the plastic flap into the employee only area, I'm already shifting. My fur tickles as it retracts. The squeezing pain as my head shrinks hits with the force of an epic migraine, then dissipates. My bones realign, the bear's extra mass melting into the ether from which it came. The changing area is colder in my human skin and I shiver as I open my locker. Only to discover someone else's clothing piled on top of my neatly folded outfit.

The flap to the enclosure opens and the rustle of wings confirms it's the raven joining me in our changing area. I'm not particularly self-conscious of my nakedness around other shifters. They'll be naked after their shift too. I'm more concerned with the fact they shoved their clothing in my locker, since the other one is locked.

Clothing that smells like citrus, vanilla, and feather dust. Well, of course it belongs to the raven. I turn to confront them, holding up the offending articles of clothing. Only to gape at Bram from the coffee shop as their all too memorable form unfolds from the feathery little nuisance standing behind me.

Our eyes meet and they tousle their flop of inky black hair, as dark and glossy as their raven feathers, leaving the strands standing up every which way. It reminds me of a disgruntled bird. Or a sex-tousled lover. I try to shake that thought away. Where the hell did that come from?

"You!" I accuse.

At the same time, Bram steps toward me with a chastising finger pointed at my broad chest. "You're the one who spilled my coffee and made me late!" Bram squawks.

The minor show of aggression is laughable. And quintessentially corvid, emboldened by the knowledge of their ability to fly away from danger. Still, if I catch them, I could snap the lithe little twinkie in half. Mm. Twinkies are not the best thing to be thinking of when I'm in serious need of an after-work snack. If Bram weren't so irritating, they would make a delightfully tasty morsel. Whatever else I feel about them, Bram's human form is entirely my type. I lick my lips and tear my eyes away from the attractive enclosure mate who I already can't stand.

"Me?" I repeat, trying to recapture my incredulity at their impertinence. I plant my feet and cross my arms. "You nearly scalded me! You're a menace."

"And you're a hazard, just appearing out of nowhere and tripping people with all your... you-ness!" Bram flaps both arms toward me, as if to encompass my bulky build. I'm a bear in every sense of the word and from the way Bram is eye-fucking me, even when we're fighting, they appreciate the view.

I snort. "You should try watching where you're going. And while you're at it, stay out of *my* tree."

"Your tree? It's *our* tree now, bucko. Jolene said we're sharing the exhibit until the pavilion reopens in March."

"March!" I splutter. "That's preposterous."

"Big words for a grumpy old bear. Why don't you just hibernate until spring and we can have the exhibit for the interim?" Bram taunts me.

"Shifters don't hibernate. Our body mass... you know what, no. I'm not wasting my breath on a featherbrain," I snap.

I try not to let it affect me when Bram's shoulders droop at the insult. It's a common enough insult for avian shifters, but I instantly regret the hurt it clearly causes them. The fight goes out of them. I find that irrationally irritating; it's not my fault if they've got a thin skin.

"This is my exhibit, and I have a contract," I say as I turn my back on the bird shifter. "I'll just tell management this is a mistake and we can't share. The zoo can surely work out another arrangement for you birds."

"Please don't." Bram's voice is small. "I'll leave you alone, perch somewhere else tomorrow, whatever you need. Just don't lodge a complaint."

"Why not?" I want to scowl at them, but I also don't want to look at them any more. I've always had a weakness for omegas of any primary gender who are more than willing to stand up to an alpha when it counts. And yet still vulnerable enough to ask for what they need. That's what made me fall for Myra's omega bearer, Arnie. Even though he's a grizzly shifter and his sleuth would have never accepted our mating.

"Because I can't afford to have my hours cut while they alter a different habitat to accommodate us. Please, Ty?" Bram reaches for me, fingers warm on my elbow.

For a moment, I'm shocked they know my name. But then again, I'm the only bear alpha to work the woodlands loop. The weekend shift omegas are Clara and Stacy. The zoo has our names plastered around the exhibit. Of course Bram saw the labels, and made the correct assumption of which name belonged to me. I glance back at the pleading expression on their face and sigh, defeated. An uncharitable part of me wants to call bullshit on their needing the hours. The zoo pays well, but I have no idea what their circumstances are like at home, so I let it go and lay out my terms.

"Fine. But tomorrow you're leaving my scratching tree alone and I get first crack at the enrichment snacks. Oh, and no hiding food in my enclosure."

"Deal on the first two. The third is an instinct thing. My raven will be an asshole if I try to suppress it for too long. And Theron and Freya won't be able to help it, either."

I sigh, understanding their point despite myself. The animal instincts our shifted forms rely on to survive are hard to suppress. "Fine. Nothing that will stink too bad when it rots if you forget about it."

"Deal. I won't accidentally forget a stinky fish in one of my caches." Bram almost sounds amused as they agree to my terms.

I notice the wording. They aren't ruling out doing it on purpose to further irritate me, but I take the temporary truce. Our argument is already threatening to make me late to pick up

Myra from my alpha mother's place. "That will have to do. See you in the morning, bird."

I dress hastily, ignoring the lingering traces of their citrus and vanilla scent and the mint from their morning coffee on my shirt. Bram's clothing rustles behind me as they also dress.

"Try not to be late again; we have keeper talks in the mornings and those usually draw a crowd." I glance back at them with one hand on the employee exit door.

"I'll see you bright and early, bear." Bram offers me a mocking salute. Somehow, the infuriating creature looks positively edible, even with their clothing rumpled from being crammed in my locker. They smell vaguely of me from the proximity of our belongings all day and my alpha nature stirs at the mingled pheromones.

If we'd met somewhere else, under other circumstances, I might let go of my irritation, put it behind us to approach them with an overture of friendship. I could offer to buy them a coffee to replace the one that our earlier collision spoiled. Or I might suggest we grab a post-work drink, but they've filled my entire day with one irritation after another. Besides, I don't have room in my life for drinks with an omega, no matter how attractive. I will not let instinct trick me into going soft on the nuisance. No way, no how. I bolt from the building and all but jog back toward my car.

🐾🐾

"Papa!" Myra's gap-toothed grin when I arrive at my mother's tidy little bungalow erases all my lingering frustration. My daughter runs to me the moment I open the door with my key and flings herself into my arms. I scoop her up and spin her in a circle, kissing her cheeks as she giggles in delight. Work doesn't matter when my little angel has her arms around my neck while she babbles to me about her day.

"Gramma says I have to ask you if we can order pizza for dinner. Can we? Pleeease?" Myra drags out the last word into a whine.

"That sounds perfect, baby," I agree.

I settle my daughter back on her feet and guide her toward the living room. My mother is sitting on the sofa working on her sewing machine. She's piecing together her latest commission project. Mom has always been industrious like that.

Myra's favorite show is streaming on the television. The familiar music and steady whir and clack of Mom's sewing machine signify the sounds of home and family. The two people who matter the most to me are right here in this room.

"Hi, Mom." I sit on the couch next to her sewing chair. Myra snuggles into my side, immediately engrossed in her show.

"Mhm. Just a second," Mom mumbles a greeting as she finishes the seam she's sewing. A moment later, the machine stops and she clicks the switch to turn it off as she trims the threads and holds up her project to inspect her handiwork. As she turns the piece right side out, I recognize it for what it is. The shell of a large bear plush toy with fur striped pink, blue, and white. "What do you think?"

"More pride bears?" I ask, reaching to pat the fuzzy toy.

I have the first pride bear she ever made. Byron is pink, blue, and purple. When I first came out to her as bi, I blurted it out at the school drop-off one morning back in middle school. Then I bolted out the car door before she could respond.

By the time I saw her again after school—anxious to know how she would react—there was Byron. The teddy bear still lives in my bedroom, alongside the genderfluid flag themed bear that Mom made when I shared that label with her years later. Around the time Myra was born.

"I've got some new designs that I'm working on, too." Mom reaches behind her for a stack of cloth doll shells and smooths them out on her lap. They're roughly the same size as the standard bears she makes. And then she pulls out one that's already finished to show me. The back fastens with a velcro seam, and with a twist of the plush fabric, the stuffie flips inside out for the human doll to become a bear.

"Did you see, Daddy?" Myra claps excitedly. "They shift! Like me."

"I saw, that's so clever, Mom. Shifter plushies for shifter kids?"

"Exactly. Myra gave me the idea a few weeks ago, and I've been experimenting with the design. Think they'll be a hit?"

"Absolutely!" I nod, flipping the toy back to its human form.

"And it's not just bears." Myra squirms across my lap to pick up a finished plush toy from near Mom's feet. "Look, she made a bat too! And a wolf." My daughter shoves both toys into my face.

"I see." I push the toys away.

The aromatic lavender inside the bat toy is soothing. Mom's top tier stuffy commissions include customizable scents, and the synthetic alpha pheromones coming off the toy wolf make me want to sneeze them out. I'm sure the omega who ordered the plushie will find the scent comforting, which is the point, but it's irritating to my sensitive alpha nose.

I'm not sure how Mom can stand to work with the scents as a fellow alpha. Then again, mom never made a secret of the fact she is equally interested in alphas and omegas. Perhaps the artificial pheromones don't bother her the way they do me. It probably doesn't smell like much to Myra since she's too young for alpha or omega pheromones to stand out to her.

"Wow. These are great, Myra. Did you tell Gramma how much you like them?"

"Yes! Gramma said I can have a rainbow bear shifter for my birthday. I can, right?"

"That's between you and Gramma. Her bears are special. Did you know that?"

"Yeah. Gramma said she makes them to show shifters that she loves them. Just the way they are and to give them big hugs whenever they need it."

"That's right." Mom nods.

"Do Byron and Lux give you hugs, Daddy?"

"They do." I smile at my kid. She settles back on the couch, head resting on my shoulder, eyes on her show again as a song draws her attention to the screen. The music apparently requires her to dance along with the characters, because Myra slips away and goes to bounce around in front of the TV. I can't help but smile as she flails her limbs along to the beat.

"*And* she's a screen zombie. Shall I order the pizza to share with you here, Mom? Or pick it up on the way back to our place?"

"Stay for dinner. Myra already did her homework." Mom pieces together the bear she just finished with one of the doll shells to sew them together. "I don't see enough of you, dear."

So I order our dinner while Mom sews and Myra dances along to her show. They both chat with me despite being absorbed in their own interests. I zone out on the couch, content to just be with the two of them in a way I'm not comfortable with many people.

CHAPTER 4

Bram

Featherbrain. The casual slur against my species rings in my head. I try not to dwell on it. It's not like Ty actually knows me. I've had similar and worse words flung at me often enough not to let it bother me most of the time.

Besides, static birds are more intelligent than people give them credit for. Static ravens use tools and can speak human languages. I'd like to meet the static human who can speak bird! But no matter how thick my skin has gotten, it still stings to hear the insult coming from an attractive alpha.

So of course I replay our argument in my head all the way back to the apartment building my rave owns. We're the sort of old-fashioned shifter group that includes multiple families of the same species living in close quarters in a tiny little town filled with similar shifter enclaves. I'm one of the few with a steady job in the nearby static city of Portland. Most of the other shifters who live in Four Corners, regardless of their animal form, prefer to stick to our own kind.

The largest other group is the local wolf pack. Four Corners is also home to a small sleuth of grizzly bears. We're neighbors with a mated pair of cougar shifters and their cubs. There are several other avian flocks and a variety of small animal dens and burrows and whatever else they call themselves. There's even a cul-de-sac near the school that's known for being welcoming to mixed shifter matings. The point is, shifters of all kinds can thrive when we carve out our own little communities. Even asshole alphas.

I don't want to find Ty sexy, but I do. Sexy and irrationally irritating. And now we have to work together, albeit in our animal forms. That should make things easier, but I'm afraid it won't. I've gone out scavenging with the local bear shifters and some of the wolf pack. Our little town functions largely on a barter system and we frequently supplement the flock's dwindling winter supplies with nature's bounty.

Scouting alongside larger predators is one way to get the best possible payoff for a day's hunting and gathering. Sure, we don't get the choicer bits of meat, but it's still enough to season a stew and stretch out to fill hungry bellies. I've gotten used to their wary acceptance of our presence at a kill. I can read a bear's body language, at least a little, and Ty seemed agitated to have me in his space.

An agitated bear in the fall can be a dangerous bear. I know that. Their instincts want them to pack on enough pounds to survive their hibernation until spring, and the animal instincts don't go away just because the shifter doesn't actually hibernate. His bear will want to, and it might make him unpredictable. Dangerous. Most bear shifters I know don't actually shift during the winter months unless it's to nap or birth cubs.

I don't have a choice but to go back tomorrow, though. My flock isn't well off, so even if the elders don't approve of my work at the zoo, they allow me to continue the job. Mostly because the team at Willowdale Zoo helps their employees get into clinical trials to find a cure for creep. And ever since I started working there, they've helped us access the hormone replacement therapy my brother needs.

Some days it still seems unreal that my brother developed the mystery illness that afflicts omega shifters and messes with our fertility. It makes the threat of the disease more real, in a way. His diagnosis shook my certainty that one day the three of us would get to start families of our own and that my kids would grow up close to their cousins. These days, I doubt Seb or Winny will ever settle down enough to think about kids, but it's still what I want. Someday, when I don't have to worry about my clutchmates' wellbeing quite so much. When they aren't dealing with their own crises.

Not that I can blame Seb for how much the diagnosis changed him. Creep is a devastating condition. For all that it's not widespread, most omegas are at least aware it could take away our fertility.

The shifter illness is still poorly understood, and there isn't a cure. It's one of those things we don't talk about in polite society. Like miscarriages and other causes for infertility, it only gets whispered about in hushed tones, a looming specter that you only seem to learn about once it has you or someone you love in its terrible clutches. Creep presents differently in different species, and with early diagnosis there are fertility preservation options, but it's something I've learned to dread since it struck Seb.

Among avian shifters, creep destroys the dominant ovary. Without the omega hormones it produces, the remaining—undeveloped—ovotestis is more likely to produce alpha hormones. We can apparently thank static bird anatomy for the way it all unfolds. The changes cause the shifter to develop alpha-like characteristics, regardless of whether they want them. For all intents and purposes, they physically and chemically become an alpha.

Except, that their seminal fluids don't actually contain viable sperm most of the time. The medical folks called it sex reversion since apparently alpha is the embryonic default.

Without his meds, Seb would revert to an alpha, which is something he doesn't want. My job means I have connections to help him access the medication cheaper. And I need the money I'm earning there to help Winny get the reconstructive shoulder surgery she needs to fly again. An accident last year resulted in a lengthy hospital stay that we're still paying for. Winny refuses to talk about what happened to her and she can't fly because the shoulder healed wrong and it screws up her wing when she's in her feathers.

I shudder at the thought of something happening to my wings. It's a nightmare that my sister has been living with for over a year. The static doctor who set her broken bones fucked up. Now she needs to have the limb surgically repaired if she wants a chance at being able to fly ever again.

The accident that stole her flight changed so much about the sister I knew. I don't think she'll ever be the same person she was before. And since it happened off shifter lands, she's furious at me for keeping my job at the zoo. Lately, it seems like all we do is argue about the surgery and whether we can afford it. It's gotten to where Winny barely acknowledges my existence.

Seb is the first one to greet me when I let myself in to join the family for supper. He and I don't live in our parent's unit anymore, but we still usually dine with our parents, Winny, and our three younger siblings. Seb, Winny, and I are clutchmates. The three of us have always been inseparable. We do everything together. From learning to fly and control our shifts to school, to having our first heats within a week of each other.

After school, we even moved out of our parents' place and into a tiny studio apartment to live together as unmated juveniles, just the three of us. It was perfect. Until Seb started to revert, Winny got hurt, and I took the job at the zoo to protect them both.

Winny moved back in with our parents after the hospital. To have more help while she healed, at first. But now she's staying with them because she's too afraid to leave our rave's building. She needs more than the surgery to heal her, but I can't make her see a shifter-friendly therapist to help work through her fear. And I can't make her talk to me. I can't make her do anything.

All I can do is everything in my power to provide the funding for her to get the surgery and rehab she needs to fly again. A bird that can't fly is… well it's a nightmare.

Seb still nominally lives with me. But he spends most of his nights sleeping with half the alphas in town and as many omegas as will risk fucking an omega who has creep. The doctors and scientists at the zoo say it's not spread through sex, but plenty of people are still superstitious about it. I love him, but it's probably not the healthiest coping mechanism.

So anyway, I slip into my seat after the family meal is well underway. Grandad shoots me a reproving look for my tardiness. My alpha mom's omega dad is joining us today, and he mutters about impertinent younglings under his breath. I try not to let it bother me, he's just a stickler for punctuality, always has been, and that has never been my forte.

Winny pointedly ignores my presence, excusing herself to her room as soon as it's socially acceptable to do so. My omega mom gives me a chastising glance for showing up late on a night I knew Grandad would be at the table, and my alpha mom reminds me to wash up before I sit. It feels like a slap at the fact I've been around statics all day. I don't question the rule, though, just go wash up before taking the seat next to Seb. Mom doesn't mean it that way, even though Grandad would.

My three youngest siblings talk a mile a minute to anyone who will listen. Seb is the only one who smiles at me, passes me my favorite food from down the table, and murmurs that he's glad to see me. The two youngest, Cory and Elric, clamor over each other to tell our grandad about school. Briony, at sixteen, is engrossed in the phone she's got poorly concealed in her lap, likely texting with her friends.

After the meal, Seb takes off to meet his latest conquest and I stay to help wash up. As Grandad points out, it's the least I can do since I wasn't around all day to help the family with any other chores. Once the kitchen is clean, I say goodnight to everyone, and head back to my apartment. As I walk past Cory and Elric playing video games without so much as a glance my way or a good night, I question why I even bother with the pretense of family dinners. Except they usually talk to me more. It's just been a bad day, and I felt Grandad's palpable disapproval over my career choices more keenly than usual. The fact everyone else just tried to change the subject made it feel like I was alone.

That isn't really true though. Sure, Mom and Mama worry about me going off shifter lands as often as I do, but they love and accept me as I am. I know they're both grateful for the financial help I provide. They were just stressed about Grandad's visit tonight since he can be difficult to please at the best of times.

My apartment is too quiet and I spend most of the night tossing and turning and replaying the words Ty threw at me in anger. Well, fuck him. I get quite enough judgment from people who actually care about me. I don't need to take it from him too.

I fall asleep with the restless resolve not to let

Ty dictate anything to me. He has no right to make me feel worse for everything I'm doing to help Winny. And unlike my family, I can give as good as I get with a random asshole bear alpha. Just because he's a territorial twat and I'm an omega doesn't mean I have to take his bullshit. I won't.

Tomorrow, Ty is going to get a double dose of his own rude medicine and I'm going to enjoy dishing it out to him. That settled, I flop onto my stomach and finally drift off toward sleep around dawn. Before I'm fully unconscious, Seb lets himself into the apartment and snuggles in next to me instead of climbing up to his rarely used top bunk.

My brother reeks of sex with a strange alpha. And my nose twitches at the hint of grizzly bear musk lingering on his skin. Gross. Why did he have to pick a bear tonight, of all creatures? And yet, having his warmth pressed against my side is too comforting for me to push him away, even if I want to tell him to go shower first. Despite the strange alpha bear's musk thick in my nostrils, I sleep easier with Seb beside me.

CHAPTER 5

Ty

I always feel like the eyes of judgment are upon me when I get to Myra's school late for the morning drop-off. The playground is deserted, so I have to walk her into the office for a late pass. She was tired this morning, not unusual for bear shifters at this time of year anyway, and we got home from Mom's late last night. Well after Myra's bedtime, so we only had time for one quick story that she fell asleep halfway through.

Dad guilt is a thing, and I have it in spades as my little girl looks up at me through a sleepy yawn. Her long auburn hair is in a messy tangle because we didn't have time to brush all the snarls out before putting it in a ponytail this morning. At least she's got clean clothes and a full belly.

Myra's lunch and extra snacks are in her bag, along with a note that she's a bear shifter, and she needs extra snacks at this time of year. I've already spoken to her teacher about that more than once, so hopefully this time he'll remember to make an exception to the usual rules for my girl.

"You have your granola bars, right?" I remind her as we leave the office, pass in hand. "And the trail mix I made you?"

"Yeah, Papa. I've got it. And the crackers and cheese, and the extra apple slices in my lunch. I'm good." She pats the straps on her school bag. "Next time no cherries in the trail mix though. They're too sour." She wrinkles her nose. I suppress a frustrated sigh because she was the one who picked out the dried cherries for the trail mix, but arguing won't get me anywhere.

"Sure. Thanks for telling me," I say. "Have a great day."

She starts toward her classroom, letting her hand slip from mine. I miss her already. It feels like only yesterday she clung to me when I came to drop her off for her kindergarten class. Now she's almost halfway through third grade and she doesn't need me at all for this. She smiles back over her shoulder at me.

"See you later, Papa Bear." At least she still uses the cheesy nicknames that have become our inside joke ever since she was obsessed with Goldilocks as a toddler.

"Have fun today. I love you, Baby Bear." I blow her a kiss. She rolls her eyes like she's already a teenager and far too cool for the likes of me, then skips off toward her classroom.

"No running!" I remind her.

"Bye, Papa." She waves without looking back at me, but she slows her pace to a walk.

I watch until Myra reaches her classroom, feeling the eyes of the school secretary, Mrs. Schmidt, on me all the while. I wave at Myra's back before I go.

The few minutes we were behind schedule add up, and then there's the time to sign Myra in as late. It all means I don't really have time to stop for coffee on my way to work. Then again, if I have to spend the entire day with the infuriating Bram, I need to make time to caffeinate.

My stomach growls as I'm taking the off ramp. I need a snack too. Breakfast was a rushed affair this morning and half of the eggs fell out of my breakfast sandwich and onto the garage floor as we were leaving the house. No salvaging that in front of tiny eyes.

So I swing by Wild Bean, even though I'm late and there's a line. Again. Fine. A few extra minutes won't make or break my day. But then someone gets into the line behind me, and I'd recognize their scent anywhere. Bram.

Not just Bram, but Bram mingled with faint traces of an alpha bear's musk. Something about that combination gets under my skin like nothing else could. I steal a glance over my shoulder at the raven.

They've got bags under their dark eyes. Like yesterday, they accented their generic jeans and a cotton tee with dozens of baubles. Shiny loops of beads around their neck, glittering rainbow hued pins, sparkly rings and clacking bracelets.

The raven is bejeweled the way Myra would be if I sent her into one of those kiddie jewelry places unsupervised with a no-limit credit card. If my kid saw this shifter, she would tell them how much she loves their style. The thought softens my feelings toward them. Makes me see them as having the same fierce confidence in their skin that I love about my daughter. The way they carry themself, almost makes the cheap, fake gems look like the real thing.

Despite all the ostentatious ornamentation, today Bram looks haggard. The swoop of their glossy dark hair is flat, the tousled disarray looks more unkempt than styled. Did they seriously spend the night with a bear shifter? It's none of my business, but it feels... wrong. I stare too long and Bram catches me looking.

"Oh! I thought that was you, Ty. Hi." Bram waves at me, bubbly and cheerful despite the exhausted bags under their eyes.

I grunt at them. "Morning."

"Listen, I wanted to chat before our shift. We got off on the wrong claw yesterday. Can I buy your coffee?" Bram asks, extending an olive branch, maybe?

"Large Black Bear Special and a honey cruller." I grit my teeth, but accept the tentative gesture of peace. If they want to make amends, then I should at least hear them out. And I really ought to find out what their pronouns are at some point, if we're going to be working together. And tell them mine. Ugh. People are exhausting and I don't want to deal with Bram or any enclosure mate.

"Great. So. I just wanted to clear the air and say I appreciate you sharing your habitat with us while our exhibit is closed. Otherwise, I'd have had to dip into my PTO for this week and I really can't afford to burn through that right now, so thanks, Ty."

"If you care so much about the job, why are you late again?" I grumble the first thought that pops into my head. A small voice that sounds suspiciously like my alpha mom is mortified at the rudeness of that comment. I want to facepalm, but taking it back would be too awkward. This is why I need my morning coffee; unfiltered Ty can be an epic asshole.

Bram bristles. "I'm no later than you! I didn't sleep well, and it's a long commute from Four Corners." They name a mixed species shifter commune about an hour outside of Portland, the nearest city.

I wonder how an omega from such an insular community ended up working at the zoo, but hadn't they already said they need the money from the job? They probably have creep or something. I remember hearing avian shifters need lifelong medication if they've got it. Their shifter commune probably couldn't provide for them, since those places aren't the most affluent.

Myra's omega dad is from a grizzly bear shifter sleuth with even stricter shifter-only views. His family made him choose between the sleuth and Myra and me, all because I'm a black bear instead of a grizzly like them. Myra knows about her other dad, but she doesn't know the exact reasons that side of the family isn't involved with our life.

Thoughts of Arnie sour my mood further. I don't regret anything that brought Myra into my life, but I wish her bearer had made different choices. Choices that let Myra have two loving parents to raise her. That isn't really the grizzly bear shifter way, though. Alpha bears aren't often directly involved in child rearing, and they are missing out, as far as I'm concerned. Instead, multiple generations of omegas raise their cubs in tight-knit family groups, with only occasional alpha involvement in those groups. Times are changing, but I still get odd looks among bear shifters when they find out I'm a single alpha parent.

My own parents defied conventions to raise me together until the day my omega mom died and left my alpha mom to raise me as a single parent. I've known I wanted to be an involved parent for ages. And Myra is the best part of my life. If Bram really does have creep, I feel bad for everything that might mean the omega could miss out on.

"You're right. Forget I said anything."

The person ahead of us finishes their order, and the barista beckons us up to the till, saving me from sticking my foot any further down my throat. Bram places our order and pays and it isn't long before I'm sipping from my dark roast coffee, sweetened with honey and nibbling my donut. With a mouthful of sweetness, it's easier to banish my grumpier side. "So, you're from Four Corners? Don't see many folks from out that way coming to Portland."

"They're traditional," Bram agrees.

I incline my head toward them. "I've heard that. So, would it be forward for me to ask what your pronouns are? I use he/him most of the time, but some days it's she/them. You'll probably be able to tell based on how I present. Unless I'm in my fur, then you can default to he/him until I can tell you otherwise."

"I use he/him. I, uh, wouldn't have guessed that about you." Bram strokes his cheeks and stares at my meticulously sculpted facial hair.

My big bushy beard and mustache in the same rich auburn as my muzzle when I'm shifted certainly draw attention on my more femme presenting days. But most people think twice about harassing a bear shifter roughly the size of a linebacker, no matter their opinions on my femininity. I can defend myself, even without shifting.

I bristle at Bram's reaction, though. His assumption that I must be a certain type of person because of how I look. I hate that. Hate that it's the norm and I'm the weird one for defying it. I shouldn't have expected anything more of a shifter from the boonies. Of course he's set in his ways. I scowl into my coffee.

"We should get to work before Bob has to do the keeper talk solo," I mumble as I pivot to leave. Big as I am, I can usually push through a crowd.

Bram doesn't immediately follow me, but when I pause at the door to glance back at him, he's watching me with something like regret in his expression. Well, we made a hash of making amends. So much for getting along better. I insulted his home and family, and his reaction to my coming out tells me everything I need to know about his attitudes. Bang-up job all around, and more fool me for hoping he'd be different.

CHAPTER 6

Bram

As soon as the words leave my lips, I know I've fucked up with my response to Ty telling me he's queer. His face might as well have turned to stone when I said I wouldn't have guessed about his pronouns. I kick myself over that the entire way from Wild Bean to the employee entrance to the zoo.

I'm late enough now that patrons are queuing at the gates. And we've got a keeper talk at our exhibit, so I need to get my feathery ass in gear. I gulp my coffee as I speed walk from the parking area to the woodlands loop.

It's not even like Ty is the first trans person I've met. Far from it. My older cousin Linda is trans. She came out to us ages ago. And her mate is a trans secondary gender alpha who opted not to go on hormones after creep rendered her infertile. So I know better. Or I thought I did. I'm just used to people like Linda and Philippa who fit the stereotypes of their gender.

Ty looks like a manly-man alpha bear in every sense of the word. And now I'm wondering if he's entirely as alpha as he seems, or if he's secondary genderqueer too. That is none of my business, and frankly, I doubt he'd ever trust me with the information if he was, considering my response to his pronouns. I should apologize again when I see him. I know I should. But that might just make my faux pas even worse? I don't know.

All I know is that for a second, things were better between us. Not perfect, but tentatively not hostile. And now I've made them so much worse and we still have to work together despite all that.

In my haste, I barge right into the locker area, and get the most glorious view of said sexy alpha's plump round ass. It's jiggling as he steps out of his snazzy chinos. He folds them and hangs the pants next to the matching blazer inside his locker. He's clearly preparing for a shift and doesn't seem to notice me at all.

I can't help wondering what Ty's luscious ass would look like in one of the ruffled mini-skirts Winny's school friends used to wear. Back when she went to clubs with Seb and me. Not that I saw her that way, because ew, but the skirts were objectively hot. Even better if he's got some lace hugging his curves and peeking out under the hem. He said he presents femme sometimes, so it's not too much of a leap to speculate if that extends to his drawers.

I lick my lips at the mental image of Ty in the place of one of the alpha bear pinups—gay bear, not shifter—I have tacked to the underside of Seb's bunk. Where I can look up at them when I'm rubbing one out before bed. Yeah, Ty is totally my type, and it's really easy to swap him into my usual wank-fodder fantasies. It's too bad my first work enemy is far too enticing for my own good.

I stare shamelessly at him. He's covered in freckles, almost the same color as his beard. His broad back is hairy too. He looks so strong. The sort of alpha I'd love to be with. If I dated. Which I don't—for reasons. Mainly having to do with the fact that every alpha I've ever dated inevitably gets weird about how close I am with my clutchmates. Just because we're close to the point of sharing a bed doesn't mean we're co-dependent.

It's all a moot point since Ty doesn't seem to like me, much less want to date me. And I'm being a creeper now, ogling his biteable ass. I don't want to objectify him. I shouldn't want him, but he is sexy as fuck and no matter how badly we're getting along, part of me wants him. And that part has control of my dick.

I am extremely aroused by the time Ty's mass expands and thick, dark fur sprouts all over his burly body. His bear form drops onto four paws and he turns partway toward me to grunt disagreeably at me before lumbering out into the exhibit yard through the plastic access flaps.

The loudspeaker system chimes with the warning that the zoo is open and everyone needs to be in their exhibits for the day. I chug my remaining coffee with a grimace at the lukewarm dregs. Then I strip hurriedly and leave my clothing in a heap in the locker that's hanging open next to Ty's.

They had it locked yesterday, so I helped myself to sharing his. I'll need to get the combination for the lock from the keepers later, but at least they unlocked it for me today. One less way to irritate Ty and fuck up our working relationship.

I remember what Ty said about finding a different perch. So even though his scratching tree has the best vantage of our entire habitat, I convince my raven that we don't need to be on high alert here. The corner nearest the otter enclosure has a pretty good view. So I settle in to enjoy watching the trio of playful juveniles as they frolic in front of the guests. Until they dive into the icy river. It's far too cold to play in the water.

The skin of ice forming along the shore of the artificial stream that runs through our area makes me shiver just thinking about a bath. Watching the trio makes me fluff out my feathers to hold in my body heat. By then, Bob has already started the keeper talk in the large open area in front of Ty's concrete den.

Ty hams it up for the keeper talk. When Bob talks about how bears mark their territory, Ty rears up to give himself a good scratch on his favorite tree. Even with us both shifted, something about his grunt of pleasure hits me right in the libido.

Ty seems to be in a better mood as he shows off for the audience. Until Bob talks about me, and ravens in general. Then Ty sulks. Bob seems to have embraced having me here, at least. He even holds out a padded falcon glove, like what Jolene uses with us, so I can perch on his arm without having to be careful of my talons.

I'm not exactly a raptor. Technically, we're passerines, but we're similar enough to other predatory birds to be grouped with them. Either way, my feet can kill prey if I need them to. I could hurt my human friends without meaning to, so it's a nice precaution. I glide down to land on the offered human perch. When I glance over at Ty, he's moping in his den. His big furry bum is the only part of him that's visible in the shadows.

Bob holds out a nice big shelled walnut for me, and I gulp down the treat. It's unsalted, but the raven is far less picky about food than my human side. As I'm chowing down on my snacks, Ty makes irritated grunt-grumbles that I recognize from hunting with the local sleuth of bear shifters at home. He wants me to back off his territory. Bob's treats are his kill, at least to his bear mind's logic.

I shuffle around on Bob's arm to keep an eye on the artificial den as I finish my snack. Bob is still talking about us, but he has an eye on Ty and he stops offering me food. I tune out whatever he's saying.

I've worn out my welcome, and it's time to get back to my perch and away from the grumpy bear. Still, I can give the crowd a good show first. I mantle my wings, showing off their span, before hopping aloft to reclaim my new perch.

A defiant loud croaking call rips out of my throat. I just can't help taunting Ty as a parting shot. To let him know he didn't scare me off; I *chose* to leave. I'm sorely tempted to fly up to perch in his scratching tree to see if that will get him to stop pouting in his den.

The only thing that stops me from being petty like that is that my new spot in the corner also affords a decent view of the looping footpath. So I get to gaze my fill at all kinds of shiny baubles. My talons itch to swoop in and grab several of the items I see carelessly dangling from bags or strollers or dropped and kicked to the edges of the path.

I enjoy watching the families best. They make it easy to fantasize about what it would be like to take my own kids on an outing like this. I want kids someday. When I'm not so busy trying to get my clutchmates' lives on track.

Surely raising a baby would be easier than trying to get Seb to stop drowning his sorrows in every shifter to look his way. Not to mention convincing Winny to venture out of our family home again. I don't want to think about their troubles, or just how distant that hope of starting a family of my own seems right now. Lucky for me, the raven is distractible.

The static visitors always seem to have lots of the shinies my raven side loves to collect. From sparkly sequin shirts to key chains to shiny foil wrappers on their food, I see it all from my perch. It's a corvid thing, that instinctual draw, but I seem to be particularly bad at resisting the impulse to gather the shinies when we go out. It's a problem, even in my human form.

Seb and Winny won't let me go anywhere near the costume jewelry places at the mall when we go out together. Though they rarely come shopping with me at all these days. The stuff there always seems so affordable until I get up to the register with my haul. I miss the way things used to be with them, so I try not to think about it.

It's easy to lose the better part of my day in people watching. When the crowd thins in the late afternoon, time crawls. I wish Theron and Freya were here to keep me company, since Ty's dozing away the day makes him boring. He doesn't come out of his den, which, from what I know about bear shifters, is pretty normal if they take their animal form around this time of year.

It's too bad the other two ravens who work the weekday shifts with me took Jolene up on having the entire week off. Maintenance is taking their sweet time about updating our accommodations for the renovations. At least they've already brought in two new lockers for us to use in the employee area of the bear enclosure. Taking the time off to wait on additional perches seems silly.

I need to save my PTO and my money. Not that I've got much in the way of savings with hospital bills to pay back from the accident. And I'll need to take time off to help Winny. When she gets the surgery, she's going to need help with her recovery.

Seb and I are the only members of our family who are comfortable spending time outside Four Corners. We'll be the ones taking her to physical therapy once she's healed enough to build up her wing strength again. It's going to be hard, but it will be worth it to fly with my sister again.

I have to believe it's a *when* and not an if. And that she'll regain the confidence to go out again once the doctors restore her flight. She's so pessimistic that she'll never fly again; it breaks my heart, but I have faith that the surgical team Felix got us referred to can work miracles.

There's nothing quite like flying together. When we show off our aerial prowess, it's one of the few times I really connect with Theron and Freya here at work. But flying alone is less exhilarating. So I sit in my new tree and idly preen my glossy feathers.

Bob brings more enrichment toys out in the afternoon. I give Ty a chance to have first crack at the rotten log, but when he slumbers on for what seems like ages, I swoop down to peck at it. There's not much of interest to me hidden within. The wood crumbles easily in my talons and my beak carves an opening easily. The fat grubs that scuttle deeper into the wood don't look very appetizing.

I break the log open, more out of boredom than interest. Unfortunately, I make too much noise to hear Ty approaching. He growls out a low threat. I squawk in surprised alarm to see the bear looming over me. Puffing out my feathers and extending my wings to seem bigger is laughable in the face of such a large predator, but instinct is what it is. I caw and fly at his face, just barely holding back the impulse to rake at his eyes with my talons as I wing my way out of his reach.

I perch as far from him as I can get, heart still racing, body trembling. Ty scared the crap out of me. And now his rumbly bear noises sound like he's laughing at me. So, once my pulse slows out of the stratosphere, I glide over to his favorite tree to watch him finish breaking apart the rotten log. Ty takes his sweet time devouring whatever bear delicacies he finds within. He might be sexy, but he's still an alpha asshole, no matter how attractive I find him.

CHAPTER 7

Ty

Bram startles me when he swoops in through the plastic curtain just over my head as I'm going into our changing area. I growl at him, the wind of his passage ruffling my fur and making me flinch. Bram caws a retort I don't care to parse and alights on the ground with a few awkward hops.

Bram ruffles out his feathers, like he's trying to brush off the clumsy landing. I snort in amusement. Much as I appreciate watching the little nuisance being anything less than graceful, the concrete can't be comfortable for him to land on. They should probably put a perch in here for the ravens, if they're going to be bothering me for a while. Which all signs indicate they will be.

Bob pointed out the temporary placards describing the birds that they've added around the spectator areas of my habitat. Of course, Bram doesn't spend long pretending to be utterly poised. It's pointless to act like he's not as ungainly as any other bird when he's stuck on the ground. He hop-skips toward his locker. And this is awkward.

We have changing rooms because, while sharing our animal forms with strangers after a shift isn't particularly taboo, the actual shift is an intimate act. One that I rarely share with others outside my family. The fact we have to share our little changing area has been one of the stressful aspects of having Bram in my space. It hasn't been an issue yet. We've been late or otherwise occupied before and after our shifts and during breaks thus far, but now I'm standing here staring at him, unsure whether to wait until he leaves or just shift and be done with it.

He doesn't seem to share my trepidation. Maybe things are different in the shifter commune where he lives. One little jump, and then he's shifting, feathers melting into smooth human skin, size expanding as his entire physiology morphs back into human. His beak recedes into a sharp nose over full, kissable lips. Glossy feathers at his crown extend into his similarly glossy hair. He completes his shift, and I'm caught staring into the dark, intelligent eyes of a very naked, exquisitely attractive man.

That's awkward as a bear, so I hurriedly reclaim my other form too. And then we're both standing there in nothing but our human skins, scowling at each other. Eyes locked.

He's so slim I didn't realize that we're nearly of a height. Unlike most folks, I don't have to look down to meet his eyes. And as he crowds into my personal space, it's not really his eyes I'm looking at. It's his lips.

I'm not suave. And I'm not used to getting up close and personal with other shifters. Or even statics for that matter. My social skills are a bit rusty in general. If he'd been a fellow alpha, I might have taken the invasion of my personal space as a challenge on instinct alone. But he's an omega, and he smells amazing. Citrus, vanilla and a hint of pineapple.

Bram snakes an arm around me, hand brushing my hip. If I close my eyes, this reminds me of being intimate with Arnie. Sweet and loving. Except there is nothing tender between Bram and me.

I blame what happens next on instinct. No one who isn't close enough to kiss gets up in my face like this. The only person, other than my baby girl, who has ever shoved his face into mine like this is Myra's omega dad. And that always presaged a kiss.

Sure enough, Bram tips his face toward mine and he's inches away from me. His breath ghosts over my lips. His eyes bore into mine with so much heat I could burn from it. No, there's nothing tender there. But there is an intensity, a spark of connection, that I've missed all alone in my bed. So I lean in, closing the last inch, and kiss him. Hard. Full on the lips.

Bram tenses. For a terrible moment, I think he didn't want this. That I overstepped. I almost jerk back, stammering an apology... except before I can, Bram moans.

His fingers that were brushing my hip curl around, grabbing me and pulling me closer. My hardening cock bumps against his rigid erection and I moan too. I take his face between my hands and deepen our kiss.

Bram's mouth softens against mine, his tongue caresses my lips, and I open to him. As our lips meld together, all the bubbling irritation over having a virtual stranger in a space that I've considered mine turns into passion. I pour it all into that kiss. That glorious meeting of mouths and tongues and bodies coming together.

It's been so long since I've been with anyone, and Bram's lithe body feels so good pressed against me. He's a fraction of my bulk; I doubt he could overpower me for real, but I let him back me up against the lockers. Both of us moan as the kiss goes on and on. The passion of that kiss lights a fire inside me that has lain dormant for years. I still don't particularly like Bram, but oh, how I desire him.

When he breaks off the kiss, I'm pinned between him and our lockers. He rakes his gaze over my body, and I instinctively try to suck in my big hairy gut. Bram snorts.

"Don't do that; I like it." He runs a hand over my belly as if to prove it, lazily stroking down toward my cock as he makes eye contact. "Look, we keep getting off on the wrong foot. Should we try blowing off some steam?"

"How?" I ask, licking my lips and trying to banish the filthy visions that his words conjure in my mind as his fingers curl around my cock.

"You got any condoms?" Bram asks flippantly. As though he doesn't care either way.

I could curse the fact that I don't, but I just shake my head, biting back another moan when he strokes my dick with his elegant fingers. Why would I carry condoms around when the last time I got laid was before Myra was born?

My bear isn't the only part of me that's been hibernating. But my dick is wide awake now. Dribbling pre-cum onto his fingers as he gives me another leisurely stroke. I hold back a whimper at how good it feels to be touched by another person.

"Too bad. Well, I'm on heat blockers and birth control, but they aren't perfect. So, pull out before you knot, yeah?" Bram says.

"But..." What am I doing? Protesting when I could be burying my dick inside the sexy shifter? I must have lost my mind.

Except I don't want to go through what I did with Myra's omega dad ever again. And at least with him, we had a relationship. I thought we were going to raise her together until Arnie bailed on us shortly after Myra's birth. Bram and I would be terrible co-parents. I can't even share a tree with him, let alone a kid.

Bram rolls his eyes. "We're both shifters, so it's not like you can give me anything a static has to worry about. And it's not like creep is actually an STD; they've debunked that theory. So, just don't knot me and we'll be fine."

"You can get pregnant without a knot," I growl, because I learned that the hard way.

He shrugs. "Outside a heat, the risk is pretty small for avians."

Bram loops his arms around my neck and kisses me again. Clearly, it's a risk he is willing to take. I'm not. Even though his hand on my dick is so good, and I want to bury myself inside him, fuck him. Feel another shifter's pulse beating in time with mine, the way I sometimes got to when I was tied with my ex after we fucked. The heat and comfort of being locked inside him. I miss it.

I want to hold Bram while he wraps his legs around my waist and shows off all that avian grace as I fuck him pressed up against the lockers. Instead, I shake my head and break out of his grasp.

Bram looks crestfallen. He balls his fists at his sides and I can tell he's got harsh words for me on the tip of his tongue. I rush to make my counter offer before he can say something that completely shatters our lust-fuelled truce.

"You can fuck me instead."

Bram stares at me like I'm speaking a foreign language. He licks his lips. "For real?"

"Yeah." I nod, eager for it. "I want you to fuck me, Bram."

He scrutinizes my face for something and then, apparently satisfied that I mean what I said, he nods. "Okay. Sure. Face the lockers and bend forward?"

I assume the position, pushing my ass back toward him. Bram's fingers brush lightly over my ass cheeks, parting them gently as he fingers my crack.

"Come on, bird, give it to me," I demand as his fingers tease my hole, making me squirm for more. "I won't break."

"No, I'm sure the big, strong alpha can take anything," Bram drawls sarcastically as he continues his gentle probing. "Have you done this before?"

"Taken a dick up my ass? Yeah." I grunt as he presses the dry tip of his finger against my rim, finally touching where I want him. And I have, but the digit hurts, reminding me it's been a heck of a long while since I've done this in any capacity.

"Mhm." He clucks skeptically. "New plan, squeeze your thighs together." He nudges my outer thighs and I do as he says. I'm too turned on to question him as the sweet citrusy scent of caramelized pineapple fills my nose. It's not his natural slick, I'd recognize an omega's slick anywhere, but whatever he's using for lube has his cock nudging smoothly along my crack as he presses between my thighs. The mystery of where he got lube can wait until later. Right now, Bram has me so turned on I can barely think.

I inhale deep, the pungent tang of his vanilla and citrus pheromones mixes with the sweet pineapple smell, amping up my arousal to heights I haven't allowed myself in years. I squeeze tight around him as he thrusts his dick between my legs.

"That's it, Ty; let me fuck you." Bram grabs at my love handles and drives forward. I'm still not entirely sure what he's using for slick. He most definitely isn't in heat, but I'm too turned on to care beyond that as he fucks along my crack from behind.

For that moment, while he's fucking me, there's no pressure to perform as an alpha for him. I might be big and strong, but that isn't what he wants from me. He's perfectly willing to take charge of this and we're just two horny bodies coming together to find mutual pleasure.

All I want is to give him pleasure, to be the one who makes him come. I squeeze him tight and rock along his slick length to meet his sharp, hard thrusts.

His cock rubs between my thighs, over my sensitive hole, and teases along my perineum.

The friction is a delicious buildup that will drive me wild, if I let it. I brace myself against the lockers with one hand and stroke myself with the other. It takes an effort to keep my legs together, forming a nice, snug channel for him to fuck as my pleasure builds.

"Someday I'm gonna take this tight little alpha pucker and make it mine." Bram grunts as his cockhead rubs against my hole, then slips forward, nudging toward my balls. I bend, trying to give him more room to work with. He hauls me back to meet his next thrust, and the next and I can imagine the rough fuck he'd give me, if I was taking his cock inside me.

The fantasy of the lithe omega claiming my ass has my balls drawing tight, but I hold off on coming for as long as I can. I don't want this to end. Need to put off the messy aftermath for as long as possible and just revel in connecting with another person while it lasts.

"You love this, don't you? Powerful alpha like you being reduced to an omega's fucktoy?" Bram emphasizes his words with hard thrusts, his balls slapping against me.

"Yes, fuck me harder, bird," I growl my encouragement.

Bram is righter than he knows. Being nothing but a slick hot channel for him to fuck turns me on more than anything has in ages. This is something I didn't realize I needed. A reprieve from all the frustration of the past couple of days for both of us.

If I'm honest, it's a relief from all the stress in my life. A moment to just let go of any and all responsibility and drink in a physical connection I've been denying myself for far too long.

Bram's hips snap forward. He adjusts his firm grip on my flanks, and then he pounds his cock home between my thighs. He uses me shamelessly until his hot cum spurts all over me. His omega pheromones, mixed with the musk of my arousal, tip me right over the edge as I paint our lockers in ropes of jizz.

Bram rocks against me a few more times. He rides out his orgasm, enjoying the aftershocks. I work my shaft a few more times, then squeeze my knot when the lack of pressure there starts to ache. I'm not ready for Bram to pull back when he steps away, withdrawing his softening dick from between my legs.

Bram reaches around me, and for a second, there's a warm glow in my chest at the thought he might snuggle close to me. It's not something I have the courage to ask him for. A quick fuck to let off steam is one thing. Cuddling afterward is something else entirely, but I can't deny how much I want it, in my heart of hearts. But he's only reaching for the nearest article of clothing to wipe himself clean. I try to ignore the crushing disappointment when he retreats, putting distance between us.

I slump against the lockers, catching my

breath. Neither of us makes eye contact, the air thick with the scent of sex and panted breaths as we both come down. Bram shoves my cum-stained shirt into my hands.

"Thanks for the lay, bear. Might want to secure your locker now that we're sharing quarters. Ravens are notorious snoops."

He winks at me, then shrugs into his loose t-shirt and starts putting on his bling.

I watch as he admires each shiny addition to his outfit. Blame it on the glowy post-sex haze, but I can't help softening toward him as he dresses himself. Once again, his taste in adornments reminds me of Myra and that can only make me warm to the vain creature.

He catches me watching and shoots me wary glances as he dresses. "What?"

"Nothing. I just like your baubles, bird."

Bram sniffs, like he thinks I'm mocking him. "They're my shinies."

"I know."

"You can't have them." He clutches at his gaudy necklaces as though he suspects I might try to snatch them away from him.

"I'm not going to take them." Only my years of practice keeping a straight face with Myra stop me from cracking a smile at his antics. Maybe the comparison shouldn't endear him to me, but it does.

"Well. Good. I'll see you tomorrow, bear." Bram slams his locker, shimmies into his tight, blinged-out jeans and pivots toward the exit. Damn, he's sexy.

"See you tomorrow, bird," I call after him.

Bram raises a hand above his head in a lazy wave of acknowledgement. His gaudy bangles clack together on his wrist and send off spangles of light. Then he leaves. And I'm left scrambling to get cleaned up. I wipe away as much of his lingering scent as I can so that Mom won't notice his omega pheromones on me when I go to pick up my kid. Or more realistically, enough so it won't be obvious what we were doing to get his scent on me. I can't waste time thinking about sexy-as-sin omegas. I've got responsibilities.

This was clearly a temporary loss of self-control. A one-off hate-fuck that we cannot repeat. Surely Bram will agree, considering how quickly he fled the scene of the—well, not crime. I find an old package of wet wipes at the back of my locker. I got so used to their convenience during Myra's infancy that I have the things stashed everywhere to this day, and swab his cum off my nether regions. Then I dress and leave to pick up my baby girl. She's got to come first for me, no matter how much I enjoyed my little interlude with Bram.

CHAPTER 8

Bram

"**Y**ou stink of alpha and preen oil," Seb remarks, the words a whispered hiss right into my ear. He is leaning into my space to grab the rolls at our family dinner table.

I try not to flush at the reminder that he knows exactly why I smell like preen oil. He's the one who figured out the trick of a partial shift to use the oil as slick for masturbating when we were teenagers.

Still, his hissed comments put me on the defensive. My gut reaction is to shove him away and tell him he's one to talk. He comes home covered in a different shifter's pheromones almost every night. And I would know, since he seems to have forgotten that he's got his own bunk. He ends most of his nights with a drunken middle of the night stumble home into my bed.

But then he straightens up with the rolls he was reaching past me on the pretense of grabbing and cuts his eyes meaningfully toward our sister. Winny is pointedly not looking at either of us. My heart clenches. Oh. That's why she was frostier than usual toward me when I hugged her earlier. She sniffs and asks one of the younger kids to pass the salt.

Seb's smile turns sympathetic. "So, you never said how the new habitat is working out."

"Oh. Uh. It's fine. Just the new coworker is an overbearing alpha bear shifter. So, he's a bit aggressive with marking his territory." I pick at my roast. Bless Seb for giving me an opening to explain away the scent in a way that might earn back Winny's trust.

"I just bet he is." Seb's tone is dripping with innuendo. So much for giving me plausible deniability about having Ty's scent on me. Seb can't help himself.

"Don't be disgusting, Sebastian!" Winny snaps.

Our alpha mom clears her throat meaningfully and exchanges a look with our omega mama. Like she's pleading with Mama to do something.

"Elric, did you tell everyone that Howard invited you along for the pack's next big hunt?" Mama says in an obvious effort to redirect the three of us from our squabbling.

Our little sibling beams at the recognition,

setting down their fork. "I'm scouting for the wolf shifters! Me and Jimmy Alvarez. We're splitting five percent of their prey. That's a lot, right?" Elric looks between our parents for approval and they both shower the kid in praise. The rest of us join in too. It might not end up being much, but every bit helps, especially with winter approaching and Winny's hospital bills looming over us.

The payment plan we're currently on for her stay last January is technically affordable, but it means food might be tight in the winter months when there's less forage to supplement the groceries. And that's without the new surgical costs tacked on yet. I try not to worry about that. We should have plenty of time left to raise the funds we need. Jolene's biweekly employee newsletter will help.

"That's wonderful, Elric." I reach over to ruffle their hair. Elric squawks a protest and scowls at me as they fix their coif. When did they grow up and get all particular about their grooming? At almost twelve, they aren't *really* grown up, but they aren't a baby anymore either. When did that happen?

"It will help a lot when Winny's recovering," I continue. Mom and Mama exchange looks and then Mama tries to signal me to stop, but the damage is done.

"I've lost my appetite." Winny shoves away from the table, almost toppling her chair over in her haste, and flees to her room. I stare after her in stunned silence, and her door slams before I can gather my wits enough to so much as stand to follow her. Seb rests a hand on my shoulder. To comfort me or to keep me in my chair, I'm not sure which.

"What did I say?" I turn my bewildered gaze toward the rest of the family. Granddad grumbles into his mug of tea.

"She got offered a surgical date." Mom stands from the table and grabs a wrinkled, stained paper from the counter.

"Why is that a bad thing?" I ask.

"Read it." She smoothes out the worst of the creases, then offers the letter to me. It looks like something she dug out of the trash after it got crumpled into a ball. Mama chivies the younger kids into eating as Mom clears away the serving dishes and wraps up Winny's plate in case she comes back for it once her temper cools.

I read the paper and my heart sinks. My eyes flick back up to the official hospital letterhead. This is the real deal. The surgical team has an opening for Winny during the first week of December. Months sooner than we'd expected. Way too soon for us to have a hope of raising enough to cover the quoted costs our insurance won't pay for. It's far too soon, and we aren't financially ready to cover the bills.

The only plus here is that we already paid the outrageous deductible after the accident, so our upfront out-of-pocket costs will be lower this way. If the surgery date listed was after the new year, then we'd be out the entire deductible again, which is unavoidably high with Winny on a community health plan, since I can't legally put her on my work plan through the zoo.

The team warned us that if we had to cancel for any reason once they gave us a date, we'd go back to the bottom of their waiting list. It could be years before she gets another chance. Years of muscle atrophy that she'll have to overcome through physical therapy. The old Winny would have fought, but this new, timid version of the sister I love, I'm not so sure she has it in her to keep fighting for years.

If we can't make this date work, I don't know that I'll ever get to fly with her again. I can't imagine a permanent loss of flight. Sure, minor injuries have grounded all of us at one time or another, but the sky was always waiting for us at the end of our recovery.

The note crumples easily under my fingers. It's already creased all over. "I'll make it work."

"How?" Seb asks, voice bleak. He squeezes my shoulder in support, but I know he doesn't believe it's possible.

"Tell Winny not to worry. I'll make this happen. I've got the money," I lie.

My boss has connections. He'll pull strings. I can just ask Felix, and he'll fix this. I know he will. Maybe I can ask for my holiday bonus early or something. I've got some savings that should cover a chunk of the costs. And the online fundraiser will get a boost when Jolene shares it with the rest of the Willowdale staff. Sure, I might not have the money now, but I'll get it. I have to. For Winny.

"Dinner was the first time she came out of her room since *that* arrived this morning." Mama juts her chin toward the paper. "Don't make her false promises, Bramble."

"It's not like that. I'll take care of it." I puff up my chest, willing them to believe me. To accept the date because we don't have any other choice. It's now or never. And never isn't an option. Not if I want the sister who laughed with me back.

Mama stares into my eyes for a long time. I don't back down. In the end, she nods and takes the balled up paper from me. "If you're sure. That's your money, Bramble. You don't have to pay for this."

"I know. But I want to," I insist.

And I want to help, no matter how much it might set back my own plans for the future and having a clutch of my own. I've got time. Those dreams can wait. It's not like I even have an alpha to share them with yet. The flash of Ty's handsome face that flits unbidden through my mind at that thought is unwelcome, and I force it down.

After an interminable silence where Mom and Mama exchange that silent communication of a long-mated couple, Mama presses her lips into a tight line and nods. "I'll call them in the morning to confirm the date."

Mama and Grandad disapprove of me using my job among the statics to help the family, but it's enough that they accept the help. I know Mama thinks it's exploitative. It might well be, but I don't mind showing off my feathers to the guests at the zoo. It's my decision, and I can spend the money I make there, a good living wage, however I choose. That's a fight we've already agreed to disagree over.

We finish eating in a somber silence. Seb and I congratulate Elric on their job with the wolf shifters again before we leave. Seb relates some silly stories about his time scouting for other shifters in the conclave. It's a rite of passage among the young ravens.

Winny and I have stories, too. But I'm not in the mood to share, and she refuses to leave her room. The room the three of us shared until we moved into our own apartment, just down the hall.

Seb pokes fun at me. Making our littlest siblings cackle with delight at the story of how I got distracted by Christmas tinsel during a hunt and let a fat, juicy static rabbit get away. That was the last time I got to scout for the wolf pack. The grizzly bear shifters still took me on sometimes. Mostly because I had a thing for the shiny foil packets of toaster pastries humans sometimes throw in dumpsters behind their food stores. Most bear shifters are fond of pastries.

Just like Ty with the honey crullers that I saw him buying at Wild Bean. The thought of the bear and the imagined hint of honey on his lips when we kissed makes me smile. It felt so good to be with him. To take charge of our pleasure, forget about bills to pay and responsibilities and just enjoy being with another shifter.

When we get back to our place, Seb rounds on me. His jaw is set in an angry line and he shoves at my chest.

"Why would you promise her that?"

"What other choice did we have? Even if we tell them we can't do it now, the result is the same as if we realize we can't make the deadline; we still go to the back of the queue for priority."

Seb rubs the bridge of his nose. "You really believe they treat saying 'not yet' the same as a last-minute cancellation that leaves a hole in their schedule? Do you think there's even a shred of hope that we'll just find a small fortune between now and the end of the month?"

I cock my head, picturing a hidden treasure trove of glittering gold pirate coins and precious gems like the ones the three of us played at searching for as children. Gold the same soft molten color as Ty's eyes when he offered to let me fuck him. I shake the enticing images out of my head. That isn't what Seb meant, and it's not a practical plan.

"I said I'd make it happen and I will, Sebastian."

"Whatever you say, Bramble. I've got plans for tonight."

Sebastian clearly doesn't believe me, but he stalks across our tiny apartment and rummages in his drawers for a change of clothes. I watch as he gets ready for another night out.

He paints on his makeup until his entire face shimmers, and layers a long sweater over his see-through mesh shirt. It covers the ass of his skintight pants, which leave almost nothing to the imagination.

Disappointment lodges low in my belly. He's going to go out and sneak back in the wee hours of the morning smelling of another stranger. If he bothers to come home at all. I don't like it —the constant worrying if he's safe—but I can't control how he copes with things. Only be there to support him when he snuggles into my arms in the wee hours of the morning most nights. And tonight, I've got too many other things on my mind to worry about Seb too much.

He's an adult who can take care of himself. And clearly I don't have any moral high ground when I fucked an alpha I can barely stand, while standing with him propped against our work lockers. I won't get a wink of sleep dwelling on that, so I write an email to Felix, apprising him of the change in Winny's situation and pleading for his help.

If anyone can help me figure out a way to help Winny, it's Felix. The head of zoo operations who handles getting Seb's HRT from the company that manufactures the synthetic omega hormones avian shifters need when creep hits us. He even offered to help Seb sign up for a clinical trial, if and when he decides to start a family. Seb scoffed at the offer. He told me it's a fairy tale that can't happen for someone like him.

Sebastian and Winifred are both different lately, and I bury myself in my raven for hours most days, even when I'm not working, to avoid having to confront that. Tonight as I stare at the ceiling in the quiet emptiness of the tiny apartment all three of us once shared, I can't help thinking about everything I'd rather avoid.

They should be here. Their vibrant scents of family and home mixed with mine instead of having to sniff around for the stale traces they leave behind. I should be able to fall asleep to the even breathing of my clutchmates. The way I have since we were hatchlings, too young to shift at will or leave the laying nest.

Between Winny's accident and Seb withdrawing ever since he got diagnosed with creep, nothing is the same as it was. We aren't living out the dreams we shared when we moved out of our parents' place. The three of us are drifting apart the way we swore we never would. I'm all alone and the weight of trying to help them be happy again is crushing me.

CHAPTER 9

Ty

Myra has nightmares again. I wake up sweltering under the warm weight of a shifted grizzly cub on my back. She's big in that form, even as a juvenile. That's probably why she chose it. Her black bear shift is smaller; a grizzly cub can defend herself. Even if the only thing she needs to protect herself from is bad dreams and the nasty words of a schoolyard bully.

I wish I could shield her from cruel words from the other kids. I wish Arnie had loved us enough to leave his sleuth and be a family with us. As Arnie's lover, I understand why he couldn't cut ties to his community. As Myra's dad, I don't know if I can ever quite forgive him for the way she cries sometimes when the other kids ask about her omega parent.

At least she goes to a shifter school. So they aren't constantly asking about a mother she never had. It's just unfortunate that the bully in question is also a bear shifter. Wendle is well aware that more often than not, bear omegas raise their cubs in multigenerational omegalineal homes.

If I'd been a grizzly instead of a black bear, I'd have moved into Arnie's sleuth. Lived with him under his omega grandmother's roof along with his omega dad, and his unmated omega sister. But that isn't how life worked out for us. So I've got Myra, and she's got me and my alpha mom.

I pat my daughter's back and soak in her warmth. She snores loudly; her bear form's natural exhaustion this time of year will make waking my girl a feat. I crane my neck to check the time. Shit. It's still dark in my room, but only because of the overcast fall skies.

We slept through my alarm, and I'm going to be facing more eyes of judgment from the secretary. A tiny part of me is relieved that will mean not having to face Bram in his human form this morning. We won't have time for an awkward conversation about letting our animal sides get the better of us last night. It was a meaningless quickie, and it should stay that way, unremarked upon and unremarkable.

Even if I *did* jerk off last night to the memory of Bram's slender cock thrusting between my thighs. His firm grip on my hips and the heat of his cum shooting onto my skin were glorious. I can't seem to forget the stirring of my long-dormant libido when he offered himself to me. Or stop imagining what it would be like to fuck into his lithe body with the air redolent of his burnt pineapple aroma. Was that him? Some strange lube? It didn't smell like any slick I've encountered before.

Myra's loud snore as she rolls off of me pushes all thoughts of Bram from my mind.

"Time to get up, baby girl." I scruff the thick fur at her neck until her snoring breaks off. Myra rolls irritably onto her back, batting a platter-sized paw at the bothersome human who dares disturb her rest. My cub is getting big, growing far too fast.

I let a partial shift roll over my forearm to block the blow and let my bear's deeper resonance into my voice as I growl a reprimand. "Shift, baby. It's time to wake up for school."

Myra squints bear eyes up at me and grumbles disagreeably. She's adorable in all her forms, but that exhausted, fuzzy face tempts me to let her take a sick day. Except then I'd have to take a day off too. Or make Mom cancel her plans to watch my cub.

It's not something I can do just because she slept poorly. Even if it is that infuriating Wendle teasing her again, staying home won't solve the problem. I'm not sure how to solve it, to be honest. But I can't fix it right now.

"I know. But you've got school and I've got work and we're already running late."

Myra arches up to nip at my arm, but she rolls onto all fours, shakes out her fur, and shifts into her human form. "I don't want to go." She pouts as she rolls, pulling my blankets up to her chin.

I stand and pad over to my closet to get dressed. The masc outfit I laid out last night isn't going to work today. I need something more femme. Flowy fabrics and feminine cuts. "That isn't an option. School is important, Myra." I flick through the hangers until I find the perfect pale green blouse to fit my mood. The shiny brass buttons will appeal to Bram's avian nature. That detail has nothing to do with my selection.

"It's stupid. I'm stupid." Myra plucks at the blankets.

"You aren't stupid. Language, Myra. You're clever, kind, and creative. You know my rules about name-calling."

"Ugh. That's *so* not the point!" Her eyes dart to the skirt I just pulled out of the closet. "Mapa!"

"I know, but I won't ever let anyone put you down in front of me, kiddo. That includes you." I step into my skirt. The soft fabric caressing my legs grounds me in my body, banishing the floaty sense of dissociation that swamped me when I reached for my dude duds. "Say three nice things, please."

"Fine. Grr. I'm smart and perfect and wonderful." She rolls her eyes again, clearly not taking my rules seriously. There's still a hint of a smile in her voice as she says she's wonderful, though. As if saying it makes her believe it, at least a little. Good. "So, since you think I'm already so smart, what do I need to learn multiplication for? I can just work at the zoo with you and be a bear all day."

"See? You *are* clever, trying to use my words against me. I have no problem with you working the exhibits once you're old enough, my girl. But you still need math. And reading and everything else you're learning. Static bears might not do much math, but you still need the skills to keep track of your pay and your living expenses and manage a budget. You need to understand contracts, and stay on top of current events." I turn to watch her as I do up the shiny buttons on my blouse.

Myra rolls her eyes. "I know, Mapa Bear. Shifters don't get to not care about politics."

"That's right." I fix my cuffs. "Now, get dressed and I'll warm you up some waffles."

Myra rolls onto her feet with a heartfelt groan. As though it's a huge imposition to stand. She takes my fluffy comforter with her, wearing it like a robe as she trudges toward her room. I reserve comment, knowing full well that it's hard to shake off the bear's lethargy immediately after a shift this time of year.

We're late for drop-off again. The secretary gives me the evil eye, but hands Myra a hall pass without a word. Myra takes it, gives me a quick hug, and makes a beeline for her classroom so she won't miss the morning snack in her class. I wave sheepishly after her. I turn back to face Mrs. Schmidt, ducking my head as if that might minimize my height. Apologies are already on the tip of my tongue. But she isn't the one who addresses me.

"Ah, Mr. Orville, a word?" Principal Daily calls from the doorway to her office.

My mouth goes dry and my heart sinks. It's not just the racing worries about why she needs to see me. It's the title. She called me mister because she sees me a certain way. I experience a moment of stomach-churning vertigo at having her tacitly saying I'm something I'm not. Even after I've asked the school not to use that title for me.

At the start of the year, Myra moved from the kindergarten through grade two school to this one for third grade. Amongst the stack of start of year papers, I crossed out the pre-filled option on their contact forms and checked the other box to fill in 'Mx' instead. I thought that meant the school would at least try to use the correct title. The principal is standing in her doorway now, arms crossed and a pinched expression on her face as she looks at me.

I clear my throat and rub my sweaty palms against my flowy skirt, trying to cling to the confidence I felt while pulling it out of my closet this morning. It's a futile effort; I look as fierce as my baby girl's grizzly form, but inside, confronted by a potentially hostile authority figure, I'm small and scared.

"Of course," I agree. "Now?"

"If you have a moment, that would be best." Principal Daily turns on her heel and goes to her desk, moving as though she expects me to follow.

Mrs. Schmidt smirks after me as I navigate around her desk and into the small office. Or it's possible I'm imagining her hostility. Projecting because I feel so judged and exposed here from years of hiding huge parts of myself to fit in at schools like this one. Guilty over our habitual lateness.

I'm already late for work, but she said it would only take a moment. And this way, whatever the principal has to say won't be looming over my head until my day off on Friday. And with Bram in my exhibit, I'm not even leaving the habitat completely abandoned for however long this takes.

Principal Daily gestures for me to take a seat, which I do while she settles in behind her desk. She steeples her fingers and looks at me over the rim of her glasses.

"As you know, Myra has been arriving late to class more often than not recently."

"She's been having trouble sleeping," I explain. That's a big part of the problem.

"And is there a reason for that? Is her home life

stable?"

Her meaningful look at my clothing forces me to hide a wince. Is she judging me? Implying I'm not a fit parent?

"She's a bear shifter on both sides, right?"

Or maybe she's just looking at me. I'm just already on my guard here. After all the issues we've been having with Wendle since the spring and the way Myra's teacher has done little to curtail the bullying. Her old teacher kept the kids separated after the disastrous party at Wendle's house that started him taunting her over Arnie's absence from her life.

"Yes. So, you'll understand that this time of year she gets easily overtired. It will get better in the spring. Myra has a stable and loving home," I say, dreading what might happen if her school believes otherwise.

"I understand, but we have other bear shifter students who are still able to arrive on time for school."

I want to growl that the way those other bear shifter children treat my daughter—shunning and excluding her over her familial differences—are a part of the problem. Instead, I keep my tone calm, unwilling to live down to alpha stereotypes of being quick to anger.

"Yes, well, perhaps if those other children didn't tell her that living with her alpha parent is unnatural she'd have fewer nightmares. If they didn't get away with telling her that there must be something wrong with her for her omega dad not to want her, she would have an easier time sleeping at night." I try to stay calm, but I can't keep the acid from my tone. I clench my fists on the chair's arms, stopping when the plastic creaks ominously.

It's not the kids I'm mad at. Until this year, Myra's friends never cared that she lives with me. A few of them asked about why she calls me Papa some days and Mapa on others, but it was never a problem before.

Not until Wendle's birthday party. When his omega grandmother greeted Myra as a cousin because of their shared animal form, then asked why Myra's omega parent wasn't dropping her off. She explained about Arnie's sleuth not being in contact with us.

Ever since, Wendle has been making her life difficult at school. Her teacher is aware of the issue. She promised to monitor the situation and keep me apprised. The weekly reports Ms. Potts sends home only mention that Myra seems withdrawn and prefers to play by herself.

Myra says Wendle hasn't stopped bothering her. Just that he's switched to quiet comments when the adults aren't around. Pinches, shoves, stolen snacks, and broken pencils. Nothing big enough to be worth escalating on its own. Just constant, relentless picking that makes me dislike the little boy with an intensity I never thought I'd feel toward a child.

I don't blame Wendle so much as his parents and grandmother. But I blame both Ms. Potts and the principal for not taking my child's safety as seriously as they seem to take her lateness.

"Perhaps Myra would have more incentive to arrive on time if she wasn't being bullied. Your school claims to have a strict anti-bullying policy."

"We do. We take bullying *very* seriously, Mr. Orville." Principal Daily puts on an air of faux-outrage.

I suppress my snort of disbelief. Barely. "And yet, she comes home with bruises on her arms, hungry from that boy stealing her snacks, and she cries herself to sleep asking me why her bearer didn't want her. She tells me that Wendle and his friends say it means she's defective."

"I was unaware of the situation with Wendle," she says, and from the way her entire demeanor shifts, softening toward me, I believe she means it. "Thank you for bringing it to my attention. Has Myra reported this to someone at school?"

The principal leans forward and sets a pen to paper on her desk. Perhaps I misjudged her and her outrage over the situation is real. I didn't think to escalate the issues to the principal when Myra's teacher proved less than watchful. I should have. Only Ms. Potts said the administration was aware of the issue and working to fix it.

The gnawing worry that I'm not enough for

my girl rears its head, telling me that Wendle's Gran might have a point. She doesn't, though. My alpha mom was all the parent that I needed after my bearer died. And I'm enough for Myra. The three nice things rule applies to me too. So I tell the voice of doubt that I love my daughter, I'm the best parent for her, and I am handling this situation for her to the best of my abilities. I am good enough for her.

"Ms. Potts. She promised to monitor the situation, but Wendle just stopped picking on her in front of their teacher. Now when my kid tries to report anything, the teacher calls her a tattletale."

Principal Daily shakes her head and makes a tsking sound. "That is *not* our policy. I will have a word with Myra's teacher today, and we can arrange a meeting for all three of us. If the issue persists, would you care to reach out to Wendle's family to mediate something? Or we can move Myra to the other third grade class. Mx. Adams will stay on top of any bullying in their class."

"I'm not opposed to mediation, but I'm not sure if that wouldn't make the problem worse? The first I heard of this issue was when his family met me and the first rude comments came from his omegiarch."

The principal nods. "Very well, I will sort this out; I promise if I'd heard of the issue sooner, we would have investigated. In the meantime, I can fill out paperwork to move your daughter into

Mx. Adams's class if you can wait five minutes?"

"Yeah. I can wait." It occurs to me that while we've spoken, Daily has had no problem using the correct honorific for her staff member. That makes me wonder. "Did Ms. Potts pass along the beginning of the year paperwork they had me fill out for Myra?"

"I believe so; is there a problem there as well?" She arches a brow at me.

"Only that I asked to have my information listed as Mx. Orville on the form. Her old school allowed it, but the form I had to fill out online didn't. I sent a corrected paper form in with Myra and she said she passed it along to her teacher. Ms. Potts said she would try to remember, but she hasn't actually made much of an effort on that front."

"I see." Daily's lips purse, and she scowls as she looks for something on her computer. "My sincerest apologies, Mx. Orville. Let me update your file. And I will look into how the form got misplaced as well. I'm glad we could clear this all up. I'm sure Myra will be happier and more rested once we resolve this, hm?"

"Yes. I think so. And I appreciate you taking this so seriously. I wish I'd thought to bring my concerns to you sooner."

"Well, I can see where you might have gotten the idea we wouldn't listen, all things considered." She reaches for the printer and grabs a change of class form, which she fills out, then passes across her desk for me to read.

It occurs to me that I should discuss the change with Myra first, but I already know this is the right decision for her. Her best friend from last year, Jenny, is in the other class already and she adores her teacher. The best way for Myra to show Wendle that his family is full of shit is for her to be happy and thriving. Preferably with a teacher who actually listens to and respects her. I scrawl my signature.

"I'll be in touch, and I'll let Mx. Adams know about the change, so expect a welcome to the class email from them. How about we move Myra on Monday to cause minimal disruption?" She files away the signed form and I rise to leave. "And I will dig into the situation with Ms. Potts as well. I assure you, we do take bullying seriously here."

"That works for me. Thank you." I'm still a little dazed to realize the issues I've been having with the school since Myra started here two months ago could be resolved so easily. All that stress and tension over nothing. Well, nothing but the misfortune of dealing with a single bigoted teacher, rather than a school that only pays lip-service to their anti-bullying policy.

"Thank you. I appreciate you taking the time to meet with me. I'll be in touch regarding the bullying issue to be sure it stops. And I apologize again about the paperwork mixup, Mx. Orville."

I shrug it off with a vague platitude. "Just

glad we could fix it." It's awkward to have to excuse the oversight, but clearly she isn't the one at fault for the misgendering in all the school communications. I have a good feeling about Myra switching classes.

Then I get back to my car and realize I'm going to be late for the keeper talk. My good feelings evaporate as I merge into rush-hour traffic to get to the zoo. I'm already late, again. And I have to face Bram after what we did last night.

I don't regret the sex. We're both adults and it was so nice to be wanted like that again, after so long going without sex or romance of any kind. Between work and my kid, I just haven't made myself a priority. I should do that more. Just not with my coworker. In our locker area, where anyone with an access pass could have walked in on us. And certainly not when it means missing out on family time with my kid, but I should try to make myself a priority too.

That starts with talking about what happened like adults. That's what my therapist would say. If I'd kept up with seeing her. In one of many instances where self-care comes in dead-last after caring for my kid, I stopped going. It wasn't practical once Myra got too big to come along with me and sleep in her baby carrier during my sessions.

Mom would have offered to watch the kid for those extra couple hours a month, but I already felt guilty about imposing on her for the coverage gaps in my workday childcare needs. So I let it slide. Anyway, the point is, I know what I *should* do about the situation with Bram.

Bram and I need to get along for the next several months while we're stuck sharing an exhibit. So whatever else I might think of the bird, I can't just ignore him or blow him off. And I shouldn't give in to temptation again. No matter how tantalizingly close he gets to me. Or how amazing it felt to be with another shifter again.

There's really only one reasonable solution. We'll discuss what happened like two responsible adults. It can't happen again. I'll keep things professional going forward.

Still, the heavy traffic that ensures I won't be on time to speak with the raven until the end of our workday comes as a relief. Even as I'm frustrated at the clock crawling inexorably further and making me late enough to get written up.

Good thing my bosses at the zoo are understanding of my family situation. At least I don't have to worry about losing my job over a few late mornings. Or over screwing around with my coworker.

That isn't against the rules. It's even subtly encouraged, given that part of the zoo's mission is to preserve shifter populations. Still, getting involved with an omega I barely know isn't a wise choice. I need to remember that. No matter how hard Bram makes me—er, remembering

—no matter how hard he makes *remembering*. Right.

CHAPTER 10

Bram

Wednesday morning, I pry myself out of Seb's clinging hold earlier than usual. Felix should be in his office before my shift starts. If I can just speak to him in person, I'm certain he'll have a plan to help Winny.

Word around the zoo is that he's the one to talk to about omegas in need. His mate even runs a foundation to help omegas affected by creep. Felix will help. Just like he helped me with getting manufacturer rebates for Seb's hormones.

Although, from the vaguely woodsy scent of him lately, he might need his dose adjusted. Sometimes I'm not sure if he smells of alpha because of whoever he was with before he came home or if it's his natural scent changing. The way it did before he got on hormones. Either way, I need a shower after sleeping with him wrapped around me. Probably can't hurt to erase any lingering traces of Ty's scent still on my skin either.

I rush through my morning ablutions and get to the zoo early enough to catch Felix in his office. Patty, his receptionist, gives me a sympathetic smile. They're always on top of everything going on with zoo staff, so I'm sure they know I'm here about Winny.

"Bramble, dear, how are you?" Patty greets me with a warm smile.

"I'm alright. Is Felix in? I need to talk to him about Winny's surgery."

"Oh? Has something about her status changed?"

"No. Not precisely. They scheduled her dates. It's sooner than we expected and I don't know if we have time to raise the funds, but if we turn it down…" I trail off at Patty's sympathetic nodding.

"You go back to the end of the waiting list. I understand why that is a problem. The sooner corrective surgery occurs, the better the recovery rates with this kind of injury, no?"

"Yes." I nod, relieved at their understanding.

"Let me tell the boss man that you're here. Help yourself to coffee and donuts and take a seat."

Patty gestures to a small break room with a

carafe of fresh coffee and a big box of donuts. I help myself to the treats while they step into Felix's office. I've just got my coffee doctored to the perfect sweet and creamy consistency when Patty tells me I can go right in to see the boss.

Felix waves me toward a chair.

"Ah, Bramble, good to see you. I got your email. As we've discussed, the zoo insurance doesn't cover siblings, but if your sister could take one of the open weekend shifts, we could cover the costs of her surgery directly."

"I've told her that, but she isn't comfortable being shifted for long periods, you know, with the injury and all." I downplay just how little Winny is willing to spend time in her avian form ever since her injuries stole her flight.

There's no way my sister would make it through an entire work shift, even on a part-time schedule, and that's not what he's offering. The weekend crowds are even busier than the Monday to Thursday shifts I work. If she took a job, we could swap schedules, so that I worked the busier weekend shifts. As if I could convince her to do anything.

I refuse to acknowledge a pang of disappointment as I realize that plan would mean not seeing Ty anymore. That should be a perk of this plan. Sex isn't going to make us suddenly get along. It might make things more awkward. All the more reason to swap shifts with Winny, if only I can convince her to take a contract with the zoo.

"In that case, there are other options, but none that are so straightforward. We don't currently have any administrative roles open that do not require shifting, but if one were to become available, I can have Patty keep your sister's resume on file. Otherwise, I can send the link to your fundraising site out in our donor newsletter. Many of our loyal patrons are likely to see it and spread the word about a shifter in need. And I can speak with Thurston about alternative means of funding the surgery. It's possible he knows of options I am unaware of."

"That's a start. Thank you, sir."

Ever since Jolene posted about the site in the keeper's breakroom, I've seen an uptick in donations. Nowhere near the tens of thousands of dollars we need to pay her outstanding bills. Let alone the expected costs of the new surgery. Not to mention private physical therapy at an expensive flight-focused rehab center afterward. But anything is better than nothing. And the old debt is on a payment plan that I'm just able to keep up with.

I didn't tell the rest of my family about that. How I got the bills put in my name when Felix helped me negotiate with the hospital administration last spring. Getting the fundraiser in front of more eyes sympathetic to shifters, and preferably with deep pockets, can only help.

"And if your sister changes her mind about working the exhibits, I'll do what I can to waive the waiting period on her company insurance. We've done that in the past for omegas who needed time-sensitive treatments, so I am familiar with the process if it comes to that. I can even make allowances for if she prefers to shift offsite, if that would ease her troubles with being seen in animal form?"

"I'll see what she says. Thanks for the offer. I guess I should get to my habitat before the gates open."

Felix glances at the time and nods. "I won't keep you. How is the new habitat working out?"

"It's fine. Ty doesn't seem too thrilled to have an enclosure mate, but we'll work it out."

"I'm sure you will. Don't let the grumpy bear act fool you; Ty is a giant softie." Felix sorts through the papers on his desk and hands me a brochure. "Oh, here, it won't cover the surgical costs, but this organization helps with skilled nursing care post-operatively and transportation to and from physical therapy. In case that's something your family needs."

I pocket the colorful flier and offer Felix my thanks. Then I turn and leave, less confident in a solution than when I walked in. I'd hoped for more. A miracle. But now it appears my choices are limited. We can hope for a rich benefactor to be moved into opening their wallet based on what little information Winny was comfortable sharing on our fundraising page. Or I can convince her to work for the zoo alongside me. Honestly, I'm not sure which outcome seems more improbable.

I sip my coffee. I'd have a better chance of convincing Seb to take enough shifts to qualify for insurance. Of course, he'd never take the work for his own benefit, but for our sister... and then it hits me. Convincing Winny to take a shift at the zoo might be a lost cause, but Sebastian would do it for her. And unlike most non-avian species, it's not as though anyone could tell at a glance that Seb wasn't my sister once he gets in his feathers.

All three of us share a familial similarity of scents that anyone might expect. If Felix can get Winny a dispensation to come and go from the zoo in her avian form, well it would be easy for me to bring my brother in her place. The only issue would be that they'd expect her wing to appear damaged. Seb and I can work something out. Like getting a wing splint for him to wear. That would serve the dual purpose of helping him remember not to use her bad wing.

My half-baked planning absorbs my full attention as I make my way to the woodland loop. I'm running late after the stopoff to Felix's office, but Ty still isn't there yet when I card into our changing area. I glance at the lockers where he let me fuck him last night and have to adjust myself. At least unwanted boners aren't a thing in my bird form.

There's two new lockers set up for Freya and Theron in the employee area. They're not supposed to be back at work until Monday. Once they're here to share the exhibit, I'm sure I won't get another repeat of last night's shenanigans. That should be a good thing.

Ty and I don't get along. No matter how good the sex was, it can't go anywhere. Still, I kind of wish he was here. So we could at least clear the air. I suppose we can chat after hours. I hastily strip, stuff my belongings into my locker, and shift.

When I push through the plastic flaps, it's immediately clear the maintenance crew visited our habitat last night after hours. They added some new perches in prime viewing locations around the enclosure so that the zoo guests can admire us birds in all our plumage. There's a roosting box as well, for if we need a moment out of the elements. And a few shiny enrichment toys hanging from the tallest branches of the tree I spent the day perched on yesterday.

I glide up to one of the silvery chimes that's twisting in the slight breeze and cock my head to admire the shiny colors. Bob enters the enclosure for the keeper talk as soon as I arrive, so I must have been later than I thought. What could be keeping Ty? He was a grump about me being late, and yet he hasn't been on time once this week. Not that I'm one to talk. But I'm not a grouch about it when other people show up behind schedule.

Bob mixes up his usual speech to give the crowd raven facts first, since the bear he usually talks about is conspicuously absent. I fly to the perches near the front to give the crowd an up-close view of what he's saying.

Ty lumbers through the plastic barrier into the habitat half-way through Bob's presentation, much to the delight of the visitors. The spectators 'ooh' and 'ahh' and snap photos. Ty mugs for them, even going up to his scratching tree to rub his back. It occurs to me as I'm watching him I didn't actually see how he's presenting in his human form today, so I might be using the wrong pronouns. I peer at the bear and wonder if there are any indicators of how they're presenting in their furry form. Should I ask? Or wait to see what they wore to work today?

I don't know, but I vaguely recall him saying that he/him worked in his fur if I wasn't sure. And then Bob brings out some berries and I'm thoroughly distracted from wondering about Ty at all.

When the chimes sound to announce that the zoo is closed to visitors, I swoop down from my comfy new perch near the observation windows at prime people watching height. Today went well. I had a better napping spot and a place to hide from the weather when it rained early in the afternoon. Bob even brought out some forage snacks for me to enjoy in my temporary roost.

And now I get to leave. My plan for the night is convincing Seb to pose as Winny so we can get her primo insurance to cover most of her hospital expenses. Granted, she's technically got health care through the shifter commune, but my policy through the zoo has better coverage and a much lower deductible, so it would help to get her on the same plan. We'll still need the fundraiser to do well to cover the private rehab, but every bit helps.

I'm distracted as I push the plastic aside with my beak and strut into the employee area of the exhibit. All thoughts of potential insurance fraud evaporate at the sight of Ty's gorgeous round ass framed in satin panties. He bends to step into his—no, *she* bends to step into *their*—skirt. I'm going to get their pronouns right. It's the absolute least I can do after my less than stellar reaction to learning she isn't cis. How was that only yesterday?

I hastily shift into my human form too, instead of standing there gawking and unable to talk. She's between me and the lockers, so I'm left standing awkwardly naked behind Ty as they get dressed. Is that the right name, when she's not masc presenting? I need to ask. But not until after I've apologized for my foot in mouth response to their coming out yesterday.

"Missed seeing you this morning." I make awkward small talk.

Ty startles at my voice, turning to see me before tugging their skirt hurriedly into place, covering the shimmery satin. She reaches for her blouse and I can't help admiring the shiny buttons.

Her shoulders hunch defensively as they say, "I had a last-minute meeting. It won't happen again."

"Oh, no worries, I was late too. Also to attend an impromptu meeting." I edge around her to my locker so I can cover up my boner. That is very much going to be a problem if I keep looking at them in a pretty skirt and shiny buttons. Or fixating on their lush ass covered in silky soft satin. I hastily tug on my boxers to cover up the issue. "Um, this is awkward, but about yesterday, should we talk about it?"

"There's nothing to talk about; it was a one-off lapse in judgment." Ty shuts her locker decisively.

"Okay, but it doesn't have to be a one-off. I don't have a lot of chances to meet alphas between work and family obligations. It was nice to be with an alpha who respected that I'm not just a hole. So, yeah, I'd be down for a repeat." My shirt is inside out, so that takes a minute of clumsy fumbling to fix. "If you wanted to, uh, blow off steam together."

"I've got other obligations too, bird." Ty retorts with the same self-important gruffness that makes them seem grumpily unapproachable. After last night, I'm not as intimidated by her. So I press on toward my goal. I pull my shirt on, part of me hoping that it won't stay on me for long if Ty agrees to my proposal.

"Right. We could make it quick, just meeting a need after hours. Freya and Theron like to fuck at work too. I keep my mouth shut about it, so I bet they'd give us privacy as long as we return the favor."

Ty groans. "I forgot I've got more of you birds moving into the enclosure next week, don't I?"

"Afraid so." I tilt my head to admire the way her buttons sparkle in the fluorescent light. Pretty. Just like the burly alpha wearing them. Ty's next words break me out of my reverie.

"Well, in that case, I better take you up on the, uh, unorthodox stress relief." There's a twinkle in her eye as she says, "looks like I'll need it."

"It might improve morale," I agree, bobbing my head.

I lick my lips, then plunge ahead. There isn't a delicate way to apologize, that I can see. But I need them to know I respect every facet of their identity as much as they showed me she respects mine.

"Um, it might also help if I apologized for yesterday morning? You took me off guard, but I want you to know that I'll always respect your pronouns. Is there a different name you prefer to be called when you present more femme?"

"Ty is fine. It's me either way." She eyes me, as if gauging my sincerity, then adds, "sometimes I use Tyson for more masc days, but not when I'm presenting femme."

"I'll remember that. My full name is Bramble. Bramble Korbin. So, since we've got the lockers to ourselves... can I interest you in a bit of below the skirt action?" I gesture toward their nether regions with my balled up pants, then toss them back toward my locker. No sense putting on clothes if I'm just going to take them back off. I *hope* that's where this is heading, anyway.

"You want to lick my big fat alpha clit?" Ty quirks one of their auburn eyebrows at me. They've got a very expressive face.

"Yes, alpha," I agree, appreciating that they gave me the terminology they use before I could stumble into saying something that makes them uncomfortable. I'll have to remember to follow their lead on what to call body parts and sex acts, if we're doing this. We should talk more at some point, but I have more interesting plans for my mouth just now.

I sink to my knees in front of her and brush the hem of their skirt with my fingers. "May I?"

Ty nods. "Go ahead. Make your alpha feel good." She makes no move to lift her skirt out of the way.

I gaze up at them above me, and I want to

memorize this moment for later. Her full beard contrasts with the soft femininity of her blouse and skirt. The outfit is all flowy fabrics that would billow in a strong breeze, little folds in the fabric giving tantalizing glimpses of shifting shapes and colors. It reminds me of alpha birds displaying their colors to attract a mate, and I like the idea of her wanting me like that after just one taste.

I can imagine that; Ty dressed up just for me. As though they can't get enough of me. Even if their outfit has nothing to do with me and what we did last night, I cling to the idea of it. That someone appreciates me, and I'm not entirely alone. In all my efforts to help my family and keep my clutchmates from self-destructing, I have somewhere to turn for solace, the way Winny ran home and Seb keeps running into the arms of any shifter who will have him.

I need to forget, and with her, I can, at least for as long as it takes for us both to come. Ty clears their throat, as if to prompt me from my inaction, so I lift the hem over my head and position myself in front of her. Ty's clit is hard and leaking pre-cum when I pull the satin panties she is wearing down enough to access it.

I lick experimentally over the crown and Ty moans, encouraging me that I'm on the right track with how I'm touching her. I remember my cousin's mate, Philippa, giving a drunken tutorial on finger-fucking trans women. Linda called it muffing and said it was the best sex of her life. Once I tried it on myself, and it was weirdly uncomfortable. I wonder if Ty would like that sense of being penetrated though? I'm not sure how to ask her that.

"Can I touch you?" I check. "Like, to finger you?"

"I'd prefer if you did, yeah." Ty nudges me closer to her genitals.

If I can find the right spot, I'm pretty sure she'll let me know whether to proceed. I lick patterns over her clit, using one hand to hold it in place, and I explore between her thighs to find the spots Philippa described with the other. It's weird to think of my cousin's mate while I'm doing this, but I need to show Ty I see her and I care about making this good for her.

Just like they made it so good for me last night. My thumb and first finger find the two indentations where her thighs meet the soft skin of her scrotum—her inguinal canals. I wince internally, wondering if she calls the folds of skin something else, but from her moaning, I don't think she'd appreciate me stopping what I'm doing with my tongue to ask just now. Ty opens their legs more, leaning back against the lockers with a grunt as I press against the twin skin-covered openings simultaneously.

"Oh, you really meant you're gonna finger me, huh?" Ty sounds breathy. "You know what you're doing, don't you?"

"Mm," I moan against their clit. I'm still reluctant about stopping what appears to be working, judging from the steady dribble of excited juices my attention garners, but I need her full and enthusiastic consent for this. "Want me to fuck into you here?" I press against the dual hollows. It's different from anything I've done with a partner before, and I want to see how Ty responds to the sensations.

"Do it! Fuck your alpha, bird," Ty demands.

So I fuck into them, my own arousal rising as the full length of my fingers slips inside. The tender, flexible skin makes the motion easy, moving with me without any need for lubrication. I go slow at first, to be sure they like it. Ty paints my tongue in their arousal, humping the tip of their clit into my mouth. She tastes like alpha musk mixed with a subtle sweetness I wouldn't automatically associate with bears. Except, after having seen their coffee order, I know she has a penchant for sweet things.

I'm in heaven, cocooned in the gauzy confines of their skirt, senses full of the hedonistic pleasure of being with an alpha. Her scent is intoxicating in my little fabric bubble. The thrill of power at being the one to make a capable shifter come undone just for me. Her body is tight around my fingers as I fuck her harder and her thighs tremble as she holds back her pleasure. Ty's hands land on my shoulders, molding the skirt to the back of my head, pinning my face closer to her clit.

"So good, bird. I'm close. Going to come on your face."

"Mm," I moan my assent.

It won't be the first time an alpha has painted me with her jizz, and I hope it's not the last time that I make Ty lose control for me. I don't let up on my frantic pace, driving them toward her release with every fuck into their body and every stroke of my tongue.

Ty squeezes my shoulders, then moves one hand to cup the back of my head and hold me in place. She folds over me and uses me to keep herself upright as her knees buckle and she cries out my name.

"Bram! Oh, fuck, bird, you... fuck me!" Ty babbles as their clit pulses and unloads onto my tongue, the musky cream dribbling over my lips in jets of raw need.

I try to swallow it all, but some inevitably spills onto my chest and thighs. At least it doesn't stain the gauzy skirt tented over me. I slow my fingers once the shudders of Ty's orgasm fade. I lap lazily at them a few more times, until they shift their hips away, as though my touch is too intense now that they've come.

"Give me a second to reciprocate," Ty says with a shuddery breath. I withdraw my fingers and duck out from under her skirts to look at her. I instantly miss being surrounded by the musky scent of her. My own happy little sex bubble, too bad it had to burst. I lick my lips, getting another faintly sweet trace of her.

"Mhm. You taste good, bear," I say when I catch her staring at my wet lips.

"Didn't you know? Bears are full of honey and sweetness. It's why they sell the stuff in bear-shaped bottles," Ty teases me, their breathing more even.

I chuckle in reply. I don't have a good comeback and my dick is achingly hard after getting her off.

"Take out your dick, omega. I want to see it."

Ty steps back and straightens out her panties. She resettles her skirt around her, as if she didn't just come her brains out, pressed against my greedy mouth. My dick twitches in my boxers at the memory. I can still taste her on my tongue.

"Yeah, okay." I rise to my feet and free my erection. "Hope you want to do more than look at it."

"What did you have in mind?" Ty asks, glancing at my crotch and licking their lips.

"I was thinking of putting your mouth to good use," I say, gesturing at my erection. Ty doesn't need me to spell it out. She sinks to her knees, and sucks me into her mouth, deep-throating my slim length like a champ. Damn, I wasn't expecting that from an alpha, but maybe I should have realized Ty would be a generous lover after yesterday. Their obscene moans leave no doubt they enjoy the act too. I can't help pumping into the wet warmth of her mouth, loving every moment of this, being with an alpha who cares about my pleasure as well as their own.

After getting her off and fantasizing about a repeat with her since last night, it takes no time before I'm ready to empty my balls down their throat. I hold off my orgasm as long as I can, relishing every stroke of Ty's tongue along my length.

The spicy alpha musk of her arousal lingers, mixing with my scent into an intoxicating blend that has me breathing deeper. Their strong shoulders feel so solid under my hands as I cling to them to stay upright while pleasure builds to a peak inside me. Like Ty can be my bulwark against all the worries waiting for me outside this stolen time together.

When I can't hold back a second longer, I gasp their name, in an abortive attempt at a warning. "Ugh, Ty, can't— "

Ty swallows down every drop of my release and holds me in their mouth until I've recovered enough to gently withdraw, wishing that we could stay in this moment forever, where the only communication we need to exchange revolves around giving each other pleasure and nothing else has to matter.

Afterward, we both clean up hastily with the wet wipes she inexplicably keeps in her locker. My stomach rumbles as I'm pulling on clothing, reminding me I skipped breakfast in favor of my meeting with Felix. I should have grabbed one of those donuts when they were on offer in his office. Too bad I've still got a long commute ahead of me before suppertime.

"Here." Ty's voice is gruff as she presses a granola bar firmly into my hands. It's one of those healthier ones with dried berries and nuts added in.

"Thanks. Are you sure you don't mind?" I ask, even as I rip open the packaging to break off a bite.

"Always carry extra this time of year." Ty shrugs as they tear open their own snack. "Don't worry about it."

The shiny foil of the wrapper catches my eye. That's why I stare at her eating it; no other reason. I'm not infatuated with the pretty alpha. Not at all.

CHAPTER 11

Ty

Once again, my evening commute feels like the drive of shame. I'm later than usual to pick up my daughter from my mother's house, with the lingering taste of an omega's cum in my mouth.

I'm not sure I should make a habit of fucking my coworker. It's not my usual style to have a quickie at work. But then again, I haven't been with anyone since Arnie, so maybe I owe myself some grace.

My ex was the furthest thing from the brashly outspoken Bram. The raven is the loudest voice in any room I've seen him in, even when he's not saying a word. Arnie's problem was that he went along with the loudest voice in the crowd.

For a while, that was me. I thought we agreed on so many points that I later found out he only went along with to placate me. But then his omega grandmother and dad laid down the law about mating a grizzly shifter or not coming home to the sleuth, and that was the end of us. Not right away, but it put the writing on the wall.

I should have seen it coming. When he asked for my knot a few weeks after his heat, I thought little of it. We'd been together a long time, had even talked about him moving in with me, since his family didn't want him bringing a black bear alpha home to the sleuth.

I thought we were forever. It didn't register that he was saying goodbye, even when he cried. I thought it was just an emotional night for us both, since I'd told him I loved him for the first time earlier in the evening.

It didn't cross my mind that he might end up pregnant. I still don't know if it crossed his. If he thought a great grandchild would sway his grandmother in favor of our mating. Myra didn't change a thing. Except to break Arnie's heart when he left her with me rather than raise her in a family that would always look down on half of who she is. That much he did right by her. I don't know for sure that it hurt him, but if he was at all the shifter I thought he was, it would have. I just wish he could have chosen us instead of the family who would reject her.

These days, I don't think about Arnie nearly as much as I used to. The recent bullying issues with Wendle coupled with having another omega on my mind have me remembering. Little things that I'd rather forget. I don't want to remember our first kiss under the stars after a high school football game.

Arnie and I were both on the cheer squad. He convinced me to join because they needed strong alphas for their acrobatics. I had fun lifting him into the air and watching him fly. I used to get such a thrill out of touching him, tossing him around like he weighed nothing, catching him before he hit the ground.

Only, he's not the omega I want to be there to catch anymore. I want to see Bram's face lit with joy. His smiling eyes sparkling at me as I kiss him silly. The tinkling clink of his bauble collection as he lifts his hand to cup my jaw is music to my ears. I want to relive our parting kiss all evening long.

Bram's heated gaze as he reached for my skirt like a supplicant on his knees before me will forever be one of the hottest moments of my life. And he must have meant it when he said he'd accept all of me. He had to have looked up that thing he did with his fingers, or he already knew something about pleasuring a trans femme partner.

Bram muffing me almost made me melt into a sated puddle of goo from the force of being fucked in such an affirming way. I was willing to believe he'd respect my pronouns, but it's a whole new level for his actions to prove his acceptance. Bram made me feel so very seen on his knees, lathing my clit with his tongue while he fingerbanged me into the stratosphere.

I don't know how long this thing between us will last, but—despite all my noble intentions not to complicate matters between us—I'm glad he doesn't want to stop doing it until we've both had our fill. Instead of letting parent guilt consume me, I spend the drive in evening traffic to Mom's place grinning like a fool over the omega I like. That has to say something about my feelings for Bram. I'm just not sure what.

Mom has Myra watching a video in the living room when I arrive. Myra's engrossed in the film and clutching one of Mom's bear plushies tight to her chest.

"Everything alright?" I ask as I step into the kitchen to greet my mother. I miss the bouncy greeting I usually get from my kid, but I can see her on the couch from here and she looks tired.

"She's fine, dear. I was about to put on the kettle. Would you like some tea?" Mom putters about rinsing the pitcher and adding water.

"Sure. Decaf, if you've got it," I agree, grabbing a second mug to set beside hers on the counter.

"Is chamomile alright?" Mom asks as she reaches for the tin of loose leaf.

"Sure. School went well? I met with the principal this morning about moving her into the other class."

"That's wonderful. I assume because of the

bullying? She'll be thrilled to be in Jenny's class, even if she shouldn't have to be the one to move when that boy is the one being awful to her."

"Yeah, my thoughts exactly. If the teacher was taking the issue seriously, I'd prefer for Wendle to be the one facing consequences. But the main thing is that Myra won't have to be around him as much this way. And the principal is looking into the entire thing."

"Good. That reminds me. Speaking of that awful Wendle boy, he invited several kids over for a Denning Night party and Myra's upset that Jenny said she's going," Mom says.

Jenny is a rabbit shifter, so I doubt very much that she will take part in the shifted portions of the party. She is probably just going for the feast and the storytelling and games the grizzly bears play during the early hours of the vigil.

"She asked why we don't have Denning Night plans yet."

Simple answer; it's a grizzly tradition. In the past, I did my best to recreate those traditions for her. I've always tried to give my kid the big cultural celebrations Arnie told me about when we were together. But when Wendle invited her to Denning Night last year, before he realized Arnie isn't in her life, Myra said she didn't want to celebrate the grizzly shifter pre-hibernation rituals.

At first, I figured it was because she missed the neighbor kids who used to join us before they moved away. So I let her skip it instead of trying to give her the small family celebration we'd done with a few other families in our cul-de-sac up to that point. It broke my heart when Myra told me the real reason she wanted to cancel. That those holidays only make her miss the connection she lacks with her omega dad and his family more. It hurts to know I can't give that to her, no matter how hard I try.

I've always offered to take her to meet other grizzly shifters, but then everything with Wendle soured her on the notion. When she was smaller, I arranged playdates, and took her to mixed species celebrations. We read books about grizzly shifters all the time. I still take her for weekend brunches with Mrs. Grund, an elderly grizzly shifter who recently moved from our cul-de-sac to a retirement community. Mrs. Grund is like an honorary grandmother to my daughter. She used to babysit Myra before Mom retired and could handle all Myra's after school care for me.

Among grizzly sleuths, Denning Night is a big deal. They have a ceremonial feast, followed by an overnight vigil. Then, at dawn, all the shifters old enough to participate make their last shift before the hibernation season to spend the day napping together in their fur. They return to their human form the following evening. Most grizzly bears prefer to remain strictly in their human form until the spring thaw, when our bear form isn't as lethargic as during the winter months.

Some pregnant grizzly omegas choose to stay in their bear form and hibernate away the bulk of the pregnancy like a static bear. Arnie joked he wished he could do that with Myra, so he could hibernate through the physical demands of growing our baby bear.

The shorter timeline of a shifter pregnancy makes it extremely physically demanding. I empathized with his desires, but we needed his income to afford his prenatal care without insurance. The pregnancy was unplanned, and we were both newly out of high school and scraping by on retail work, so that dream wasn't possible. Arnie had a lot of dreams about a family. Truthfully, so did I. We both wanted a large family. I thought those were dreams we'd get to live out together.

Sometimes I wonder if Myra has younger half-siblings and if Arnie got his hibernation births. And I can't help being bitter at knowing Myra won't ever get to feast with those siblings or her cousins on Denning Night. She'll never cavort with the sleuth's other cubs under her omegiarch's watchful gaze. Or doze away the first day of winter in her fur, tucked close to her bearer's side.

At least I can give her the black bear traditions I grew up with. Our family always made a bigger deal of the spring thaw. We feast to the reawakening of spring and the bounty of summer. The closest thing I had to a Denning Night tradition was Mom's lazy family brunches to honor the bear's needs in the fall. And we set aside one weekend a month during the winter to be bears together and remember to take the time to rest. Right here in this familiar kitchen with the cream and tan subway tile backsplash and the painted tan cabinets.

Not much has changed in this room since my omega mom designed it when I was a cub. We had a lot of traditions here. Traditions that became too painful after my other mom died and only trickled back into our lives years later, when Mom dusted them off to share with Myra. We have our pancake brunches again now. And we can have a Denning Night celebration, just the three of us and some close friends. The kettle bubbling and hissing as it reaches the correct temperature draws my attention back to the here and now.

"I suppose we can celebrate it as a family again this year. Or I can try to find a sleuth that puts on a public Denning Night feast," I say.

"Or you could call Arnie," Mom suggests, her voice soft. She glances toward the living room, as if to be sure Myra isn't listening. I check too. She's not paying us any attention, though I get a lazy wave when she sees me. The movie wins out over actually talking to her mapa, though, so Myra sits on the couch looking dozy-eyed at the screen.

"No." I shake my head, and though I don't allow venom into my tone, that is not a line I will cross.

If Myra ever asks to meet that side of her family, I won't stand in her way. Heck, I'd do everything in my power to support and facilitate her having a relationship with them. But I will not be the one to initiate contact after the way we left things.

"I won't let them hurt her any more than they already have with their rejection. I'll see if Mrs. Grund knows of any local Denning Night celebrations that are more inclusive."

"Excellent idea." Mom fixes her mug with honey and a splash of cream as the tea steeps. "And if not, we can always throw a feast here, with Mrs. Grund and any other shifters who don't have family to celebrate with."

"You wouldn't mind hosting?" I asked.

"Not at all, dear. I still have the recipes from when Myra was little." Mom gestures toward the drawer where she keeps a stack of disorganized hand-written recipe cards. Someday we should get those all filed better.

"I'll look into our options. We have two more weeks to plan, right?" I add a generous helping of honey to my mug, no cream.

"We do," Mom confirms with a decisive nod. "Though if we *are* hosting, we'll need time to plan and get the word out."

"I'll do some research into our options tonight

and we can discuss the plans tomorrow, if that's alright?"

"Sounds wonderful, dear." Mom pats my hands, and it's as comforting now as it was when I was a cub needing her reassurance.

The tea timer beeps. Mom pours the hot brew into our mugs, stirring in the sweetener. Then she says, "Myra's half-asleep watching her movie; why don't you join her? I think you could both use the closeness. You look frazzled, and I can make spaghetti before I send you both home."

Mom cups my cheek with one hand and presses the back of the other to my forehead, like she did when she suspected I had a fever as a child. The gesture makes me feel unburdened and cared for, as though all the world's problems are still simple enough to be solved by my mother kissing my brow.

I've known for a long time that isn't true. Ever since I was Myra's age and my omega mom kissed me goodbye for the last time without either of us knowing that she'd never make it home that night. It's still a pleasant fantasy that Mom can fix everything.

I take my mug of tea, and let Mom chivy me toward the couch beside my daughter. Myra doesn't respond to my greeting with more than a few monosyllabic grunts about her day. When I sit next to her, she readjusts to be closer to me, leaning into my side and pulling my arm around her narrow shoulders. Within a few minutes of sitting down, Myra sprawls across my lap, still enthralled by her movie.

I set my steaming mug on the side table and consider where I might start my search for inclusive multi-species shifter holidays as I card my fingers through her hair. We need to brush out her tangles properly. The beads on her necklace clink when the buttons at my blouse cuff tap into them. The sound reminds me of Bram's baubles clacking together as he covered his delicate wrists in bangles earlier.

Thoughts of the bird remind me of the shifter enclave where he said he lives. A mixed species enclave. And ravens often roost in territories with large predators. Like wolves. Or bears. I think he even mentioned living near bear shifters. Or he came in smelling of another bear shifter alpha, at any rate. I won't soon forget that scent, lingering on his clothing with the rank musk of a rival alpha.

Bram's community might have grizzlies living in it. And they might celebrate Denning. I should ask him. And possibly reach out to Felix, the zoo administrator, to see if he knows of any options for my girl. In the future, the zoo could consider adding Denning Night as one of the big cultural diversity events they hold throughout the year. They do similar events to raise awareness of different shifter traditions and holidays that vary from the mainstream static ones.

Myra would get a kick out of spending the

night at the zoo. Especially if they were to open up some of the more interesting habitats for visitors to explore during the vigil. I can see Felix appreciating the idea. And it would be good for other young grizzly bear shifters like Myra, who don't have a connection to the grizzly community to connect with their heritage in some small way.

My daughter falls asleep on my lap well before the final credits roll. While she dreams away the evening, the heavenly aroma of sauteing garlic and onions. Mom's cooking entices me into staying for supper when I might otherwise bring Myra home to sleep in her own bed if she's exhausted enough to fall asleep this early. We both need to eat. It might as well be here, and this way I can let her rest for a little while before waking her.

I dig my phone out and write an email to Felix about my idea for a zoo Denning Night celebration. I wish I had an easy way of contacting Bram. On a whim, I punch his name into my social media and click on the first profile to pop up. He's got a raven photo set as his avatar. I'm pretty sure it's him, after spending the last three days with him in his feathers. I hesitate over whether contacting him unprompted is entering creepy stalker territory.

Then I dismiss the concern. Bram gave me his full name, knowing that it would be easy to look up his online presence. And I can still practically taste his spunk on my tongue, seasoned with the sweetness of his promises that it won't be the only time that happens. So really, this is hardly more personal or private than that. At the worst, if he is uncomfortable with me contacting him, I can just stop messaging him.

Still, never hurts to ask permission in my first message.

Ty: Hey Bram. I looked you up on here because I have a question. If it's not too weird that I'm contacting you out of the blue?

I set my phone on my lap and watch a few minutes of Myra's movie before my phone buzzes with a reply. The giddy thrill of pleasure at hearing from back from Bram doesn't have to mean anything.

Bram: Not weird at all. Why did you think I told you my full name?

I don't have an answer to that question, so I ignore it and cut right to the chase.

Ty: Does Four Corners have any grizzlies? Or more to the point, is there a community Denning Night celebration?

Bram: There is a bear sleuth here. A grizzly omega, her three grown omega sons, several cubs, and a handful of their alpha relatives and extended family. You know bear shifters better than me, but you all don't seem to be much more sociable than static bears.

I chuckle at that. We actually are far more social than our static counterparts, considering that most wild bears are fairly solitary once they reach adulthood. At least, they are outside of mating season. They each have their own range out of necessity; a fully grown bear needs a ton of resources to survive the winter. It makes us territorial. But I understand his point and as shifters, we've got our human side's more sociable nature to contend with.

Ty: I'm sure that seems like a small group compared to you avians with your huge clutches.

Bram: Three isn't a huge clutch. And most of our omegas take meds to limit the size of our fertile clutches.

Bram: But I suppose I have several siblings and heaps of cousins. As do most of the raven shifters in our rave.

Ty: That is an apt term for a large group of you, bird.

I can't resist teasing Bram. He makes me smile and I hope he'll grin at my words too.

Bram: You're infuriating, bear. Anyway. I know they always have a big party around the holidays. Let me check with one of my oh so many siblings about the details. I haven't gone in a few years.

There's a pause while I wait for him to get an answer.

Bram: Seb says the grizzlies have a big pre-hibernation party in a couple weeks. It's one way they find potential mates from nearby sleuths, if they haven't yet. You looking for an invitation?

Aren't you a black bear? I didn't think bear species mixed their celebrations?

Bram: Not that it's any of my business. We're both free to sleep with whoever we want, right?

Is that jealousy? It makes me smile, even though I shouldn't be glad that he'd be averse to my seeing someone else. The unwelcome curl of envy in the pit of my stomach at the words should tell me everything I need to know. I'm getting far too invested in him. In our sex life.

It can't go anywhere, we barely know each other. I'm not ready to tell him about Myra yet, and until he knows about her, dating isn't really an option. I'm protective of my baby. Mom says it's gotten to the point I use that as an excuse never to get serious with anyone I've dated since Arnie. Even if she's right, there have been precious few dates for that to matter, all of them casual and none going beyond a goodnight kiss.

Ty: We didn't explicitly promise each other exclusivity, no. But I'm not looking to pick up. I'm just trying to help another shifter connect with some fellow grizzlies for the holiday.

What am I doing? Am I asking him to go steady? This is a terrible idea, but I've already hit send and he's typing a reply. I could take it back. But I don't want to.

Bram: That's kind of you. They have a potluck feast in the community event hall, followed by a festival with storytelling and carnival games that lasts from dusk to dawn. They let any shifters who care to attend, but if your friend wants to eat with the grizzly bears, they should bring a dish to share. Large carb-based casseroles are popular. And berry-based desserts get overrepresented. There's more to the celebration the next day that's just for the grizzlies. That part isn't open to outsiders unless they're invited to join in by the sleuth.

If we go, I'll have to approach the omegiarch and see if they would welcome Myra among their cubs for the bear-only part of the festivities. That's if my girl is comfortable shifting with them. If they—by some miracle—aren't as insular as the other two grizzly sleuths I've dealt with. At least the fact they live in a mixed shifter community implies some level of acceptance of close dealings with other shifter species.

I'll have to see if Mrs. Grund will accompany us. That way, Myra won't be alone without a trusted adult if allowing a black bear into their ceremonial shift is a bridge too far for them. Of course, I'd prefer to be there to keep an eye on her, but it's already a long-shot that they would let a strange cub join them. I doubt they would accept a black bear among their ranks. But two new grizzly shifters might prove more palatable.

Bram: So, you're welcome, I guess?

Shoot, I didn't want to make him feel like I was just using him, but the bird's latest message definitely reads as petulant. And I can't blame him after I've left him on read mid-conversation, as soon as he got me what I needed.

Ty: Thank you, Bram. I appreciate the information.

Ty: And to clear up any confusion, you're the only omega I'm seeing for stress relief purposes ;)

Bram: I'm not seeking stress relief with any other alphas, either. Or omegas. So that's good to know.

Ty: No other alphas for me, either. You like both?

Bram: Yeah. I pretty much like everyone. So, uh, awkward question, but are you always alpha?

Bram: You can tell me to drop it if I'm getting too personal.

Ty: Yes, that part doesn't change for me. Just the masc-femme part of the equation. And I've found the occasional alpha attractive, but I've only ever dated omegas.

Ty: And coming from most people, yeah, that's sort of personal, but you've had your mouth on my junk, so you can ask me personal questions.

Bram: Cool. Good to know.

Myra snorts in her sleep and snuggles up onto my chest and I almost drop my phone on her when she knocks into my hand. I should wrap up this conversation.

Ty: Well, thanks again for the information. See you tomorrow?

Bram: Yep, I work Monday through Thursday most weeks. You'll meet the other two weekday raven shifters on Monday. But that shouldn't change our evening plans much. Not if they stay true to pattern and sneak off for an afternoon 'break' to have their usual quickie.

Ty: I didn't need to know what they do on their breaks, bird.

Bram: And I'm sure they won't care what we do after hours.

Ty: I can't stay much later than we have been.

Bram: Obligations, I know. We've both got them. Speaking of which, I've got to go now. Glad you reached out. And that we've got one more day before the weekend. By Monday, I'll be very glad to see you. ;)

Ty: See you in the morning, bird.

The symbol by Bram's name goes dark, showing he's offline. I tuck away my phone instead of giving in to the temptation to snoop around in his profile for pics of the pretty omega. We aren't anything to each other but coworkers who get off together. No matter how wonderful it felt for him to fuck me like he really saw through to the heart of me.

After the way he responded to my coming out, I'd never have guessed that I'd have the most affirming sex of my life with Bram. But contrary to that first impression, he didn't bat an eye at seeing me in a skirt for the first time. That's not something I take for granted, much as I might wish I could.

Most of the time, I'm fine with my body as it is. It's an alpha body, whether I present femme, masc, or somewhere in between. But the way I use it differs depending on where I fall on my personal gender axis. Bram followed my lead on how to treat my body. He touched me with not only respect, but with some knowledge of how to make me feel like he really saw me as myself. When I told him to pleasure my clit, he treated it like a clit and that made all the difference to my enjoyment of the act. Not to mention the muffing. That was a very pleasant surprise.

The surprise wasn't in the actual act. I've known I enjoy that since I figured out how to finger myself as a horny dysphoric teen. There were days when touching my junk killed any libido I had and figuring out fingering for those femme days was a revelation. No, it was the fact that Bram knew what to do with me to embrace my anatomy as it is that made for the pleasant surprise.

In light of that, it makes sense that he isn't picky about the genders of his bed partners. It's a pleasant change from the more traditional bear shifters I've been with in the past. I'm not in any position to pursue a relationship with the bird. But the idea of sharing my habitat with him at work for the foreseeable future no longer seems like so much of a hardship as it did on Monday morning. Funny how in the span of a week, I went from dreading Bram's presence to looking forward to seeing him again. I might have misjudged him at first.

Before I can contemplate that possibility more, Mom comes into the living room to call Myra and me into the kitchen for supper. We eat together as a family and for a short while, I'm not guilty about all the things I can't give Myra. Instead, I focus on what I *can* give her. My kid has the same loving home life I grew up with. Our cozy little family dinner makes me feel like it's enough.

CHAPTER 12

Bram

"**H**oney, that's insurance fraud." Sebastian dismisses my idea as he applies shimmery blush to his cheekbones, then twists to check his makeup in the mirror. Seb shifts his focus to make eye contact with me for a second.

"Some things you can't fix," he says

"I know."

My gut clenches around the dinner we just ate at our folks' place at the reminder. I can't fix whatever drove Seb to seek solace with a different stranger every night. I can't fix the trauma that keeps Winny's social wings even more clipped than the badly healed break to her shoulder that has her grounded.

"No." Seb sets down his mascara tube and twists around from his vanity to level an accusing gaze at me. "Don't you go blaming yourself for our garbage, big brother. You do more than anyone would reasonably expect for us." He wags the mascara wand at me. "You aren't responsible for us or our choices. That's what I'm trying to tell you."

Seb quickly curls the wand along his lashes, fluttering them at me and almost making me laugh at his makeup related facial contortions. It reminds me of better days, when all three of us were inseparable and we dressed up to go clubbing together.

"I *am* responsible for you two though," I insist. "We're clutchmates. We're supposed to be—"

Seb tsks loudly, cutting me off. "No. You. Are. Not. Our. Keeper." He sticks the wand back into the tube with a forceful jab, twists it shut, then slams the tube back onto the counter. "Seriously, it's not just that we aren't your problem, Bramble. Lately, it feels like all you see when you look at us is how much we need to be fixed. I don't need you to save me from my choices and Winny doesn't need you to badger her into a surgery she isn't even sure she wants."

"Of course she wants it! She'll never fly again without it, Seb. Who wouldn't do everything in their power for flight?"

Seb sighs heavily. "Please try talking to our sister before you do anything you can't take back in the name of helping her."

Seb gives his flawless makeup a final check,

then reaches into a drawer for a selection of shiny metal bands for his wrists. I got those for him on our hatchday. They match his aesthetic more than mine, but I couldn't resist them at the store. Four thin bands, all in different metals that catch the light and clink musically together when he moves.

The bangles don't sparkle half as bright as my brother. I consider going out with him. Finding a different outlet for blowing off steam. One that isn't my prickly coworker. Except, I want another taste of Ty.

"If I can just convince her to take the weekend shifts, they're only thirty hours a week. Three days." I try to pull my attention back to helping Winny.

"Sorry, did I say talk to her?" Seb claps his hands onto my shoulders and looks me in the eye. "I meant *listen* to her. Really listen to what she wants instead of projecting what you think you'd want in her situation. You will never convince Winny to work outside the community, let alone in her feathers."

"Okay. I'll ask her what she wants. Sorry. I just"—I give a helpless shrug—"want to help."

"I know you mean well, Bram. But good intentions can still hurt."

I don't have a response to that. And my phone buzzing in my pockets saves me from needing to find one. I pull it out and check my notifications. A new message request on social media takes me to a tentative question from Ty.

"Hey, Seb, random question?"

"Shoot."

"Do the grizzlies have a holiday coming up?" I know they do, but I haven't gone lately and he's more likely to know the details.

"Yeah. Their big hibernation party. Denning Night? There's always a big open bar and I'm definitely going to get laid," Seb says as he laces up his fiercest boots for the club.

I admire the shiny patina of the faux leather, but I'd have gotten the ones that come with rhinestones, if they were mine. I relay the Denning Night information to Ty, grinning to myself at thoughts of the grumpy bear letting loose at a party. Until Seb mentions that bears use it to hook up. That has me frowning. I don't like the idea of Ty finding another bear to be with instead of me.

"Lo? Earth to Bramble? You have your eye on a certain bear or something?" Seb teases me. He scents me like he did the other night. I know I still have lingering traces of Ty's scent on me, no matter how well we cleaned up with those wipes afterward.

"No. We just work together." I tuck my phone against my chest to shield the screen from my brother's prying eyes. My discussion with Ty about letting off steam together in the locker rooms belies my words. No reason for Seb to know that.

"Uh huh. Have fun with that." Seb leans in to kiss my cheek. He clearly sees right through my obfuscation, oh well. "Don't wait up for me tonight, yeah? I'll have my phone if you need to check in, and I'll text you deets if I pick up."

He usually does that. Most mornings I wake up with Seb snuggled next to me, and a photo message with his partner for the night's ID in my inbox. He deletes them if he gets to my phone first in the morning. But it gives me peace of mind to know there's some record of who he left his hookup spot du jour with until he's home safe. If not me, then his best friend, Rollie, gets the deets. That's probably where he'll be sleeping, if I don't wake up tomorrow tangled with my brother in my bed.

"Have fun tonight, Sebastian."

"You know I always do." He winks at me, hanging on the door for a second. "Love you, bro."

"Love you too." I wave.

Seb laughs as he blows me a kiss, then saunters off to meet up with Rollie and hit the shifter clubs in the Old Port. He leaves the door open for me to shut, and I can't help staring after him and wishing I could bear to go along for the ride. But I've got work in the morning, and I can't stand watching him self-destruct with every vice to come along. It's not about the sex. I don't care if Seb sleeps with every shifter in the state; he's my brother and if that makes him happy, then I'm happy for him. But it doesn't.

It's obvious he's miserable in the way his smiles never reach his eyes anymore. And how he mumbles things I pretend not to hear when he wakes me with whimpers in his sleep. Seb and Rollie won't bother with the local bar on a Wednesday night. Not when the clubs in Portland will have more options for them to find anonymous hookups.

I shake my head at myself. I must be getting old for all of that to sound more like a bothersome chore than a fun evening. Once Seb disappears down the stairs, I lock up behind him and I pull my phone back out, contemplating more flirting with Ty.

Seb's words have me second-guessing everything. He's probably right that I should go listen to what Winny has to say about her surgery. If nothing else, she's the smartest of the three of us. She might have a better idea about how to make the money we need in the reduced timeframe we have to work with now.

I tap out a goodbye for now message to Ty, then get up to find Winny. My folks don't lock the door to their apartment. No one in the rave does, since this entire apartment block is ours.

Much like our static cousins, our nesting grounds are communal. We might be attracted to shiny things, but the rave is family, to be cherished and protected. No one in the rave would enter an apartment they don't belong in for nefarious purposes.

Elric and Cory glance up from playing video games on the couch when I step inside our family home. Briony, sitting in the armchair with earbuds in and homework on her lap, ignores me entirely.

"Is Winny in her room?" I ask as I ease the door shut behind me so as not to disturb—or more accurately, alert—our parents.

"Yeah. Hasn't left since after dinner," Elric says with a half-shrug as they tap intensely on some buttons to knock Cory off the stage in whatever fighting game they're playing.

I pad past the younger kids and to Winny's door to knock. I wait a few seconds, to no reply, and then tap again.

"Win?" I call through the door. She might be listening to music. It's possible she isn't just ignoring me. "Can you hear me? It's Bramble."

Still no reply.

"I wanted to apologize for being so pushy with you."

More silence. Just when I'm debating between trying the handle and accepting that she doesn't want to talk to me, the floor squeaks under her tread. I pause there, all but holding my breath for her response. A moment later, the door opens a crack to reveal a narrow slice of Winny's face.

"What?" she asks warily.

"I'm sorry. Seb says you might not even want the surgery, and it made me realize I haven't been listening to you. So. I came to listen. If you want to talk?"

Winny gives me a hard look, then eases the door open enough to admit me and turns her back to me.

"Come in," she says grudgingly.

When I join her inside, she shuts the door behind us. I watch as she shuffles to her bed. I stand awkwardly by until she pats the mattress for me to sit next to her. We sit there until I'm squirming with the urge to fill the silence, and Winny is watching me with that knowing look of hers.

"You're really here to listen?" Her lips quirk in an almost smile, as though I've passed some unspoken test. Or I proved to her that I'm genuinely not here to tell her what I think is best for her, yet again. Sitting there while she looks so uncertain of me and my intentions, I realize I fucked up big time. By being so ardent in pursuing what I'd want in her shoes, I forgot these are her choices to make.

Browbeating Winny into something she doesn't want is the last thing I want to do to her. Not after the accident that we all know was anything but accidental. That's what she calls it, though, so we agreed not to contradict her. I could kick myself for pushing so hard to protect Winny that I forgot it's up to her to choose her treatment path.

Winny takes a deep breath, and she talks. For

the first time in a long while, she opens up to me, and I listen.

"I don't want to fly again, Bram."

I gasp at the pronouncement, muffling my protest. She must not mean it, but she purses her lips, ready to shut down again, and I hold my tongue.

Winny shakes her head at me. "Okay, fine, no, what I mean is, I'm not clinging to impossible dreams. And it *is* impossible, Bramble. They'll need to replace the joint in a way that will require immobilizing it when I'm in my feathers. And I'm okay with that. I know that's hard for you to believe, but flight isn't everything. Okay?"

She gives me a moment to interject, but I just nod for her to continue.

"So. I've accepted that there was too much damage to the wing for them to fix it. I still need the surgery because my shoulder hurts all the time after the way it healed. They say replacing the joint will help with that, but I've already accepted it will never be the same. Okay? I can't go back. I'll never be the same person I was before, and I need you to understand that."

There are tears in her eyes, but in that moment, I catch my first glimpse of the fierce sister I remember. The Winny who would take on dragons and win. And that's not what I need to take away from this at all. She doesn't need my paternalistic coddling. What I think Winny's trying to tell me, what Seb has been saying all along, is that she needs more than my understanding and support. She needs me to love who she is now, not the person she was before. She needs me to accept even the broken bits. Even if it means never flying together again.

"Okay. Whatever you need, I'll be there to support you."

"Yeah? You aren't going to push me toward the next breakthrough surgical technique? Or the most expensive miracle PT cure money can buy?"

"No. That's not what you want, is it?" I ask, realizing it's true as I say it.

"It's not," Winny confirms. "I don't need all the fancy bells and whistles the shifter orthopedist was talking about."

"Okay. I'm sorry I didn't listen." I was so intent on fixing things for Winny I didn't realize how much it would hurt to be seen as a broken thing by the people who love her.

"Yeah. I get why. And I'm sorry I gave you reason to think you had to make me keep holding on. I'm going to be okay though, Bram. Even without flight."

"Well, I guess that will make the surgery less complex, huh?"

"Yep. We'll still have out-of-pocket costs, but lucky me, I used up most of the deductible in January with that inpatient stint, so we'll manage."

I wince at her glib mention of that stay

after she overdosed on her pain meds. It was on purpose. We all knew it was, though we pretended otherwise. And I can't blame her for wanting a way out of the pain. I just hate thinking she was that desperate, and we all missed the signs. Our folks and Grandad scraped together the money to cover the out-of-pocket costs when she had an inpatient stay afterward.

Winny promised not to make another attempt. And she's mostly been doing better with regular therapy. But fear for her was part of why I latched onto the idea of this surgery. I begged Felix to get her in with the top shifter orthopedic surgeons. My logic was if we could give Winny back the skies, she might not hurt so much anymore. I feel foolish for not asking what she wants sooner.

"I still want to help pay for your PT, even if it's not for flight rehabilitation; you'll need it as part of recovery, right?" I say.

"Yeah. And thanks, Bram. I really appreciate how much you've helped and getting my case in front of Doctor Cressida. I think that's part of why it made me so mad. Because I hated being upset with you when you clearly are only pushing me because you care about me, but like, it's still my life and my choices, you know?"

"Yeah. I love you, Win. Nothing will ever change that." I open my arms, and she lets me hug her.

It's not the same as before; she's more guarded.

There's a tense rigidity to her embrace, whereas she used to cling on like a limpet, taking for granted that I'd hold her tight. But that doesn't matter because no matter how much she changes, she'll always be my clutchmate and I'll always love her.

Even if I have to learn not to cling too tight to her and Seb, if I want to be close to the people they're becoming now that we're grown. It's a tough reality to swallow, but I'd do anything for them, and that includes giving them space. And maybe, just maybe, if I do that, I'll have room in my life to focus on what *I* want for a change. Such as the big strong alpha bear who wants to bring a guest to Denning Night here in Four Corners.

CHAPTER 13

Ty

Bram and I hook up again after work on Thursday, swapping blowjobs before going our separate ways for the weekend. I ignore the twinge of disappointment at the thought I won't see him again until Monday.

Things will be different with the other raven shifters joining us in the habitat. I'm low-key nervous about that, but not nearly as put off at sharing space with more of the birds as I was when I first learned of the arrangement.

It's funny how quickly I've gotten used to having Bram in my space. It helps that he mostly keeps to the perches high overhead and leaves my scratching tree alone now, as promised. He also leaves my enrichment games alone. Now that Bob and the other keepers have added similar activities suited for his beak, talons, and curious nature to the upper branches of our exhibit, there's no need to share.

It's kind of interesting to watch him try to work open the more complex foraging puzzles. He's funny when doing so forces him into undignified dangling from his claws, or flapping to stay balanced. Watching him contort his body to preen is more interesting than staring at the static spectators who come to see us.

I might just be associating Bram with sex, but the display of avian flexibility gives me all kinds of ideas. And I take a while, but I recognize the whiffs of a vaguely fruity scent as he carefully grooms his feathers. I wouldn't have guessed he could produce enough preen oil with a partial shift to use it as lube, but it's a clever trick. More and more, I enjoy just being in his presence. I might even miss the bird once the forest pavilion reopens in the spring. Not that I'd tell him that.

We message sporadically over the weekend. Bram sends me weird shifter memes and random videos he says remind him of me. I find myself smiling and checking my phone more often than usual in between a video game marathon with Myra and taking her to get a few school supplies that she needs for the switch to her new classroom.

Sunday night, Myra has a hard time getting to sleep, caught between excitement over the new class arrangement and worry that she'll have a hard time adjusting or catching up on assignments. I do my best to reassure her, but once she's asleep in her room, I have to admit that I'm nervous about the changes too, and second-guessing whether I'm making the right choices as her parent.

When I asked Mom, she agreed that a more inclusive teacher and some distance from Wendle would be good for Myra. And Mx. Adams sent us a lovely email to welcome Myra to their classroom and assure us both that they take their anti-bullying policy seriously.

But I couldn't leave well enough alone, so I poked around on parenting forms to see how other families handled similar situations. So now I'm worried that I'm teaching her to run away from her problems instead of standing up for herself or something. Or that we're letting the bullies win.

Of course, I also want her to know she can rely on adults she trusts to help her if she comes to us for help. As with so many other parts of being a parent, it feels like there are no right answers, and I resent Arnie for leaving me to make those choices alone. I hate resenting him, but I do.

I can't sleep. So I open my message thread with Bram. There are some new messages and when I open them, it's a series of animal pirate memes with increasingly raunchy jokes as captions. I snort at the last one, 'show me your booty and prepare to be boarded.'

Then it occurs to me he might actually want

me to send nudes. That's a thing people do, right? I'm not ready to go there. The parental part of me has to resist the urge to lecture him about internet safety, which is *so* missing the point. Bram is old enough to make his own choices about who he sends dick pics to. And the idea he wants to send them to me is undeniably arousing. I palm myself through my flannel pajama pants.

Ty: Excited to see you tomorrow too ;)

I hedge my bets. No nudes, but he can read my meaning into the words.

Bram: Me too.

There's a brief pause and I try to work out what to say next. I could leave the conversation at that. Leave it sweet and chaste. That's certainly more romantic than what I really want to do with him. But saying, 'I want to lick your butthole and fuck you,' seems so crude. Then again, we aren't dating. Romance has no place between us, right? We're fuck buddies. Does that mean I should take the hint and try sexting him?

Before I can figure out how to take that step, Bram messages me again.

Bram: Um, I hope this isn't too forward, but would you want me to pick up condoms? I know you were worried about knocking me up, so you could fuck my hole if I grab some?

My dick achingly hard at the prospect of being buried inside of him, I just stare at the message. I want to fuck him, and he wants the same. I squeeze my eyes shut and pinch the base of my cock so I can try to think through my response. Condoms can break. I shouldn't agree to this. I know that's paranoid, but I can't shake my worries after what happened with Arnie.

Bram: Or not. I'm happy to keep doing what we've been doing.

Ty: I want to. It's not that I don't want you. But you could be the one to fuck me?

Bram: You don't like to top?

Ty: It's not that. I enjoy it either way. It's just not everyday I find an omega who wants to top. Might need to work up to taking a dick again, but I enjoy it.

Bram: Oh fuck, now I'm imagining you stretching your tight little alpha hole for me. That's so fucking hot. Do you have a plug?

Ty: I might have one around here somewhere. ;)

Bram: Pics please?

Ty: I'd have to find it first.

I'm not sure about sending him nudes, but a picture of my sex toys seems innocuous enough. There's always plausible deniability there. I pull the box of sex toys out from the back of my closet and dig around until I find a slender silicone plug. Then I lay it on the white plastic box lid and send him the image.

Bram: Fuck, Ty.

Bram: Now I'm picturing it peeking at me from under your pretty panties. Those satin ones you wore the other day have been driving me wild all weekend. Do you have lacy ones too?

Bram: I've been wondering about that. Like a lot.

I laugh at how eager he sounds. But it also fills me with a genuine warmth. Bram likes my pretty panties. Fantasizes about them. For half a second, I consider answering with a picture of my underwear drawer. The jumble of utilitarian cotton briefs on one side, juxtaposed with the other half of the drawer where my selection of nicer underwear lie tidily folded. Satin and lace and all things pretty.

I can't bring myself to expose something so intimate to him yet. Not with a picture that he could do anything with once I hit send. Funny how the plug that I actually plan to stuff up my ass while I masturbate to fantasies of him feels less intimate than the undergarments I routinely leave lying around in my locker at work, but there it is. Sharing that is too much. It feels like it's about more than sex. It's about him liking things about me that have nothing to do with orgasms, and I can't let myself go there.

Ty: You'll have to stick around if you want to find out what I've got in my underwear drawer. ;)

Bram: Fine by me. I'll just have to keep imagining the possibilities for now. ;)

Ty: Have you been thinking of me when you touch yourself, Bramble?

Bram: Duh. You're hot, bear.

Bram: Um, hope that's okay?

Ty: It would be hypocritical to say no. I've been thinking of you too.

Bram: Are you thinking about me now?

Ty: Yeah.

I reach into my flannel pajamas and stroke myself. Now that I've got his explicit consent, there's no reason not to let the conversation run its course. I hesitate for a second longer before locking my door in case Myra wakes up. That done, I shove the toy box back into its hiding place, and bring the lube and the plug to bed with me.

Bram: Me too. If you were here, I'd bury my face between your thighs, push your panties aside, and lick your hole.

Bram: Um. Is it a she day or a he day? And do you wear pretty panties on boy days?

My heart beats faster at his innocuous question. It's such a basic thing that shows he cares enough to want to gender me properly. Another little way to show he respects all of me. And even if that level of care should be the bare minimum of respect, I still appreciate it. This bird is hazardous to my heart.

Ty: He today. And sometimes?

Bram: Cool. So, I'd lick your hole until your rim gets all soft and desperate to be filled. Play with your cock and balls and just go to town on you until you're begging me for more. You know that feeling? Where you can't take another second of foreplay or your balls might explode?

Ty: Yeah. Right on the verge of coming, with my balls tingling to come.

Bram: That. And then I'd finger you with my spit while I slurp all up along your dick, kiss the tip, tongue your slit and suckle on the head of it.

Bram: Just play with you while I plunder your booty with my fingers. Get you all hot and bothered and stretched out for me.

Ty: Fuck, Bram. You've got a filthy mind.

Not that I'm complaining. Far from it, I'm imagining that it's his tongue stroking my rim instead of the lube-slick plug I'm teasing my ass with. I set the phone down for a moment to wrap my fingers around my shaft. I want to beg him for his cock, to feel that connection of bodies again. It's been far too long. I yearn to be close to another person in those ways I haven't been in years.

I pick up my phone when it chimes again.

Bram: You like it.

Bram: Right? Do you like it?

Ty: I do. You know that plug? I'm going to fuck myself open with it. Get my hole all ready for your dick.

Bram: Yeah? You want me to fuck you with my cute little omega dick?

Ty: It's not that little. You're thicker than my plug and it's doing a damn good job of stretching me open about now.

I'm not exaggerating either. The plug is about

as big around as my little finger at the tip and maybe thumb sized at its widest. Not huge, but it's still more than I've put inside my body in ages. I'm damn well going to take the entire thing though. I want to be ready for Bram when I see him again.

He's got a lovely cock, slender with a graceful arch to it when he's aroused. I enjoy watching his broad rosy head poking out of the foreskin when I jerk him, or painting the smooth tip over my lips so I can taste his pre-cum. Omegas might not have fertile semen, but they still produce ejaculate. His tastes good, with a similar fruity undertone to the preen oil he used as lube our first time together.

I add more lube to my plug and fuck the tip inside my body. Deep enough that it nudges against just the right spot to make my cock leak on the brink of coming. That makes it easier to handle the widest bit before it narrows and the flared base settles along my crack.

I fuck it into my p-spot, pleasuring myself until I'm panting and struggling not to moan too loudly. And then I hold myself there, gently fucking and jerking and thinking about Bram doing those things he just described to me. Would he pin me in place? Take me deep? Boss me around?

If I asked him to, would he penetrate my front bits again? Sheathed in the loose skin of my sac, his fingers sliding up into my body were heavenly. I've only ever done that to myself before, too afraid of their reactions to ask anyone else. Even Arnie. He wanted me to be the strong alpha stereotype he could rely on. To take charge and take care of him in bed, so it never came up.

The fact Bram's the one who offered that to me, without my having to ask, might be the most thoughtful thing a partner has ever done for me in bed. I'm not sure what that says about my sex life. And I don't want to think about just how intensely close to him it made me feel. Still makes me feel when I think about it, the tender care he took with me.

I just want to lose myself in pleasure with him. No strings sex. Like we agreed to provide for each other. I fuck the plug in and out of my hole. Each twist of my wrist drives it right into the spot where I need it. When the building pleasure gets to be too much, I jerk myself furiously until I spurt over my hand, panting and biting my lip to keep from crying his name.

Fuck. I shouldn't be calling out his name. Still sticky with lube and cum, I turn my phone screen back on. There's another message from Bram waiting for me.

Bram: Aw, you like my dick. You can kiss it later.

I grab a wet wipe to tidy up before I reply.

Ty: I'm going to do a whole lot more than kiss it, bird. I'm going to let you fuck me with it.

Bram: Yeah? How do you like it? Tell me how

you want me to pound your gorgeous ass, bear.

I know he's goading me into sexting him more, but I just got off to his filthy fantasy, so fair's fair. It's perfectly healthy for me to have a sexual relationship with an omega. I take a deep breath, and then just let myself type before I can second-guess what I'm saying. There's nothing filthy or wrong about this. Nothing inappropriate, it still gives me an illicit thrill when I hit send.

Ty: I want you to bend me over, take me from behind. You reach into my pants and find lace. It makes you so hard; you finger me through it, rub all over my rim.

Bram: Heck yeah, it does. So hard for you, bear. I grind against your ass, desperate to be inside you. Kiss your neck until you squirm against me, just as needy as I am.

Ty: You pull my pants down, part my cheeks, and lick me there until the lace is a wet mess.

Ty: Then you push the panties aside, not off, just out of the way so you can fuck me while I'm still wearing them. Neither of us wants to take the time to strip.

Ty: We need to be joined, and you slip inside of me in a single slow slide, taking me all the way, until you're balls deep.

I pause there, waiting to see if he has anything to add. When he doesn't reply right away, I can only assume he's doing what I just did to his words, jerking himself off. I want to give him more, finish painting the picture, in case he's still reading while he masturbates.

Ty: My ass cheeks are both still covered in lace, rubbing against your thighs and belly with every thrust.

Ty: More lace traps my dick in place, the pattern digging into my erection. It's all sticky with pre-cum. I'm so ready for you to pound me and fill me up with your hot load.

Ty: You hold on to my love handles as you fuck me silly, pulling me back to meet your thrusts. And you gasp my name when I squeeze tight around you, milking out every drop.

Ty: My lacy panties are a sex soaked ruin by the time we're done, and it's totally worth it.

There's a few more moments of nothing from him after I send that barrage of messages. Instead of obsessing over whether I took it too far, or said something that turned him off, I drag myself out of bed. Might as well clean up and take care of my plug. It wouldn't do to leave it lying around if Myra needs me in the night.

When that's done, I come back to bed to a message from Bram.

Bram: Are we doing dick pics? Because I kind of want to send you a picture of what you just did to me, bear. But only if you want it.

I hesitate, visions of my kid accidentally opening the message thread making my stomach roil. But I want to see him, and I can always delete the picture, or save it into a hidden folder for later.

Ty: Sure.

The next message I get is his dick, covered in jizz. My cock twitches in a valiant effort to get hard again at the sight. As much as I appreciate the evidence of his pleasure, I'm not in rut and another round so soon isn't happening outside of that. I still save the image to my password protected spank bank folder in my photos. Part of me wants to return the favor. I could send him a picture of my spent cock. But I already cleaned up, and I'm still not quite ready to hit send on something like that.

Ty: Very pretty, bird.

Bram: Thanks. You can see it in the flesh tomorrow.

Ty: Again, I'm going to do much more than just see it ;)

Bram: Yeah, you are. So, condoms?

Ty: You can't knock me up, bird. No matter how hard you try.

Bram: Hmm. I'll just bring the lube then, so we can test that theory. Thoroughly. You know, just in case.

Ty: Just in case, sure. See you tomorrow.

I almost tack on a cutesy good night message. Something flirty and sweet, but I don't want to blur the lines. This is just about getting our rocks off. I don't have room in my life to offer him more than that, and it's not fair to either of us to pretend I can.

Bram: Sweet dreams, Tyson.

Damn. So much for my resolve not to make more of this than it is. His affectionate words on the screen do things to my heart, twisty beat-skipping sorts of things. That fluttery hope of finding that elusive happiness with a partner that I can't take a risk on. Not when my hands are already more than full with being Myra's dad. I can't leave Bram hanging either though. I try to leave things on a neutral note.

Ty: Good night, Bramble.

Sated and with my head full of pleasant thoughts about what tomorrow holds, I drift off to sleep.

For all that we're both excited for Bram to fuck me, it doesn't happen on Monday. For one, we've got his usual coworkers joining us in the enclosure today. They're polite enough, but I don't want to worry about the logistics of sex while they're trying to get ready to leave alongside us tonight. That's not exactly the first impression I want to give Freya and Theron, even if they spend our morning break getting frisky in the locker area.

Instead of squeezing in a tryst after work Monday, Bram and I sneak off for a lunchtime quickie in the back of his car. His because I've got Myra's booster seat in mine and I don't want him asking questions I'm not ready to answer. The back of his sedan is cramped, but the confined space makes it more fun, in a way. Even if it means anal is out of the question. There just isn't room for that.

There's something deliciously naughty about fooling around where there's a chance we'll be caught. With nothing but window tint and the fact there aren't many people in this part of the employee lot at this time of day to hide us. Both of us laugh and shush each other's hilarity as we struggle to move our pants out of the way and get our mouths on each other's junk.

Bram full on guffaws when he finds the surprise I'm wearing for him under my chinos. It was a pain to get my lacy blue panties on after I shifted without him seeing, but totally worth the effort.

"You're a delight, bear," he says through his laughter. His hand is rubbing my dick through the lace as he kisses me deeply. It doesn't take either of us long to come, despite having to contort for car sex. We have to get back to our habitat as soon as we're done, but we grab a quick lunch from the zoo cafe along the way, even though that means swinging through the edges of the polar bear alpha's territory.

Feeding my omega makes my alpha side swell with pride. That's how it should be, providing for my mate. Taking care of him—I shut those thoughts down fast. Bram isn't my mate. This is still just sex. Even when I savor every trace of his scent as I kiss him once more, up against the lockers. He fondles my ass through my panties when we should both be stripping. I press him more firmly into the lockers and a paper tears loose and flutters to the ground.

We both glance down to see what it was, then Bram pushes me gently away to retrieve the colorful flier. I recognize the header as his eyes lock onto the large color picture front and center on the page.

Jolene puts out the biweekly employee newsletter in all the break areas. And this time, the featured article is about Bramble's sister. I read the headline while he continues to stare. There's a QR code with a link to a medical fundraiser. He has made off-hand remarks about helping out with his big family, but not specifics before today. I read over the fundraiser description, giving him a chance to collect himself.

"So, you didn't tell me your sister needs reconstructive surgery when you mentioned saving up to help her," I say when he stands staring at the grainy photo that appears to be printed from the fundraising site.

The picture is of him with two other smiling raven shifters around his age. They have to be the clutchmates he rambles on about whenever something reminds him of them, which is often. Winny and Seb.

Bram and his brother both have an arm around their sister's shoulders in the picture and they all look happy to be together as they mug for the selfie. Bram is notably younger in that image. There are less worry lines around his eyes.

Bram tears his gaze away from the photo, his usual good humor vanishing, shoulders slumping. Even his usual array of shiny costume jewelry seems muted with his face so twisted up in misery.

"Yeah." He swallows thickly, like this is hard for him to discuss. "She had an accident last year. Sort of. It's complicated, but a static doctor treated her and her shoulder never healed right, and we're still paying the bills for her hospital stay after that fiasco. Meanwhile, she *can* shift, but it hurts when she does, and she can't fly." Bram shivers like even saying those words hurts.

"I'm sorry." I rest a comforting hand on his shoulder. "If there's anything I can do let me know. Even if you just need someone to listen."

"Thanks." Bram twirls in closer, turning my supportive hand into a hug that he snuggles into, as though my arms around him offer all the comfort that I can see he needs right now. I wrap my other arm around him too as he sniffles against my shoulder.

"Sorry." He swipes away tears. "I just...she hasn't smiled like that picture in so long, Ty. None of us have. I think she's depressed. Or more than depressed. She barely leaves the house anymore. We fight a lot, mostly because I've been pushing her toward the experimental procedure that I'd want in her place to restore her flight, instead of the one that she actually wants."

"But you did listen, right?" I prompt him when he pauses on that note of self-recrimination. He mentioned that they've been fighting, but didn't give me the details until now. His confession makes me feel so much closer to him. Like there's more growing between us than mere orgasms. It also makes me feel guilty that I haven't shared as much about my life outside of work with him yet, but this isn't the time to spring Myra on him. "You told me you had a good talk with your sister the other day," I remind him.

"Yeah. We did. She says she just wants to live without constant pain, and I feel like a terrible brother for not listening to her sooner and putting all this extra pressure on her when she's already going through so much. But at the same time, I can't help wondering if she'll regret not taking a chance on the more expensive experimental technique that she is refusing."

"You don't want her to have regrets?" I ask.

"Yes, exactly. They warned us that, because of scar tissue, it might not be possible to try this option later if she changes her mind. But I promised to listen to her and respect her choices, so I'm working on keeping my mouth shut and just offering her support."

Bram grimaces, and I can imagine the outspoken bird struggling to hold his silence.

"And then there's Seb. I told you he lives with

me right?"

I nod. It's easy to recall the scent of another shifter on his skin and how irrationally jealous it made me before he explained the situation.

"Well, he was already struggling with creep and needing to take hormones, but everything with Winny feels like it's made him even more fatalistic. He takes stupid risks getting drunk and going home with strangers every night and stumbling home at all hours, so I worry about him constantly. I don't think he drives when he's drunk. He swears he doesn't, but he's gotten a DUI in the past, so I don't know for sure."

"I can see why you would be concerned, Bram." I give him a gentle squeeze.

"It feels like they're both falling apart and I'm desperately trying to hold us together, but after I talked with Winny the other day, I'm starting to think that what I've been doing to help might be more selfish than helpful."

"That's a lot to unpack," I say, rubbing between his tense shoulder blades. And we are supposed to be back in the exhibit, having already pushed the limits of our lunch break with backseat blowjobs, but Bram knows that. He just needs a minute to deal with all the emotions that picture brought up. "You aren't selfish, though, bird. Far from it. It isn't selfish to want the best for the people you love."

"Yeah, but what if the best they want isn't the same best I want for them? Like I wanted us to stay close, the way we've always been. I always had this picture in my head of raising my family next to theirs, lots of kids and cousins and love, but that's not how things are going to turn out and it's hard to let go of those dreams."

"But you are. You're a good brother, Bramble. I'm sure that Seb and Winny both know you'll be there for them no matter what. You can't fix their problems for them, though. Just be there to support them."

Bram sniffles. "Yeah. I guess I'm figuring that out. Gah. I thought when Seb got diagnosed with creep, that it was the worst thing that could happen. You know?"

I nod. "I'm sure that was hard for all of you."

For avian omegas, in addition to the devastating effects on their fertility, creep can cause a spontaneous change in their secondary gender traits. And unless they are trans secondary gender, the changes usually bring on severe dysphoria. No wonder his brother seems troubled.

Thankfully, hormone replacement can stop the unwanted alpha-izing effects of the illness, but it's still an added trauma on top of an already difficult diagnosis. It's also uncommon enough that most people, even among shifters, aren't well informed about creep and the ways it can manifest in different shifter species. I only know all that from stumbling upon an omega vlogger who went through the heartbreaking condition when I was exploring my gender and looking up videos about how other shifters view and express their genders.

Videos of other trans shifters were a huge help in deciding whether I wanted to pursue medical changes. I opted against any medical transition, but I learned a ton. Now I wonder if Seb would appreciate the videos I found of other avians going through similar experiences to his, but it sounds like half the problem right now is Bram's innate desire to fix things, so I just listen. I can always pass the link along to Bram later, if he thinks Seb would appreciate it.

No wonder Bram's brother is struggling with the diagnosis though. At least it sounds like he's got access to hormone therapy to stop the unwanted changes and a supportive family.

"Yeah. Mostly it was hard for Seb. But we all took the news hard, I think." Bram takes a deep breath. "Anyway, seeing that picture caught me off guard. I knew Jolene was going to send this out, so I'm not sure why it hit me so hard. Sorry to babble all over you, bit of a mood killer, huh?" He forces a chuckle as he swipes at his eyes.

The bangles on Bram's wrist clink together, and a tiny curl of genuine happiness flits over his features as the sparkles catch his eye. I can't help smiling at how quickly he bounces back from his reaction to the photo.

"Not at all," I say, squeezing him tight. Just long enough to convey I care and I don't entirely believe everything is magically better just like that, while still letting him put on a brave face to get through the day. "You needed to get that off your chest; I'm happy to listen. Anytime."

"Careful, bear, I might just take you up on that." Bram traces his finger up my chest, then boops me on the nose and gives me a quick kiss before he turns back to his locker to strip and stash his clothing, gently stripping off his shinies to lay atop his crumpled clothing with exaggerated care.

Nothing mood killing there at all. To keep myself from staring at his cute butt when I should be changing too, I hastily scan the QR code on the printout to get to the fundraising site. At a glance, they're making progress, but still nowhere near their fundraising goal. I hope Jolene's sharing it in the newsletter will help. I chip in and post the link on my socials, but I wish I could do more.

Bram shifts, then flaps up to one of the newly installed perches beside the lockers to croak at me to hurry up. He tilts his head toward me and I can't resist giving his soft feathers a quick scritch, I don't often get to touch him in his bird form. We're usually in a hurry to shift and screw around during our breaks and after work.

It would be nice to have more time for tender explorations. After his confessions and now with him letting me pet his animal form, I feel closer to him than ever before. His feathers are softer than I'd imagined under my fingers. He croaks again, startling me into action. Right. We have to get back to work so Freya and Theron can take their lunch break. No time to pet his pretty feathers or let myself indulge in more than the hot and heavy action we got up to before we got back to the lockers to see the newsletter. We go back to the enclosure to relieve their other two ravens.

Neither of us lingers at the end of our work shift. As much as I enjoy my time with Bram, I'll see him again tomorrow, and I'm eager to learn how Myra's first day in the new class went. Besides, I'm sure he wants to share the progress on getting the word out about their fundraiser with his family.

When I get to Mom's, Myra comes running up to greet me with a beaming grin on her face.

"Papa! Mx. Adams is my new favorite teacher."

Tension I've been carrying since she started the year evaporates. From day one, when she came home in tears over some nasty comment from Wendle, this year has been a nightmare. And now my girl is excited to tell me about her day. She gushes about a book they read in class with a kid being raised by a single alpha parent like her. Her smile is contagious and I've missed seeing it as much.

She and Jenny are working on a science fair project together, and the only time she had to see Wendle was on the playground at recess.

When he tried to hassle her, Mx. Adams saw and stepped in to shut that shit down. They also sent home a note about the incident to both families, according to Myra. I sign that I've read it, along with checking her homework log when we pack up her bag.

The next morning, Wendle's alpha mom catches me in the drop off line to make sure her kid gives my kid a hand-written apology. I didn't realize she was in the picture, considering how traditional his family is, but I resolve to be polite.

"Sorry, I've said mean things to you, Myra," Wendle says. He doesn't look entirely contrite as he sullenly offers her an envelope. Myra doesn't look convinced of his sincerity, but she pinches the note gingerly between her fingers and nods.

"Okay?" she says, and I'm absurdly proud of her for not letting his apology pressure her into saying the way he's treated her is alright. It's not. I rest my hand on her shoulder in silent support.

"And?" Wendle's mom prompts when the boy just stands there shuffling his feet.

"And I was wrong to repeat speciesist things my gran says. I shouldn't have invited everyone in the class but you to our Denning Night party; you can come too. If you want."

I have to clench my jaw not to point out how the way he just invited her was meant to sting. More about reminding her he didn't want her there than an actual invitation. My kid is smart enough to see through that BS.

"Oh!" Myra says with wide-eyed innocence and what I know to be feigned regret. "Sorry, I can't make it. We've already got family plans."

I squeeze her shoulder, so proud of her for not letting him get under her skin.

"I'll see you tonight, Mapa!" Myra turns to wave at me and runs off to play with her friends in the schoolyard. Wendle slinks away to join his friends at the other end of the yard. I'm left to stand awkwardly beside Wendle's mom.

"She really is welcome at the party. Wendle's grandma won't be around the kids," she says. I actually believe in the sincerity of her overture, but it's still too little too late in my book.

"That's kind of you, but we have other plans already."

"That's too bad. I can't tell you how mortified we were to learn what was going on. I've told my mother-in-law I don't want her talking about these things with the kids. There's no talking to that woman sometimes."

"Ah. I know the sort. Myra's great grandmother and her grandfather were the same way when I was in contact with them."

"Well, I can see why you wouldn't want her around people like that. After this incident, we're finally moving out of the sleuth's house. I told Wendle's omega dad that the kids and I were leaving, and he agreed to come with us. I guess he didn't want to believe it was this bad. And honestly, I haven't put my foot down before now because I wasn't sure if he would come with us."

"I'm glad he is sticking with you and the kids." I give her a wan smile, even though the fact that Wendle's omega dad is choosing his kids and mate over his sleuth feels like a punch to the gut. Granted, Wendle's dad is an adult and Arnie was just a kid, fresh out of school, when we had Myra. It still hurts, more for Myra's sake than my own, and I stumble through a few more pleasantries, trying to extricate myself from the conversation as quickly as possible.

At least it seems like Wendle's parents are serious about him not repeating his grandmother's bile and genuinely don't share her bigoted views. Just the fact that Wendle's alpha mom is here handling drop off is testament to that fact. I'm still glad we already made our plans to go to Four Corners for their festival. Myra will have more fun at an inclusive event, I'm sure of it. She knows it's where my coworker lives. I've told her that much about him. Now I just need to tell Bram about her before Denning Night.

Somehow, it's hard to find the chance. The next two weeks pass all too quickly with Bram's proximity as a constant temptation. We don't *just* fuck, despite my best efforts to remain casual, we talk more and spend all our breaks together.

I can't seem to get enough of the sexy omega. That might be my libido making up for lost time, but Bram and I have found stolen moments to fuck most days since we first agreed to continue hooking up.

He's a considerate lover, and he doesn't press or pry when I turn down his less than subtle suggestions that we should make plans outside of work sometime. Dinner or coffee on a day off. So far, he just accepts that I've got other responsibilities and I can't date right now. But if not now, then when?

It's hard to accept just how much I want to take Bram up on those dates. It *would* be dating though, and I'm still not ready to share about Myra with him, even though the timer is ticking down to the festival. There's no guarantee he'll actually attend. Or that we'll see him there if he does.

I've told Myra that my new friend from work is the one who invited us to the festival and she might meet him. She noticed that I've been coming home smelling like a stranger, so I had to tell her about sharing my enclosure and becoming friends with Bram. She doesn't need to know that our friendship mostly entails getting each other off.

Granted, I still need to tell Bram that I'm a parent at some point. If we're going to be more than fuck buddies, but that's precisely why I haven't let the emotions lurking inside me take the reins yet. Instead, I've gotten in the habit of offering him post-coital snacks. I've got no shortage of treats in the stash I carry around with me. It's been part of my routine ever since Myra was old enough to require food for longer outings.

As a bonus, it's harder to blurt out my growing affection for him when our mouths are stuffed full of granola bars, or the freeze-dried cherries he loves. The ones that Myra decided she no longer likes after I made a big batch of trail mix with them. And yet they are back in my snack stash because of the way Bram picked them out of that trail mix to devour them first.

I can tell myself I bought more out of habit as much as I want, but it doesn't stop the warm glow I feel when the omega beams at being offered more of his favorite snack. I don't want to admit, even to myself, that I care about Bram more than I should.

The way I feel about him is a messy tangle. One that gets messier with every little detail he shares with me about his life and family that I dodge reciprocating. It's all colored with the intimacy of post-orgasmic happy hormones and fears that my past baggage has inked indelibly into my psyche. I fell for the high of a new relationship before. When I thought Arnie was it for me. I refuse to repeat the mistake of confusing good sex with love.

My daughter has to come first, and dating has to take a back seat for now. Except, that rings hollow now that my kid is doing better with school. She's been sleeping better and her anxiety about going to school is almost gone since she moved to her new class. She adores her new teacher.

Maybe Mom's right and I do use being Myra's parent as an excuse not to put myself out there. These past few weeks with Bram have shown me how freeing it is to be completely myself with a bed partner for the first time, probably ever. Arnie's traditional family upbringing made it hard for him to understand my dysphoria. Since I was still working out who I was back then, it was hard for me to explain. In the end, it hardly mattered to him, since I've always been an alpha foremost and that was what Arnie needed in a partner.

Bram is so different from that. He makes the effort to understand and affirm me. I don't want anything to burst my bubble of happiness with him. Because we might not be dating, but we're still texting every night. We've started eating lunch together—even when we can't sneak away to get our hands all over each other. We meet at Wild Bean each morning, and whoever gets there first orders both of our coffees. And those darn cherries he loves are next to Myra's favorite chocolate-covered granola bars in my pantry and my work backpack, silently mocking any illusions I have that I'm not gone for the bird.

I'm still not ready to face my emotions, or risk breaking this fragile bond that's growing between us. So I put off upsetting the status quo for as long as possible. Right up until it's the morning of the Denning Night party and I realize that I've run out of time. So I guess he's going to find out by meeting my kid unless I call ahead.

I'm tempted to risk it. Bram might not even be there, and he can't get too mad about my withholding the truth in a public venue with said kid right there in the room. It might actually diffuse any anger or hurt feelings he has to meet Myra. But that might be a dick move.

In his shoes, I'd want the courtesy of being told before the kid is in the room. If he's not interested in being with a single parent, better to know that up front. Or as up front as possible at this point. He needs to know if I'm really thinking that this could be more than sex.

And if he's still interested in me once I explain about Myra, then I want them to meet. Not as anything more than a friend for now, but I want her to know the sweet omega who makes me laugh over the most mundane things. Who loves all things shiny as much as she does, and who looks at me like I'm one of his precious baubles. And I want Bram to know the girl who will always have a giant chunk of my heart firmly wrapped around her little finger.

It shocks me to realize that I want to give my kid the chance to approve of Bram, and I want to see if he could care about Myra the way he seems to care about me. Tonight will tell me if that's possible. I just need the courage to tell him and avoid springing the situation on both of them.

Now or never. I dial Bram's number; this isn't something I can do over text.

CHAPTER 14

Bram

It's been a few years since I've been to the local grizzly bears' Denning Night potluck. It's the sort of big community gathering that most the shifters in Four Corners partake in. Most shifters who don't have a connection to the sleuth will drift away from the more culturally focused parts of the festivities, giving the grizzlies their space to celebrate without gawkers.

As a child, the stories about grizzly bear heroes and their spiritual beliefs around hibernation just seemed like any other fanciful story, but as I grew older, I realized those tales had a deeper significance to the grizzly sleuth. It's humbling that they're willing to share such a huge part of their culture with the rest of Four Corners and that they make the evening festivities fun and engaging for our entire community while they hold their vigil.

Denning Night—and other shared celebrations like it—is part of what I love about Four Corners. It's a way to share in all the rich cultures among the different species who live here. From the traditional dishes that all the different shifter groups bring to share to the grizzly elders recounting the origins of the holiday to any who care to listen, it's part of what makes our mixed species community feel special.

As a teen, I always looked forward to playing carnival games in the town square and the dancing and music that persists late into the night. When my clutchmates and I were small, the lure of filling our bellies to bursting with sweets was more than enough to make it a celebration. As we got older, we crept off into the woods with the other teens to shift and play in our animal forms. I still have fond memories of those long-ago nights.

I'm not sure why I stopped attending, but this is the first year in a while that I'm giddy at the thought of going to the festival. I wake up the morning of the event thrumming with anticipation.

If I'm honest with myself, I know that champagne bubble feeling in my chest is because I get to see Ty tonight. No work constraints or other responsibilities to rush us along. I'm excited to see the alpha. And if I'm even more painfully honest, I've been catching feelings for my fuck buddy from the first time he bent over and offered to let me fuck between his thighs.

I'm not ready to put it into words yet, and certainly nowhere near declaring myself in love with the bear, but I like Ty as more than a fuck buddy. How to ask if he feels the same is a problem for another day.

We have time to just enjoy this thing between us without worrying about it becoming something more. I mean, sure, I want kids and a big family someday. And, yes, creep is a thing that might speed up my timeline for pursuing those things, like it did to Seb. In his case, the condition derailed any plans he might have had for kids, but that doesn't mean I'm going to let fear dictate my life. When it comes to Ty, I'm happy with our stolen moments together at work for now. But I *really* like Ty.

Which might explain the butterflies in my stomach when I get a call from Ty while I'm trying to decide what to wear tonight.

"Hello!" I don't even try to hide that I'm excited to hear from the alpha. We text a lot now, but phone calls are rare. "Pronouns?"

"He today."

Ty's warm rumble is music to my ears.

"Cool. To what do I owe the pleasure?"

I wonder if I can convince him to upgrade our next sext session to phone sex. I'd love to listen to his voice while I jerk off to thoughts of thrusting between his luscious thighs again. Or feeling his knot pulsing hot inside me.

His next words bring that fantasy up short and I can't quite believe I heard him properly.

Ty says, "I'm a dad."

The words don't quite penetrate. I'm not sure what he means. If he's got kids, that seems like the sort of thing I should know already, even if we've only been getting closer for a few weeks. It's still pretty stinking huge. He knows about my family since I talk about them a lot. Heck, he let me spill my guts to him after Jolene sent out the link to Winny's fundraiser in her biweekly staff letter.

How could he just not mention having a kid? I mean, sure, he's always talking about how he can't go on dates with me in the evenings because of responsibilities, and he's such a nurturing alpha. Haven't I enjoyed the protective way he cares for me after we come? Cleaning me up and feeding me snacks?

I tried not to scavenge all the decadent cherries from his trail mix the first time he offered me some, but the alpha must have noticed because the next day, he showed up with a bag full of just the cherries. Is it any wonder I'm falling for the shifter when he's so caring?

"What?" I ask, teetering on the edge of anxious laughter with my pulse pounding like I've run a race because I'm not sure what it means that he's telling me this. Is this him breaking things off? Does he have a mate too? One he wants to hide me from tonight? Am I having an affair? No, wait, he'd be the one—no, the semantics don't matter.

"I have a daughter," Ty says. And even through my own racing thoughts, I can hear how anxious he is about telling me this. Somehow, that relaxes me, makes me want to soothe his nerves. Obviously, this is as huge to him as it is to me.

"Oh, wow. What's her name?" I ask, with genuine curiosity that I hope will ease his mind. The news he has a kid makes me like Ty more, makes it easy to see him as parent material for my future children.

"Myra. She's my universe, so I just needed you to know before this goes any further," Ty says, and just the fond way he says her name has me all swoony over him. My emotions and thoughts are pinging all over the place about this huge news.

"Are you mated?" I ask, trying not to make the question an accusation. Or let my heart go racing ahead off a cliff because he wants this to go further.

"No. Myra's bearer hasn't ever been in the picture. He left us when she was a newborn."

Relief floods through me, banishing the last vestiges of tension and fear that he may have been lying to me about everything. At the same time, I can't even imagine walking away from a clutch and leaving them with my mate. It makes me want to scoop Ty into a hug.

"Wow, that must have been hard. I can't imagine what that was like for you, Ty."

"It was, but I got Myra out of it. I wouldn't change that for the world."

"I bet you're an amazing dad, I can tell how much you love her. How old is she?"

"She's eight. And I'm sorry I didn't say anything sooner." Ty sounds sheepish.

"It's okay. Your kid comes first. I get it." And part of me does. Another part is still trying to process everything, but I have all day to work through exactly how I feel before I see him in person. Ty didn't lie to me, but he kept something monumentally huge a secret. Sure, it's only been a few weeks, but the shifter I'm falling for has a kid. A whole life outside our job I know nothing about. Absolutely nothing. Except that's not true either. I *do* know him, and he's exactly the sort of person I can picture raising a family with. A family with an eight-year-old bear cub.

"So, Myra? She's part grizzly?" I ask.

That has to be the reason he acted so cagey about the 'friend' he was asking about Denning Night for. She's probably a mixed shifter child, considering he needed help to find an inclusive grizzly celebration.

Is it still considered mixed if the kid is bear on both sides? Probably. I suppose our part-crow cousins have varying traditions from ours, even though we're all corvids. That bears out what he said about the kid's grizzly parent not being in the picture at all. Ty is the one making sure she gets to experience both sides of her heritage. That's the sort of question I probably shouldn't blurt at him.

"Yeah. For what it's worth, I'm just protective of her. You're the first person I've really dated since Arnie and when we were just hooking up, it wasn't something you needed to know."

That 'were' sends my pulse racing for a much more pleasant reason. I bite back a delighted little shriek that he wants us to be dating. He thinks this has moved beyond convenient sex to the point he wants to let me into his life.

No, not just his, his daughter's life too. That's huge. And that's when it truly hits me that being with Ty doesn't just mean the possibility of having kids and a family someday in the future. If Ty and I get serious, that would mean having an active role with his daughter too. Myra might one day be my step-daughter. Is that something Ty would want? I'm afraid to ask that so soon, but I want him to know that I'm open to it. More than open, that I'm enthusiastically supportive of her place in his life and any family we might form together.

"Well, I'm glad you told me now. Thanks for trusting me, Ty. You won't regret it. I'm really excited to meet her tonight. Assuming I get to meet her?"

"Yeah. Of course," Ty says, and I can hear the warm smile in his voice. "I'm not sure about telling her that we're dating yet, but I want you two to meet. We'll have to figure out the details as we go."

"That's fine. We can *wing* the whole single dad dating thing together." I tease him, once again giddy at the prospect of seeing him tonight. If anything, I've decided the fact he told me about Myra now has to mean he's as serious as I am about us.

"In more ways than one, bird." Ty catches on to my bird-themed teasing, his droll tone humoring me.

"I'm hilarious."

"You sure are something."

"Thank you. So, that's why you turned down my dinner offers? Needed to get home to the kid?"

"Yeah. But if we are doing this, I can get a sitter."

"I can help pay, if it means I get to see you more."

"No. That's sweet of you, but you've got your sister's medical stuff. I wouldn't ask that."

"Okay, but like, totally worth chipping in a couple bucks if it means I get to see you more."

"It's not really about the cost. More, I don't like to disrupt her schedule or miss the time I have with her."

"How about a lunch date on a Friday when we're both off work, then? So she'll be at school."

"Sounds perfect. And I'll see you tonight?"

"Yes," I agree, determined to go now more than ever. "I'll see you both tonight."

I take my time picking an outfit once we hang up. And then, just before I planned on leaving, I change my mind again. It has to impress Ty without looking like I put in too much effort. Attractive without being too obvious. Kid-friendly and still alluring.

In the end, I pick a comfy pair of stretchy bedazzled jeans and a slouchy green shirt that reminds me of the blouse Ty wore with all the pretty little buttons. Just before I leave, I layer on a bunch of my costume jewelry, because I figure that might give me something to discuss with Myra. The glittery pink and gold bear charm I put on last makes me smile. A little cub, just like her.

I always see loads of kids around her age when I go to accessory stores. Seb likes to point out there's a reason for that, and tease me over having a pre-teen's taste in jewelry, but I like what I like. I don't know why I'm nervous about impressing an eight-year-old, but I am. I want her dad to keep liking me.

When I finally get to the party, dinner is already in full swing. Olga, the omegiarch of the grizzly shifter sleuth, presides over the feasting from a table at the front of the room. Her raven shifter mate sits beside her. The laden buffet tables line two walls of the community room, potluck style. All are welcome, but I still shuffle into the gathering feeling weird about arriving late.

At least I didn't come empty-handed. The paltry packets of cookies I picked up at the store hardly seem like a fair exchange for all the delicious food others have contributed. Enticing aromas waft from chafing dishes set over little Sterno burners. I deposit the cookies with several similar packages on the dessert table despite its inadequacy. Then I grab a plate and join the line of guests as I help myself to little portions of everything that catches my eye.

I'm far from the last to arrive, so that relaxes my nerves a fraction. I'm mostly nervous about meeting Ty here. It's our first time really interacting in person outside the zoo. My first time seeing him as a dad. And until this morning, neither of us had acknowledged that there is a palpable something special growing between us.

I scan the crowd for the familiar form of my big burly bear coworker. His stature should make Ty stand above the crowd, but I don't see him at first. I finish filling my plate, then search for a seat among the crowded trestle tables. Cory runs by me brandishing some sort of toy. They're pursued by a passel of other young kids from all different species. The group includes several cousins from our rave and a few of the grizzly cubs I vaguely recognize as their friends.

They're all laughing and their party clothes show evidence that they've been through the buffet line already. Elric and Alphonse, Olga's alpha grandson, and two of the wolf pups from the pack Elric is going on their first hunt with are filling their plates. The older kids watch over Cory and the younger kids. I smile at their carefree laughter as the gaggle of children makes their own fun.

My younger siblings being here is proof my parents are already in attendance. I catch sight of a large group from the rave, several raven shifters enjoying their meal and taking up most of a trestle table.

Winny is there with them, head down and focused intently on her plate, but leaving the apartment is an enormous step forward. Before our talk, I might have gone over to suggest we enjoy the dance floor at the far end of the hall, the way we used to as kids. I'd have pushed her to do more. Now, I can just be proud that she's stretching the boundaries of her comfort zone on her own. If there was more room, I might go join the other ravens. But I can't escape the jittery excitement bubbling inside me that Ty is here somewhere. So I wave to Mama when she sees me, then keep searching the crowd.

Seb's brightly dyed hair catches my eye from

across the room. At first glance, he seems like he's canoodling with someone. But then I recognize the person who he's huddled close with is Rollie. So the two of them are probably scheming.

Seb is smiling, and he doesn't seem to notice me watching, so I'm not about to interrupt whatever those two are plotting. Probably scoping out who to flirt with tonight. Which is exactly what I don't want to admit to myself I'm doing. Scoping the crowd for the alpha who I want nothing more than to flirt with tonight. Well, maybe not *nothing* more. If Ty wasn't here with his kid, I'd want to do way more than flirt.

I make it about three quarters of the way around the room when I spot his familiar auburn hair. Ty. My eyes skate over his outfit to confirm he's still presenting masc like when we spoke earlier today. He is. And he's dapper in his burnt orange blazer and matching chinos. His bushy beard looks freshly shaped, and I want to dig my fingers into those wiry curls while we kiss.

My raven has the urge to preen his pretty hair. In my human form, I want to run my fingers through it. I want to bask in the post-coital haze we never get to relax and enjoy together with the way things are between us. It's unfair of him to be so handsome when I can't touch him. He isn't ready to tell his kid we're together, which is totally fair, since we haven't actually agreed to be more than fuck buddies. I can treat him like a friend for one evening.

As I'm considering the implications of mixing two totally different spheres of my existence, Ty rests a proprietary hand on his seatmate's shoulder and I freeze. His daughter is a pint-sized replica of him. The same twinkling eyes and coppery-brown curls that shine with a warm luster in the fluorescent lights. A couple of years younger than Elric. It all clicks into place as he leans over to listen to something the child is saying and removes a tomato from her salad for her.

Ty is a dad. Theoretically I knew that, but it's different seeing it. I shouldn't be gawking at him as he helps his child. I shouldn't intrude on their family time. Should I just walk away? It's not as though anyone is going to miss me here tonight. I could take my paper plate and go eat the feelings welling up inside me. The realization crashing down around me at seeing Ty with his kid isn't a pleasant one.

He already has the family I hope to create some day. The kid and the baggage of a mating gone terribly awry. Is that something I can even be a part of? I'm not sure. After sitting with these thoughts all day, all I've figured out is that if Ty wants to be with me, for real, not just for orgasms, then I want to try.

I want to meet Myra and see if she's as much like her daddy as she appears. I want to make them both laugh, watch Ty's eyes crinkle the way they do when he's amused, despite trying to pretend to be above my silly jokes. And maybe, someday, the three of us could be a family together. It scares me to think that so soon, but from everything I know of him, Ty could be the alpha by my side in all my hazy dreams of the future.

Before I can tear my eyes away from the pair, an elderly shifter on the child's other side catches me staring. Her benign smile turns into a concerned moue as she gestures toward me, drawing Ty's attention. I hunch my shoulders as he swings a worried parental look my way, because, duh. No one with good intentions stares at strange children, right?

I'm not really staring at the kid, though, so our eyes lock and I can't read the emotions that flicker in his gaze. Ty lifts his napkin and wipes his mouth before rising from the bench seat with a murmured word to his companions. The elder puts an arm around the child's shoulders and Ty swings his leg over the bench.

I stand, frozen in place as my crush approaches me.

"Hi." I go to wave, nearly overbalancing my plate in the process since the flimsy paper is holding a lot of food.

"Hi, I didn't realize the entire community would turn out here." Ty glances self-consciously around the room.

"Oh, yeah. We enjoy a good excuse to

celebrate." I shuffle in place, unsure if I should actually join them with my food or not. "Um, didn't mean to stare at your kid. She's as pretty as you."

"You might need your eyes checked, bird." Ty chuckles. "Myra is much prettier than me."

"Um. If you say so, bear." I hesitate to say anything, but he came over to me. Interrupted his family time to acknowledge me. "So, the in-laws didn't invite you to theirs?"

"They were never my in-laws," Ty says.

"Sorry, they're a sore spot?"

Ty scowls, then he shoots a terribly fond glance toward his seat. As if he wants to be sure his daughter won't hear whatever he has to say next.

"You could say that. Myra's omega dad is from a traditional grizzly family, and they didn't want a non-grizzly alpha-in-law. The family omegiarch refused to acknowledge Myra if she took her black bear form and we agreed that wasn't a good way to raise her. Arnie let me have full custody. He went back to them, mated another grizzly, and for all I know, they've got cubs together by now. We've got my mom and our neighbor, Mrs. Grund—the grizzly shifter who is sitting with us—for family. I send Arnie pictures of her twice a year and he doesn't respond other than to send me a terse thank you note."

"Bet he regrets it," I say, glancing between Ty

and his child. Who wouldn't regret walking away from this alpha? Let alone their own child? I can't imagine leaving a clutch over my family objecting to my chosen mate. Then again, I can't imagine my family forcing me to choose between them and my mate and child. "I'm sorry."

Ty shrugs, as though he didn't just share an old wound with me. "He has shown no signs of that. But I appreciate the sentiment. Myra deserves to know every part of herself, so I try to help her connect with grizzly traditions. We used to hold our own Denning Night celebrations. We invited another family who didn't mind my being the wrong kind of bear, but they moved away. The other grizzly sleuth near us has more traditional views on alpha and omega roles."

"Meaning they didn't think a single alpha should raise a child?"

Ty nods, his expression tight.

"Well, that's bullshit. I'm no expert, but I'm pretty sure kids are best raised by a parent or parents who adore them, not someone who would choose anyone else over them."

"Arnie isn't the bad guy here. He made the best choices he could for himself and Myra," Ty defends the prick of an omega and I can't help falling for him even more. Because of course that's the sort of person Ty is. Someone who can forgive and empathize with a person who clearly hurt him. And more to the point, also hurt his kid.

"No matter what I think of his choices, he's still Myra's bearer, and I don't like for people to assume he just didn't care. He did. That's why he agreed to let me raise her. Instead of taking her into a situation where she would always have to hide a part of herself or be seen as less," Ty says.

"That's, uh, a unique way of looking at things. I don't think I could forgive someone who hurt me like that."

Ty shrugs. "Like I said, he isn't the bad guy. Just a person who had no options that wouldn't hurt someone. He made the decisions he could live with. And I'll be forever grateful that he gave me Myra. But enough about that. Come join us?"

I hesitate. Even though I planned on meeting Myra tonight, this feels monumental. Even if he isn't telling Myra that we're together yet, her opinion about us is going to matter to him more than anyone else's.

"She wants to meet the omega who saved her trail mix from the curse of the dry cherries," Ty cajoles. And doesn't his insistence send warmth radiating through me? He's going to introduce me to his kid. That's huge. And I'm ready for it. I take a deep breath to steady my resolve. Then I nod.

"Yeah, okay, I'd be delighted to meet Myra."

Ty beams at me, obviously pleased, as he offers me his hand.

"She and my mom have both been asking about my new coworker, so I'm sure that's mutual," Ty says with a rumbly chuckle.

His comment reminds me of what he said earlier about introducing me as his friend and coworker. My bubbly excitement dims at the reminder that we aren't officially more than that. Not yet. "You'll tell her about me if we keep seeing each other, won't you? I don't want to be a secret you're keeping from her."

"Yes. It's just for now, Bramble." Ty cups my cheek gently, angling his bulk to block the intimate gesture from the view of his family behind him. Even if he's being discreet, his touch renews the fizzy excitement that I get to spend the evening with him and he wants the same things as I do. "I want to date you, but I don't want Myra getting too attached too soon if things don't work out. We might not be taking things slow between us, but that doesn't mean I want to put her heart on the line yet."

"Right, that makes sense." I swallow down my disappointment, because I truly do understand. Even if I wish he didn't have to be cautious, that we could be reckless and throw ourselves headlong into romance. But he has to worry about his kid's heart as well as his own, and I can only respect him for it.

"I'll follow your lead with her," I say.

"Thank you." Ty's genuine smile melts my heart. He takes my elbow and turns toward the table. "Come meet my daughter."

Ty steers me toward his little group and I revel

in the stolen touch. As we walk toward his kid, he leans close enough to murmur into my ear, his breath a warm tickle that goes right to the butterflies fluttering in my belly. "Relax, bird, I know she'll like you. You are something else."

I know he means it in all the best ways. I feel like his sweet words are a glowing ball of warmth in the pit of my stomach. The grumpy bear likes me on more than a superficial level. Ty likes me and he trusts me enough to introduce me to his kid. My dreams of having a mate and family have never felt so close as they do tonight.

CHAPTER 15

Ty

I'm not sure why I left Myra sitting with Mom and Mrs. Grund to go greet Bramble, but I don't regret the impulse. Bram beams at me as I approach him. His entire face lights with joy that makes my heart swell with pride that I make him happy just by being around him.

As we chat, I realize I needed this moment to connect with him, just the two of us in the crowd, with no pretending I'm not falling for him. Bram's smile when I cup his cheek says he feels the same. No need for words. The bird wears his heart on his face; I swear. Or his sleeve, whatever the static idiom is. He's easy to read and the naked longing when he looks at me is an undeniable ego boost.

He's not the first shifter to look at me like that. But he's perhaps the most earnest about it. There isn't an ounce of guile in Bram. When he looks at me like I'm the juiciest berry on the bush, it's hard to resist him.

Turns out, it's even harder to resist him after catching him watching my interaction with my daughter with the same sort of soft longing I imagined from a mate. The way Arnie would have watched us in another lifetime. As though Bram appreciates the sight of me with her, in total dad mode, as I helped her perform a tomato-ectomy on her salad.

Mrs. Grund thought the bird was watching my kid, but from my angle I could tell that he only had eyes for me. And in the crowded event hall, he stands out with his ever present baubles and his lanky-limbed gait. His laden paper plate looks in danger of spilling despite his firm grasp. All I could focus on as I rose from my seat was that I might not see Bram again tonight if I let him slip away with his dinner, so of course I went to him.

Bram keeps on smiling at me. And I can see he really isn't mad that I kept being a parent close to my vest. I didn't intend to deceive him in any way. It's just that I don't tell dates about her. I've always known that anything romantic would be temporary by necessity.

My dalliances since becoming a parent have been few and far between, and the idea of introducing anyone new into her life makes my skin crawl. It's just too much of a risk. First, because I'm protective of her safety with any new adult in her life. But also because if things don't work out, I never want to hold her while she cries about another adult walking out on her without a backward glance. It would break my heart all over again to hear her ask why Bram, or any other person I might introduce her to, doesn't want her.

Then again, Bram works at the zoo. Which means I know he's had a background check. If he was on any kind of registry, he wouldn't be able to work around kids as we do.

We might spend most of our time together in our animal forms, but I still feel like I'm coming to know the shifter. He's kind, playful, utterly enamored of all things that sparkle and shine. And he shines. Like Myra, he shines bright with a zest for life I can't match, and I want to bask in both of their glow.

"Come meet my daughter," I insist when he hesitates. The words seem foreign on my tongue. As though someone else said them. But I mean them with all my heart.

This is still early days with him, but I don't want to spend all evening avoiding him. Besides, introducing my coworker to my daughter at a public festival he pretty much invited us to attend is reasonable. Normal. The sort of thing I should be able to do.

Bram follows me to the table with a spring in his step. We have to shuffle around some to make room for his plate next to me.

"Hey, everyone, this is Bram." I sweep my hand toward him as I move Myra's plate of dessert to make more space.

Mom smiles knowingly at me when I introduce him. "Pleasure to meet you, Bram. Are you the raven shifter we've been hearing so much about recently?"

"If by that you mean this one has been complaining about me invading his territory, then probably?" Bram jokes self-deprecatingly.

"No, Ty hasn't been complaining. Far from it." Mom leans conspiratorially close to him, resting her fingers on the table just in front of him. "My cub seems rather enamored of you."

I stifle a cough in my fist. Acting embarrassed will only encourage her to play matchmaker. She already knows there's something between us. The way she subtly scents the omega and shoots me a softly knowing smile tells me she knows he's the one I've been seeing. The one I've been texting and smiling over. There's no use denying the truth. Mrs. Grund keeps Myra engaged with her food while Bram and Mom chat.

"Oh? He does? You do?" Bram flushes and shuffles the food around on his plate, he won't look at me. "That's uh, good. Right?" He glances between Mom and me, as though seeking our approval.

"Very good." Mom nods.

"I may have misjudged you when we first met," I allow. "Bram, this is my alpha mom, Mavis, my daughter, Myra, and Mrs. Grund is Myra's honorary second Gram."

"I was their neighbor for years, and I've babysat this little one since she was a squalling cub."

"I don't squall." Myra pouts. "What's a squall?" Myra tugs on my sleeve.

"It just means you cried as a baby," I explain.

"Oh. I guess I might have been a squall then." She spoons up another bite of Mrs. Grund's bacon macaroni and cheese from her plate and sucks the utensil clean.

"It's nice to meet you all," Bram says. "What grade are you in, Myra?"

Myra makes a yuck face. "Third grade."

"Oh, nice. My youngest sibling is in second grade this year. What's your favorite subject?"

Myra considers for a while, spoon poised against her chin. "Art."

"Oh yeah? Do you like to use loads of glitter?"

"Yes." Myra nods. "Lots of glitter. Papa says we can't use it at home though. He won't let me get it because it's like herpes."

"I did not say that!" I stifle the urge to cover the kid's mouth and wish the ground would open up and swallow me.

"You did!" Myra waves her spoon at me. "You said it to Gramma while I was finishing my picture last week and she said I could bring the glitter home and you said no."

I *did* say that. But we'd been in the living room

while she finished her picture at the kitchen table. With music playing far too loudly for me to hear her, but of course she overheard me when I said something not meant for cubs' ears. "I meant it's like a harpy, showing up where you don't expect it," I temporize.

Bram has none of my compunctions about laughing. He bursts into a spirited guffaw, head thrown back and eyes dancing with mirth. "I think you and I could be good friends, Myra. Glitter is my favorite."

Myra nods. "It makes my flowers really pop." She points at one of Bram's bangles. "I like your glittery bracelet."

Bram lifts his hand and twists the bauble around so it will catch the light. "Mhm, this one? I like it too. See, it's a little teddy bear." He cocks his head toward her. "Say, that's just like you, right? You're a bear shifter like your papa?"

"Yeah. Only, I'm special 'cause I've got two different bears." She holds up two fingers proudly, her grin showing off the gap in her teeth where she lost her latest wiggly tooth.

I love that smile and I love the pride in her voice as she claims both of her shifted forms. We've had to work on that. Not every mixed species child inherits two animal forms. I half-expected her bear to be a hybrid form of the two species. That happens sometimes with mixed shifter kids.

If she has kids of her own someday, there's

no guarantee which of her animal forms they'll inherit. I've worked so hard to help her take pride in herself—fighting against the ingrained attitudes of more traditional shifters like Wendle and his family. It's gratifying to witness her claiming both of her bears like this.

"Would you like it?" Bram slips the stretchy plastic bangle off his wrist. It's that corkscrew plastic kind that can double as a hair tie. It's got enough spring that it should actually fit her smaller wrists. The plastic is glittery pink and gold and the bear in question is a small acrylic charm, also glittery.

Myra gasps and looks between the offered bangle and me for permission. I incline my head. There's no harm in the little gift, and considering how possessive Bram is over his pretties, I know the offer has a deeper meaning.

"May I, Papa?" she asks.

I nod and Myra snatches the bracelet from Bram and holds it in my face for me to admire. He smiles indulgently at her.

"Look, papa bear!" Myra waves her prize around. "Your friend gave me craft harpies! See how sparkly it is?"

Bram looks like he might choke to death trying not to laugh. Mom looks just as amused as she sips from her punch to cover her smile. I'm mortified at my daughter's pronouncement.

"He gave you a bracelet, baby girl." I take the object in question because she's holding it half an inch from my eyes. I look at the charm and smile. "It's a cub, just like you."

Myra giggles. "Daddy, I'm not pink! Or glittery."

"Oh, my bad. Here, go like this." I hold up my hand and she mirrors the gesture so I can slip the bracelet around her wrist. Myra holds her hand in front of her face to admire the charm.

"Oh, I have an idea! Can we dye my fur sparkly pink like this cub?"

"Absolutely not." I can just picture her shedding glitter over every inch of our house. They make hair chalk if she wants to tint her fur. That might not be too much of a disaster. She can even invite Jenny over to play salon with the stuff. I can sense a stint as a fur stylist in my near future. "We'll see about getting you more of that fur chalk you like, though."

"I want rainbow fur," Myra says.

"We'll see what they have at the store." I know they don't make rainbow and the odds that they will have every color in stock to DIY a rainbow fur look aren't in my favor.

"Rainbow." Myra does jazz hands at me, smiling when her new bear charm catches her eye. "Thanks for the new bracelet, Bram."

"You are very welcome, cub. We should all eat up now. Before they set out the ice cream and cut the Denning Night cake." He demonstrates by scooping up a big bite of his food. Myra doesn't take much reminding, devouring the rest of her favorite dish with frequent glances at her new bangle.

Bram definitely won my girl's heart with that kind gesture. To most adults, it probably wouldn't mean much of anything. My heart squeezes a bit because I know how much his costume jewelry means to him. The gift is as meaningful coming from him as it is to Myra. And watching the man who has been on my mind more and more often win over my daughter with his kindness melts my heart toward him even more. It's unfair just how much this shifter can make me want him in my life for the long haul. Especially when a few weeks ago he was nothing but an inconvenient barrier to my daily caffeine fix.

I eat my dinner while I've got the chance and Myra is distracted dipping pieces of chicken into the cheesy sauce remnants on her plate. She finishes her meal and gazes longingly at the plate of cookies I let her select for afterward.

"Go ahead." I nudge the plate in front of her. Myra devours the treats in record time. A grizzly at the head table announces they are bringing out more desserts as she finishes her cookies. Volunteers are gearing up for the carnival part of the evening.

"That's Olga, the omegiarch for the sleuth," Bram says in a soft undertone.

Mrs. Grund rises shortly after a couple of grizzly shifters bring out a cart with ice cream along with cut up sheet cake. She offers Myra her hand.

"How about we go get some ice cream and see if we can find some other cubs for you to play with?" Mrs. Grund asks.

"I can introduce you to my sibling, Elric, and a few of the grizzly cubs, after you finish your cake," Bram offers.

Part of me is anxious at the idea of letting my girl out of my sight. Even if this is a community gathering, it's not *our* community and I don't know anyone who isn't seated at our table with us. And they don't know Myra to look out for her.

"I can ask my little siblings to keep an eye on her. They're used to babysitting fledglings younger than her." Bram correctly interprets my misgivings before I can voice them. I swallow the protest that's on the tip of my tongue.

"Are you sure?" I ask.

"Yeah." Bram waves me off. "They're used to looking out for the younger kids from the rave at community nights. It's sort of a raven shifter rite of passage. Seeing as how between all the mated pairs in our rave, there's always a bunch of nestlings of all ages around. The older ones look out for the younger ones."

"She's not a nestling though," I point out.

Bram snorts. "Seb and I as much as invited you to this shindig. So, you could say that means you're here as guests of the rave. We'll look out for your cub the same as if she was our nestling.

I promise." Then he stands and flags down a passing child with his lanky build and the same flop of dark hair on their head. "Elric, you see the cub with the pink glittery tutu dress?"

The tween glances over toward the ice cream cart, squints, then nods. "Yeah?"

"That's Myra. She's my coworker's kid; watch out for her tonight?"

Elric's chest puffs up, sort of like a strutting bird alpha, and I have to stifle my amused grin. The tween reminds me of their older sibling. I bet Bram looked very similar at that age. Though the omega likely was a bit more keen on keeping track of other people's shiny baubles than watching over a passel of younger kids.

"On it! We'll take her over to the face painting with us once they set up the booths. If that's okay?" Elric glances toward me for permission.

"She'd love that. Thank you, Elric," I say.

"No problem, Bram's friend. Catch you later, bro." Elric tips Bram a saucy mock salute, then leads their entourage away. A half dozen rambunctious young shifters follow them. Several smell like ravens, interspersed with a few wolf cubs, and one with the distinctive scent of a young grizzly alpha's musk.

I'm still not entirely sure I'll be able to relax with my kid out of my sight. Luckily for me, I can keep an eye on her while she gets swept up in the crowd. The kids get their bowls of ice cream and squares of cake on flimsy plates before most of the adults go up for dessert.

"That's your sibling?" I ask after Elric leaves.

"Yep," Bram says, pride in his voice. "The middle one after our clutch. There's two more you haven't met. Elric uses they/them. Briony's older and uses she/her and the youngest, Cory, is six. They haven't settled on their pronouns yet."

"Oh. That's an avian thing, right?" I ask, recalling the tradition.

Bram chuckles. "Yeah, how much do you know about avian shifters?"

"Not much," I admit sheepishly.

"Well, most avian shifters lay eggs, so our babies start out as chicks. Occasionally, a clutch is born in their human form. In that case, they can't shift into a chick for the first few months."

"They can't shift right away? What about if they hatch in their avian form?"

"Nope, they can't shift from the form they are born in until they're old enough to digest a crop feeding in their human form. Or milk in their bird form. So usually between four to six months. I guess it's different with mammal shifter babies?"

"Yeah. Myra could shift right away. I think she was shifted in one of her ultrasound pictures, since cubs and human babies are comparable. Static bear cubs are tiny at birth, but shifter cubs gestate longer so they're roughly the same size as static human babies at birth."

"Aw. I bet she was adorable in all her forms,"

Bram says, and the bird knows just how to burrow right into my heart, saying sweet things about my baby.

Then he explains the reason behind his raven traditions. "But that's why we don't really assign pronouns to babies. Our hatchlings aren't sexually dimorphic, so we tend not to assign a gender even once they take their human form with their first shift. We just let them tell us when they're old enough to pick pronouns that fit. Most of the time, they pick pretty young, but some nestlings take longer than others, and some switch a few times before settling on something. And sometimes they're fluid, like you. So yeah, it's not too uncommon for a nestling's pronouns not to match their static human gender norms."

"Ah. Cool." I guess that explains how easily Bram accepted me. And how he already knew ways to have affirming sex with me without me having to explain or guide him. I should have tried dating avian shifters a while ago. "So I guess it's really not a big deal to you?"

"Nah. I'm not fussed much about that sort of thing. Most of our rave isn't. I told you my cousin and her mate are both trans too, right? My family wouldn't bat an eye at your pronouns changing from day to day, other than to be sure they're using the right ones."

"And Myra?"

"They love kids." He shrugs.

"No, I mean, she's got two animal forms."

Bram shakes his head, a flare of anger entering his scent. "We care even less about that. Some of my cousins are cravens, that's crow raven hybrids. And among static birds, ravens prey on baby crows. So, if we can overlook those differences, we sure as shit don't care that your kid has two different bears."

His anger on Myra's behalf seals the deal. This omega is too perfect for words, and I want him to be mine. Enough to take risks with my heart that I haven't allowed myself to consider since Arnie. Enough to trust him not to hurt my baby if they get to know each other.

It helps that she's old enough now to tell me if he ever makes her uncomfortable. I might even trust him enough to believe that even if things don't work out between us, he won't abandon her the way Arnie did. Much as I won't tolerate a bad word about my child's bearer in either of our hearing, I can't help resenting the ways he hurt our child.

Tonight is one of those bittersweet nights where I regret what might have been with Arnie and his family. Myra should be running around her family's Denning Night festivities with her cousins and siblings instead of being folded into a group of kids she's only met today. She should have dozens of watchful adult relatives to dote on her and annoy her by exclaiming over how much she's grown.

I can't give her that. But I can give her the party she would have had if I weren't her alpha parent. Or if I were a grizzly like her. I can give her my mom and Mrs. Grund, and Bram and his riot of siblings and relatives. Other mixed species shifter kids to play with.

I watch her beam at Elric and a grizzly cub called Alphonse. The three of them laugh at jokes I can't hope to hear from across the crowded room. The trio bonds over big bowls of ice cream so smothered in toppings you can't even see the scoops of strawberry underneath them all.

I can watch as she listens with rapt attention to the grizzly omegiarch telling the traditional Denning Night stories once the last of the food gets cleared away. After dessert, the festival spills out into the town square where there are booths with games, activities, and craft sellers set up.

We gather our jackets before venturing outside. Bram stays close to me, and despite my reservations about telling Myra about us, I can't resist holding the handsome omega's hand as we stroll around the square. Everything is decked out for the celebration and other winter holidays. There's even a face painting booth and a band playing music. It's a perfectly magical night, the first snow of the season sifting over the scene like glitter in a snow-globe.

We stay at a distance from the children, keeping a weather eye on my kid while preserving the illusion that she's got free rein of the celebrations. I love giving her the chance to run wild with the other kids, the way Arnie described his Denning Nights as a cub.

It's a good night. Bram stays by my side, pointing out his relatives and introducing me to people as his coworker. Mrs. Grund hits it off with one of the grizzly shifter elders. Myra, Elric, and Alphonse stick together even as the younger kids with them peel off to rejoin their families over the course of the evening. The three of them are thick as thieves as the rest of the mob of mostly raven shifter children around them seems to shift and change throughout the evening.

Myra finds me in the wee hours for a nap. As soon as she wakes up, she rejoins her new friends, and all three of them finish the vigil strong. At the end of the night, when the grizzly bears gather outside to ring in the dawn with traditional songs, most of the remaining other shifters disperse. Bram picks his way back over to me from talking with his brother, Seb. He sits next to me as my child joins the other grizzlies as they all take their bear forms.

The actual change is usually a private thing, but it's communal on Denning Day. A way of connecting with their fellow grizzlies. There are a few shifters at the doors to the event hall to help get them open for those who prefer privacy to shift inside. More volunteers gather up discarded clothing and belongings to bring them inside, out of the light snow.

Most of the gathered grizzlies eschew privacy and strip to shift wherever they can find a spot in the square. Myra wore a dress that's got enough stretch in the fabric that she can wriggle out of it after her shift, and Mrs. Grund helps her before stripping to shift as well.

My chest aches at not being able to do this with Myra. Bram nudges me toward the other bears as Myra and her new grizzly cub friends paw playfully at each other, all of them already in their fur.

"Why don't you go join them?" he asks.

"I'm not a grizzly." I try to hide my bitterness at the memory of being told in no uncertain terms I wasn't welcome to join the sleuth on Denning Day during their shift when Arnie and I first became friends. His omega grandmother doubled down on that message later, when we were dating.

Bram gives me an insouciant shrug and gestures to where a large raven shifter swoops down to land on the omegiarch grizzly's back. The bird settles in and preens the old bear's broad head. To my surprise, Olga leans into the bird's beak, grunting a soft familial little sound at the other shifter.

"They're mates?" I ask, unable to keep the incredulity out of my voice.

"Yep," Bram agrees. "Mixed shifter pairings are more common here, since we all live together.

Anyway, it's a second mating for both of them. They won't mind you joining your cub."

Sure enough, Mrs. Grund lumbers toward us in her bear form. Her grizzly bear is huge as she approaches to collect Myra, bigger than mine. She stops in front of me and nudges her bluff head into my side with a plaintive growl. She's gentle, in deference to my size as a human, but it still rocks me back onto my heels.

I look between Bram and the grizzly bears, over to where my kid is enjoying herself, and strip down at the outskirts of the crowd. Bram takes my discarded clothing over to one of the trestle tables the grizzlies brought into the event hall's entryway after the feasting, where the other shifters stashed their belongings.

I don't dawdle in the icy air. Letting my bear out is second-nature, and my change is nothing Bram hasn't seen before by now. The familiar changes ripple over me, leaving me in my fur. I'm large for a black bear, but compared to all the grizzly bears around me, I'm small. None of them seem bothered by my differences as I follow our neighbor over to the rest of the sleuth.

Bram stays off to the side, and my bear wants him to shift and preen my fur the way the omegiarch's mate did for her. Bram shows no signs of shifting to join us, to my profound disappointment.

Myra gambols over to me, having gotten a second wind now that she's in her cub form. She rears up to paw at my face, making the shift to a black bear as she interacts with me. We play-wrestle for a moment before her new grizzly cub friend comes to join the game. She shifts back to her grizzly so the pair of them can tumble around together.

They play until another adult, who smells enough like the other cub to be his omega parent, approaches us. Alphonse follows meekly along, glancing back at Myra. Their parents get the cub to settle in with two young omegas that I'm pretty sure are the little alpha's siblings, or maybe cousins. Myra chuffs at me, as though asking permission to cuddle with her new friends.

Unsure of our welcome, we edge closer to the other family. Myra plows right in to snuggle with her friend. I settle on her other side, leaving some space between myself and the other cubs. Static alphas can be a threat to unrelated cubs, so I get why Myra's new friend's parents might be wary of my presence and I don't want to cause problems. The grizzly sow grunts a vague greeting at me and snuggles closer to the two younger cubs. I stretch out on the ground, relaxing at her calm acceptance.

Myra wriggles around to get comfortable for a while. Eventually, she presses a rear paw against mine and drops off to sleep next to the other cubs. I didn't plan on joining in, but I blink awake hours later, as the sun's last light is fading from the sky.

The other bears have started to wander into the communal hall, seeking shelter from the chilly square to reclaim their human forms. Even those who shift in the open hurry to find their clothes among the jumbled belongings gathered in the foyer.

The act of shifting is far more vulnerable and private than nakedness among shifters, so it's fairly normal for this sort of gathering to include nudity. However, it is quite cold to be outside without fur, so most people are sticking to their fur until they are inside the warm hall. Resting there with Myra, it's nice to be around a group of bear shifters who don't treat my family as though we're strange. I stretch and yawn, easing up from the bear's lethargy over the course of minutes.

Once I'm alert enough, I wake my cub, nudging her insistently with my muzzle until she stops her grumbling and gets up. She shakes herself off, and is soon a bouncy ball of energy again, ready to play. Before she can wake her friends, I grab her by the scruff and carry her inside to shift.

To my pleasant surprise, Bram is waiting inside to hand me Myra's dress and my bundled up clothing as soon as we're ready.

"Thought you might want these." Bram rubs at his neck. "Have a good nap?"

"Yeah. Thanks, Bramble," I say.

"Mhm." Myra yawns as she pulls the dress over her head and carefully adjusts her new bracelet on her wrist.

"No problem." Bram waves away my gratitude. "I'm glad you made it out for this. Did you have fun, Myra?"

"Yeah. Does my bear really have to rest until spring now?" she asks, a small frown on her face at the prospect.

"No, but some grizzly bears don't shift during hibernation season," I remind her.

Bram grins as he leans down toward her, as though to share a secret. "Did you know your papa likes to hide in his den for most of the day when the weather is cold, Myra?"

"He does?" she asks, hanging on his words.

"Yep." Bram nods. "Only comes out to put on a show for the spectators when our keeper brings out forage toys or activities for the grumpy old bear." He glances toward me as he pokes gentle fun at me.

I smile as Bram makes my daughter giggle. Watching them together should be incongruous, but it's not. It's the most natural thing in the world to smile at the two people I look forward to seeing the most every day. Despite my reservations about bringing strangers into my daughter's life, Bram isn't a stranger anymore, and I'm glad to have introduced them.

At some point over the past several weeks, Bram went from being a stranger, to my coworker who I spend ten hours a day with, to the guy I share my orgasms with, to someone I can ask for help. I'm not entirely sure what he is to me now. Certainly more than someone I know from work. When I look at him joking with Myra about lazy bears, it's easy to cast him in the role of my mate. And strangely enough, I like that vision of the future for us.

CHAPTER 16

Bram

Myra and Ty leave not long after they wake up from the big bear pile. In the watery light of dawn, I'd almost taken to the wing and snuggled in with them. Like Olga and her mate. If having a raven shifter mate is good enough for the omega matriarch of our grizzly community, then it's possible I could be with Ty.

Except that I'm not Ty's mate. Until yesterday, I didn't even know he had a kid, so what else could he be hiding? I know that's not fair. Obviously, he didn't tell me about Myra sooner because it wasn't relevant. And to protect both of them. After what he said about his ex, they've both got to be afraid of abandonment.

I'm not sure how I'd have reacted to knowing about her sooner. I might have guarded my heart better, knowing there was a slim chance of Ty and me turning into anything serious. Or I may have gotten this wild idea in my head of a family with him sooner. Can we be more than casual? If we mated, would Myra call me her step-dad someday? I'd like that, a glitter loving, happy cub filling my life with laughter.

Ty's smile when he watched Myra and me joking around on the walk out to their car warmed me to my toes. Even despite the chill of the late fall day outside in Maine. I've always known I wanted a family someday, but lately, Ty has me thinking that future isn't some far-off thing.

That could just be hormones talking. I take blockers, but I'm coming up on a year since my last heat and they recommend stopping blockers once a year to be sure everything is in working order.

I was going to push it back until after Winny's surgery and the holidays, but I *could* stop the blockers sooner. Before the remodel is complete. While I'm still with Ty, in whatever capacity he has room for me in his life and family. I've got a week of annual paid heat leave, so work won't be an issue.

Would Ty agree to spend it with me? Even though he has a kid, I want to ask him for that. I'm sure her grandmother or the neighbor whom I met last night would watch her. If he agrees. If he wants that with me. Would he ever want more kids?

I shake away the mental image of a nest full of hatchlings with an alpha like Ty. I'd always assumed my mate would be a fellow raven shifter, but Ty shares the same values as me. He's a doting parent. One who would embrace both sides of our potential future nestlings' natures. My heart aches to have hatchlings of my own. I've been considering just picking an alpha to give me a clutch for a while now. Ever since Seb's heats got sporadic, and we all pretended not to notice, since creep doesn't have a cure. Sometimes it runs in families.

Winny hasn't stopped her heat blockers since our brother developed symptoms, and the blockers can mask any signs, so she might have it too, for all I know. I want a clutch before I can't have one. It doesn't have to be this year, or this heat, or even this alpha. But part of me wants it to be all of those things.

Static ravens mate for life. Static bears don't, but shifters are human too. Our animal natures don't dictate who or how we love, even if they play a role. Some bear shifters are monogamous. Several raven shifters I know aren't.

And even if Ty and I aren't together forever, I think he'd be a good co-parent. I should at least ask him. He might say no, but there's no way he'll say yes if I don't ask. Either way, I want to give him my heat this year. Whether it's having him sire my clutch or as a sort of farewell so I can find an alpha who wants to have kids with me. I think I'm ready for a family.

As Winny said, if I put more effort into minding my own business, I won't be so tempted to stick my beak into hers and Seb's. If I wasn't so busy trying to fix the people I love, I might take a chance on asking for what I want from life. After last night, I'm certain that what I want is nestlings with an alpha who looks at me and our kids like we're the light of his life. Like Ty looked at me and Myra last night.

I need to ask him soon. Before I chicken out. There's an urgency to the thought I don't fully understand, but I know I have to act on it, so I text Ty.

Bram: It was amazing to see you last night. And thanks for introducing me to Myra. She's a delight.

Bram: So, I know you're probably still driving home, and this might be awkward, so if I'm totally misreading where we're at, pretend I didn't ask. But, there's something I want to ask you.

Bram: My heat is coming up soon. I want you to share it with me.

Bram: It doesn't have to mean anything, and we can use condoms, or avoid knotting, if you don't want more kids with me.

Bram: Only, I'd rather if we didn't. Because I want a clutch and I'm not sure how much longer that will be possible for me.

Bram: With Seb having creep, it might be a matter of time before it gets me too. And you're a really wonderful parent, so, yeah. Share my heat? We can discuss the details in person, if you'd prefer.

Bram: I think it might start sooner than I'd planned though.

Bram: Either way, text me when you get this, I guess.

There. No taking it back. I might just crawl out of my skin waiting for his response, but I asked.

I asked for something for myself and if I'm lucky, Ty might give it to me. Even if he says no, it feels good to articulate what I want. The waiting is hard though, and it's a long drive to the city, plus Ty will need to drop off Mrs. Grund and his mother. Then he'll have to take care of Myra before he can get back to me. I might be in for a long wait.

In the meantime, I need to stop thinking human thoughts for a while. I find a place to stash my clothing, a simple task in Four Corners. Since our community is all shifters, there are plenty of public cubbies for storing personal effects during a shift. No one here would touch another shifter's things inside a cubby despite the lack of locks.

I still hesitate over leaving my shinies alone. In the end the need to shift wins out and I wrap them up tight in my shirt. No one will bother my stuff. It's just that the pretty jewelry is mine and my raven feels possessive until I cache our treasures safely inside the protected cubby. In moments, I take to the wing, flying up over the town.

Below me, a few grizzly bears are still napping together in their fur in the town square. A fresh layer of snow from last night covers the open ground between the buildings and the trees of the forest where we hunt. That was the first flurry of the season to stick. Animal prints of all kinds mar the smooth expanse.

Most of them are the smaller prints of children, but plenty of older shifters indulged in the magic of the first snowfall too. Their prints mingle among the others. The air has a chilly bite to it. This is far from the time for a static raven to be thinking about a clutch. It's far too cold, and only getting colder.

And yet, my raven unerringly goes to an old nest among the trees and sets to work pulling free the sturdy sticks that form the base of the platform. The raven who built it won't reuse the same nest, but plenty of us are happy to recycle the materials that went into it. Sort of like hand-me-down baby furniture.

Not that my raven is thinking of that. He just *needs* to build the structure that will support our eggs. If I was in any state for introspection and nebulous worries, I'd stress over what that might mean. It's a sign of an impending heat. And breakthrough heats can be a sign of creep in its earliest stages. Or being around a potential mate.

My raven doesn't find those two options nearly as alarming as my human side will later, when I'm lying awake in my bed tormented by what-ifs the raven refuses to consider. Distantly, I wonder if I have time to find another alpha in case Ty turns me down.

My raven won't entertain the idea that the alpha who has been marking us with his scent will be anything but thrilled at the thought of making some eggs together. The raven can only think of finding the perfect sticks and bringing them to the ledge outside my apartment's window.

My raven mind plays on a loop of designing the perfect nest for me to lay my cub-nestlings. In my idle imaginings, my eggs will be the same soft auburn brown of Ty's fur and facial hair, mixed in with the usual blue mottling.

I hope the hatchlings will have both their parents' forms, like Myra. But part of me wonders if they could be bear cubs with raven wings, which a very tiny part of me knows wouldn't make sense because they couldn't fly or walk. I don't care how they turn out, and I'll fight anyone who does.

I lose track of how many trips back and forth I make to the woods. At some point, Seb must notice me flying to the window, because he opens it for me. He also lets me arrange my stash of sticks on top of his unused bunk.

I don't rest until the nest is a sturdy platform over the most protected corner of the bunk and I've woven a cozy hollow within the cradle of sticks. It's partly made of the materials I found in the trees and partly made from soft bits of cloth plucked from a selection Seb left out on my bed.

I'm not as good at reading human moods in my feathers, but when the nest is done, my brother climbs up to sit by me and inspect it. He doesn't seem excited about my nest. *Rude.* He cautiously scratches my pin feathers with his fingers.

"Nice nest, Bram," Seb praises my efforts. Which is much more like it. It's a very good nest. I twist around to let him preen a particularly itchy patch near the back of my head. It's a wonderful indulgence, since that's a hard spot to reach on my own. The attention makes up for his earlier lack of excitement.

I trill my satisfaction with the nest to him. And he smiles at me. His eyes are watery. That makes me puff out my chest and tail feathers with pride. My nest is so good, it brought him to tears. I'm going to make the best eggs to fill it up with too.

"You're still on your blockers, right?" Seb asks, voice all nasally and weird.

I cock my head at him, parsing the words, then bob a hesitant nod.

My brother nods back at me. "That was how it started for me too." He sucks in a deep, noisy breath. "I'm so sorry Bramble."

I don't know what he means. No, I don't want to understand. Seb renders any nuanced conversation impossible as he shifts. In his bird form, he crawls out of the loose hoodie he was wearing to join me in my nest.

Seb preens me, and I help him with the pin feathers on his head. I fall asleep with my head tucked under his wing. For once, I'm the cuddly one leaning on my brother for comfort from some nebulous and terrible weight I can't name in this form.

My fear has a name, though. Creep. It might be coming for me, and I don't know if I have time to convince Ty he's meant to be my mate. I need him to agree, before it's too late to have the life I want with him. All my raven knows is that our heat is coming soon, and our mate will be very pleased with the nest we built.

I dream of Ty and the eggs I want to have with him. The clutch I want to raise with their half-sister. The family I've barely begun daring to let myself dream could be mine one day.

CHAPTER 17

Ty

I read the message again. It hasn't changed since the last ten times I checked it. Bram wants me to spend his heat with him. No. It's far more than that. He wants me to give him a child.

As I sit alone in my room after putting Myra to bed, I'm still not sure how to process his words. He sent the message while I was driving, so I couldn't reply right away and when I tried to call him back, it went to voicemail. I hung up, unsure of what to say.

The numb dread around my heart at reading his request is fading to a dull anger mixed with a vague sense of longing. Thinking about Bram's heat has my libido raring to go. But this isn't something he should have sprung on me over text messages. I understand his reasoning. He mentioned creep and I know how much that ugly specter looms over omegas these days.

But we only agreed to try dating yesterday. We're barely anything more than coworkers who agreed to an exclusive exchange of orgasms. So the request to share a heat makes sense. Of course he'd offer to spend it with me before seeking another partner.

It's the part where he admitted he wants to use me to get knocked up that upsets me. As if I didn't tell him how much Arnie's parenting choices hurt me and Myra. This situation couldn't be more different. For one, we never planned on Arnie getting pregnant outside his heat. And the fact Bram is asking for it means that this would be.

Bram wants to be a parent, and he already told me how he and his family view mixed species children. He called his crow-raven cousins cravens. Would that make any child we created a beaven? Or a been? A ravaer? I don't know. But thanks to seeing Myra playing with Bram's little sibling last night, it's far too easy to picture her with a sibling who shares Bram's build and his glossy dark hair.

I love being Myra's dad. If life had turned out differently, I'd have been more than happy to give her siblings. As many as my omega partner might want. I swallow hard at the realization that, for the first time, the hypothetical omega mate in that picture isn't Arnie. It's Bram.

Bramble could be the omega I'd want to raise more children with. The first omega I've ever actually thought about this with, since Arnie and I weren't ready for kids when Myra surprised us.

It's too soon to be thinking about children and growing my family with this omega. He just met Myra and I'm nowhere near ready for so much as having him sleep over in our home. If he has my children, I'd want to live with him. But if what he's really asking for is a sperm donor who isn't involved with the nestlings, is that something I can live with?

No. I can't bear the thought of Myra having more siblings she never knows. Or not being involved with my kids. I can't let them grow up without a connection to their bear side, the way Myra aches to have ties to her grizzly.

I'm not ready to have kids with Bram. But I want to share his heat with him. I want to take that step and let our relationship grow to where we could raise nestlings together.

On the flip side, the idea of Bram with another alpha hurts my heart. I don't want him to find someone else. I want him. And if he wants kids, then it feels right to dream of that future for him.

What if by agreeing to spend his heat with him, and refusing him the clutch he wants, I deny him his chance at children of his own? Can I live with that? Could our relationship survive the inevitable resentment?

It's not the timeline I'd prefer. It's too soon. I

wish we'd spent the past few weeks dating for real instead of limiting our alone time to furtive after hours sex. But if Bram wants kids with me —if he's willing to work out how to raise those kids together, even if we don't last romantically —I at least ought to hear him out in person. Since he wasn't answering his phone earlier, I text him.

Ty: Sorry it took me so long to reply. I'm not sure how to respond. We just started dating. It's too soon. So. I think we should go on a date and hash out what we're doing.

Bram doesn't reply right away. I stare at my phone, check the time and wince. It's late. He's probably asleep.

Ty: Oops, didn't realize how late it got. No worries if you're asleep and get these in the morning, just reply when you can.

Ty: I want to be your alpha and share your heat with you. I'm not sure that I'm ready for more kids when we've only known each other for a month. But if you are showing signs of creep, I don't want to deny you the chance at a clutch of your own.

Ty: Can we discuss it tomorrow over dinner?

Ty: I get if that's a deal breaker. Pleasant dreams, bird.

I can't quite bring myself to put away the phone, hoping he'll message me back with an answer. Until this moment, I didn't fully realize how invested I am in Bram. In my fantasies, I don't just want sex, I want to date him. Share every one of his heats from now on. And maybe someday, with Bram in our lives, Myra won't be an only child.

It's possible last night was the first celebration of many that she'll spend surrounded by all the cousins and family I'd envisioned for her when Arnie told me about her. I fall asleep with my phone still propped on my chest. Visions of raven-haired cubs cuddling with my daughter dance in my dreams.

I wake up the next morning to my phone buzzing on my chest. My heart flutters at Bram's contact details when I lift it to look at who's calling. We slept in; no surprise after the celebrations and letting our hibernation-ready bear sides take the foreground for the better part of the day. Myra must have had a restful night too, since she isn't in my room.

Yawning, I hit accept and sit up in the bed to talk.

"Hello?" Bram sounds tired.

"Hi, bird. Is everything all right with you?" I ask, worried.

"Yeah. Sorry, pronouns today? Is it too early to call? I should have texted—"

"It's not too early. I'm glad to hear from you. He/him today. Did you get my messages?"

"I did." Bram sounds cautiously optimistic. "And I didn't expect you to be, um, so open to my suggestions? Seb thinks I'm already in the prodrome of my heat. I was planning to stop my blockers soon, but not yet. And—" His words get thicker with emotion until he can't seem to finish the thought, his voice too tight to go on.

"That's not a good sign, huh? Breakthrough heats are scary?" I prompt him.

"Yeah," Bram chokes out.

I run a hand through my hair and consider. "If we share your heat without protection, and you have a clutch, what do you expect from me?"

"Co-parents? I mean, I get we aren't in a place to be merging our lives right away. But I would want my hatchlings to have a relationship with you. We could try fifty-fifty custody, if you wanted? Like I said, they usually hatch in their feathered forms. So it's a few months of beak feeding that you might have a harder time helping with, but once they're through that stage, an even split?"

"That's fair," I say the words, but my heart aches at the thought of only spending half the time with a new child. And honestly, at the thought of Bram handling a newborn alone. I don't want him to go through what I did when Myra was a newborn, before I figured out how to ask for help from the people in my life. "I know we alluded to wanting more before the festival, but would you still be open to dating me and seeing if we could make a family together? With or without a clutch?"

There's a pause, and my heart is in my throat, hoping I didn't overstep. "Yes. I was afraid to ask if this changed that for you, but yes. I want that."

"Are you going to take ovulation minimizers? Those are a thing with all omegas, right? Not just bears?"

Bram swallows audibly. "No. I mean, they are for all omegas. But I don't want to take them. I can, if you aren't comfortable with the possibility of a larger clutch, but I'd rather not."

More eggs would mean more chances at the child he wants, so I get his reasoning. I also know how hard baby shifters can be to care for, and multiplying that for a large clutch is daunting, to say the least.

I remember reading an article to Arnie about a bear shifter having naturally conceived sextuplets before his first ultrasound with Myra. He wondered aloud if it was too late to take minimizers. It was, but we lucked out that Myra was a singleton.

"How large are we talking?" I ask.

Bram chuckles. "Well, I've got two clutchmates. Two eggs is average for a raven omega who isn't on meds to minimize or enhance ovulations. Some of the more fertile omegas in the rave can lay up to seven eggs at a time. And singletons are common enough."

"Seven?" I repeat. There is no way we can handle that many kids.

"Relax, I don't think anyone in my direct

family has laid over three. It should be fine. And if we *did* have a freakishly large clutch, I have a ton of family who would help us."

"You're sure about that?"

"Positive. That's how the rave works; we're pretty social and we like babies. I know most bears are more solitary. Is that going to bother you?"

"No. Your family was lovely, from what I saw of them. Myra loves your sibling. She couldn't stop talking about them and that grizzly cub last night."

"So, are you okay with the risk of a bigger clutch?"

I close my eyes and take a deep breath, hoping it won't be an issue. With my eyes closed, visions of chubby-cheeked raven babies fill my mind.

"Yeah. We'll make it work." The zoo pays well enough. And we even get paid parental leave to adjust to the new hatchlings. Or cubs, whichever they end up being or preferring in the early days. Can Bram birth a cub? I might have some research to do.

Either way, a larger clutch might not be so bad. If we have the help that Bram is promising. Myra will be thrilled if I give her a sibling. She's only begged for one forever. And more immediately, the idea of sharing a heat with Bram is, well, it's exciting.

My libido is raring to go. My morning wood, ignored up to now, becomes more insistent at the reminder of just how we'll make this clutch. I want to see Bram desperate to take my knot. For all that we've had sex dozens of times now, I've yet to penetrate the omega. There's just so many other ways for us to enjoy each other and I wanted to avoid an unplanned pregnancy with him.

But if he's ready to try for a clutch, there's no reason we can't be less careful. Shifters don't pass on static illnesses, and any potential STIs that affect shifters are specific to a particular host species, so the usual risks wouldn't apply to us.

"So, can you arrange childcare for Myra for a few days? If not, my folks or Seb would probably watch her, if you're comfortable with that? I get it if you're not, since you barely know them, but it's short notice…"

"Short notice?" That pulls me out of fantasies of sharing his heat. "How soon is this happening, Bram?"

"Um. Like I said, I'm in the prodrome. I shifted and forgot my blocker yesterday, so I'll probably start to really, uh, slick by tonight? Maybe tomorrow? The next day at the latest. It takes longer if it wasn't a breakthrough heat, but— well… I'm sorry to spring this on you."

"You aren't. It's not like you can control having a breakthrough heat, bird."

Bram snorts, and there is a tinge of bitterness in his voice as he says, "you'd be surprised at how many alphas think otherwise."

"They're ignorant, then. Don't you worry about Myra; my mother will be glad to watch her for the weekend."

If not, I've got other babysitting options I can call. But Mom has always come through for me in the past and if I explain the reason, I'm sure she will make a sleepover with Myra work with her schedule. The kid is old enough to help at the craft fairs where Mom sells her custom toys these days, if nothing else.

"Are you sure?" Bram asks.

"Yes. So, how long do your heats typically last? And do you want me there tonight?" I ask.

Bram huffs out a breath. "Yes, please. If you can. The earlier parts are easier with an alpha around. And mine usually last three or four days, not including the prodrome. Might be less with an alpha to help me through it? I haven't... um, tried sharing a heat before and they say the artificial hormones aren't as potent at sating a heat."

"They stink too." I wrinkle my nose.

Bram laughs. "Only to alphas."

"Well, if you want my knot tonight, you'll hold off on breaking out the synthetic pheromones while you're waiting for me to get there, bird."

"Is that a threat?" Bram teases, almost like he wants me to go all controlling alphahole on him.

"No, just the scent is off-putting, and it lingers. I don't know if I could knot you while you've got that stuff in the air."

"Noted. Anything else?" he asks.

"Prep before I get there?"

"Duh. I'm probably going to take a nice long shower as soon as we're off the phone."

"Should I bring snacks for between rounds?"

"Yeah. Or we can order in. There are a few delivery places that cater to omegas in heat here."

"Nice. You're sure you want to share this with me, Bramble? It's not just about the closest convenient knot? I mean, if that's all it is, I'll still do it. I know heats are better shared, but—"

"It's you I want, bear. I wouldn't use you for your knot. No matter how impressive it looks when we're fucking. And I wouldn't ask you to have kids with me if it wasn't about who you are."

"Who is that? I thought you said I'm a grumpy bear."

"I said that. But you're also kind. And a doting dad. And I like the way you look at me."

"How's that?"

"Like me when I'm scoping out shiny baubles. Come over soon, Ty?"

"I'll be there as soon as I get Myra situated. Get yourself nice and ready for your alpha, bird."

Bram moans at the title, and it makes me think he's further into his prodrome than I'd thought. Not so far as to preclude a discussion about boundaries and consent, but far enough that I should probably call Mom to get Myra squared away as soon as possible.

"Yes, alpha. See you soon?" The note of vulnerability in Bram's voice has all my alpha instincts coming to the fore.

I want to be there for my omega in his time of need. I want to scent his heat, lap up his slick, join our bodies. Knot him and breed him and fill him with a clutch of hybrid cubs. I want him to be mine in every sense. And I want to dote on him while he carries my cubs. Rub his back and his belly as the eggs gestate, take care of him while he lays, whatever raven traditions that might entail.

More than that, I want to be by his side while we both tend to the eggs until they hatch. I want to show Myra her siblings while we wait for them to break out of their shells. I want everything with him.

"Yes, omega. Alpha is going to take good care of you and give you a clutch."

"Mhm. Gonna get myself ready for your big, fat cock now, alpha. Hurry, please."

"I will. You take your time in the shower, get that tight little hole slick and ready for me." I palm my aching erection through my thin pajama pants, trying to ease the worst of the need this conversation is awakening in me.

Bram pants into the receiver, and the faint squelch of his slick makes me think he's getting a head start on that prep. The sounds are doing nothing to quell my desire. "Mm. Alpha."

"I'm coming for you, baby. You take the edge

off while you wait for alpha's knot and I'll be there soon."

I give myself a few languid strokes, the tip of my dick dripping pre-cum already. More than I usually produce. Almost as if I'm already entering a rut. As though my mate's voice is enough to have me responding to his heat. That only happens with mates though. And he's not my mate yet. Right? My bear couldn't care less about semantics. All my black bear side cares about now is breeding and knotting our mate.

Judging from the noises from the receiver, Bram is stroking himself with abandon. I can't bring myself to stop stroking my length. His ragged breathing and pleasure-soaked voice in my ear is hotter than any porn.

"Ty, so close. Need your knot, alpha." Bram's voice hitches.

"I need to be inside you, bird, soon. Gonna give you so many babies, as many as you want."

"Yes, Ty! Mate me."

The wet slaps of his hand on his flesh intensify. I match his pace, twisting at the crown of my cock. The motion milks out enough pre-cum that I could easily slide inside my omega with just that for lube. Even if he didn't sound slick enough to take me with hardly any prep as he fingers himself.

"How many fingers do you have stuffed in my hole, bird?"

"Three. Need more. Need your knot, bear," he

pants.

"Can't wait to stuff you full of it."

"Fuck, yes. Ty," he gasps my name. "So close."

"Come for me, omega, squeeze my cock with that hot little hole. Such a needy slut for me."

"Yes, alpha, just for you." Bram's breath hitches again. "Hn." His pained little cry as he reaches his climax transforms into a keening moan as he comes.

The familiar sounds of my omega finding his release tip me over the edge too, spilling into my pajamas like a horny teenager. Fuck. The pleasure lights all my nerves on fire, obliterating any shame I might feel at coming so fast and without even taking off my pants.

I moan into the phone as I shift my grip to squeeze my swelling knot tight. It will go down fast without his pheromones to make it last, but not having anything touching it as it swells is a deep ache. He makes a shuddery little sound in reply.

"You are so sexy, Bramble, making your alpha come for you already."

"Mhm. Hurry, so the next one can be with your knot buried inside me; I think it might be a short prodrome. Thanks for taking the edge off with me. Text Seb if I don't answer the phone when you get here. I'll send you his number, and he can direct you to our apartment."

"He lives with you, right? Will he be there?" I ask, realizing that I'm not entirely sure what his living arrangements are.

"We live together, but he's going to stay with someone until my heat passes. And he sprayed scent neutralizer as he was leaving this morning, so it should just smell like me. Um. Actually, I'll change the sheets before you get here; he sometimes comes home stinking of alpha. Just so you know, we share a bed sometimes, so that's all from him."

"Noted. Good call on changing the sheets. If I'm in a full-blown rut when I get there, I probably won't want to breathe another alpha in your bed."

"What if you do?" Bram's voice trembles as he asks.

"I might get possessive. I'd never hurt you though, Bramble," I promise, meaning it with every fiber of my being.

Bram snorts. "I know you wouldn't. I might like you possessive and forceful, alpha. Maybe I'll leave the sheets."

I growl low in my throat. "No need for that. I don't want to scent another alpha on you, bird. I'll fuck you as hard as you want, regardless. All you have to do is ask."

"Clean sheets it is. It'll give me something to do to keep my mind off waiting. You promise to hurry?"

"Yes, Bramble. I'll see you soon."

"See you soon."

I hang up first. Then I slip out of bed and

into my ensuite to wash away the evidence of our phone sex. The mental fog of a rut is already there, at the edges of my mind, but it's less intense without Bram's voice in my ears. I take a hasty shower, which mostly restores my clarity. And then I make plans.

CHAPTER 18

Ty

Once I'm dressed, in grubby rut-friendly loungewear that I wouldn't normally leave the house wearing, I call my mom to arrange for Myra to stay with her. It's a darn good thing she met Bramble last night, so I don't have to explain the sudden appearance of an omega in my life.

Then again, I know she's scented him on me when I go to pick up Myra. Still, I cleaned up enough to pass that off as coworkers sharing a small space versus what we were actually doing. Which was what? Sneakily snatching stolen moments of pleasure before going home to our families.

She seemed to like Bram, but liking him and accepting that I want to spend his heat with him so soon after meeting are two entirely different stories. It's late enough that I know she'll be awake, at least.

"Ty, dear, I was just thinking of calling you. How's Myra?" Mom answers on the second ring.

"Great. So far we've had a lazy morning after the long day, so she's still in bed. She loved the festival. I'm glad you made it out there with us."

"Of course. It was lovely to be included. I like that sleuth, don't you think? Hopefully, having other grizzly cubs to play with will be good for Myra."

"I think it will."

"I'm sure you'll be out that way more often. At least, if the way you were making eyes at a certain omega is any indication?" Mom's tone pitches toward conspiratorial, as though I'm in on her mapping out my life after one introduction.

Granted, the only other omega—or potential partner of any designation—that I've introduced her to in the past was Arnie. So her assumptions are at least a little justified.

"Mom!" I protest.

"Don't you tell me it's not like that or that he's just a coworker. I saw the way you looked at each other last night, Tyson Orville." She full-names me, knowing that I'd have mentioned by this point in the conversation if I was having a femme day.

"I suppose I don't have any room to argue that we aren't serious, considering the favor I called to ask you."

"Oh?!"

"Yeah, could you take Myra for the weekend so that I can spend Bram's heat with him?"

"I'd be delighted. Am I safe to assume this is *very* serious then? Are you considering mating him, dear?"

"It's, um, possible we've discussed exploring something serious. He wants kids, and he's concerned creep runs in his family."

"Tyson, am I watching my grandchild so that you can make me another grandbaby?"

"Mom!" My protest this time is about an octave higher than my usual voice. "I do not want to think about you knowing I'm doing *that*."

"Child, I am aware of how babies are made. I made you, didn't I?"

"You did. But if you *want* another grandchild, then discussing the process with my mother is hardly going to have me in the mood to perform."

"Darling, if your mate is going into heat, no amount of sex talks from your mother will overcome your rut. Of course I'll watch my grandbaby while you're busy. Call me when Bram's heat ends so I know when to expect you and we'll work out when you can pick Myra up. I'll get her to school next week if need be. Don't you worry about a thing."

"I really am sorry for the short notice. If it's easier, the two of you can stay here, and I'm sure Mrs. Grund can watch her for a bit if you have other plans."

"Pshaw, it's a heat, Tyson. These things rarely follow a convenient schedule. Even coming off blockers can be unpredictable. You take good care of that sweet omega and don't worry about a thing. Myra and I will have a wonderful time without you. And when you and Bram have both recovered from the heat, you tell him he's invited to family dinner, yes?"

"Yes, Mom," I agree, since she'll steamroll over me if I try to protest. And really, I don't want to. I love how she is willing and ready to fold my chosen mate into our little family without batting an eye.

"That's my cub. Just you give me half an hour to get ready and I'll come to collect Myra. Get her fed and explain that you'll be away for a few days and I'll take care of the rest."

"Thanks, Mom. I can't tell you how much I appreciate the help."

"It's always a pleasure to watch Myra, you know that. I'll be there soon."

We hang up, and I go to get my kid ready. I'm not sure how much to explain to her about this weekend. Obviously, she'll know I'm going to spend a few days with my new friend. She knows what a heat is from being around other shifters. It's just not something that happens in our household since the adults who take care of her are all alphas.

Myra is grumpy about waking up, but a bribe

of waffles for breakfast soon has her slumped at the table, watching me mix up the batter through sleep-bleary eyes.

"Can we have whipped cream on them?" She asks.

"Yes, if we have it," I agree, hoping we have some in the fridge so she won't be disappointed.

"And unicorn sprinkles?" She presses her luck.

"And unicorn sprinkles. Want to get them out?" I gesture to the cabinet where I keep the baking supplies. Myra grabs the shaker, finding some of her usual energy when sprinkles are on the line.

"Why are you dressed like that for making waffles, Papa?" She eyes me shrewdly as she sets the sprinkle shaker next to the waffle batter.

It's such an ingrained habit for her to check in on how I'm presenting before addressing me by title that I don't think she gives it conscious thought. I cherish her simple acceptance, and I hope she always feels that same unconditional love from me. As to her question, I would normally make a lazy weekend breakfast for us in my nice cozy matching flannel pajamas. It's reasonable for her to ask about the deviation from our norm The ratty sweats and an old slubby shirt that I don't care about ruining during my rut aren't anything I wear unless I'm feeling under the weather and need extra comfort.

"Are you sick? Can you put sprinkles inside

and on top?" Myra presses.

"I'm not sick. And I can put sprinkles in the batter for yours." I check that the waffle iron is hot enough to start the first waffle.

Is it a cop out to address the softball question first? Butter the kid up with sweets, and hope she'll take the news better? I'm not sure why I'm worried about this. I've always been an open book with my kid. But her opinion matters. More than anyone else's. If I want a future with Bram, Myra has to like him and be okay with me spending time with him.

"So, you remember Bram?" I ask.

"Duh. He gave me my bracelet. Elric says he's nice. Are we going to visit them again? I want to play with Alphonse, if we are," Myra mentions the alpha grizzly cub she hit it off with at the festival, and I'm glad she has a grizzly friend to relate with.

"Not today. You are having a sleepover with Gramma this weekend while I spend a few days, um, getting to know Bram better." I feel myself flushing at the vague description of my weekend plans. I hope the kid isn't too curious about the details.

"Can I come too? If he's special to you, I should get to know him better, right?"

"You're right, but you can't come along for *this* visit." I manage not to cringe at the thought of my kid tagging along to Bram's heat.

"Why not?" Myra asks, the portrait of

innocence.

"Because it's his heat, and he asked me to help him," I admit.

I focus my attention on pouring the batter into the iron and swirling in Myra's sprinkles, so I don't have to look at her reaction. I set a timer for when to flip it.

"Oh. So you want privacy? Jenny says if an alpha and an omega want to mate, they share a heat. And after her omega dad has a heat, she usually gets a new sibling a few months later."

"Um, yeah, rabbit shifters are known for having large families, so I'm sure that's true."

"Elric says ravens like having big families too. Does that mean you and Bram want to mate? Will that make Elric my—Papa, what do you call an aunt or uncle if they aren't a girl or a boy?" She wrinkles her nose at me, deep in contemplation.

"Good question, baby. I'm not sure there's one specific term, but we can ask Elric what they'd prefer the next time you two hang out. Since you're close in age, 'cousin' might work?" I latch onto the new topic to avoid awkward heat talk with an almost nine-year-old when I'm on the verge of a rut.

"I'll ask them. Does this mean you and Bram are getting mated?"

So much for her changing the subject to something with a simple answer.

"We've talked about dating for now. Is that okay with you?"

"Yeah. He's nice and you smile more since you met him." Myra props her chin on her hands and watches me as I try to hide how flustered I am that she noticed his scent on me. It seems awkward, considering how his scent got on my clothing. Not that she has any way of knowing the details, but still. It's strange to realize my kid noticed I was seeing someone, however casually, before I told her.

"He makes me smile more, yeah." I grin just thinking of the flashy bird.

My waffle timer beeps to be flipped. As I'm turning the hot metal of the old stove-top wafflemaker over on the burner, Myra strikes with her next question.

"So, if you're spending his heat with him, does that mean I'm going to get a new baby sibling soon?"

I choke on my spit at that gem of a question. Kids. "Um, it's possible. But I don't want you to get your hopes up about it."

"If you and Bram have a baby, does that make him my step-dad? Calvin has a step-mom, and she takes him for brunch and bowling with her other kids every weekend. Would the baby be my sibling? Or my step-sibling?"

"Technically, you would be half-siblings. And I would hope the distinction won't matter. But, again, baby girl, I don't want you getting your hopes up. It might not happen."

Myra pouts and crosses her arms sulkily. "Why

not? Doesn't Bram want to be part of our family? Don't you want him to be?"

"Because, my dear, babies come when they're ready, and sometimes all the wishing and trying in the world isn't enough to bring them about."

"Oh. But you *are* wishing and trying?"

"That's complicated, dear. We are still figuring it out, but how about this: if we find out there's a new baby on the way, you'll be the first one we tell?"

"And I can help pick their hatch name? Elric said ravens use gender neutral hatch names until the baby is old enough to pick a name of their own."

"Hold your horses, Myra, there is nobody to name yet."

"But you're considering it?"

"We are."

I plate her waffle and cover it in a lavish amount of whipped cream, hoping that will distract her from awkward questions about babies. The ploy works. Myra adds more sprinkles to the whipped cream mound, then digs into her breakfast while I start the next waffle.

It's not like we've never discussed where babies come from. She knows the basics. And that she can come to me with any question, big or small. It's just that discussing this is a reminder that it won't be long before puberty reveals whether she's alpha, omega, or beta. I don't like thinking about my baby growing up. We could have had her genotyped; plenty of families do. I didn't see the need. Her secondary gender doesn't matter to me.

In shifters, it's the secondary gender that determines gametes. Primary genders, or what the statics view as sex, is a form of mimicry. The genitals we have in our human forms basically let us blend in with our static counterparts. Secondary gender determines our gametes. Alphas produce sperm, omegas produce eggs, and betas encompass any variance from that binary. Not every shifter identifies with their anatomy, and among most shifter populations, we accept trans primary or secondary gender shifters for who they are. There aren't enough of us to reject family over things they can't change.

Shifters in general have a more nuanced take on gender anyway, since between our primary and secondary traits, it's impossible to stick to a strict binary like static humans. Though some try, like the persistent stereotypes among bear shifters, particularly grizzlies, that omegas make better parents. I hated hearing that as a kid with an amazing single alpha mom, and I hate it even more now that Myra has to deal with the same stigma.

If Myra presents as an omega, she'll be at risk for creep. Like Bram. It doesn't present the same way in mammals and it seems to be less common among bears, but it still impacts fertility. I don't want that worry for her.

At the same time, among grizzly bear shifters, omegas are celebrated. Even more so, with creep lowering our fertility rates. That's why Arnie's omega grandmother wanted us to have Myra genotyped at birth. If she's an omega, I've got the lurking fear that his family might change their minds about their lack of contact these past eight years.

Not that they'd have a leg to stand on as far as legal custody. Arnie signed the paperwork to relinquish his parental rights after he left us. I mostly pushed for it because his grandmother was badgering us about the genotyping to see if Myra was omega. He hadn't seen her more than a handful of times in the first year, so he went along with my request.

The judge signed the necessary papers to grant me full custody and cut Arnie and his family out of the picture, on the grounds of abandonment. Even if she turns out to be an omega now, the fear of his family trying to stake some sort of legal claim is groundless. It's already been settled that Myra is legally mine.

"Papa?" Myra's question pulls me out of my worries over her omega dad and his family. Arnie is the last person I want to be thinking of right now.

"Yes, baby?"

"How long is a heat?"

"It varies. Bram says four days. I'll be back as

soon as I can."

"Okay. Papa?"

"Yes?"

"When do omegas start having heats?"

"It depends."

"For bears?"

I sigh. Guess we're having this conversation, like it or not. "Your omega dad had his first full heat at sixteen. Which is average. He presented as omega before that, at twelve."

"Did you spend it with him?"

"No. He used suppressors to handle the worst of it, and then he went on blockers until he was eighteen. That's pretty common."

"Will I need blockers if I'm an omega?"

"That will be your choice to make. If that's how you present, we'll find some other omegas for you to discuss your options with, all right?"

"Okay. Alphonse says I smell like his older omega sisters."

I suck in a sharp breath, because I'm not ready for her to be interested in an alpha cub's scent, or vice versa. And pheromone changes are one of the first signs to present. I haven't noticed a change in her scent, but could she have started a subtle shift already? Her ninth birthday is coming up in the spring. Is this too soon? It feels far too soon. It's really not though.

"Well, you're growing up, baby. Lots of things change when you present, no matter how that looks. How do you feel about it?"

Myra licks some whipped cream off her fork with a contemplative look. "I think I'm omega. Even if I don't present that way. Or if I grow a knot."

I cough at the frank mention of anatomy I don't want to associate with my kid, and plate up the second waffle. I want to rush right over to Bram's, but I should eat something first. And Mom will probably be hungry when she gets here. I start a waffle for her with the last of the batter before I answer Myra.

"Then that's what you are, baby girl. There're blockers and hormones you can take if how you present doesn't match who you are. You can always talk to me about this."

"I know. Do you think I smell like an omega?" Myra asks through a full mouth.

"Chew with your mouth closed."

Myra rolls her eyes, but she closes her mouth to finish her bite. I go around the counter and bury my nose in her hair. At first, all I detect is the familiar scent of my baby. Myra's scent is home and family and everything good in the world.

There is a hint of a sweeter undertone mixed in, now that she's asked me to look for it. One that owes nothing to the sugary breakfast she's eating. The sweet comfort of an omega who shares kinship with me. I want to cling to her, soak in every moment of her childhood. Who knows how much longer she'll let me hold her close to my heart? But I never want to hold her back either. "You do."

"Cool." Myra cranes her neck to beam up at me. "Maybe that will make my omega dad regret leaving us, huh?"

My heart wrenches at the forlorn hope in her voice. These are the moments when it's hard not to hate my ex for the ways he hurt our kid. For her sake, I can't hold that grudge. "Baby, his choices have nothing to do with you."

"Yeah. I guess. Do you think Bram will be happy I'm omega?"

"Any potential mate I bring into our family will adore you regardless of how you present, baby girl." I assure her with perfect conviction, because I would never mate a shifter who ever made my daughter feel anything less than perfect over things she can't control. Before we can delve into anymore conversational topics that I'm not remotely ready for this morning, Mom knocks on the front door. Considering that I'm tired and riding the edge of my first rut in years, it's a welcome reprieve. She lets herself in, since I'm expecting her.

"Are you two in the kitchen? Something smells delicious," Mom calls to us.

"Papa made waffles!" Myra calls back. "And guess what?"

"What?" Mom asks as she joins us. She gives me a side hug in passing. "Good morning, dear."

"Morning," I say.

"I'm an omega, Gramma. Wanna sniff?" Myra holds her wrist out toward my mother, the bear charm dangling from the bracelet Bram gifted her. She's still wearing it, and I still can't help the warm sense of rightness at the sign of them getting along. Mom takes Myra's wrist and scents her with exaggerated care.

"Hmm, you do seem sweeter today. Think you're starting to present?" Mom asks.

"Yes!" Myra nods. "Papa says it will still be a long time before I get to have a heat, is that right?"

"Yes, dear." Mom pats her hand. "Most omegas don't have their first heat for years after their scent changes."

"Oh. I guess that's good. I don't want to have a mate anytime soon. Alphas are kind of stinky."

"We are." Mom agrees sagely.

"Not you and Papa," Myra rushes to assure us. "You smell like family."

"I know, dear." Mom pats Myra's cheek.

"And Alphonse smells good. Like the forest and fall leaves."

Mom and I exchange a look. Myra has talked about crushes before, but this is the first time she's mentioned being attracted to another shifter's scent. I am so not ready for puberty.

"That sounds nice," I say, resisting the urge to cling on and never let go at this new evidence that my baby is growing up right before my eyes. "Once you present, it's normal to notice new things about other shifters. That doesn't have to change how you play with other shifter kids though, okay?"

"Yeah. Okay." Myra nods. "Can we visit Alphonse and Elric again sometime? I liked them."

"I'm sure we can," I agree. And part of me wants to shield her from grown up concerns. From childhood crushes, first loves, and what it's like to fall for your best friend before you realize what love even is. The way I fell for her omega dad. But the bigger part just wants to be there for her, even if a friendship with an alpha grizzly cub might grow into puppy love and her first heartbreak. It might not, or she could fall for another omega or a beta, and it's for her to decide.

Still, I'm having all kinds of conflicting emotions over my baby growing up as I wrap a napkin around my waffle and leave my family to finish their breakfast together. Mom and I quickly touch base on the logistics of my impromptu weekend getaway with Bram. She reminds me to leave a message with the zoo about taking a week of rut leave. Then I grab what I need for the next few days. I hug Myra and Mom goodbye on my way out the door, and leave.

I punch in the address for Bram's community. It takes an effort of will to use the GPS instead of calling Bram again. I can reason the urge away as wanting to ask him what it was like for him when he presented. I want to know so I can help Myra through the awkwardness of puberty and presenting. And because I want to know everything about Bram. But most of all, I just want to hear my omega's voice, because the rut has me in its grasp already. I need him with a burning ache in my chest and low in my belly.

It doesn't take long for thoughts of Bram to lead to memories of this morning and anticipation of what we're about to share. I want him. Everything about him. I want to feel his body tight around me, milking my knot. That train of thought needs to be derailed if I want to hold off my rut until I get to him.

No amount of unsexy thoughts will hold my arousal at bay now that I've opened the floodgates. I reach surreptitiously between my legs to give my balls a painful twist and that tamps things down. Enough to focus on navigating to the road that will take me to Bram.

Once I'm on the highway, the traffic doesn't require as much of my focus. I try to count by threes to occupy my mind. That helps until I get to sixty-nine and the mental image of Bram's mouth wrapping around me as I lap up his slick has my hard-on raging back to life. I groan and palm myself hard through my sweatpants. Pre-cum is already making them damp. Ruts are a pain in the butt.

I turn on the radio, singing along to Myra's favorite sugary pop station. Thinking of my kid takes my mind off the rut at least. The music distracts me until I get to the exit for Four Corners. I find parking in the same public lot near the town square where I parked for Denning Night. Was that really only yesterday? Then I call Seb for directions to Bram's apartment so I can go to my omega.

CHAPTER 19

Bram

I smell Ty's alpha musk before he knocks. I scramble off the bed at the soft rapping, my largest dildo still wedged firmly inside of me as I hobble to the door to let him in. Every step presses it into me more, barely scratching the surface of what I need from my alpha. His pheromones are divine, even with the door separating us. I need him here right now.

The door swings open quietly when I turn the handle, revealing Ty standing there, hand raised as if to knock again. I leave the door wide open as I throw myself into his arms. It's impossible to resist the drive to be as close to him as possible. I wrap my arms and legs around him, our lips crash together, and I shove my tongue into his mouth.

"Oomph." Ty lets out a soft little sound. It's

clear I took him by surprise. His immediate reflex is to wrap his arms around me, holding me tight. It's indescribably wonderful to feel secure in an alpha's arms as the waves of my heat roll over me.

Instead of resisting the pull of my hormones, as I've been doing since it became clear this was coming, I give in to it. The heat crashes over me, and I kiss my alpha with quiet desperation. I tug at his clothing, wishing it were out of the way and he could slide his fat cock inside me unimpeded. Already, I'm kicking myself for not stripping before he arrived.

I wrap my legs tighter around his hips, pressing my erection against him. The motion tugs my underwear tight over my ass, pushing the base of my dildo further inside me in a pale imitation of what Ty has to offer. I want to feel the warm pulse of his length deep within my body, the contrast of softly rigid flesh instead of the unyielding firmness of my toys. Need his knot swollen and shoved past my rim, plugging me up and keeping his cum where it's most likely to get to my eggs.

How I want to make a cub with him. A whole clutch of cubs. The absurd thought of hatchlings fuzzy with downy bear fur makes me giggle against his mouth. I haven't touched his bear in my human form yet and I suddenly want to with a fervent intensity that almost rivals my need for him to fuck me. Will our cubs be soft or wiry? Will they have my glossy black feathers?

Or perhaps a tinge of his auburn? I don't know. I want to find out.

"Alpha." I squirm free of his hold, and Ty releases me with care. I take a moment to drink Ty in with my eyes. He's so sexy. I take another moment to be sure I'm getting the pronouns right. My alpha is usually an impeccable dresser. Today, he's in a loose tee and sweats.

Ty plucks self-consciously at the clothing. "Figured it was best to wear something easy to remove that won't wrinkle," he, at least I'm pretty sure that's right, explains sheepishly.

I nod. "Yes. Ready to remove it? He/him today?"

"Yes, and yes, you asked on the phone, heat making you fuzzy, bird?" Ty takes my words as the instruction I intended and tugs the shirt over his head even as he teases me. He steps out of the sweats to reveal a distinct lack of underwear. His dick—already hard and leaking for me—bobs up from his groin. It's making a valiant effort to defy gravity despite his impressive size.

I lick my lips, eager to taste all of his naked skin. Before I can drop to my knees and take him into my mouth, Ty pivots to swing the open door shut and give us privacy. Slick gushes out of me at his decisive movements. My damp underwear and a loose robe are the only clothing I was still wearing. My heat already has me firmly in its grasp.

Ty steps into my space and kisses me,

maneuvering us back toward my bed with its fresh sheets. Part of me wants to lead him up the ladder to Seb's bunk, so we can fuck near my nest. But Ty's a big burly bear of a shifter in both his forms, and I don't want to risk breaking the bunk. Besides, my bottom bunk is a full, compared to Seb's twin.

Ty walks us backwards until my legs bump against the mattress. I squeak as he eases me down onto my back, lifts my legs to his shoulders, and pulls my underpants out of the way to reveal my dildo. He growls a frustrated protest and withdraws the toy.

"Need inside you, Bramble." Ty's voice is low and rumbly with lust. I arch up toward him, fully on board.

"Yes! Breed me, alpha. Need you so bad." I writhe and wriggle closer to the edge of the mattress.

Ty adjusts his stance to line up and pushes past the waistband of my panties to nudge his cockhead against my rim. I try desperately to fuck myself onto his length. Ty chuckles, one big hand going to my lower back, slipping beneath the silky robe to touch my skin and support me. He holds me in place as he eases inside of me for the first time. I grasp at the blankets as the perfect curve of his cock and the angle of my body light every nerve on fire with pleasure.

Ty moans, driving all the way inside of me. He's gentle, but neither of us wants to take this slowly. His knot stretches me wider, even before it swells with his orgasm. His heavy balls slap against my ass. I try to drag him closer with my ankles on his shoulders.

"Mhm. Alpha. Yes! Oh, yes." I pant as I make further uncoordinated efforts to fuck myself harder with his dick. Ty pins me down and pulls back, only to thrust in again. "Yes, harder, fuck me harder!" I demand.

Ty isn't as rough as I'd be if I was riding him. But he doesn't try to make me take a slow, gentle coupling when I need him to make me feel it. Need him to anchor me and make my heat burn through my entire being.

Ty's scent gets stronger as he pistons into me. Sweat glistens on his furry chest. He's glorious as he loses himself in his rut. Our mingled heavy breathing and the potent scent of our mutual arousal signals that he's already consumed by it. I moan my pleasure again, his pheromones making my heat even more intensely pleasurable.

Ty fucks me hard until his knot swells and we both come. My cock pulses in time with the way he releases inside of me, over and over as my ass clenches around him. It's so perfect, like his knot and my hole are two pieces of a puzzle, always meant to come together like this.

The perfect swollen bulb of it locks his juices inside me. Keeps him right where I need him to be as my body milks another load out of his full balls. I need him to keep fucking me, and he does, rocking our bodies together through the tie as he spurts his cum into me. The rut lets him come repeatedly, far beyond his usual limits.

The first tie lasts a long time before his knot goes down. An eternity of our bodies moving together, locked into a tandem dance of pleasure. The pressure inside me builds higher and higher and every time I don't think I can take another drop, Ty proves me wrong. I can take everything he gives me. My body sings with each orgasm that wracks through me. Each one is better and more intense than the last, until I'm floating on a blissful cloud. Every one of my senses is full to bursting with my alpha's presence.

I savor his kisses on my tongue, though the angle makes it difficult for us to bring our lips together right now. I want more, so I tug him down toward me. Ty moves gingerly to avoid tugging too hard at our tie, where his swollen knot joins us together. Even with his tender care, his knot tugging against my rim is super sensitive.

Ty cradles me against his chest, his brawny arms supporting my entire weight so he can move us. I sigh contentedly as my big strong mate settles us both onto the mattress on our sides with minimal jostling. Once we're both comfortable, he thrusts into me with the slow shallow strokes that are all his knot will allow, triggering another wave of pure bliss to crash over me.

I breathe in deep, filling my nose with our combined pheromones, heat and rut melding into a potent aphrodisiac unlike any other. Ty's scent is perfection mixed with mine, a blend of the forest where both our animal forms make their homes. Musk and loam and sharp piney notes, the sweetness of ripe berries and clean river water mixing with my citrusy scent and the dusty vanilla notes of my feathers.

His tender touches on my skin make me ache for more of him. The swell of his cock, huge and hard inside me, presses on all my pleasure centers. His knot stretches me deliciously wide.

"Bram. My perfect Bramble, so good for alpha." The ragged panting of his breath plays counterpoint to squelching wetness as he moves within me. I love the low sound of my name on his lips, praises reverent as a prayer washing over me like warm honey.

I babble back at him, needing to reciprocate. "So good, Ty."

I reach out to caress his beautiful face. His bushy hipster beard is wiry under my fingers as he gazes at me with such tenderness I could melt. His body moves beside me and inside of me. I meet his every thrust. It's easy to fall into a place where we may as well be one entity rocking in sync to a unified goal. Not just sex and orgasms and a pleasure so blissful that nothing else can come close to comparing. My clutch.

Ty's going to give me a clutch. That's a surety in my bones. It won't be long before I get to watch him gazing at our hatchlings with that same tender sweetness that's been growing the last few times we've been together. His care for me shines in his eyes, hinting at the possibility of so much more, and I'm greedier for that than any other treasure in the world.

CHAPTER 20

Ty

Between bouts of his heat, Bram naps. Sometimes I join him, especially when he's still tied onto my knot when he dozes off. I love sleeping nestled inside his body. My bear is convinced the two of us should always stay joined this way.

Bram is slick and tight and wonderful. I love fucking him. I also loved when he fucked me in the changing area of our habitat. But during his heat, he's less interested in anything that doesn't include my knot in his ass, breeding him over and over again.

When I'm not napping with him, I use the time while his heat ebbs to call in a food delivery to our door. Good thing Seb gave me the number when I first got here and needed directions up to the apartment. That way I can nourish my omega without disturbing his rest.

I also check in with Mom a few times to make sure she and Myra are alright. She scolds me for it, telling me they're fine and to take care of Bram. Just, with him begging me for a cub, I needed to check on my cub. Otherwise, I'm glued to my omega's side. Bramble is pure perfection.

He's also horny as hell, even in his sleep. His breathing is still soft and even when he starts rubbing against me again. My cock nudges against his slick hole until I can't take another moment of not being inside him.

"You awake, Bram?" I grip his hip, steadying him.

"Mhm, knot please, alpha," Bram mumbles sleepily. He emphasizes the request by pushing his ass more firmly against my groin.

I groan as his slick coats my length. I dig my fingers into his flanks, holding him still as I use the other hand to guide my dick inside of him. Bram moans and ruts against me.

"Yes, alpha, more. Please. Need you."

It's my pleasure to give him exactly what he wants. I want the same things. To be as close to him as is physically possible. To breed him and stay buried as deep inside my lover as I can reach. I want to give him my cubs. I fuck him slow and gently this time. His body strokes my cock and I thrust at an angle that has my omega slicking and panting with pleasured little gasps of breath.

"There, Ty, right there. Need you alpha, need

you so bad. Give it to me. Want all of it," he begs me for more and I give it to him. I'd give him anything. Everything that matters.

I fuck him harder, rolling him onto his belly and moving to cover him from behind. He moans and begs and arches up to give me better access.

At this angle, it's easy to fuck him deep. I drive right into the core of him. My body presses against him. I love his back. Love the way his powerful flight muscles translate into an expanse of toned and sculpted shoulders. His body writhes under me as he rides back on my cock, taking me harder and faster. I pin him more firmly in place and take my time with him, hugging him close. My round belly—softer than usual with my bear's hibernation fueled hunger —rubs over his lower back. We're a perfect fit with the way Bram arches for me, lifting his ass to meet my every thrust.

My pecs rub against his shoulder blades, the firm jut of his bones stimulating my nipples in a deliciously affirming way. I love how he plays with my chest during sex regardless of how I'm presenting, but sometimes having that part of me touched makes me feel more femme. This is one of those times when I need it. With my knot stretching him wide open, it's good to feel like that isn't the only part of me he wants. Even if he isn't trying to touch my nips, it still feels good and right.

He's so perfect for me; my precious omega.

"Bram, gonna knot you."

"Yes, Ty. Do it. Breed me. Need your cum inside me."

"Gonna knock you up, omega, make you a papa."

"Yes! Fuck, yes." Bram's channel squeezes me tight as he comes, as though his body is consciously trying to make my words a reality. It's too much for me to hold back. I fuck in hard and deep, pressing every inch of my knot inside my omega and filling him up like he asked.

I come inside of him, like I've done more times than I can count since his heat started. Like I plan to keep doing until it ends. It feels so good to know that he wants me, wants this. Wants the potential cubs we might make together. I squeeze him tight as I pump my release as deep inside of him as I can reach. My knot swells to keep it all in place for as long as possible.

As my knot locks us together, I find myself hoping more and more for a fertile heat with him. I was leary when he asked for a clutch with me. But the longer I spend knotted inside of him, breathing in his scent, holding him in my arms, the more I hope he'll catch.

Part of it is hormones, I know that. Basic shifter biology. But just because I'm in a rut doesn't mean it's all hormones. Part of it is the tender way my omega touches me. The way he feeds me bites of his food between bouts of sex. How he shares more than just his body with me.

He's mine and I want him to stay that way well beyond the end of his heat, regardless of whether he gives us a clutch of eggs.

My dick aches from the number of times Bramble and I fucked over the past—however long his heat has lasted. I've long since lost track of time. All that matters is being buried inside my mate.

We haven't agreed to that level of commitment yet, but I want it. It's easy to imagine a future with my sated omega dozing in my arms and our bedsheets perfumed with his slick and my scent. Sharing a heat comes with that sort of intense emotional connection. It will fade once the heat passes. Probably.

Or, it does if there isn't a relationship to go with the shared sex. At least, that's what I've always heard. I've only had heat sex with two omegas. Arnie, and now Bramble. I loved Arnie long before we shared his heats. And I've been feeling something stronger than lust toward Bram for a while now.

I'd never have agreed to father a child with Bram if I didn't care about him on a deeper level. I wasn't quite ready to call that love before this, and I refuse to declare something like that while we both still reek of sex. Once our ardor cools, if I still feel this way after my rut and his heat fade, then I'll say it. When the moment is right.

Bram snuggles closer to me in his sleep, pulling me out of thoughts of love and commitment. For now, it's enough to care about him.

Still, if his heat is over, we're going to have to face the real world again soon. More than to place the occasional order for food delivery with the local restaurants that cater to omegas in heat and their partners. Food sounds good.

Bram's stomach rumbles, so I'll bet he's hungry too, but I'm not ready to disturb our cocoon of warmth. My limp dick is nestled perfectly between his pert ass cheeks, like I belong pressed naked against his body. As if we really are mates in every sense. I don't want to shatter that moment of closeness.

I nuzzle my nose into the back of his neck, scenting him. Shifters can smell a pregnancy without a test. That is, if they know the pregnant person's usual scent well enough to recognize the subtle changes the hormonal fluctuations cause. Even so, it's far too soon for that. I still breathe in deep, as though I can memorize him and this moment with the two of us together.

Bram rolls to face me and snuggles closer to me. "Morning, alpha."

I wrap him tighter in my arms and press a kiss to his forehead. "Good morning, omega mine."

Bram grins at me. "Think you can get it up for one last round?"

I groan. "My dick aches, Bramble. Your ass

can't feel any less chafed now that your heat has passed."

"I suppose." Bram looks wistful, sadness clouding his bright eyes. "I hope we get to do that again. You know, before…" He shudders, not finishing the thought. He doesn't have to, his meaning hangs heavy in the air between us. Creep. He's worried creep might steal that part of him away.

I gather him more firmly against my chest. "It will be alright," I assure him as I finger comb his hair. Bram leans his head into my touch, like a bird accepting a mate's preening. How many times have I watched him watching Freya and Theron grooming each other in our habitat with a longing I could see even in his bird form?

The gesture reminds me of our differences. Hopefully, I can give him what his bird side needs. The way I couldn't give Arnie—I need to stop comparing them. I can't constantly be caught up in the past if I want a future with Bram. And I do want a future with him. It's not just the residual heat hormones or my rut talking.

Bram forces a brittle laugh. "I suppose if there's a clutch, it will be a while before my next one."

"How long before you know?" I ask, unsure if it's different for avians.

Bram squirms free of my arms to look at me. "You really want this? To be a parent with me?"

"Yes. I really do. I'd have more cubs already, if things were different."

Bram swallows hard and nods. "Okay. I don't know if it's different with hybrids. Or rather, it wasn't much different when my cousin had her clutch, but even static crows and ravens can interbreed, so of course it would be a compatible timeline. Bear cubs gestate longer, right?"

"Sort of? We have delayed implantation like static bears. So a spring heat might fertilize an egg that only starts to develop in the fall, around Denning Night."

"Huh, that's neat. I wonder if that's part of why grizzly shifters celebrate it so prominently; it marks the time when their cubs grow," Bram muses.

"I think that's part of it, yeah. So, most bear cubs are born in the late winter or early spring. But for shifters, if an omega has a fall heat, or gets pregnant outside of a heat, then the cub usually implants without as much delay. Basically, bear shifter cubs are born in the spring at the end of hibernation season. When food gets more plentiful in time for them to wean, and their parents aren't already exhausted from needing to hibernate."

"Oh, yeah, I wouldn't have considered that. Sleep deprivation from babies and your bear would be a double whammy, huh?"

"Yep. Static bear cubs develop in about two months. It's a little longer for our omegas. I think

Myra took almost four months from Denning Night. I'm not sure how that works with cross-species matings that aren't other bears."

"Ah, so, her birthday is in April? If we have a clutch, the eggs probably won't hatch until May, so she wouldn't need to share her celebration." Bram rests his hand low over his belly.

I lie there beside him, struck speechless that he's already taking Myra into account. Already seeing her as a big sister to the baby he's dreaming of having. It's so completely Bramble to worry about her feelings, and his thoughtfulness toward my kid makes me want to scoop him into my arms and kiss away all his worries.

Maybe I should be anxious at the idea of such a huge commitment so soon, but all I feel in his presence is peaceful. I want to plan a future with this omega.

"That would be great."

"Yeah. So, the delayed implantation thing sounds sort of like having a clutch and waiting to incubate them until all the eggs are laid. Only, you know, with a significantly longer delay for you bears."

"Is that a thing?" I ask.

"Yeah." Bram nods. "Laying is strenuous. Most static birds only lay one a day or even every couple of days. With shifters, we sometimes only lay one at a time if we have a larger clutch. So, if you incubate them as you go, then the last egg laid can hatch significantly later than the first. So, it's better for the youngest hatchlings to wait, so they all come at the same time and don't have to compete with much stronger older siblings for food."

"That makes sense."

"Also, since our static counterparts have vastly different biology from our human sides, there's a longer gravid period. The eggs develop internally for around four months, and then we lay them and the eggs require another few weeks to develop externally before they hatch. Usually, they fledge and get their shift around four months after their hatchday."

"Huh. That's still weird to me."

Bram shrugs. "It's not that weird. Bear cub shifters take milk in both forms," Bram asks.

"True. Does that matter?" I seem to recall him mentioning something about food last time we discussed this, but I'm having a hard time wrapping my head around how to care for a newborn baby bird who can't shift. Bram's clutch will be even more tiny and delicate than Myra was at that age.

"Yeah, the best we can tell, that's why the delay with avian babies. Hatchlings can't digest milk. So if they take a human form too soon, it is harder to keep them fed for the first few months. By four months, they don't puke every time they shift with a full belly, regardless of which way they're shifting. Rarely a hatchling will shift early and it's hard to keep those ones fed without the entire rave to pitch in and help. That, or medication to keep them in one form until they are old enough for it to be safe. Sometimes that can delay them getting control of their shifts, but better than being chronically underfed."

I hadn't considered that, and a part of me secretly hopes the baby he wants so badly will come in their human form, so I can help with all the tasks I'd be clueless about with a baby bird. I don't want to miss out on all the little bonding moments I got to share with Myra as a newborn. This time I want to share them with my mate as well as our baby.

"So, they'll definitely hatch into avians?" I ask, unable to entirely hide the note of hope in my voice.

"As far as I know? I suppose it's possible to gestate a hatchling in their human form. In that case, they stay human until the point when it's easier for them to digest things that aren't milk. Makes it easier for crop feeding their fledgling form."

"Then, with a hybrid cub, it's possible you might birth our cub in their bear form?"

"As far as I know?" Bram shrugs. "Hopefully, it wouldn't be an issue if we had a mixed clutch." Bram bites his lip. "Like, if the cub needs more time to develop and there's also an egg that only needs three months, what would happen?"

"I don't know." I hug him tighter, not liking

the idea of having two cubs with incompatible needs. "It might be good for us to use meds to be sure you only have one cub at a time in the future, so that won't be a problem. And if you are pregnant, then we should see a shifter specialist as soon as possible." I rest my hand over his abdomen, wishing I could tell already if he was carrying our cub.

"I'll ask around at work tomorrow. Felix is on top of all the latest shifter reproduction news, so if anyone would know how mixed avian-bear babies work, it'd be him."

"Are you planning to go in tomorrow?" I ask, because they usually include a few days of recovery in heat leave. Part of me wishes I could languish in bed with my omega now that the urgency of the heat is behind us. Another part is anxious to check on my cub after several days without contact. This is the longest I've been apart from Myra since she was born.

Bram sighs. "Can't afford time off that I don't need. Besides, if I stay here, I'll probably just obsess over whether we'll get to use the nest I made or not."

"You will." I kiss his temple. "Even if this heat didn't take, we'll try again. And speaking of this nest, do I get to see it? Or is there cultural stuff I should know about it?"

Bram laughs. "You can see it. Raven alphas help to build the nest with their mates, so it smells like both parents. It's not like it's a surprise or taboo for you to see it or anything."

"Yeah? So I should get my scent on it?"

"Sure," Bram grins at me, as he gets up and goes to the ladder up to the second bunk. I trail after him.

"Watch your head."

His warning comes as my head and shoulders brush the ceiling. Seb's bunk only has a couple feet of clearance for headspace. I hunch to crawl onto the mattress, wedged in next to Bram. Under us, the bed groans ominously. I don't think it was intended to hold an alpha bear shifter, let alone two adults and the huge pile of sticks and wrist-thick branches that I'm pretty sure are Bram's nest.

I wasn't sure what to expect when he mentioned it, but this is bulky and has lots of pointy bits sticking in all directions. My gut reaction is that it might be hazardous to a human baby, but he's looking at me like he's about to burst with some combination of pride and worry. Like when Myra shows me a new art project she's not sure I'll approve of. I'm not entirely sure what I'm looking at, but I can see it's important to him, and that makes it a masterpiece to me.

"It's perfect." I say, laying a palm on the rough wood. Bram beams and bobs his head excitedly.

"You like it? We usually recycle the materials from old nests. But not the nest structure itself. It's all bird instincts really. I think it might be too small, if you wanted to shift and join me while I'm incubating the clutch?" He flashes me a shy little smile as he tosses out the pseudo-invitation.

I didn't know that was a thing before he said it, but now I really do want to sit with him while he's keeping our eggs warm. I want to be by his side for as long as he wants me there. Bram glances back at the nest, eyes full of wistful longing as he rearranges a little basin made of smaller twigs near the center. That must be where the eggs go. It looks much more baby-friendly, so that's a relief.

"I guess my raven side didn't get the memo that our alpha isn't a bird shifter," Bram says, following my gaze.

"We can make it bigger, together." I place my hand over his inside the nest, giving him a reassuring squeeze. "And maybe build one at my place too? So the eggs can come over with you. If that's safe?"

"Moving them too much isn't ideal, but we'll figure it out. You really want to have kids with me?" Bram sounds so hopeful, I want to wrap him in a hug and kiss him until he doesn't have a single doubt about how much I want with him, but there's barely room to move up here.

"Yeah. Now that it's out there, I really do." I settle for squeezing his hand again.

"Even though it's so soon?" Bram worries his lip between his teeth.

"You want kids regardless, right?" I ask.

"Yes."

"So, I want you to have that."

"Before creep takes away my chance." Bram rolls away from me, arms wrapped around his middle, no small feat in the tight confines of the crowded little mattress.

"It might not." I reach for him, rubbing the curve of his back.

Bram hunches in on himself more. "Sure, but this is how it started for Seb."

"We'll make it work, Bramble. I'm here for you," I say with a pang. I know he's scared and I can't actually promise him that his fears won't come true. All I can do is hold him through it. The words, 'I love you,' are on the tip of my tongue. But I can't say them now. Not when he's upset, and I'm not sure how much of my feelings are just the afterglow of our weekend together and my rut. I have to be completely sure I mean it first.

"Yeah. We'll make it work." Bram rolls toward me and buries his face in my chest to cry out his emotions.

I'm not sure if that's the comedown from his heat or the culmination of his fear and sorrow over what he stands to lose if he really is developing creep. Either way, I don't let go until long after he's cried himself out next to the beautifully lopsided structure he built to cradle his dreams for our future.

CHAPTER 21

Bram

The days after my heat as we wait to see if I'm knocked up are stressful. Ty and I talk more. He invites me to his home for dinner after our work shifts a few times, and I go. I enjoy the time with him and his daughter.

Myra doesn't ask if I'm going to be her dad's mate, or clamor for a sibling after the first time when Ty chides her for being rude. But I catch her watching my belly as though it might show signs of a pregnancy before we tell her. It doesn't, and that's not the only thing that has me stressed.

Winny's surgery is coming up fast. I spend way too much of my spare time anxiously refreshing our fundraiser page to see if we've got enough to cover the out-of-pocket costs. We have enough to cover the upfront copay. But I'm worried about having to work out yet another lengthy payment plan for the balance that her co-op insurance won't cover. Not to mention physical therapy while she's recovering.

Ty is good at distracting me when we're together, pulling me out of my phone with sweet kisses. I haven't spent the night yet. Myra already seems pretty invested in us working out. Neither of us wants to get her hopes up about that so soon. But I wish I could. I hate going home to my empty apartment now that Seb and Winny have both moved out. Seb hasn't made it official, but he hasn't been back overnight since my heat, so I know it's only a matter of time.

I wake up bleary and alone on the morning that the quarterly zoo newsletter goes out. It's a little over a week after my heat, and I've been down in the dumps. I know Felix included the fundraiser I set up for Winny, as promised. I saw an uptick in donations after Jolene shared the link with the staff, but we're still short. As I've made a habit recently, I refresh the fundraiser page. And then I have to double check that I'm really seeing what I think I'm seeing.

I want to roll over and poke Seb awake to make him confirm the numbers, but he's stopped sleeping in our apartment. My next thought, as I catch a stray whiff of my mate in my pillows, is that I wish Ty were here. I want to share the news with him.

I screencap the huge number at the top of

the page. The total already exceeds our goal by enough that we can pay down most of the old debt and cover the new procedure along with the private rehab for her recovery. And it's still ticking up as I refresh to be sure I'm not seeing things. Felix came through. All my efforts to help are paying off and I don't have to worry so much anymore. Not about Winny, anyway.

As much as I long to tell Ty, I text the picture to both of my clutchmates and our moms first. I hesitate over sending it to Ty, too. I want to tell him in person, and I should check in on how Winny is taking the news. As I'm getting dressed and picking out my shinies for the day, Winny calls. I can't remember the last time she called me; it's been the other way around since before her accident. Her number on my screen gives me hope that we'll find a new normal.

"Is that for real, Bramble? They didn't misplace the decimal point or something?" Winny asks.

"It's for real," I say, and the weight of the medical debt that's been crushing us since last year falls from my shoulders as that fact sinks in. I don't think I realized just how much I was stressing about the costs of the rapidly approaching surgical date that I badgered Winny into accepting until now.

It's like I've been carting that worry around with me ever since we got that first eye-popping hospital bill that I knew we could never pay without working in the static world. It has felt like everything relied on me for months now. Our homes are owned collectively through the rave, but that doesn't mean debt collectors couldn't try to take our family's portion of the value from us if we fall too far behind on our payments. My moms both help, but they have jobs in Four Corners that pay just enough to cover household expenses and not much else.

I don't think they meant for the debt to fall on my shoulders, but it did. And now that there's a way to pay it off, I feel so much lighter. Without the specter of debt collectors coming after my family and the rave hanging over me, I can finally breathe easy.

"Thank you, Bram," Winny says.

"You don't have to thank me. If anything, thank my boss for getting his rich mailing list to chip in."

"No, not for the money."

I scoff. "You sure? It's a heck of a lot of money, Win."

Winny snorts a laugh. "Okay, but not just for the money. Thank you for never giving up on me."

"Never. For what it's worth, I'm sorry I pushed you about the surgery."

"We already had that conversation. I get you want the best for me; you just have to let me define what that means. And I hope you know that we all want what's best for you too."

"Huh? What do you mean?" I ask, puzzled by

the subject change.

Winny huffs out a breath. "Just that if you're only working at the zoo to help us, I don't want you to feel like you have to keep doing that. I've been picking up odd jobs online and I'll be okay without your financial help now that the medical stuff is covered. You've seemed so stressed, and I feel bad that I've been so wrapped up in my own stuff that I barely noticed."

"Okay. I have been stressed about the bills, but I like my job, Win."

"Right. I just thought... you know what? Nevermind. I think I've been listening to Grandad too much. You like it there, huh?"

"Yeah. I really do. It's a good job. And I enjoy having my feathers admired every day."

That makes her chuckle. "Classic Bramble. I guess I should listen to you more too, huh?"

"Just a little, yeah. So, are we good?" From the gentle teasing in her voice, I think we really are going to be okay again. For all that's changed, she's still my sister.

"We are so much better than good, Bramble. I can't believe you really found a way to cover the entire cost. Even the PT afterward. I don't think I'll really believe they can fix me until after I actually get out of the surgery."

"First of all, *you* aren't broken; your wing is just screwed up. And second, Felix says they're the best shifter orthopedic team in the NorthEast. You're in the best of hands, sis."

Winny takes a long moment to answer. "Sure, Bram. Listen, I don't want to make you late for work, but Mom and Mama are asking me to tell you they want to celebrate tonight with that black forest cake you like from the bakery. Any other requests?"

"Nope, I'm happy with my cherry cake."

"Cool. See you tonight?"

I think about it, because lately that isn't as much of a given as it has been for most of my adult life. Part of me wants to celebrate the good news with my family, but another part longs to see Ty and Myra too. Since it's good news about my family, I should probably join them tonight. Not for the first time, I consider inviting Ty and his daughter to my family's dinner, but that might be one of those things where Ty doesn't want to move things with Myra too fast.

"Yeah, see you tonight, Winny. I love you."

"Love you, too."

We hang up. Seb and my parents texted back while I was on the phone so I reply to them. By that point, I'm running late if I want time to chat with Ty before work. I rush out the door, excited to see my alpha soon.

As soon as I step into the locker area, Ty hands me a little tupperware full of chocolate lumps, before I can even open my mouth to tell him the news.

"I saw the fundraiser page this morning. Congrats, Bram!" Ty pulls me into a big bear hug, burying his nose in my neck and breathing in my scent.

I kiss him, unwilling to face his disappointment on top of my own, if my scent still hasn't changed. Today we are celebrating, so there's no room to angst over whether I'll get to have a clutch with him.

By his feet, Ty has an entire picnic basket with him that has me very curious about its contents. He shoves the insulated bag into his locker, then turns back to face me.

"What's this?" I hold up the box of chocolate between us.

"Nothing much. Myra and I dipped those cherries you like in chocolate. She said we should make you a treat since the fundraiser was doing so well, so we did a quick job of it before I dropped her at school."

"They look delicious." I pop one into my mouth. And they might look a bit messy, but they taste divine. I kiss Ty again, chocolate lingering on my tongue. Kissing leads to touching. I grope his firm, round ass. Ty moans, grinding us together. I've got a hand down his pants and one leg hitched around his waist when Freya and Theron walk in on us.

Freya clears her throat pointedly. "Keeper talk starts in less than half an hour, you two."

"Save it for your lunch break." Theron winks at us.

Ty and I step apart, adjusting ourselves. He

seems flustered at the interruption, but after a moment to compose ourselves, all four of us shift and enter the exhibit mostly on time.

On our lunch break, Ty and I finish our celebration with the picnic-style lunch that he brought. It's a meal that goes largely uneaten as he lets me fuck him in the locker area before we bolt down a few bites at a picnic area. I can tell by the way he scents me while I'm driving my cock between his lube-slicked thighs that he's still hoping we'll have more news to celebrate. I try not to be too disappointed that there's nothing. It could still just be too soon, though that hope fades more with every passing day.

A week later, I'm itchy and restless as I drive into work. I've been meeting Ty at our enclosure instead of the Wild Bean, preemptively avoiding my usual morning caffeine fix in the hopes of a clutch. Despite that avoidance, I feel jittery enough to have downed half a pot of coffee already. I'm squirming in my seat to the beat of a pop song on the radio. Feverish and horny and I know what it means, even if I don't want to acknowledge it.

Today marks two weeks since my last heat ended, and I know for sure it didn't take. It's obvious from the prodrome symptoms of another heat starting. These past few weeks with Ty as my partner have been incredible. I've gotten closer to him now that he's not hiding anything about his life. We've gone on dates, talking about our future long into the night after Myra goes to bed. I still leave to sleep in my bed for now.

Each morning, I get to see Ty at work, and the sight of him makes me smile. Sets butterflies loose in my stomach to frolic and flutter and make me believe I can have everything I ever wanted. I love knowing Ty wants the same future as me. A mate and a big family.

It's even kind of cute that Ty thinks he's been subtle when he scents me each morning before we shift in the locker area. He greets me with a hug and nuzzles into my neck, inhaling deep. He's not subtle, and he's not good at hiding his disappointment that my scent hasn't changed. I'm disappointed too.

The heat symptoms sneaking up on me again make me anxious about what back-to-back heats might mean for my health. Rebound heats can be normal. Especially after going off long-term blockers. They can also be a sign of creep. No way of knowing which this is until I either develop more symptoms or I don't.

It could be nothing. I haven't been taking my blocker prescription, in case Ty knocked me up. They can be harmful early in a pregnancy and I want to go into heat again if I'm not pregnant. This might just be my body's way of self-regulating my hormones. Or it could mean I'll never have a clutch of my own. The uncertainty makes me irritable. Unless that's just the hormones. Ugh.

By the time I pull into the parking lot, I can't really deny the symptoms and what they mean. I pop some low-dose, short-term heat suppressors that I keep in the car's console as a just in case, to forestall the inevitable until at least tonight. A couple of doses should get me through my day. If I can last through today's work shift, then I'll have three days off for the weekend to deal with my heat without taking more unexpected PTO.

Winny's surgery is next week, so the timing could be worse, all things considered. This way I'll get the heat behind me on my days off and I'll be fine to take my scheduled time off next week to support Winny while she's recovering.

This morning, when Ty hugs me, I cling to her. She's wearing one of her flowy blouses and subtle makeup today, cluing me into their pronouns. Instead of a single inhale and a sad smile—which is how this played out every other morning this week—today, Ty breathes in deep. Then they snuffle along my pulse point. Her tongue darts out to sample me, and I shiver at the intimacy of her mouth on me.

"You're coming into heat," she murmurs, mouth pressed to my ear.

"Yeah." I swallow hard. "It didn't take."

"Do we get to try again?" Ty asks.

"You're sure you want to?" I ask, afraid she'll

have changed her mind. Now that she's had more time to consider.

"Yes." Ty grips my hips, grinds against me and I inhale a sharp breath. Her scent is a little different from usual. Muskier, like an alpha in rut. That's not ideal.

I don't want to miss this shift. I need all my PTO to support Winny. Sure, I no longer need to pinch every penny to get her an experimental prototype replacement joint and put her through a rehab program she doesn't want on the slim chance it might restore her flight, but I still want to support her in any way I can. Winny deserves the best I can give her, and that includes being there for her as she recovers. I can't let her down.

"Can your mom watch Myra again this weekend?" I ask.

Ty shakes her head, not saying no, just clearing away the lusty thoughts. I guess mentioning their kid is a surefire way to cut through the urgency of her rut. "Yeah. I'll call her. And I might need to get scent blockers from the kit if we're waiting until after work to start."

They grab the plastic first aid kit from its spot on the wall next to the lockers. The velcro that holds it in place makes a loud ripping noise that makes me cringe and itch at my skin.

"I took suppressors this morning to hold it off."

"Scent blockers should be enough to keep my rut at bay," Ty offers.

Ty's already rummaging through the kit for the meds. The zoo keeps a supply of common meds stocked for each habitat. She comes up with the blockers that will dampen her sense of smell and mute her own pheromones for a few hours. That should help. Otherwise, breathing in my alpha's rut hormones for hours would dramatically reduce the suppressors' effectiveness. Already, I want them. Badly. Fuck, maybe if we just take the edge off before the zoo opens to guests...

Freya and Theron arrive before I can act on that impulse. They're chattering to each other about something to do with their rave.

"So, she said—" Theron stops talking mid-sentence, scrapes his eyes down my body and tuts.

"Heat leave exists for a reason, Bramble," Freya says in her snootiest know-it-all tone.

Ty growls possessively, sidling closer to me. As though their imposing bulk can shield me from unkind words.

"You do sort of reek of it." Theron fans his face, as though to wave away my stench.

I fidget uncomfortably. My skin is fever-hot and I itch at the rough fabric on my sensitive skin again. I want to go home and spend the day fucking my alpha. But I can't. I ignore the other raven shifters and remove my clothing so I can take to my feathers. Before I can, Ty grabs my wrist and turns my hand palm up to tip a scent blocker tablet out into my grasp.

"Wait. Take this first," Ty says as she takes her dose of the medication.

Freya sniffs after me. She's an alpha, so she doesn't seem put off by me. At least I only stink to Theron's nose. He nudges his mate's arm. Probably grumpy that she's expressing any sort of interest in my scent. "What? I find slick enticing; doesn't mean I'm going to fuck him." Freya scowls at Theron and rubs her arm.

"Are those scent blockers?" Theron reaches for the pre-dosed packets of pills that Ty found in the first aid kit and grabs two, handing one to his alpha mate.

"We'll be fine for a few hours if we all take these. In the future, though, you really should stay home when you're in heat, Bram." Freya rakes her eyes over me again. She licks her lips, then glances toward her omega and takes the pill. "You should take suppressors, too, if you don't want to trigger a heat."

"Sorry." I stare sheepishly at my feet.

Freya's right that the pheromones I'm putting off could trigger a heat in another omega who has to share close quarters with me. Especially if there's any perception that I'm competing for his alpha. I'm not. Freya isn't my type. At all. I only have eyes for Ty. That won't help Theron if he has a reaction to my heat.

"It's fine. We're trying for a clutch anyway, so an unexpected heat wouldn't be the end of the world." Theron bumps my shoulder, his earlier attitude thawing.

I glance up and the other two ravens are exchanging besotted smiles.

"Sure, but you didn't want to be gravid during the winter holidays, Theron," Freya says.

He shrugs. "We'll make it work, alpha."

"We always do. Now, get in your feathers, both of you. The job doesn't stop because you've both got eggs on the brain." Freya waves us toward the habitat, like an overbearing elder shepherding youngsters with mantled wings.

I shift, squawking at her bossy attitude. Ty waits until I'm through the plastic slats to strip and shift. Their protectiveness makes my raven preen. She keeps a wary eye on me all day, growling her rumbly bear sounds if our enclosure mates get too close to my favorite perch. We get along better than this most of the time. Sometimes they'll even include me in their preening. Not today.

When Bob delivers our enrichment activities for the day, Ty sets aside the choicest treats for me. They rumble out a contented sound when I swoop down to indulge in her offerings. Most of my heat symptoms aren't bothering me as much in my bird form. The raven just wants to nest. Since I already built a cozy nest that smells of me and my alpha, my raven instincts say we should go to the nest.

Since that isn't possible with us all being here

in the enclosure, the raven is restless. I want to pluck some of my alpha's fur to line the nest and cushion our eggs. I hop closer to Ty. We usually keep our distance during work hours. At first because of the animosity between us, but then later to maintain professional boundaries.

Even with the suppressor and scent blockers, I can't entirely resist the urge to be close to her today. Ty lets me flutter up to perch on their broad shoulders. The coarse bristly guard hairs that rise when someone gets too close to her territory stay flat when I'm in her space now. They let me preen their fur.

Her trust at having my sharp beak near her neck makes my inner bird want to preen her all over. My raven wants to shower them in affection until I've covered them in the caramelized pineapple scent of my preen oil. She sniffs after the preen oil when I gather it from my glands to rub into her fur. I suspect they recognize the odor from my trick of using the oil from a partial shift as lube. And she only makes a token protest when I pluck a clump of her thick downy undercoat for the nest.

I tuck the nesting material into my tail feathers, a trick I picked up from watching lovebird shifters here at the zoo line their nests. I spend a long time balancing on my mate's back, trying not to dig my sharp talons past their fur and into their flesh. Ty doesn't seem bothered as I alternate between preening her soft fur and collecting it for our egg.

Our keeper has more scent blockers stocked around lunch when Freya ducks into the private area to take another dose. She makes sure the rest of us take our doses too, including suppressors for both Theron and me. The second dose helps me to stop fantasizing about Ty naked and in their human form for a while. I still can't quite bring myself to put space between us, though. Not when she's already called her mom to make sure Myra is all set for a weekend at her grandmother's house.

At the end of the day, the tone sounds to tell all park visitors that the zoo is closed. Ty and I go through the flaps to the changing area as soon as the last lingering visitors walk away from our habitat. Freya and Theron swoop down to join us. I fret over the bear fur I've collected, plucking a tuft free and then considering the best place to store it until I have hands for gathering it together.

The other two ravens shift and are half-dressed before I give up on trying to gather all my nest lining materials from where I tucked them into my tail feathers for safekeeping. Ty shifts and puts on her blouse and skirt. I shift too, but then I get distracted, staring at the lacy panties they're wearing today. And the way her clit fills out the front panel. I want to lick them all over and take them inside me.

"You two have a fun weekend," Theron says

with a cheeky wave. His words distract me from my sexy thoughts, and I just stare after him dazedly.

"Might want to take the edge off before either of you gets behind the wheel," Freya says, her tone amused. "That, or take a cab. Bye now."

They leave arm-in-arm, and much as I hate to admit it, Freya is probably right that I'm in no fit state to drive.

"Hotel?" I suggest, even though I really want to get home to my nest. I need to add Ty's fur to the interior. We'll have the softest, warmest little cub hatchling. I'm not sure which I want more. A tiny, furry bear cub mewling for milk or the big-eyed, begging-beaked, bald baby bird. Either. Both, if things go well and we can have more than one clutch. I want to experience both, though maybe not at the same time.

After my last heat, Felix confirmed that while the gestations for raven and black bear omegas are similar, a mixed clutch could cause complications. They don't have enough information to say for sure whether it's safe. He helped me get a prescription for medication to make sure I only release one egg at a time.

I don't want to take the meds. I know I should, but reducing the number of potential eggs seems like it will reduce my chances of getting to carry a child. And with my symptoms pointing to creep, I just couldn't make myself take them. So they're sitting on my bathroom counter untouched. And that's how they'll remain for now.

Ty crowds closer to me, and I rub my naked self against her body. Their blouse is silky smooth against my chest. I like it. The gauzy skirt is rough against my hard dick and I don't enjoy that. I tug it up, trying to expose the panties underneath, wanting to rub us together through the pretty barely there lace.

"We can go to my place; it's closer." She takes my hands, gently removing them from her skirt. I whine and hump their leg. She squeezes my ass, which both turns me on more and stills my needy movements long enough for me to process their suggestion.

Oh. Yes. I want to go to my alpha's nest. Er. Den? Home. Her home where everything is marked with her scent. "Yes. Your house. Now." I try to kiss their neck. Ty gently nudges me away.

"You'll have me in a full rut if you keep that up and I'd rather breed you in private, bird. Did you have a reason for plucking my fur all afternoon?"

"Needed it for the egg."

"Ah. Well, gather up your nesting materials while I call us a cab. We can leave our vehicles here in the employee lot. Bob knows the situation with your heat." Ty nudges me toward the tufts of fur littering the ground and pulls out her phone to order us a ride.

I bend to gather their fur, and I'm not the least bit shy about showing off my ass while I work.

The dose of suppressors I took at lunchtime is the only reason I'm not dripping slick all over the place, but I can already feel the wetness building inside me.

The medically mediated reprieve won't last much longer. Not with my sexy alpha right here, talking about taking me home and breeding me. Giving me a cub. The thought has me stroking myself with one hand while I add more bear fluff to my growing pile of it with the other.

"Save that erection for your alpha, Bramble. It will be better at home."

Ty scoops up my pile of fluff and bundles it into a baggie she got from somewhere. Their locker? I don't know and I don't care. They shove a bundle of my clothing into my arms and I struggle into it. Even the softest material scrapes over my raw, heat-sensitized nerves. I want to be naked. Too bad I can't ride to their place in my raven form. It would be easier to resist their allure. Most car services frown on allowing wild animals, even if we are shifters.

Ty helps me to get my shirt and pants on, then guides me toward the front entrance. Our cab arrives, and I resist the urge to climb in and straddle my mate's lap. I could rub their firm clit between my wet cheeks. Slick all over their lap. Make her knot me. I want them to knot me so badly it hurts. I can feel my pulse throbbing there, the ache of needing to be filled. The suppressors aren't helping anymore.

The cab driver has to be a static, since he shows no response to my increasingly potent scent. Not that I'm paying much attention to him. But if he was a shifter, he'd probably notice and say something. The drive to Ty's place lasts an eternity.

I paw at her thighs, rub between her legs. Kiss their neck. She gently rebuffs my every advance, settling my hands back on my lap when I touch them too insistently. Nudging my mouth away from her skin. The rejections sting. My eyes burn with unshed tears by the time the car stops in front Ty's adorable little house on her familiar cul-de-sac.

Ty pays, while I almost trip over a kid's bike with pink streamers that's tipped over on the front walkway. They steady me with a hand on my lower back. I scowl at her. Now they want to touch me? I want to yell at her for pushing me away earlier. I want to be mad, but all I have room for is horny.

Ty leans in, breath tickling my neck. Tendrils of arousal shoot to my core as she speaks into my ear, voice a sexy rumbling purr. "Do you know how hard it is to keep my hands off you right now, Bramble? The only reason I didn't impale you on my knot in that cab is so that the driver would actually get us home, where I can breed you in peace."

"Yes, alpha," I breathe, the anger and hurt draining out of me in a rush. Ty wants me. She wants me as bad as I want her. Wants to give me a clutch. And that's best accomplished inside instead of on their front lawn. "Breed me, alpha."

"As soon as we get inside." Ty squeezes the back of my neck and I shudder at the possessive alpha-ness of the gesture. They guide me toward their front door. She lets us inside, fingers caressing my neck as we hasten through a living room strewn with toys. Down a narrow hallway to the bedroom at the end. The bed is unmade, the sheets rumpled and smelling strongly of my alpha. I couldn't care less about the state of my mate's housekeeping. I wrench free of her grip and turn to face her.

Unable to handle another rejection, I tip up my chin, offering them my lips. I long to throw myself into a kiss. It takes all my restraint to ask for it first.

"Kiss me?" I ask. I don't like how plaintive the request sounds, but I'm in heat and I need her and I can't think straight.

Ty steps in close and kisses me. Our lips meet and meld and it's just like my last heat, connecting with her so intensely that it's easy to lose track of everything else. I tug at their clothing and she pushes my pants down. Ty's bear strength is more than up to the task of lifting me and carrying me to the bed, laying me down on the soft mattress. She kisses along my thighs while she fingers my hole until I'm begging her to fill it up properly.

Then, instead of taking off their skirt, they ruck it up around their waist and let the fabric settle over me as their big alpha clit rubs between my cheeks. I can't help the gush of slick her fluids trigger. Their lacy panties are soaked with our combined fluids as their engorged clit pokes out of the waistband, ready to breed me.

Distantly, I'm aware that this might play out very differently if my lover was a static human. Someone who might not be comfortable using her anatomy to penetrate me on a femme day. But Ty's an alpha. Regardless of whether she's rocking a clit or a cock, penetrating an omega in heat is an affirmation of their alpha-ness. I think. I don't know for sure. But Ty told me last time that she'd still enjoy knotting and fucking me regardless of pronouns.

They rub the tip of their clit along my crack, and I coat them in another gush of slick. I rock up to meet her as she thrusts against my hole. I need their knot so badly it aches.

"Need you, alpha. Put your clit inside me. Please." I grip her shoulders tight, try to get them where I need them.

Ty presses inside of me. She moans, eyes fluttering shut as I engulf her in my slick warmth. I moan too. Being stretched open by them is everything I need. Their skirt slithers over my skin with every sinuous roll of their hips, adding more sensations that make me shiver and writhe on her length. I like the way it pools around us, creating a personal privacy bubble. Almost as if we could have fucked in the back of the cab with no one the wiser.

"Such a sexy omega, Bramble. Can't wait to see you carrying our clutch."

"Yes, alpha. A whole clutch. Want to give you cubs and hatchlings. Give us everything."

I arch as she sparks more sensations deep inside of me. Their clit throbs with their pulse, close to release even though we've barely begun.

CHAPTER 22

Bram

My second heat in a month doesn't last as long as the first, only two days. Ty's Mom gives us a ride to the zoo to pick up our cars when she drops Myra off at home. It's awkward greeting the little girl after spending my heat with her papa. Even though Ty and I showered thoroughly before she came home, his scent feels like it's permeated my skin.

I smell like her dad. Not in a gross sex way. Just the way a shifter carries another's scent after spending several days wrapped around each other, bodies entwined. Like mates. We aren't mates though, not officially. No matter how much it felt like we could be as we were jostling elbows in front of Ty's vanity after the shower.

I could picture us getting ready together like that every day. Watching as Ty applies her makeup on their femme days. Maybe even having some of my shinies here, so I can mix things up after a sleepover. That would add some sparkle to the neatly organized bathroom counter.

Ty says he wants to be with me, but part of me worries that he'll change his mind once he knows me better. Or if I can't give him a clutch. It's an insecure part that is particularly vulnerable after leaving his warm embrace, but it's there nonetheless.

The weepy tide of emotion that wells up inside me as I think about Ty and his daughter and how my heart ached to drive away from them is familiar. I get this way after a heat sometimes. It helps to connect with people, so I call my folks as I drive. I texted between rounds of sex to let them know I wouldn't be home for a few days and why.

"Mom?" I say when she answers the apartment's landline. I'm not sure which parent picked up, but usually my siblings don't get that phone if an adult is home.

"Bramble, is your heat already over?" my alpha mom asks.

"Yeah." I nod, even though they can't see me. "Is that a bad sign?"

"Not at all, dear. Rebound heats after an attempt at having a clutch are usually shorter. We had Elric after a rebound heat." Mama interjects. I must be on speaker so they can both listen in on me.

"Does that mean I'm more likely to have a

clutch?" I cling to the little spark of hope that gives me.

"Sadly, no. It doesn't seem to factor into fertility, and it's not a sign of creep, any more than any variation from your normal cycle is a potential symptom."

"So, all I can do is wait and see?" I sigh, knowing the answer, but frustrated by it nonetheless.

"I'm afraid so, Bramble. Did you eat already? I can reheat leftovers if you're hungry?"

"Thanks, but we ate," I say, and I'm tearing up for no reason again.

Hormones are a pain. Why am I getting weepy over Mama offering to warm up food for me? Or is it that insidious little 'we'? The implication that I can be a unit with Ty and Myra. Like they're becoming family to me.

Ty's kid is a delight. She was regaling me with stories about one of those games Elric loves, and apparently she's been playing online with my sibling since they met. It made my chest all full and fluttery to hear it, but now I'm crashing back down from that high of warmth and acceptance and it's miserable.

I exchange a few more pleasantries with my parents. They extract a promise that I'll join them for family dinner tomorrow and invite Ty and Myra to come along sometime soon. Then we hang up and I drive the rest of the way home in silence.

I can't help the emotional letdown I experience in the aftermath. That's normal too, for the crash of hormones to make me melancholy.

It's worse after this heat cycle. A couple of days spent in my alpha's arms makes coming home to an empty apartment ache of loneliness. The empty nest I set up in Seb's unused bed is a constant reminder of the family I want to have, and might never get. I still add Ty's fur to the inner cup where I hope to lay my eggs, even as I'm wishing I was still with him.

Another day or two of heat sex at Ty's is far preferable to coming home to an empty apartment. The discovery that Seb still hasn't come home since my first heat is even more unwelcome. There's no sign he's been home at all, other than to pick up some of his things. His clothes aren't in our shared closet and his makeup is gone from the bathroom. It seems as though he's moving out without bothering to tell me first, and that stings.

There's an empty pill bottle with his name on the label in the bathroom trash bin. One that shouldn't be empty yet, based on the dates. But maybe he just put the rest of his HRT into one of those pill box things. He takes some daily vitamins and a heat blocker with his hormones, to stave off the random pseudo-heats he gets sometimes, so the empty bottle doesn't have to mean anything.

I'm not sure why he's distancing himself. Unsure if he's found other places to sleep or if he's found one particular other place to stay. He didn't move back home like Winny. I'm not so sure that wouldn't be better than wherever he's staying, but he still comes to family dinners, and he says everything is fine. More of my fussing won't be appreciated. I can't force myself not to worry though.

At least my sister is talking to me again now that we've discussed what she wants out of the surgery. I was so preoccupied with giving her back everything that was taken from her, I never stopped to ask what she wanted until Seb reminded me I should. I'm glad I asked before her surgery.

She's nervous about it, but at least the cost won't be an issue. I really have the best boss and an awesome job. Between the funds we raised and my savings from working at the zoo, Winny will get the care she needs.

My siblings aren't my responsibility. They've both told me that. Old habits are hard to break, and—my problem or not—I do worry about them. Sitting alone in my empty apartment with my empty nest and the stale scent of my alpha lingering on the pillow he used can't be healthy for me, but I just don't have the energy for anything else. For once, moping alone, I'm more worried about my own life than my clutchmates' choices. It's not a welcome change. Introspection with a side of post-heat mood crash is miserable.

I end up shifting to sleep in my nest, dreaming of the eggs that I'm afraid will never get to fill the soft interior. At least it smells like Ty with my stolen stash of bear fur. My sleep is fitful. When I get to work on Monday, Ty greets me with a big hug, but he doesn't scent me like he did last time.

My mind jumps to the idea that it's because he's changed his mind, or given up on us having a cub together. The fact he no longer seems charmingly eager stings more than I'd have imagined it could. I don't bring it up, because I don't want to hear my fears confirmed. Logically, he's more likely just trying not to put extra pressure on me to be pregnant, but logic can't take away my insecurity over this.

It's a relief not to have my shift at the zoo on Tuesday. I drive Winny to her surgery, and wait with our parents in the waiting room while she's there. Seb stayed home so someone will be around when the three younger kids get home from school, even though Briony is old enough to look after the younger two. All of us are anxious for word of how Winny's surgery went as we wait for her to be finished.

Not even fretting over Winny can fully distract me from the gnawing worries plaguing me over how my heat might have changed my fledgling relationship with Ty. I trust her surgeon to take care of her and fix the joint that's been causing her so much pain and suffering.

Ever since my rebound heat ended, I've got this constant gloomy cloud over my head. As though I'm walking around in a fog, unsure even whether to dare hope I could be pregnant. I don't want to dwell on my worries about what it might all mean or whether I'm moving too fast. The squirmy roiling in my belly at the thought that I'm already too late to start the family I wanted doesn't help. I can't shake the fear that I'm setting myself up for heartbreak.

CHAPTER 23

Ty

After Bram's second heat, I do a better job of not getting my hopes up about whether he's pregnant. Or carrying a clutch, whatever raven shifters call it. It's easier not to dwell on the question when Bram is busy with his sister's surgery, but I miss him.

He took most of the week off from work, so I'm no longer seeing him every day. I miss his constant presence in the enclosure, the clanks of his jewelry and the colorful prisms of light it refracts onto the changing area walls as he gets ready before and after our shifts. His smile, his hugs, the way he shines all made my days so much brighter.

We still text daily, so I know he's doing alright, if stressed about Winny's recovery and Seb not being around as much. He seems down though.

And he takes longer than usual to reply to my texts, but I chalk that up to being busy with his sister.

While Bram handles his other responsibilities, I focus on spending time with Myra instead of worrying about how my mate is doing. She's happier about going to school with her new teacher. And ever since she let word get out that she's an omega, Wendle has kept his mouth shut about her parentage entirely.

Traditional grizzlies don't mess with an omega. Not even one who is still a cub. She's happier than she's been since starting third grade at her new school this fall. Or maybe since Wendle's birthday party last spring. When the other bear cub and his family made it clear that she didn't belong with them. All because they don't approve of a single alpha parent.

Now she's found places where she belongs. Other grizzly shifters who don't care about her species. People outside her immediate family who include her and let her connect with her heritage.

"Papa, is Bram going to visit again soon?" Myra asks as I drive her home from Mom's on Thursday evening. It's been a long week of not seeing him at work. Funny how fast I went from dreading his presence in my habitat to missing him. My bear wants him close, even just for a moment, to reassure myself that my mate is alright after his heat. I want to bury my face in his neck and breathe in his sweet vanilla, citrus, and burnt pineapple scent.

"Do you want him to?" I glance back at her in the rearview mirror. It's not a long drive, but I always appreciate these moments where we can have each other's full focus. Not counting that I have to pay attention to the road. Luckily, there isn't much traffic on the residential roads between Mom's place and home.

"Yeah. He's nice," Myra says.

"He is."

"Gramma says that just because an alpha and omega mate during a heat, it doesn't mean they want to *be* mates."

Myra squirms in her seat, the motion drawing my eye. She looks concerned, but not upset.

"She's right. And lots of shifters have multiple mates or choose never to mate at all. "

"Did you choose not to mate with my omega dad?"

I swallow hard, unsure how to answer that without throwing Arnie under the bus.

"It's okay if you don't want a mate, Papa. Only, you should tell Bramble that, because I think he really likes you."

"I really like him too. And to answer your other question, I'd like to find a mate, Myra. But relationships can get complicated."

"So, does that mean you and Bram are going to be mates now? Or is that complicated too?"

"It's too soon to say for certain, but I'd like to

be with Bram for as long as he'll have me."

"And have more cubs with him? I'll be the best big sister."

"We'll see about that." I hedge. I want more cubs, but if creep changes our plans and Bram can't get pregnant, I still want to be with him.

"If Bram is your mate, can I call him my step-dad?" Myra plows on with her questions, oblivious to the melancholy turn of my thoughts.

"You'll have to ask him that."

"Okay. I will. You should invite him over for dinner again. He hasn't come over all week."

"Oh, should I?" I suppress a snort of laughter. My bossy girl certainly knows what she wants, and she isn't shy about asking me for it.

"Yes. Make your baked strawberry salmon. It's so yummy."

"You just want the strawberry glaze," I tease her.

"Papa, you want to impress him by being a good provider, right? So you should make your best dish."

"What if he doesn't like seafood?"

Myra rolls her eyes, declaring with all the certainty of a young bear who can't imagine anyone not enjoying one of her favorite meals, "Everyone likes salmon, Papa. Besides, I saw him eating fish at the Denning Night feast."

"I'll ask if he likes it," I concede.

We drive in silence for a while. As we're turning onto our cul-de-sac, Myra asks, "So, are you going to invite him?"

"I will. Have you finished your homework?"

She grimaces. "Everything but the math. I don't get it."

"I'll help you before we eat."

"But you'll call him?"

"I'll call him."

"Good."

I park the car and grab Myra's school bag. She must have brought home more than her math homework; the thing weighs a ton. Myra chatters about her school friends while she cleans out her lunch box and sets up to do her math homework at the kitchen table. I get out ingredients for dinner. Mom has a quilting circle with some friends tonight, so it's just us for dinner, like most Thursdays.

I throw together the ingredients for one pot chicken and mushrooms with noodles and spinach, and toss it into the oven to bake. While dinner cooks, I settle in to help my kid slog through her multiplication assignment. She says she doesn't get it, but she mostly just seems to need reassurance that she's doing the problems correctly. Once I sit with her, she flies through the worksheet.

There's still fifteen minutes left on the oven timer, so I give her permission to play video games in the living room until supper is ready.

"Sweet! Elric is logged into our *Minecraft* server! You should call Bram while we play."

Myra asks if she can use her tablet to voice chat with Elric and Alphonse, her new grizzly cub friend, while they play. She already told me she exchanged information with them. It's no surprise, but it still has my protective instincts on high alert.

She's not allowed to voice chat with strangers, and I'm wary of her talking to older kids online. At the same time, I want to encourage her forming connections with other grizzly shifters and Elric is my boyfriend's sibling. So I grant my permission; with an internet safety refresher that has my kid rolling her eyes at me. It's hard to believe how old she's getting sometimes, how I have to let go a little more every day to give her the independence to keep growing.

"I know not to tell strangers where we live, or like, send inappropriate pictures, Papa. We just wanted to talk about the latest episode of this ghost hunter podcast Elric told me about. We're going to recreate the haunted museum they were exploring in-game. It's a really cool podcast. Bet you'd enjoy it."

"We can listen together sometime," I agree, always glad for bonding experiences even if an amateur ghost-hunting show wouldn't be my top choice for entertainment otherwise.

"Sure. So, you're gonna call him?"

I smile and ruffle her hair. "I'm doing it now." Myra grins and pulls on her headphones as she connects to her friends and loses herself in her game.

I watch over her shoulder while she and two other characters labeled with her friends' names lay out a building foundation on the screen. There's another player, labeled Cory, the youngest of Bramble's siblings. Once Myra settles into her game, I grab my phone and duck into my room to call Bramble. The phone rings for a while before he picks up.

"Hello?" Bram asks, sounding winded.

"Hey, it's me," I say, smiling at the sound of my omega's sweet voice.

"Hey, you." Bram's tone warms. "How's everything?"

"Good. Myra is playing video games with your siblings."

"Elric and Cory?"

"Yeah."

"Ah, fun. They like to build little mini-dungeons and stuff in-game for their friends. I'm sure they'll have a good time."

"How's everything there?"

"Good. Winny is getting released from the hospital first thing tomorrow, so our moms are on a stress-cleaning kick to make sure everything is ready for her. I spent most of the hospital's visiting hours there with her. She isn't happy about having to stay the extra night, but they were worried about her blood levels or something, so they wanted to keep her a little longer."

"And how are you?" It isn't lost on me that he deflected his answer away from himself.

"I'm fine. Did I tell you Seb officially moved out of my place?"

"Oh? How do you feel about that?"

"Dunno. It's weird not having anyone to share my space. It feels too big." He forces a laugh. I get what he's not saying. That he doesn't enjoy being alone. His tiny studio apartment isn't the sort of place I'd ever describe as too big, but I understand what he means. I've been there. Experienced that moment of drinking in the echoing emptiness of a place that used to be shared and noticing all the little touches someone I loved took away with them.

"Think you'll stay living there?"

"Dunno. The lease is month-to-month, but my other option is to move back home. Winny might throttle me for hovering if I do that. I guess I could find roommates. A bunch of my cousins share places in the building, so I could see if one of them would want to move in with me or something. I might just need time to adjust. If I'm carrying, it would be good to have my own space. Seb said as much when we talked."

"But you're lonely?"

"Yeah."

"Well, part of why I called was to invite you over for dinner tomorrow."

"I'll be there. Um, can I bring anything? Is Myra okay with me being there?"

"She suggested it. She likes you." I glance down the hall to be sure Myra is still engrossed in her game. "I haven't seen her take off that charm bracelet you gave her except to shift. You won her over."

"Glitter is magical," Bram says, and there's a world of mischief in that innocuous phrase.

"You are not infecting my home with glitter, Bramble. You're invited to dinner. Craft herpes is not invited."

"Sure, okay. What's Myra's favorite color?"

"She's on a purple kick." I sigh, resigning myself to sparkles everywhere. If my daughter and my mate are happy, I'll learn to live with glitter. Honestly, the thought of Bram as part of my little family makes me smile despite the imminent threat of glitter bombing.

"Perfect. So, I'll see you two tomorrow?"

"Yes. Bring an overnight bag, if you want."

Bram inhales sharply, the sound loud through the phone. I hold my breath, hoping he isn't upset by the offer.

"That is, if your sister won't need you." I rush to backpedal, kicking myself for overstepping. He's been worried about Winny's surgery for months; of course he doesn't want to spend the weekend with me just when she needs his support the most.

"No. That's not it. Winny made it clear I'm overbearing, and that she wants her space once she gets home. Just are you sure? I don't want to, like, overstep or confuse Myra, or anything."

"I'm sure. Myra knows about us; she likes you. And with... well, everything, you're going to be a part of her life now."

"Everything?" Bram's voice is tight and I'm pretty sure I fucked up. "You mean trying to have a clutch? What if I can't? Will you still want me as a mate? What if creep—"

"Yes. I know you want a clutch, but how I feel about you won't change if you can't," I say, hoping he can hear how much I mean it.

"Even if I can't give you more cubs?" He makes the question a challenge.

"Yes." I can give him an unequivocal yes, because he's what I want for my future. "You can still be Myra's step-dad and we can look at fostering more cubs or chicks further down the line if we want more kids. Unless you don't want that with me?" I tack that on at the end as it occurs to me that maybe he's changing his mind. That might be the reason this is suddenly coming up.

"I do. I want a future with you, Ty. A family. Sorry." He sighs and I wish I could wrap him in a hug and assure him everything will be alright. He sounds like he could use that. "I've been kind of a mess since the heat. Hormones. I didn't mean to snap at you."

"It's fine. I get that you're stressed with everything going on. We both want to make this work, so we'll figure it all out. Does starting with family dinner tomorrow and a weekend with just the three of us sound okay?"

"Yeah. I'll see you two tomorrow night, then. And speaking of dinner, I should go find food."

My oven timer beeps, making me chuckle at the timing. "Sounds like it's supper time here too."

We exchange lingering goodbyes until Myra calls for me to turn off the timer and get the food from the oven for us. We eat together, and then I sit with her while she plays more of her game for a little while. Her podcast plays in the background.

The narrators pull me in more than I thought they would and the structure she's building with her friends is impressive. That might just be my parental pride talking, but Myra comes up with some clever little designs in the game, making a tripwire thing that fills a room with zombies. We listen to several old podcast episodes together before I have to remind Myra it's a school night and send her to get ready for bed. And, she's so excited about our weekend plans with Bram, the cub goes right to sleep for once.

CHAPTER 24

Bram

Winny takes one look at me as she walks through the door to our folks' place—our parents trailing behind her—and rolls her eyes.

"You're already itching to take care of everything; I can see it in your face," she accuses.

"Maybe." I try not to look too guilty at being called out. I also try not to stare at the bulky brace on her shoulder. Twiddling with the oversized beads on the chunky bracelet I'm wearing helps me refrain from reaching for the little handbag she's carrying on her good side.

Winny sees right through me. "Uh huh."

"How's your pain?" I ask, hoping to deflect the topic, even though the question itself sort of proves her point. "Don't glare; I'm allowed to care about you."

"Care, yes. Meddle, not so much. I'm actually in less pain now than I was before they put me under. It never healed well. And if it helps to validate your annoying big brother protective streak, you can run to the pharmacy for my meds. I've got this, Bram. Our moms made sure we've got a supply of ice packs for my shoulder brace. I'll call the rehab place for an appointment while you're at the pharmacy. Are you going to hover?"

"No?" I say sheepishly, since that's exactly what I had planned for the day. Not that I'd have called it that, but yeah. I started the day with every intention of being around in case she needs anything.

"Good, I love you, but I don't need you to mother me; I've already got two moms for that," Winny says.

Winny sticks her tongue out at me. That glimpse of the playful sister I've missed since her accident sets a surge of hope fluttering in my chest. I knew this would make things better. I just didn't realize how much the constant pain must have brought her down.

"That's fair enough. I'll grab your meds," I agree.

Winny ruffles my hair with her good hand. "Thanks, bro. Mama has the papers." She tips her head toward our omega mom. Then my sister heads for her room. "I'm ready for a nap, so no rush."

"I'll get it now. So you have everything when you wake up." I turn toward our parents. "Need anything else while I'm at the pharmacy? More ice packs? Anything?"

"We're good for now, dear. Thank you for running errands." Mom pats my cheek as she passes me, taking Winny's bag to her room—and I'm sure helping my sister get settled. I guess I can see her point about all of us smothering her in love. Mama rifles through the stack of hospital paperwork and pulls out the prescriptions and Winny's health card.

The community's collective health plan isn't nearly as comprehensive as what I get through work, but it will help with the cost of Winny's prescriptions. They refused to cover the surgery at first, since their adjudicators didn't consider it medically necessary. As though my sister being in constant pain and all but unable to shift from the badly healed break wasn't important enough to fix.

They called her shoulder reconstruction an elective procedure. In the end, we got a prior authorization saying it was medically necessary. It still makes me mad whenever I think about it, even months after fighting with the company and losing our initial appeals. So I try not to think about it.

The closest pharmacy isn't too far from our rave's building and the friendly alpha rabbit shifter who runs the place wishes Winny well after she fills the prescriptions. I have a date to prepare for once I deliver everything to Winny, so I don't plan to linger.

When I return to my parents' apartment, it's quiet in a way it seldom gets. My sister is still asleep and my three youngest siblings aren't home from school yet.

Mom takes the medications and asks if I'll be back for dinner. It's small talk; I almost always come over for family dinners. It's so routine that I have to catch myself on the verge of agreeing that I'll be there.

"Ye—actually, not tonight." I grin at realizing all over again I get to see my mate and his cub tonight.

"Oh?" Mom gives me one of those all-knowing mom looks. "You have other plans? This wouldn't be about that alpha you spent last weekend with?" She pauses as I flush, then adds, "The same one who spent your heat here with you a few weeks before that?"

"How did you know about that?" I splutter. I told her about last weekend, but I didn't think she knew about Ty spending my first heat here.

"Darling, the entire flock knows you weren't home last weekend. Your car was gone and everything. Elric and Seb seemed to think well of the alpha on Denning Night. He's a bear shifter, right?"

"Yeah. I might spend the weekend with him again. He invited me over."

"I hope you have a pleasant time, then." Mom smiles at me.

"We will. I like him."

"I should hope so, considering the nest Seb said you built in his bed."

Heat suffuses my cheeks and I flash back to being a little kid caught with my hand in the cookie jar. Mom looked at me with that same soft amusement in her eyes. Only back then, all I saw was the stern set of her mouth as she put the cookies on a higher shelf and sent me outside to play. Now she's smiling knowingly at me.

"Um. Yeah. I might've done that. It doesn't mean anything," I say.

Mom's smile slips into a worried frown. "Are you sure about that? You two have been seeing each other for a while now, no?"

My gut reaction is to deny it, but as I consider, I realize I *have* been seeing Ty for a while now. Longer than I've dated anyone else in ages. "Almost two months. And it's kind of serious? It started out casual."

"So it's no longer casual?" Mom asks.

I take a moment to think, then swallow hard. I'm not ready to tell my family that I want a clutch with a bear shifter who already has a child. But I want them to accept Ty as a part of my life. At least enough not to hassle me over spending time with him.

"It's not. I guess it stopped being casual when I wasn't paying attention. He's different. The sort of alpha who wants to protect and provide. He carries around wet wipes for messy emergencies and he always has snacks." I stifle a smile, thinking of the cherries I now know he carries around just for me, since Myra won't touch them.

Ty said the snack stash is for Myra, but I've seen him share with others. He's shared them with me when my stomach grumbles after we fool around.

I love Tyson. It's strange for that to hit me like an epiphany after all the time we've spent together lately. After sharing two heats with him and hoping to conceive a clutch with him.

More than love, I want him to be my mate. My partner in all things, raising our hatchlings, and growing old together. I love him, and I want to tell him as much. No more holding back feelings to maintain the status quo.

Mom is smiling at me again. She cups my cheek in her hand and I crane into the touch, sort of like offering my crown for her to preen, if we were in our feathers. We aren't, but she still cards her nails along my scalp affectionately.

"I'm happy for you, Bramble. You're always working so hard to look after everyone else. I'm glad you found someone who takes care of you too."

"Yeah. Ty does. Anyway, I'll call, but don't expect me home before Monday," I say, kissing Mom's cheek.

Then I slip the envelope of money disbursed

from the fundraiser to cover Winny's first PT session underneath the pharmacy bag, and go to meet Ty and Myra for supper.

CHAPTER 25

Ty

I spend most of Friday fretting over tonight. This will be the first time Bram spends the night while Myra is home. His heat last weekend doesn't count. We've been dating for a while, but having him and Myra both under my roof strikes me as a huge relationship milestone.

It seems like the first major step to blending our family. My girl is bouncing off the walls with excitement about having him over. She is still wearing the bracelet he gave her at Denning Night and she hasn't stopped asking me questions about raven shifters and their culture since she met him.

It's disconcerting to realize that I actually know some answers, just from listening to casual comments Bram has made over the past couple of months. For all that we claimed to want a casual fling, this has turned into anything but casual. Bram is my mate. My bear has yearned to provide that possessive protectiveness toward him for a while now. He's mine to care for.

That's probably why I need this dinner to be perfect. It's the same urge to care for my partner that I loved to indulge with Arnie when we were together. The same need to take care of Bram that I've always felt toward Myra.

Cooking for him feels right. Fussing over the presentation until the dining room looks as close to something out of a foodie magazine as I can manage calms my nerves. At least until I get home from picking up Myra from school.

Myra takes one look at my day's work. She giggles when she sees the cloth napkins I had to dig out of storage to fold for each place setting. It looks nice, with places for three. More than nice, it looks right.

"Papa, we barely use paper napkins. Do you think we really need all this?" She pokes the folded cloth, tipping it over and ruining the fan effect.

"We do. Need I remind you that impressing him was your plan?" I pluck up the napkin and flap it at her before I fix it so that it sits just right on Bram's plate. "Now, shoo; don't you have homework or video games to do until he gets here?"

Myra snickers. "Sure thing, Papa Bear. Don't be nervous, he likes you too. Elric says so." She leaves to turn on her video game console before I can follow up on that line of questioning.

The food occupies my attention until Bram arrives. I'm sweaty and anxious as I open the door. I feel like an adolescent on my first date as I invite Bram inside. Until he pulls me into a kiss. I kiss him back, holding my omega in my arms, unable to resist the urge to be close to him, to scent him.

I snuffle deep at his pulse point, and try to quash my disappointment that his scent remains unchanged. It's okay if he isn't carrying a clutch. We have plenty of time to try. This is all so new; I try to tell myself that it's probably for the best if he isn't. And anyway, it's still early. Less than a week since his last heat ended. More than a week since it began, though. He could be carrying.

"Hi." He gives me a breathless grin.

I still have my arms wrapped tight around him, and no desire to let go.

"Hi." I grin back, enjoying the comfort of his warmth pressed close to me. Myra's voice drifts in from the other room from her game's voice chat. I clear my throat and step back. "Come on in; dinner's almost ready."

Bram holds up a bottle. "I, uh, brought sparkling cider. Since, you know, kids."

For a second, I think he means that he's pregnant, but his scent still hasn't changed. I just checked. And then he gestures vaguely toward the interior of my house where Myra is gaming with his siblings. I take the sparkling cider from him.

"Oh, white grape, that's her favorite."

"I know, I had Elric ask. Is that alright?"

"Sure. I guess they'll be family, too, if this works out between us."

"Yep. So, how was work without me this week?"

"Boring. Freya and Theron took advantage of your absence to use your favorite perch. Considering the way they eye-fucked each other while I was getting dressed, I assume they, uh, made use of the locker area."

Bram chuckles. "Well, I guess we don't have much room to complain about that, all things considered."

"Not really, no. It's good that you'll be back on Monday though, since they mentioned taking Theron's heat leave soon."

Bram nods. "Makes sense."

I smile at the way the motion makes his necklaces clink together on his chest, I've missed that sound this week. He grins at me and gives me another quick kiss.

We make more small talk about work as I lead Bram to the kitchen. Myra pauses her game and runs over to see what he brought when he holds up the sparkling juice.

"My favorite! Thanks, Bramble. Papa said you're staying the weekend?"

"That's the plan," Bram says.

"Cool. Papa, can I show him my room?"

"Sure," I agree. "Dinner's almost ready, though, so make it quick."

Myra takes my mate's hand and drags him down the hall to her room. I can hear her chattering his ears off about her decorative choices and how I wouldn't let her get a glittery wall hanging, so she asked Santa for it.

She initially wanted to get this gold glittery paint for an accent wall, but I'd refused to allow it. Mostly because it seems like too big a project and the dark glitter paint might be hard to cover up if we ever need to sell this place.

The gaudy tapestry is her solution to my objections. It's also expensive. And from what her friend's parents told me, it sheds sparkles everywhere. Well, crap on a stick. She's getting old for Santa, but I don't want to spoil the magic by denying her something she's wanted for months, ever since Jenny got one for her room.

I listen to them laughing with a grin on my face. They talk about which shade of purple would go best with her style as I pull the salmon from the oven. Contentment fills me as I'm basting the salmon with the glaze once more, listening to my kid and Bram talking like they've known each other for ages. I dress the salad and set the table.

I bought an antipasto platter at the grocery store too, but looking at the spread already laid out, that might be going overboard. Fresh bread and butter, the salmon on a bed of rice, and salad are enough. We can save the platter for a picnic or something.

Bram and Myra return to the kitchen and all my awkwardness and worry fall away as my mate and my daughter devour the meal I prepared for them. It feeds my inner alpha to watch them enjoy something I provided.

After food, we all pitch in to put away the leftovers. There's a lot, which Myra teases me about as she helps load the dishwasher, but I don't mind since I know the kid will devour them tomorrow. I wash the larger pots and pans and Bram helps me dry them, over my protests that he's our guest. Between the three of us, we have everything clean in short order.

Myra breaks out a multiplayer party game on her console and ropes the two of us into playing with her. My heart melts even more, watching Bram play video games with my kid and me. As though there is nothing else he'd rather do and nowhere else he'd rather be than following the in-game dictates of an eight-year-old with a very specific architectural vision.

Myra teases me about being old and bad at games, but all three of us spend most of the evening laughing. After Myra tires of making us build her a virtual fortress in *Minecraft*, we put in a movie.

The evening is perfection, sitting between my mate and my daughter fulfills me. I've long since given up even hoping to share this sort of casual intimacy with a partner. I thought those dreams were in my past, but maybe with Bram, I can have another chance at love.

This once, I let Myra stay awake late for the movie, but she falls asleep on my shoulder midway through.

"I think the kiddo conked out." Bram gestures toward Myra.

"She did."

"Do you want to watch the rest of the movie or go to bed?" Bram gives me a suggestive smile, licking his lips like he wants to devour me with kisses. He adjusts his collection of necklaces and the gesture makes me smile; it's just so Bram.

"What movie?" I reach for the remote and turn off the TV. Bram's grin widens at my response.

"Mhm, I can think of something else I'd rather watch." He winks at me.

"I'd make suggestions, but not in front of the kid." I ease her off my arm so I can get up to carry her to her room. "Did you bring a bag?"

"Yeah. Left it in my car, I didn't want to be too forward." Bram shrugs.

"I invited you to stay, bird." I lean in to give him a peck on the lips.

Bram tips up his chin to accept the kiss. I linger, savoring his sweetness for a long moment. I am falling for him.

"Go get your bag while I tuck this one into bed. I'll be right back," I say.

He gets up, stretching onto his toes, then he heads toward the door. I gather Myra in my arms and carry her to her room. She stirs a little, rolling onto her side as I tuck her under her blankets, but she settles when I rub her back. I hum a lullaby under my breath, watching her sleep for a few breaths, savoring these tender moments.

Before turning out the lights, I make sure the nightlight she swears she's too big for now has a full charge. Then I set it to the pink LED mode that projects stars onto her ceiling. For mood light—not because she's scared of the dark. *Sure.* Last, I turn on her white noise machine and make it a little louder than usual.

I turn to check on my kiddo one last time. She's still asleep, her expression soft, breathing deep and steady. I brush her bangs out of her face and kiss her temple.

"Sweet dreams, Myra." I turn to leave.

Bram is just letting himself inside with a duffel when I ease Myra's door shut behind me. He grins and waves at me across the living room. I feel as giddy as a teenager with a crush at the sight of him there in my home. It feels right for him to be here. All the long days of missing him at work melt away as the two of us meet in the hallway, his arms going around my neck as he drops his bag there to hug me. I loved sharing family time with him earlier, but this is pure bliss.

This moment, easing shut my kid's door and stepping into my mate's embrace, could have been plucked straight from my hazy imaginings of what family life would be like, but it's something I've never had before. Bram melts against me, his beaded necklaces press into my chest. He tugs them out of the way and smiles up at me.

"Bedtime for us too?" he asks with a glint in his eye.

"Definitely," I agree.

Bram bends to scoop up his overnight bag, and I let myself ogle him. He catches me looking and waggles his butt at me. "Bet you missed this all week, huh?"

"I missed *you*, bird." I reach for his hip and turn him to face me for a chaste kiss. He opens to me. The eager way he deepens our kiss tells me that he missed me just as much. So does his needy moan as I pull away before we get carried away right outside Myra's room. I want to get him in bed and take my time loving my omega.

"You should take me to bed and show me just how much you missed me," Bram teases, echoing my thoughts. I tangle our fingers and lead him down the hall.

With a shared urgency, we retire to my bed. Where I make love to him. I love watching him relaxed and carefree as he rides me. His face an open book of pure pleasure as he comes, eyes heavy-lidded, mouth slack. I feel a fierce alpha pride deep in my chest at how bonelessly content he looks sprawled across my bed, like he belongs there. The last bit of tension leaves his shoulders as I clean us up and he drifts off to sleep in my arms. This is where I always want him to be, right here beside me as we make our family together.

In the morning, we're up and making breakfast by the time Myra climbs out of bed, seemingly unphased by my adult sleepover. If anything, her sleepy smile at seeing Bram still here says she likes waking up to the two of us in pajamas bantering over French toast and fruit salad. And it's another tiny moment that feels completely right. Cooking and laughing together like a family.

Bram spends the entire day with us on Saturday. We take Myra to her dance class, eat a picnic lunch at the park, then return home for more video games. It's all so routine, but it feels new and wonderful to do it with Bram.

My heart swells with happiness watching him laughing with my kid, teasing her playfully and making her giggle. Our eyes meet over her head as the three of us are walking home, and we both just smile. Like there is nowhere else either of us wants to be than strolling through the park with Myra as she prattles on about what she's been building in *Minecraft*.

We have last night's leftovers for dinner, and watch the rest of our movie before bed. And the very fact that there is nothing special about leftovers makes this feel so much more real. You don't feed a guest leftovers; that's for family or maybe close friends. I can picture a lifetime of this with Bram, normal days going about our lives together. Raising kids together.

I invite Bram to spend the night again, and he agrees. I tuck Myra into bed while he calls his family and check on his sister. When Bram joins me in my bed, we come together without our usual urgency. He fucks me slow and gently, both of us relishing the chance to take our time together and enjoy each other.

Bram's body is familiar by now. After nearly two months of regular sex, I know what turns him on, but I still love the chance to explore him unhurriedly. No need for either of us to be elsewhere or worry about getting caught, since the door is locked and Myra is asleep.

We can both focus on the moment. Every hitch in his breath thrills me. Every shiver of his skin as I run my fingers over a sensitive spot fills me with satisfaction at knowing another person in this intimate way. I delight in his smiles and his pleasure.

Bram takes his time with me too. He lathes my nipples with his tongue, sucking and teasing them into hard little peaks as he jerks my dick, edging me for ages. I return the favor, both of us holding back, drawing out our time together until neither of us can last for a moment longer and our slow and sensual exploration ends in mutual orgasms.

Once again, we fall asleep together, for the second time outside his heats, and I can't seem to help the secret hope taking root in my heart that someday this will be how we end every night, tangled together in a shared bed with our mingled scents all around us.

From the way Bram clings to me in his sleep like a limpet, he's a cuddler too. This weekend is making it abundantly clear to me that Bram fits with Myra and me. No matter what happens with his fertility, I want to make Bram a permanent part of my family.

Sunday morning, I wake up with my nose buried in my omega's neck, inhaling the nectar-sweet scent of him. He smells different today. Still musky with feather dust, his unique citrus and vanilla scent and what I now know is the burnt pineapple scent of his preen oil, but more vibrant. There's an underlying sweetness that's becoming more pronounced and my alpha side instinctively knows why his scent has changed.

Before I'm even fully awake, I inhale the new aroma as deep into my lungs as possible with my human form. My bear can't get enough of Bram's scent, altered by his hormones changing to support a pregnancy. My omega is pregnant with my cubs. No need for him to take a static human pee test. I'd recognize that change in his pheromones anywhere. My snuffling at his neck wakes Bram.

He giggles at my nosing and licking along his throat. My bear wants to shift and use our better senses to take his essence deep into my lungs. I long to make him a part of my essence. More than I already have.

"Hey, stop that! It tickles, Ty."

Bram shoves my face out of his neck and I try to look contrite, despite wanting nothing so much as to taste more of him.

"Sorry. You smell amazing."

Bram's mouth falls open, and he stares at me. "Are you saying...?" He presses a hand to his abdomen. I wouldn't expect him to register the changes in his own scent.

I nod. "You smell pregnant, Bramble. We're going to have a cub."

"No." Bramble shakes his head, and my heart lurches up into my throat at his denial. Terrified he might bring all my fledgling hopes and dreams crashing to the ground. His beatific smile and his pleased scent belie the words. He wants a clutch with me. "Not a cub; we're going to have *another* cub. We—er, you—already have Myra."

That chokes me up, that he already sees my girl as part of his family. That he's already saying she won't be any different to him than the cubs of his own body. I didn't think I could fall more in love with him, but it turns out that Bramble has an endless capacity to make me fall for him.

"We're having another cub," I agree. Then

I can't help but kiss my omega, tasting his sweetness and rutting my throbbing morning erection against his answering hardness. We frot until I can't resist the urge to taste him.

"Want to suck you, omega mine," I breathe out the request between desperate kisses. Bram nods, still rutting into me.

"Sixty-nine," he pants.

I turn to position myself over his body. Line up my dick with his lips even as I pull him free of his pants to lap up as much of his sweet essence as I can get. I suckle on his cock, drawing out his arousal, breathing in his musk. I savor every moment of making love to him.

Bram sucks just the head of my cock at first. When he tries to take me deeper, he gags. That has my balls drawing up tight. And the thought that it might be my cubs in his belly making his gag reflex more sensitive than usual has my knot tingling on the verge of release. This primal part of me relishes marking him as my mate. Bram lathes my length with his tongue and I push down on his cock, taking him to the back of my throat. I encourage him to thrust in deeper, swallow around him, knead his perfectly plump ass with my hands.

He bucks up, the sweeter-than-usual flavor of him bursting over my tongue. I want to drink him down, hold him in my mouth all day.

The sound of the bathroom fan turning on down the hall alerts me to the fact we might not have long before Myra knocks on the locked door. The thought of an imminent interruption lends a new urgency to our movements and I increase the suction on Bram's shaft.

Bram must have heard it too, or he's close to the edge. Either way, I need to drink down my omega's load, need to give him release and savor my time with him. He moans around the head of my dick. The same needy sound I know means he's close as his hips buck up off the bed.

Then he swirls his tongue around the head of my dick in a surge of pleasure and I suck him hard, bury my nose in his pubes. It's not enough to tip him over the edge, so I finger his hole. I find the nerves that send him flying into his orgasm.

Bram's cum spurts into my mouth and I savor every drop of his release. The sweetness of him overwhelms me. His hips thrust against my face. His voice breaks as he cries my name. It all blends with the sensation of his mouth closing around my cockhead in a symphony of pleasure.

"Bram, ungh," I moan his name, the sound nothing but humming vibrations with my mouth still full of him. I squeeze his ass harder.

I rock into his mouth. He gags again and pulls off of me, stroking me as I come on his chest in thick white jets.

I let his spent cock slip from my lips and turn to face my lover. The alpha side of me loves to see him marked with my cum. Our scents should always be mingled like that. I want to breathe in mate and family and home forever. I kiss my omega, nuzzling into his neck to get another whiff of the intoxicating scent of him bearing my cubs.

Bram sighs, then chuckles.

"What's funny?" I ask.

"You. You're going to spend the next few months scenting me every chance you get, aren't you?" He sounds resigned, but when I glance at him, he's wearing a sappy, delighted smile. And he presses my face back into the crook of his neck.

"You smell good." I lick a kiss to his throat.

"I'm really pregnant?" Bram asks, insecurity sneaking into his tone.

"Yeah, my bear is sure of it. You're bearing a cub. At least one cub. I don't know if there's a way to tell if there's more than one or which form they're in. Other than ultrasound. Not sure how soon they can tell." I shrug, vaguely remembering an appointment to find out how many cubs we were expecting with Myra. Just the one. They said that was common for younger omegas, that or having large litters.

"The doctors at the clinic back home can do an ultrasound about four weeks after a heat to see how big the clutch is. I bet they could tell if I'll be laying an egg or having a live birth. I'll make an appointment tomorrow."

"Perfect. Let me know when it is and I'll be there. If you want."

"I want. You're my mate, and you'll be the hatchling's Papa."

"You're good with that?"

"Yeah. Myra already calls you Papa/Mapa, so I figured that's what all our kids will call you, and I'll be the new baby's dad."

Our kids. Bram said *our* kids. He might just mean the cub or cubs that he's currently carrying, but I don't think so. I'm pretty sure he's already including Myra in that number. His in his heart, if not by blood. He cares about her and seems to genuinely enjoy spending time with her. My heart is full to bursting at that thought. I want that with Bram. Someone who wants to be a parent with me. Children, including Myra, who are ours, not just mine.

From now on, I'll have a partner by my side. To share the burdens and the joys of parenthood. I've always had people to help me. From the neighbors who offered to babysit and teach Myra about her grizzly heritage to my mom. But parenting with Bram will be different. More of a partnership. I can't wait to experience everything with him.

The door rattles as Myra knocks. "Can I come in?" she calls through the door.

"Just a second, baby." I call. Then I grab the wet wipes from the bedside table.

"Always prepared," Bram teases as we do a hasty cleanup job. We stand and steal one last lingering kiss before I turn toward the door.

"I'm going to shower while you break the news to her. If you want to tell her?" Bram backs toward my ensuite to rinse away the evidence of our morning sex.

"Nothing to break. She's going to be thrilled. She'll want to name the cub and start calling you her step-dad."

Bram's eyes widen. "Step-dad?"

I shrug self-consciously. "We're mates, right?"

"Yeah. And you two are a package deal. I just don't want to move too fast or step on toes. I know I'm not her parent."

"Whose toes?"

"Myra's and yours. And maybe her omega dad's?"

"Arnie abandoned her as a newborn." I shake my head at the idea of Bram taking a place that Arnie's actions have made it clear he doesn't want. "She doesn't have an omega parent. But with you in our lives, I think that could change. If that's something you want. She'd be thrilled to call you her step-dad. You've already been more involved with her after a couple of weeks of knowing her than he ever was. I don't expect you two to blend seamlessly into a family overnight, but she likes you."

I don't warn him not to break my baby's heart. He's not the sort of person to take his responsibilities lightly.

"I'm glad. And I'll follow your lead on how involved you want me to be with her." Bram strokes my cheek.

"You're doing fine," I assure him, capturing his hand to kiss his fingers. "I'm going to let the kid in. Are you ready?"

"I will be once I rinse off." Bram grimaces and gestures to his chest.

My bear appreciates seeing how I marked him, but I can understand why he'd want to get cleaned up properly as soon as possible. I drag him into one more lingering kiss before going to see what Myra needs from us. I'm going to be all glowy about that 'us' for the foreseeable future. Bram and I are an 'us', and I love it.

I love him, but I don't think right after finding out he's pregnant is the best time to tell him. That probably ranks up there with declarations made during sex, the sort of thing that you almost have to brush off as a heat of the moment blurt. No, I want him to know without a shadow of a doubt that I mean it when I tell him I love him for the first time. I am going to tell him. Soon.

CHAPTER 26

Bram

Ty and Myra invite me over more often after Ty scents the clutch growing in my belly. First every weekend, and then a week night here and there, until, by the time the pregnancy is showing, I'm spending most nights with them.

The doctor at the shifter clinic that most of my rave sees did an early ultrasound. She took one look at the screen and declared herself uncomfortable handling a mixed species pregnancy. I hadn't even told her that the alpha parent is a bear yet.

Turns out, I didn't have to, since the ultrasound revealed that my clutch consists of an egg and a baby. She wrote me a referral to a shifter specialist who handles high-risk pregnancies. Felix pulled some strings to have the zoo get me telehealth appointments with the top doctor in the field when I asked him who he'd recommend.

So I get regular follow-ups to be sure the cub and the egg are both developing at a compatible rate. Since we don't know much about mixed species clutches, I've got all kinds of doctors involved in my care. Both the zoo's regular staff medics and the high-risk doctor who seems fascinated with detailing every aspect of my babies' growth and development.

The doctors I've seen all agree that I'm incredibly lucky to have conceived during the denning season. My cub implanted right away instead of the usual several month delay if I'd had a spring heat. They're not sure whether delayed implantation would actually happen, since I'm an avian omega. But I've been scolded enough to believe it's not worth taking the risk for future heats.

Now that I know I can conceive, I'll definitely take ovulation limiting medications next time. If there is a next time. With my clutch growing inside me, the fear of creep taking my heats away for good isn't as sharp. I want to share as many heats as I have left with Ty, but we've discussed it and we'll still be happy together without heat sex.

The immediate implantation means the almost four months that the raven egg needs to mature before I lay my clutch should coincide nicely with the cub's development. I get regular growth assessment ultrasounds, just to be sure. And to document the unique nature of my clutch. My raven preens at the idea of my clutch being special, so I was happy to agree to the scans.

When I go in for my appointments, Ty comes with me to all of them. Nominally to hold my hand, but I think he's more worried than I am about the clutch. Granted, after the first month passes, I can feel our little cub kicking my bladder at all hours and the egg's quick pulse beats against my skin.

The cub means I had to stop shifting sooner in the pregnancy than would otherwise be necessary, just in case my bird form isn't compatible with their anatomy. Which means I'm on leave from work. It's paid leave, at least. Since part of the zoo's mission is to support shifter fertility, they offer generous parental benefits for alphas and omegas alike.

That's another reason I've been spending more time with Ty and Myra. Since I'm home anyway, I've been picking her up from school. At first, it was just a day here and there. Then alternating days with her grandmother, but lately I pick her up three days a week. Myra's grandmother takes the fourth. Ty and I pick her up together on his Fridays off. We've bonded a lot and I love that she's excited to meet her little siblings.

She reads her books aloud to them most

nights, or sings them songs. She loves putting her hands on my belly to feel the cub kick and trace the smooth shell of the egg. Both babies are getting uncomfortably large toward the start of my third month. But I still try to do fun things with Myra. Even as the rapid changes to my body from the accelerated timeline of a shifter pregnancy throw off my balance and create near constant aches and itchy skin.

When we're together, Myra and I have fun. From art projects that her grumpy dad would veto over their messiness, to video games, to shopping for her room. I also help with organizing Myra's ninth birthday party.

She's getting to an age where the cutesy cartoon prints and stuffed toys in her room are being replaced with pop star posters and gadgets. I suspect my mate is having a hard time watching his baby grow up, because he keeps putting off the changes she wants to make to update her style. I still ask before we buy anything major, and Ty wasn't opposed to her requests, just not ready for change.

Recently, I started bringing sticks over with me. A few from my nest, so it will smell like my family. I don't want to impose, and their place is cozy, so I stash them out in Myra's disused treehouse in the backyard. The ladder is rickety, so I bring a hammer to secure the rungs better. And replace a few of the loose boards.

Before I know it, I've moved the entire nest

structure and filled the bowl where my egg will stay with Ty's fur, scraps from Ty's mom's sewing projects. An old stuffy that Myra said I could borrow. There are bits of my family in there too. Feathers, mostly. A lock of Winny's hair, since she doesn't like to shift as much anymore, though she's healed enough that she can shift without pain at this point. She says that's enough, and I agreed to take her at her word about it.

I've collected all kinds of things to make the nest soft for my egg and the cub. Myra got me some more of her and her dad's stuffies from her gramma, Byron and Lux, to add to the bowl. They make it extra special, but it's still not quite complete. Actually, surveying the finished nest, I can see that my initial worries about the nest being too small were right. It needs to be bigger for a cub. Much bigger since I won't be able to shift during labor. Not until our cub is born.

Myra is inside finishing her homework and Ty will be home soon, so I really don't have much time to work on the expansion tonight. But the big round swell of my belly gives the task a certain urgency. I need a safe place for the clutch. And soon. My doctors say that, at just over three months, the clutch could safely be born anytime now.

The egg will need to incubate after that, but the cub should be healthy and whole and able to shift into their human form within the first month. That worried Ty, since Myra had her shift pretty much from the start. Our doctor explained that sometimes hybrids take longer to find their shift.

I want to meet my babies, but I'm also relishing the time with them connected to me. Growing safe within my body, where I can protect them from everything and nurture them. Where my alpha can hold all three of us safe and warm in her big, strong arms.

Ty finds me still in the treehouse, rearranging sticks to expand the nest structure. She's got her long winter jacket on, it's still a bulky winter coat, but it's cut to emphasize curves more than the one they wear on their more masc days. She gathers me into her arms and kisses me.

"Darling, what are you doing out here in the freezing cold?" They ask, concern furrowing their brow and making my stomach roil that I'm worrying my mate.

"Nesting."

"I can see that, and your nest is just as lovely here as it was in your apartment, but I think we should consider moving this inside." Ty wraps an arm around me, as if to guide me into the house.

"There's not enough room. The babies don't have a room."

To my utter mortification, I burst into tears at the overwhelming weight of my dilemma. It's not just that I want to expand the nest. It's about making physical space for the babies. And for me. This is Myra and Ty's house. They've never done anything to make me feel unwelcome in it— quite the contrary—but it's still not my space, no matter how good I feel when I'm with them and how much I've come to treasure our increasingly common sleepovers.

My space is a tiny studio apartment that smells stale with disuse and my own scent. Now that Seb has moved out, it's not a place that smells of family at all. I hate going there alone. Another reason I spend most nights wrapped in my alpha's embrace these days.

Ty holds me tight, rocks me from side to side, takes my sudden emotional outburst in stride. "It's okay. We'll make room for them. For our whole family. Bramble, it's okay."

"It's not!" I wail, surrendering to their hold despite my defiance.

"Okay, yeah, it's not. But we'll fix it, and until we do, I'm here." She rubs my back and lets me cry myself out, clinging to their jacket like my life depends on it. When I'm reduced to the occasional sniffle, and less overwrought, I pull away from their embrace.

"Sorry." I wipe away my tears. "Didn't mean to blubber all over you."

"Nothing to apologize for. Want to tell me what's bothering you though?"

"The nest is too small for a cub."

"So you want to make it bigger?"

"Yes."

"Okay. Can I ask you something?" Ty asks.

"Yeah."

"Will you move in with Myra and me officially?" Ty doesn't stop touching me, rubbing my arms to offer much-needed comfort.

I hesitate. This is what I've wanted. She's hinted about me living with them since my heat, but I've always deflected. I'm not ready to move away from the rave and all the supportive shifters who live in my community. It's struck me as a catch twenty-two that I couldn't solve from the start. I want to be close to my family, but which one? The family I'm making with Ty can never replace my flock. I need them both.

I don't know what to do. The idea of bringing my babies home to the studio apartment where I nominally live is impractical. But I still want to raise my babies surrounded by the rave's tight-knit shifter community, like I was.

Family dinners and living wing-to-beak with loving cousins, aunts, uncles, and their doting grandmothers. Even my crabby grandfather is excited to welcome my clutch. It would be perfect if not for the lack of Ty and Myra in that equation. I want my babies to grow up under the same roof as their sister and other parent too.

But moving in with them means cutting off my daily ties to my family—not just for me, but for the two babies I'm carrying. I can't imagine a scenario where I'm no longer involved in the life and community I've been a part of from my hatching. I can't do that.

Ty wants to be an involved parent. So, if we live apart, it would mean leaving our kids with them —at least some of the time—when I'm home with the rave. I try to imagine kissing my babies goodbye and leaving them here with Ty and Myra.

Saying goodbye to all of them every time I want to see my family is even worse than the idea of exiling myself to the suburbs of Portland. It's like a pit of despair opening inside my belly. I know I should have realized this sooner. Should've talked it out with Ty when that first heat didn't result in a pregnancy at the least.

It's no excuse, but I got swept up in baby fever and stress over whether I'm developing creep and having my dreams so close I could touch them. Now I'm worried that I might've jumped from the nest before my feathers were properly fledged on that one. It's been like that for a while, but I haven't been able to give voice to the problem.

I haven't wanted to push Ty for more. Not when I already pushed about having a clutch together so early in our relationship. I can't ask Ty and Myra to move too. So I've been pushing back the living arrangements conversation that I know we need to have. To avoid the tough choice of what to do.

"What's wrong? I thought... I mean, you spend

most nights here already. We agreed that we'd raise the babies together. I thought this was a formality. Don't you want to live together?" And now I'm hurting them with my indecision.

I shake my head. "It's not that I don't want to be with you. I just… this is *your* home. The two of you."

Her features soften with compassion as understanding dawns. "You don't feel like there's room for you here?"

"Yeah. I'm sorry. I want to live together. All of us." I cradle my round belly in my arms. Ty rests their warm palm over my hands.

"What if we all find a new place together?" they ask. "In Four Corners. So we'll be close to your family."

Relief swamps through me, hope filling the empty chasm of sadness that's been growing for months now. Since Seb moved out, really. "You'd move for me?"

"*With* you. Yes. I want to live with my family, bird. My entire family. Make a home with you and our cubs. I own this house outright, so it shouldn't be a problem to sell. Let me talk about it with Myra and ask a realtor about our options. Okay?" Ty rubs my belly. I give her a watery smile. My raven loves the idea of them helping us select the perfect place for our nest before the clutch arrives.

"I can ask around about family properties in Four Corners. There's an area with a lot of mixed species families that might be a good fit. What about Myra, though? I don't want to interfere with her school."

"She can finish the year here and start at the shifter school Alphonse and Elric and Cory attend in the fall. This past year has been rough for her anyway, and she's gotten closer with those three. It would be a good move for her. To be with other kids who accept all of her. And she can still keep in touch with Jenny. Her best friend's family lives near Mom."

My elation dims at the reminder that she and Myra have family too. They're as close to their mom as I am with my parents. "What about moving further from your mother and Mrs. Grund?"

"We'll still see them plenty. Four Corners might be a bit more of a drive, but it's still close enough to the city for frequent visits. And Mom has mentioned downsizing for a while now. Who knows, she might even move to Four Corners too. And Mrs. Grund moved to a retirement community last year, anyway. We still call her our neighbor and go to visit regularly, but there's really nothing to keep us in this house. Not if you aren't comfortable. Let's look at houses. I can't promise that we'll be moved in before the babies come, but we can start the ball rolling. And we can start making space for our entire family by moving your nest inside where it's warm and there's room for everyone."

I hold my breath as she reaches for the bowl of the nest, where the eggs will nestle. I expect my raven to bristle at anyone interfering with it, but my mate is different. They're helping, and it's a welcome aid. A relief that she's improving the nest for our kids. It really is too small for a cub. And far too cold out here.

The nest should obviously be inside. Even if I do prefer the security of being up in a tree to any of the potential spots inside my mate's ground level home. Still, with a big strong alpha bear to protect our clutch, it will be safe enough.

I hug Ty awkwardly from behind, my belly keeping me from getting as close to her as I'd prefer. They turn to hug me tight and nuzzle into my neck, still unable to get enough of my scent while I'm carrying our clutch.

I'm just considering the logistics of a quickie out here—and whether Myra will remain occupied long enough for us to try it—when her voice calls for us.

"Dad? Are you out there? Is Mapa with you? They brought in groceries, but I can't find her now."

Ty and I exchange a look and I know my eyes are comically wide and probably wet with unshed tears at hearing her call for me. It's the first time she's called me that. Dad. Before today, she called me Bram. Or referred to me as her new step-dad. Or as the dad to her baby siblings. Dad. Her dad. I love the sound of it. It's as though she's inviting me into her life and her family, sharing Ty with me. Myra's words and acceptance of me as her mapa's partner plays a key role in transforming the three of us into a family unit.

I choke down the swell of emotion and call back to her. "We're in the treehouse."

Ty gives me an adoring smile. "Is that the first time she's called you Dad to your face?"

"Yeah." I wipe away a happy tear. Darned pregnancy hormones have me crying at the drop of a hat. Yeah, I'm planning on blaming the babies for as long as the excuse holds water, but really this is huge.

"She's been saying it to me off and on for a few weeks now. Asking if 'Dad' is coming over and saying 'Dad' helped with her homework. You good with it?" Ty checks, a wariness in her gaze.

"Yes. I love it. I love her."

"Good." Ty presses a soft kiss to my temple, their lips warm on my chilled skin. "We're a family now, Bramble. And we're going to live together. We'll start the search for the perfect house with room for all of us tonight. We're raising our cubs together."

"All three of our cubs?" I ask, sure I know the answer, but needing to hear it.

"Yes." Ty agrees.

"I want to adopt Myra, if that's okay with you both? I know it's only been a few months, so we can wait. But, eventually, I want to be her dad on paper too. If she agrees to it."

Ty kisses me properly then, and a few moments later, when Myra pokes her head inside, we're still kissing. I love having my alpha's hands pressed flat to my belly, where our cub is rolling, pushing our egg into my ribs. As a raven shifter, home has always been synonymous with family for me. And with Ty holding me while our eldest gives us the universal yuck face of a kid watching a parental PDA, even the drafty treehouse seems like home.

Today can't get any better. Except, as soon as I think that, it does.

Ty breaks the kiss, her forehead resting on mine, to say for the first time, "I love you, Bramble."

My heart is fluttering and my eyes sting with more of those happy tears that I can't hold in any longer.

"I love you too, Ty. And you, Myra." I turn and reach for her, to pull her into a group hug. Myra makes another overdramatic grossed out face, like she's too cool for this, which has me laughing through my snot-faced joyful weeping. Myra melts into the group hug all the same. We hold each other for a while, all of us basking in the warmth of family. I love them, and they love me back. It's everything I wanted and more.

Moving to a new house while heavily gravid with a high-risk pregnancy is a terrible plan. I do not recommend it to anyone. But the perfect little three story three-bedroom condo came on the market just as we were starting our search and Ty and I jumped on it. The thing about living with the rave is that raven shifters are inveterate gossips.

The moment I told my folks that Ty and I were thinking about buying a place in Four Corners, they both had friends who they simply couldn't wait to call. In a matter of hours, they had a lead on the townhouse condo. It's in the same neighborhood where most of the mixed shifter couples with kids live. Close to the school, so Myra can walk with the neighbor kids if she wants. And it's affordable with both our salaries at the zoo.

It's also conveniently close to the building where most of my rave lives. A short walk and an even shorter flight. So we can still have our family dinners. We've even got a big enough kitchen and dining area to invite people over for family dinners at our place with Ty's Mom and my big boisterous family.

The entire process happens at whirlwind speeds with a direct sale between us and the young wolf shifter family who are selling because they've outgrown the place. Part of me hopes we'll outgrow it too. Maybe have another clutch or two in the future.

For now, Myra will have her own room and the babies I'm carrying will share the room across from hers once they're old enough to leave our spacious top-floor suite. There's an unfinished basement that we could remodel to add more bedrooms when the cubs are older. Or turn into an in-law suite for Ty's Mom if she opts to downsize and move in with us.

I'm not supposed to lift anything, so I'm mostly relegated to directing where boxes go and instructing our helpers as they set up our furniture. I tear up at the sight of the nursery. The two cribs ready and waiting for my babies somehow make their imminent arrival seem more real. Myra's room, with all the little touches she and I picked out together, makes me cry.

I love seeing her making her space here in our shared home. Her grandmother and Elric are both helping her hang her new curtains while she makes the bed with the new, more grown up bedding set we picked out together.

When I go upstairs, my mate is fussing over our nest. That was the first thing we moved in once the sale closed. My head is still spinning that we went from talking about a house together to closing the sale in just under three weeks. Now that we're moved out of his old place, he's working with a realtor to stage and list it.

The family who lived here were motivated to sell fast, with their own new baby on the way. It worked out perfectly for us to be moved in before our babies' arrival. If I take into consideration all the false contractions I've been having over the past week, we might be cutting the move close.

It's a relief to have the nest ready at last. Ty helped me to expand it so that it's big enough for our cub. Now the softly padded divot in the middle is large enough to fit my human form and our human-shaped cub. Since I won't be able to shift until the baby is born, we needed it large. With as huge as my clutch is growing—and as much as it hurts like they're already trying to punch their way out of me—I'm hoping they arrive soon.

The sight of my mate next to our nest makes me want to jump him. If we didn't have a house full of family and friends here to help us with moving everything in and unpacking, I'd be all over him.

Even with the full house, I'm tempted to lock the door to our massive third-floor suite behind me and take a break for him to fuck me. He smells divine, all sweaty and covered in alpha bear musk.

The fantasy of licking the sweat off his firm pecs, down his round belly to his jutting erection, pulls me up short. I always find my alpha mate sexy, but I haven't been very horny for the past little while.

Between stress over the move and the babies making me achy and uncomfortable, sex has been the last thing on my mind. Until now. Odd. I rub at a cramp low in my belly and sidle up to my mate.

Ty wraps an arm around me and pulls me close, burying his nose in my neck. I'm used to the way he likes to inhale me deep like this, so I tip my head aside to let him have his fill.

"Huh." Ty says.

"What?" I ask as he snuffles along my collarbone.

"Your scent…" He gives me a puzzled look. "You smell like slick."

When I step back to look at him better, I notice the wet dribble of it on my thighs. Thinking back over the morning, I've sort of felt like I do at the start of a heat. Achy and cramping and restlessly horny. And even a whiff of my alpha has me wanting to beg for his dick. That's something several other omegas have said could happen, mostly because pregnancy hormones are a rollercoaster ride of weirdness.

They called it a birthing heat and said it's pretty common. It's also totally safe to let my alpha knot me to help stretch everything out and make it easier to birth the clutch. I wasn't sure how to process that, but now that it's here, sex sound like a good way to ease the heat-like cramps low in my belly.

The doctor mentioned slick during the birth is normal and said if I wanted to have sex during labor, it could speed up the process. It's also not a true heat, so despite the slick, I shouldn't be fertile for a while after giving birth.

Which is good, since with my alpha's musk filling my nostrils and my hole achingly empty and slick, all I really care about is getting him naked and inside me as fast as possible. I want him. And for our nest to smell like us when we welcome our hatchlings into it.

Desire courses through my body with the urgency of a heat. I press my awkwardly swollen belly against him, loop my arms around his neck and kiss him hard.

"Fuck me, Tyson," I beg.

I wish my bump wasn't keeping me from getting the friction I need. Then I immediately get weepy over the fact that soon the babies will be here and I'll miss the bump. Miss having them move in my womb and knowing exactly where they are and that they're safe at every moment of the day and night. At least I won't miss all these wild hormones and their mood swings.

"Now?" he asks, eyes wide, hands on my hips to hold me still.

"Yes, now. This minute. I need you, alpha. Need to be together in our nest."

He looks even more like a deer caught in the headlights now. First, he kisses my lips, then my belly, and then he makes a dash for the door to lock it. I giggle despite myself as I watch him strip on his way back toward me. I fumble at my stretchy pregnancy pants and loose shirt. Ty helps get the shirt off and bends to kiss the curve of my belly. He steadies me as I struggle free from my pants to finish getting naked.

"Are you in labor?" Ty asks, cupping my cheeks. He searches my eyes, his own brimming with concern.

"I think so? It's like a heat, only with worse cramps." I rub my belly.

Ty kisses me, all his excitement and joy at meeting our babies at last, and all his worry for me communicated through our lips moving in tandem. His tongue dances with mine, twining and moving together and making me moan into his mouth with rising need.

Ty's fingers grip me, holding me tight like he never wants to let me go. I can't help trying to rut against him like a wanton. Ty breaks off the kiss and drops to his knees in front of me to cradle my belly in his big, warm hands and kiss me all over.

"Can't wait to meet our babies." He kisses my bump over the shell of our egg. "I love you Bramble." More kisses, this time where our cub has turned their back to pummel my insides as they protest the way my body is squeezing them.

Ty's fingers trace under the curve, lower to my dick. "Love every curve and stretch mark and bit of you." More kissing as his fingers slide past my dick to my hole, slipping easily inside of me with all the slick I'm making now. He pushes in gently, stretching me with two, and then three fingers.

"Love you too." I arch into his touch. "Need more. All of you. Ty!" I wail his name and clutch at him as he adds a fourth finger. He fucks into me, slow and easy, spreading his fingers to stretch me more.

"Nest," I pant the demand. "Now."

Ty hits a spot inside me that has my slick gushing to coat his hand. I gasp and cling to his broad shoulders. He grunts and rubs the spot harder until I'm reduced to leaning on him and moaning incoherently for more.

Ty presses a little harder. He's still gently fucking his hand inside of me, in a way that's only possible at this angle because of my copious slick. I can't hold back my release a moment longer. My cock spurts between us, the jets of cum hitting my big, round belly. Ty keeps up the pressure and I clench hard around his hand, reveling in just how far inside me he can reach.

I've never felt as connected to him as when I take his entire fist inside me like that. Stretching me for something even more intimate than sex, in a way. There's something beyond satisfying about having him help me like this. He helped put the clutch inside me, and now he's helping to ease our babies into the world. I whimper as he withdraws his hand, my rim clenching hard on the empty air.

When the orgasm passes, the cramps in my belly intensify. It's unlike anything I've experienced before. Like my insides are trying to squeeze their way free. Or expel two fully formed tiny shifter babies. One or the other, the thought forces a pained giggle out of me.

Now that I'm not distracted with pleasure to balance it out, this hurts. I need Ty to keep doing what he was doing. Or fuck me properly. I need to be filled up and stretched wide.

"No, don't go, need you." I scrabble at his shoulders, wishing I could push him back inside of my body. I need him to open me up.

"Sh, I've got you Bramble." He brushes our lips together. "Do we have time before we go to the clinic?"

"Huh?" I ask, the pain and need making my thoughts fuzzy. It's only as I ask that I remember they wanted us to go to the zoo clinic for this, because my pregnancy is technically high risk. They even mentioned meds so that I wouldn't shift by mistake. Fuck. Too late for any of that now. It will be fine. Most shifters in the rave lay their eggs at home without a doctor.

My clutch will be fine. They have to be. I can't even contemplate sitting in the car with the way my belly aches and with as slick as I feel already.

"We're supposed to call when you're in labor, remember?" Ty says, worry furrowing his brow.

"I don't think we have time. I need you now, Ty. Need you to fill me up and help me have our babies. I want to at least try having them here."

Ty wavers, looking like he wants nothing more than to bundle me off to the doctor in case something goes wrong.

"Please?" I moan as another contraction takes my breath away. The babies are coming and I don't want to stress about trying to sneak past our house full of guests or the long drive to the zoo and the specialists. I just want to be here, in my nest with my mate, bringing our babies into the world the same way we made them, together.

"Yeah, Okay, but I'm calling to let the clinic know you're in labor, and we're getting an ambulance out here at the first sign of trouble, deal?"

"Deal." I grunt my agreement, eager to have my mate resume his earlier aid.

"Let's get you into the nest."

Ty scoops me into his arms in a bridal carry and lifts me into the cozy interior of our nest. He lays me on my back and gazes down at me with this reverent expression. Like he's in awe of me and can't believe he gets to have me. That's how I feel, too, in awe that he's my partner as I lay in our nest, gazing up at my alpha mate.

I snuggle into the enlarged cozy interior while he makes the call and leaves a message with the clinic staff.

"Good?"

"Yeah. They're going to have our doctor call us to check in and probably make a house call if you're too far along to come to the clinic."

I moan my way through another contraction, more slick gushing out of me. I can't really focus to discuss logistics at this point, I just want to feel Ty stretching me open.

"Okay. Need you now, alpha. Need you to open

me up."

"You sure you want that still?" Ty seems uncertain.

"Yes. Need it, please?"

"I'm here, bird. Right here." Ty positions himself between my splayed open thighs and presses his cock to my rim.

"Do it. Fuck me, alpha," I demand, reaching for him.

He lets me pull him down, covering my body with his. We kiss as I thrust my hips up to take his cock. Ty holds himself up over me, so as not to put any weight on my belly, making slow, sweet love to me. He doesn't last long, coming with a shuddering sigh. I don't want him to pull out, but he slips free anyway, cock going limp now that we've both come.

If he were a raven shifter, we'd both shift for this next part. So I could lay my eggs in my bird form and he'd be ready to offer comfort and take turns incubating them once the entire clutch is here. He could preen me, and be close to me. But I can't shift until the cub and their placenta are born.

Everyone made that very clear. It won't be safe for either of us, no matter how much the growing ache of contractions makes me want to retreat into my animal form. I can resist my animal instincts.

Ty still holds me, but his heat and weight soon stop being a comfort and I need him to get up and let me push. It's all too much. The contractions pick up and I nudge him away further.

"Hurts." I moan.

Ty comforts me as best he can. Just when I think I can't take anymore and it takes all my restraint not to shift, something changes. The building pressure breaks over me like a wave and I bear down hard.

Something stretches me impossibly wide, but doesn't quite slip free. The next wave pushes my limits again, stretching until I think I'll rip open. It's not quite enough. Ty looks between my legs, ready to catch the baby, the way we talked about with the doctors.

I push again, harder, squeezing until that burning stretch peaks and Ty gasps.

"I see our egg!" Ty exclaims. "It's beautiful, bird. You're doing so good. A few more pushes and Kyrie will be here."

I knew that was likely with the way the babies were positioned, but a small distant part of me is disappointed that Kyrie coming first means I won't be able to shift to lay my egg. If our cub had come first, then I could have potentially shifted between the births. But it's not important when I'm in the middle of pushing them out. All I care about is having both babies safe in my arms.

I push impossibly harder. The smooth curve of the egg's widest point splays me open. With a final effort, our egg slips free, into the cradle of the nest and their papa's hands.

I have a few moments of panting to breathe before the urge to push hits me again. And I have to repeat the entire process with our second baby, Leighton. Their giant head stretches me wide. It's a lot like birthing Kyrie's egg. Except lumpier. And a moment later, much louder than their sibling's arrival as the baby squalls with their first hungry cries.

Ty bundles baby Leighton into a diaper, wipes away most of the goopy mess from their birth, and settles them into my arms. And I'm glad to be in my human form for this meeting. I gaze down at their perfect chubby cheeks. That precious face, red and wrinkled with their hungry crying. Their dark reddish wisps of wet, messy hair already remind me of Ty with a bad case of bedhead.

Hard to believe that tiny waving fist already holds my heart firmly in their grasp, that I made this whole other person. They're perfect. And huge, at least compared to their sibling's modestly sized egg and the tiny cubs I envy static bears for delivering. Shifter cubs start out more developed than their eight ounce static counterparts, but Leighton has to weigh at least eight pounds. That's what it felt like while I was pushing, anyway.

We've been assuming Leighton is our little bear cub, but there's no guarantee either baby will have a bear form. Kyrie will hatch in their raven form, though. I snuggle their egg closer into my side and position Leighton to nurse. Hungry lips seek food as the baby nuzzles my chest.

It's a good thing we went to those birth classes, because when the urge to push doesn't stop as I cuddle Leighton and Kyrie close, I don't panic about a hidden triplet. It's the placenta. I have to deliver that too.

Mammal babies are so messy already, and they're only a minute old. Still, it's not as big or hard as the babies. And I've my hands full, so I barely notice as Ty takes care of the mess and covers me and our clutch in a blanket.

Ty calls the doctor again. I trust him to deal with Leighton's umbilical cord, and anything else that comes up. I did the hard work already; my mate can handle the rest.

Ty talks a while with our doctors, getting instructions for what we should do now while I hold our babies close, cooing over Leighton. They've quieted as they root around for milk.

I watched videos about this, but it didn't feel quite real, like something I'd be doing. Most avian omegas don't chestfeed. It's not even a real option unless the clutch is born in their human form. Still, I manage to get the baby latched on alright.

By the time Ty hangs up, our Leighton is happily suckling. My mate relays the news that our doctor from the zoo is already on the way for a house call to be sure the babies and I are healthy. He says something about the placenta too, but I'm distracted by my perfect little clutch.

Even with months of knowing Leighton would be born in their human form, I wasn't entirely certain about nursing. I'm still not sure if chestfeeding will work out for us long-term with twins, but it's sort of nice for now, cozy almost.

As though I'm still connected to my cub in some small way. Just as incubating Kyrie's egg establishes that ongoing exchange between us. My body continues providing for the little lives that grew inside me, for a little while longer. It's nice, even if we do plan on mostly using formula so Ty can help with feeding our cub.

Ty gazes at us with hearts in his eyes. "You did so good, Bramble."

"We make cute babies." I can't tear my eyes off them. Nothing in the world matters beyond Kyrie's glossy blue mottled egg nestled close to absorb my body heat, and Leighton's warm weight on top of me.

I love cuddling my cub close and breathing in their new baby scent. Leighton makes adorable grunty bear noises as they nurse and I can't get enough of those cute little sounds, the warm little fists pressed against my chest. The plan for keeping both babies fed still includes formula, but for now, this is perfect. Almost perfect.

"Want to bring Myra up to meet her siblings?" I give Ty a tired smile. He beams back at me, squeezing my hand.

"You sure you're ready for that?" he asks.

"Yeah. Want all my babies here," I say.

My mate's eyes glisten with unshed tears as he leans in to kiss me, then our busily eating cub's brow, and the smooth curve of the egg.

"I love you, bird."

"Love you too, bear. Now, get our daughter." I wave an imperious hand, hoping to make him laugh. It works. Ty chuckles as he turns to do my bidding.

"Of course. You want any other visitors?"

"Not yet. I just want the five of us to snuggle for a bit before the rest of them descend on us. If that's okay?"

"I'll do my best to keep them out until you're ready, but we have a house full of family and friends, so they might want to meet our babies."

"After the doctor visits. For now, just us," I say.

"I'll hold them off." Ty nods, and somehow he sneaks Myra back up to me without the rest of the crowd being any the wiser.

"Can I hold them?" Myra asks, bouncing excitedly at her papa's side.

She doesn't ask if she has a brother or a sister. I know a lot of non-avians will ask about the babies' genitals. It threw me for a loop when random strangers who noticed I was pregnant asked me that. That's just not something people here do, growing up among avian shifters. But I know enough mammalian shifters not to be too weirded out by such a personal question about a baby.

Ty and I already discussed this with Myra. How in avian families we don't assign a gender until babies are old enough to tell us who they are. Ty agreed to doing that with our clutch, cub and egg alike. And Myra was excited about it.

After the talk, Ty guiltily confessed that he thought it might be more about having special traditions to share with the babies than the tradition itself. I think she likes it because it's something that normalizes and honors who her papa is, as a gender non-conforming person. But I don't get into that with either of them. The reasons don't matter as much as all of us being on the same page about how to refer to the new babies.

"Once they're fed," Ty agrees. "You'll have to sit with them, so you don't drop them."

Just as the two of them climb into our expansive nest to join me, our cub finishes nursing and promptly shifts into their bear form. The stretchy material of the specially designed shifter diaper clings in place through the shift. Soft, dark fur and scratchy little dewclaws tickle my skin. Leighton is larger than a newborn static cub would be, but smaller than their human form. Myra squeals with delight and immediately takes her black bear form, too, snuggling into my side and snuffling at the baby with keen interest.

"Shall we all shift?" Ty suggests, knowing that I've been aching to take my feathers for months. He scoops Leighton off my chest, since the baby might be small for a bear, but they're still almost as big as I am in my raven form.

Once I'm free of their slight weight, I shift and settle myself over Kyrie, keeping their egg cozy and warm, and safe from their much larger siblings. Ty shifts too, moving gingerly to snuggle his bulky bear form in next to me and curling around our two bear cubs. He rests his head against me and I preen his fur, reveling in the intimacy of being together like this. It strikes me that this is the first time we've had a chance to be truly intimate in our animal forms outside the zoo, and something about that is fitting.

This is utter perfection. A moment to connect as a family unit and bond with the babies before the doctors come to poke and prod us.

Soon, the rest of our extended family will crowd in en masse to snuggle the babies. But for now, we carve out a moment to just be together, the five of us connected by love. My heart has never been as full as it is in this moment, with my mate and our children gathered around me.

EPILOGUE

Ty

Bram in my bed every morning is sort of like the opposite of waking up from a pleasant dream only to realize it wasn't real. It's like rediscovering my dreams all over again after spending years believing they would never happen.

Life hasn't panned out like I thought it would. I spent nine years raising my daughter on my own and trying not to be bitter about the mate and life I thought I'd have.

Even when the twins start their hungry baby caterwauling, it still feels like a dream come true. I take a moment to realize the sounds are different this morning. Instead of the usual avian hunger squawks at the first sign of light mingled with baby cries or bear grunts, I hear Leighton's sleepy grumbling and the high wails of a human infant.

That can't be right. I rub at my eyes, then ease my omega's leg off my hip so I can shuffle out of bed. Part of me misses the time when our babies were still gestating, and I woke to Bram wrapped around me. Lazy morning sex with Bram is among my favorite types of sex.

But the babies are still sharing our room for now, and between Leighton not sleeping the night yet, and Kyrie waking ravenous the moment any light creeps into our room, we don't have as much energy or time for adult activities. I check inside the bassinets at the foot of our bed and confirm what my ears are telling me. Since the kids are both to the stage where they could shift, the sort of bassinet static humans use is the best option, in case they shift in their sleep.

When I peer inside, sure enough, Kyrie shifted. Our little hatchling has had their first shift. Which means they can start taking a bottle in their human form to supplement their crop feeding. That will make things easier for us.

Poor Bram didn't want to use an avian feeding formula. He worries about crop infections or something, so he's been shifting to his raven form to handle Kyrie's all too frequent feedings. Meanwhile, I take care of keeping Leighton fed with bottles of human formula. Now either of us can feed both babies. That should give us more uninterrupted breaks if we trade off.

I just hope both babies won't be much longer

in figuring out sleeping through the night. Myra didn't manage that feat consistently until her bear's first hibernation season. I'm hoping the new cubs will pick it up sooner. If not, they've only got a few more months to go until longer nights trigger the bear parts of their brains to sleep. Then again, Leighton might have a cub form, but we're not sure if Kyrie does. Or if Leighton can shift into feathers. If they're able to access both sides of their shifter heritage, they should do it soon, now that Kyrie has their human form.

I scoop my youngest into my arms, admiring the glossy black curls that match their omega dad's. Even though Kyrie's egg came first, Bram assures me their hatchday is the one we celebrate. That gives the twins each their own special day to celebrate, so it seems more than practical.

With their face scrunched up in a hungry squall, Kyrie is adorably angry. Flushed with their fists balled and waving. As soon as I pick them up, their cries become less strident, letting me take in their features.

I'm already irrevocably in love with the baby in my arms, but there is something wonderful about seeing them in their human form for the first time, the familiar scent of my youngest paired with this new little face that's a perfect blend of Bram and my own features and yet entirely unique to Kyrie. I can't wait to share this moment with Bram. It's a minor miracle that he slept through the crying, so I'm torn about whether to wake him.

I hastily diaper the baby, in case they have to go after sleeping since their last feed at bedtime. Kyrie fusses again at being placed on the changing table that Leighton's been the only one to use so far. They need the fastening tabs pulled tighter than their sibling, but the stretchy shifter diapers are adjustable enough to accommodate both babies, thankfully.

"That's yours," Bram mumbles sleepily when Kyrie starts to wail again before I snuggle them to my chest. That seems to wake Leighton, the cub pokes their furry head over the edge of the bassinet to investigate their twin's distress.

I chuckle, not without sympathy for my mate's exhaustion, and scoop the grumbly cub out of their bassinet, carrying both babies back to the bed, one in the crook of each arm.

Kyrie might not keep Bram up every couple of hours like I've been doing with Leighton, but the constant crop feedings every half-hour during daylight for the first few months were exhausting for my poor mate. I did as much as I could to help, prepping a steady supply of healthy snacks and small meals for him, cuddling with both babies, and handling poop duty.

Before they were born, I was worried about how to handle a tiny chick. I was unsure whether

I'd bond with the baby the same way I did with Myra, but no matter their form, Kyrie smells like my cub, and I am just as in love with the adorable huge-eyed hungry hatchling as their chubby-cheeked twin. Baby birds are demanding little creatures though.

Even with Kyrie eating slightly less frequently now and Bram's moms helping occasionally, since I can't feed our baby bird directly, my mate has still lost weight trying to keep our chick fed. He assures me that's normal, but I'm glad things will be easier on him now that Kyrie can eat in both their forms, even if the ability to shift might mean no more sleeping through the night with a baby bird's instinctive sensitivity to darkness.

I didn't believe Bram at first when he told me avian hatchlings sleep as soon as it gets dark and don't wake until it's light, but Kyrie has borne out the truth of that statement since their hatchday. Which has meant no turning on the lights in our room to handle Leighton's middle of the night feedings, but as exhausting as the babies can be, I wouldn't change a thing about them.

Leighton is already wearing a stretchy diaper that is roomy enough to accommodate both their cub and human forms when they shift. There isn't an avian equivalent, since baby birds have fecal sacs that contain their messes and make for easy disposal. They're kind of gross, but no more so than a dirty diaper.

"Are you sure about that, love?" I set a furry

Leighton on his daddy's chest.

Leighton snuggles into Bram's body, seeking cuddles. I fed the bear cub less than two hours ago, so they aren't as hungry as their sibling.

I bounce Kyrie gently in my arms, shushing them softly. They latch onto the finger I offer in lieu of a bottle and settle slightly at having something to suck on. The reprieve won't last long, but it lets us admire our baby for the first time in their second form.

Kyrie's human side is this perfect blend of us. They have hazel eyes, like Myra's. They've got my nose. And I can't get over the sweet bow lips that remind me so much of Bram, not to mention they have a full head of dark curls like him.

Bram hugs Leighton close, then sits bolt upright and stares at the human infant in my arms. "They shifted!" he exclaims, still clutching Leighton to his chest.

The sudden motion causes the cub to startle into a shift. Except instead of having his arms full of a human baby, Bram is now holding a fledgling raven. Leighton's bird form is bigger than their sibling, but their feathers aren't as fully fledged and they're ruffled and in need of a good preening.

Bram looks between our babies, giving Kyrie's newly discovered human form a longing glance as he strokes a thumb over Leighton's feathery head. They are adorable in ugly-cute fledgling feathers. I think we could both stay there admiring our babies in their new forms for ages, except Kyrie needs food and Leighton's feathers are in need of a thorough first preening.

"Guess we're swapping babies for now?" Bram asks ruefully.

"Seems that way. Kyrie will shift plenty more, now that they've figured out they can." I lean in close to let Bram see Kyrie's human face, drinking in all their sweet perfection as he cups their chubby baby cheek against his palm for a moment. I rub a finger along Leighton's stubbly head feathers and they squawk indignantly. Raven chicks are nowhere near as sleek and poised as their adult counterparts. They're adorable.

"I know, you need help with those itchy pins, huh, baby?" Bram coos to Leighton, who seems to be pleased with the new sounds they can make in their new form. Bram chuckles at the disgruntled baby croaks. He kisses Kyrie's brow. The baby mewls and sucks harder on my finger.

It won't be long before Kyrie protests louder at the lack of forthcoming milk. Bram recognizes that fact too, and he shoos me toward the door as he removes the clean diaper that's pooled around Leighton's legs and tail. It can stretch enough to fit both cub and human forms, but not enough to stay on the baby's avian form.

"Go fix their first bottle. I'll handle Leighton."

So I sway my way to the kitchen to fix a bottle as Bram brings Leighton to the bassinet nest. He settles them inside before claiming his raven form and joining the chick to groom their feathers for the first time. It's a bonding experience for both of us, sharing moments with the baby who, until today, didn't share our animal form.

Kyrie takes a few tries before latching onto the bottle. When they do, they guzzle the formula too fast. It takes me a moment to realize I might need to switch back to the lower flow nipples until they get used to taking food this way. Once I swap them out, Kyrie snuggles against my bare chest to eat. I gaze down at their perfect little face, savoring this moment. Remembering how quickly Myra grew from a hungry baby into a pre-teen. I want to savor every moment with my family.

As though thinking of her summoned my eldest, Myra joins us, yawning in the doorway.

"Good morning. Did the babies wake you?" I ask.

Myra shakes her head and shuffles closer to me. She plops onto the sofa at my side and nuzzles her face against my shoulder to peer down at her sibling. "Good thing you're so cute, Leighton…" She coos baby talk at them, then pauses. "That's not Leighton." Myra sits up and looks between me and the baby.

"Kyrie shifted? Good job, Kyrie!" Myra tickles the baby's cheek with a finger and Kyrie spits out the nipple to give their sister a gummy baby grin.

"Aw, you're a cutie-pie. Papa, they've got hazel eyes like me!" Myra exclaims. She's as doting a sister as she promised she'd be, offering to help out more than I expected. Sure, she's had her moments of needing attention when the babies seemed to take all our energy over the past few months. I've worked hard to schedule one-on-one time for us with all the changes in our family, but overall it's been wonderful to watch her bonding with Bram and her siblings.

"They do," I agree, smiling at the pair of them. Kyrie roots for the bottle and I help them latch back on. "What would you like for breakfast, Myra?"

"Pancakes? With that blueberry syrup Dad got," Myra suggests. She's been calling Bram 'Dad' for a while now, but it still never fails to fill me with warmth. Not so much the title, just everything it means. That Bram is a part of us now. Part of our family, another adult who loves my girl and whom she can rely upon. Bram fairly preens every time he hears her call him that, like it's the finest title he's ever heard.

It means the world to me that the five of us can be a family. The sort of family I've envisioned ever since I found out Myra was on her way into my life. It might not be traditional for alpha bears to be involved as parents. More like distant providers, but my alpha mom raised me, so this is the life I've wanted ever since I can remember. I wouldn't trade this moment, snuggled on the couch with two of my cubs, for anything.

"Can I hold them? Or, like, finish feeding them?" Myra reaches for Kyrie. And much as I'd love to hold my babies forever, it warms my heart to see her dote on her little siblings.

"Sure." I transfer Kyrie into their sister's arms, help her get the bottle situated and sit with them for a moment to be sure she's comfortable feeding the baby.

Myra lets me hover at first, but as Kyrie gets about halfway through their bottle, Myra shoos me away. "Pancakes don't make themselves, Papa."

"Bossy kids don't get syrup." I snort and muss her hair.

Myra scowls, her glittery bear bracelet tinkling on her wrist as she reaches up to fix her hair. The kid has barely taken the thing off since Bram gave it to her. They've bonded even more since Bram moved in with us. They've both conspired to smuggle glitter into the house. The nursery we set up for the babies to use when they're old enough to sleep on their own has so much sparkle it's like stepping into a disco. Or, well, it's like a raven and a nine-year-old decorated it. All things shiny.

"Please make us pancakes, Papa Bear?" Myra amends her request.

"That's more like it. Want them with berries?"

"Yes, please."

I rise to cook, kissing Kyrie and Myra each on

the forehead before I leave my oldest feeding my youngest on the sofa. I've got the first batch of pancakes on the griddle and the oven preheating for a baking tray full of bacon when Bram, in his human form, joins us.

Leighton, still in their feathers, is perched on his shoulder, wide curious eyes taking in the world. I was nervous when he first let Kyrie perch like that, but apparently fledglings are good at clinging on tight. And even though neither fledgling is quite old enough for true flight, the only time Kyrie lost their grip, they glided to the ground for a safe, if ungainly, landing. Still, Leighton isn't used to having talons, much less wings.

"Stop frowning, Papa Bear. Perching is all instinct. Leighton will be fine." Bram catches my worried gaze locked on our cub.

I bite back my concerned protest, knowing that he's more of an expert on baby birds than I am, even if I'm the one who's done the baby thing before. Bram shakes his head at me, reading my anxious expression.

"They'll be fine, love," he says.

Still, he offers Leighton his hand. They test it with their beak before transferring to their dad's hand. Once there, they bob their head toward their siblings until he brings them to sit on the couch. Once Bram sits next to Myra and Kyrie, Leighton shifts into their cub form and curls up for a nap, chin resting on Myra's knee.

At just over five months old, the cub is almost ready to start sampling solid foods. Although I suppose if they are spending time in their bird form now, we'll need to crop feed them like Kyrie. I don't want to dwell on that; as a mammal, the avian diet of partially digested food isn't all that appealing.

"Berry pancakes sound alright, Bram?"

"Sure. And bacon?"

"And bacon." I smile and slide the tray of bacon into the pre-heated oven, then flip the pancakes on the griddle, content to provide for my mate and our cubs. Even if two of them are too small to enjoy the meal that I'm cooking. It's more about having all of us gathered together for a leisurely weekend brunch than the actual food.

When the first batch of pancakes is ready, I portion out the rest of the batter onto the griddle. All that's left is brewing more coffee and fixing a bottle of formula for Leighton when the cub inevitably wakes up hungry midway through our meal.

As I pour drinks, including juice for Myra, I listen to her telling Bram about what she's doing at summer camp. She finished the year at her old school with Mx. Adams.

In the fall, she'll be starting grade four here in Four Corners. She'll be walking to Bram's folks place after school, along with Elric, Briony, and Cory, the three youngest of Bram's siblings. I had my reservations about that, but I trust Myra to follow the rules and tell me if anything about the arrangement makes her uncomfortable.

Bram notices that the food is close to ready and settles the babies into their downstairs playpen, both of them napping for the moment. Then he nudges Myra to help set the table. The two of them get out a selection of syrups, butter, and whipped cream for the pancakes.

"Papa, are we still going to join the rave for dinner tonight?" Myra asks as she adds the sprinkles to the array of condiments on the table. "I'm supposed to bring my controller so Elric, Cory, and I can work on our museum."

"That's the plan. And Gramma will be there too. So you should make sure you have everything ready for camp before we head over there; it will be a late night and you've got an early start in the morning. I thought you kids already did a museum?" I ask as I stack the final finished pancakes onto a serving plate.

We spend plenty of time with Bram's rave these days, but it's always a good bet that we'll be over at his folks' place for hours at a time. He's got a large loving family, just like he told me, and I wouldn't have it any other way. Mom has already made raven shifter plushies for all my mate's siblings. And for the babies.

"Yeah, we did. But we're doing a different one this time. And it's not haunted. I'm making a replica of Sue, from the Field Museum," she explains.

I set the platter of pancakes on the table, then carry over the coffee and juice. The bottle goes in a warmer for when Leighton wakes up from their nap. Bram adds syrup and cream to his mug. I take mine unadulterated this morning. It was a long night with the babies and I could use the jolt.

"That's the *T. rex* that has social media, right?" Bram asks.

"Yeah, they're fun." Myra nods. "You should follow them, if you don't already. Because Sue has all the ham jokes."

"Speaking of ham—" I pivot to pull out the tray of perfectly cooked bacon just as the oven timer beeps. "Breakfast is served."

"Bacon is much better than ham," Myra says, reaching for a strip. Bram grabs her wrist and keeps her from stealing a piece yet.

"That's hot; don't make your papa spill the grease," he warns. I flash him a grateful smile, because I don't want her to get burned, and I appreciate Bram looking out for her safety. He makes me feel like we're a team in all the little ways and having that is better than I even thought to imagine. Someone who always has my back and loves my kids as much as I do.

Myra pouts as I set the tray on a trivet. I use the tongs to serve the kid the lion's share of the bacon before divvying the remaining slices between Bram and me. I make sure I turned everything off in the kitchen, then the three of us enjoy the food, laughing and chatting about our plans for later.

The conversation soon devolves into cooing over finally getting to see the babies in their new forms. I've worn out the joke that Leighton is making up for being born second by outgrowing Kyrie. Bram always shakes his head at me and says that of course Leighton is bigger since they were born before Kyrie's hatchday, making them the older twin. Leighton is adorably chonky in all their forms. The extra weeks of growing between their birth and when Kyrie hatched show in the size difference between the two now that they can share a form.

As I expected, Leighton wakes up for breakfast as we're finishing eating. Bram scoops them up and grabs the bottle I prepared earlier. He feeds the hungry baby while Myra and I clear away the dishes, just in time for Kyrie to wake with a dirty diaper. Life has been chaotic with two babies clamoring for attention, and that's bound to continue with the two of them both shifting and becoming more mobile now, but I wouldn't trade it for the world.

I glance up from changing Kyrie to see Bram feeding Leighton on the sofa. Our eyes meet and we share a smile. Watching him care for our kids fills me with sunshine and light. Nearby, Myra works on an art project at the clean kitchen table. This morning, surrounded by my family, is how I hope life can always be for us. Nothing makes me happier than being together with them.

We aren't sure if Bram's weird heats were a sign of creep, and we might not know for certain for a while since it should be a few more months before he gets his heats back postpartum. He's already back on his heat-blockers. We haven't decided if we want more than three kids yet, either. But that's fine. We have time to decide and I'm happy with either option.

All I know for sure is that I don't want anyone but him by my side for whatever life has in store for us. A lazy family brunch at home might be perfectly mundane, but it's precious to me. It reminds me of the tradition my omega mom started with my family growing up and I love sharing it with my family now. It might not seem like much, but it's all mine and I couldn't ask for more than I've got in Bram and our kids.

Thanks for reading! If you loved Ty and Bramble's story, be sure to leave a review. For more omegaverse from me, get a new expanded edition of the previously-released short story Squirrel Trouble at: www.amzn.com/ B0BFXLRBX5

Still want more? Seb and Winny will each be getting their own stories as well. Join my facebook group, Alex's Alcove, for all the latest updates on my writing.

ACKNOWLEDGMENTS

Thanks for coming along for the ride with Ty and Bramble, and of course Myra. And a huge thanks to Reese Morrison for beta reading this book, their input was invaluable to making Papa Bear the best it can be.

The idea behind this series came to me while visiting a local wildlife center and wondering what it might be like if the animals on display were all shifters, and so far I'm having a blast with these characters. I can't wait to get started on Seb's story.

You might have seen Squirrel Trouble as part of a free short story giveaway featuring heat sex, if you missed it, fear not, an expanded version is in the works. Those two weren't finished talking to me after Felix's heat, so I am planning on fleshing out Felix and Thurston's romance to release a novel length version soon.

ABOUT THE AUTHOR

Alex Silver (he/them) grew up mostly in Northern Maine and is now living in Canada with one spouse, two kids, and a lovebird. Alex is a trans guy who started writing fiction as a child and never stopped. Although there were detours through assisting on a farm and being a pharmacist along the way.

Visit me online at:
http://alexsilverauthor.wordpress.com/
Browse my entire book catalog at:
https://www.amazon.com/Alex-Silver/e/B07NPBW615
Join my Facebook group at:
https://www.facebook.com/groups/alexsalcove
Follow me on BookBub at:
https://www.bookbub.com/profile/alex-silver
Follow me on Twitter:
https://twitter.com/asilverauthor
Sign up for my newsletter for a free short story at: https://landing.mailerlite.com/webforms/landing/i2w6l7

And as always, consider leaving a review on Amazon or Goodreads if you enjoyed this book, reviews are of vital importance to independent authors, thanks!

Shift Work

Omegaverse MPreg Romance

Papa Bear (M/X)
Squirrel Trouble (M/M) (expanded edition)
Trash Panda (M/M)

Summer of Adventures

Kinky Contemporary Romance

Dungeon Master (M/M)
Knotty Boy (M/M)
Service Call (M/M)
Picture Perfect (M/M)
Puppy Love (F/X)
Stud Muffin (M/M/M)

Table Topped

Contemporary Romance

Roll for Initiative (M/M) Book 1
Charisma Check (M/M) Book 2
Saving Throw (M/X) Book 3
Plus One Bonus (M/X) Book 4
Dump Stat (F/F) Book 5
Party of Three (M/M/X) Book 6

Hauntastic Haunts

M/M Paranormal Romance

Dan's Hauntastic Haunts Investigates:
Goodman Dairy (*Book 1*)
Hawk Lake (*Book 2*)
Ivarsson School (*Book 3*)
Joliet Asylum (*Book 4*)

Drew's Haunted Hangout (*A Hauntastic Haunts Short Story 1*)
Rafael's Haunted Halloween (*A Hauntastic Haunts Short Story 2*)
Lee's Haunted Holiday (*A Hauntastic Haunts Short Story 3*)
Free download links to the shorts are available in my FB group: https://www.facebook.com/groups/alexsalcove

Psions of SPIRE

Urban Fantasy

Shelter (M/M) Novella 0.5
Bright Spark (MMMM) Book 1
Bold Move (MMMM) Novella 1.5
Keen Sense (M/M) Book 2
Weak Link (M/M) Novella 2.5
Quick Fire (M/X) Book 3
Clear Sight (M/M) Book 4
New Look (M/M) Novella 4.5

A SPIREverse daddy kink standalone
New Ground (M/M/X)

Shared Universe Series

Super U - Superhero Romance
Super U: Rising Storm (M/X)

Final Days - Zombie Romance
The Willows (M/M GNC)

Anthologies

Listen: The Sound of Fear
Haunt (M/M trans gothic horror)

Fix the World
Upgrade (gay trans cyberpunk)

www.ingramcontent.com/pod-product-compliance
Lightning Source LLC
Chambersburg PA
CBHW051518250626
47156CB00001B/131